The Angel of
Darkness

Also by Ernesto Sabato

THE TUNNEL
ON HEROES AND TOMBS

THE ANGEL OF DARKNESS

ERNESTO SABATO

Translated by Andrew Hurley

BALLANTINE BOOKS • NEW YORK

Grateful acknowledgment is made to the following for permission to reprint
previously published material: MCA Music Publishing: Excerpt from the lyrics
of "Julia" words and music by John Lennon and Paul McCartney. Copyright ©
1968 by Northern Songs. All rights controlled and administered by MCA
Music Publishing, a division of MCA Inc. under license from ATV Music.
Used by permission. All rights reserved.
Playboy: Excerpts from the "Playboy Panel: New Sexual Lifestyles," *Playboy*
Magazine (September 1973). Copyright © 1973 by *Playboy*. Used with
permission. All rights reserved.

Library of Congress Cataloging-in-Publication Data
Sabato, Ernesto R.
  [Abaddón, el exterminador, English]
  The angel of darkness/Ernesto Sabato; translated by Andrew Hurley.
    p. cm.
  Translation of: Abaddón, el exterminador.
  ISBN 0-345-36050-8
  I. Title.
PQ7797.S214A6313 1991   90-24991
863——dc20   CIP

Design by Holly Johnson

Manufactured in the United States of America

First Edition: October 1991
10 9 8 7 6 5 4 3 2 1

*AND THEY HAD A KING OVER THEM, WHICH IS THE
ANGEL OF THE BOTTOMLESS PIT, WHOSE NAME IS
ABADDON.*

REVELATION, 9:11

*IT IS POSSIBLE THAT I WILL DIE TOMORROW, AND
NO ONE ON EARTH WILL HAVE UNDERSTOOD ME.
SOME WILL THINK ME BETTER THAN I AM, AND
OTHERS WILL THINK ME WORSE. SOME WILL SAY I
WAS A GOOD PERSON; OTHERS, THAT I WAS A CUR.
BUT BOTH OPINIONS WILL BE EQUALLY WRONG.*

MIKHAIL LERMONTOV
A HERO OF OUR TIME

Contents

viii

SOME EVENTS WHICH OCCURRED IN THE CITY OF
BUENOS AIRES, EARLY IN 1973

◇

ON THE EVENING OF JANUARY 5,
Bruno was standing in the doorway of the café at the corner of Guido
and Junín when he saw Sabato coming down the street. But just as
Bruno was about to speak to him he sensed that something inexplicable was happening: in spite of the fact that Sabato's eyes turned
directly on him, the man continued on, as though he hadn't seen
him. It was the first time anything of the kind had ever happened—
and as Bruno and Sabato were life-long friends, it was simply not
possible that Sabato had cut Bruno deliberately, that he had walked
by without speaking because of some grave misunderstanding that
had come between them.

Bruno's eyes followed Sabato attentively, and he watched him
cross the dangerous intersection without any concern for cars, without looking in either direction or showing even the single moment
of hesitation that a person alert and conscious of the dangers would
always show.

Bruno was so shy that it was only on the rarest occasions that
he had the courage to use the telephone. But after days of finding
Sabato neither at La Biela nor at the Roussillon, and learning finally
from the waiters that Sabato hadn't been in once in all that time, he
decided to call his house.

"He's not feeling well," Bruno was told vaguely. "No, he won't
be going out for a while."

Bruno knew that Sabato could fall, sometimes for months, into
what he called "a well," but he had never before sensed so clearly
that those words might hold some dreadful truth. He began to recall
stories Sabato had told him—of curses, of one Schneider, of unfold-
ing plots. A terrible anxiety began to weigh on his spirit, as though
in the middle of some unknown territory night had fallen and he

found he had to orient himself by tiny lights in far-off huts inhabited by people who were utter strangers to him, or by the glow of a great fire off at some unreachable distance.

AFTER MIDNIGHT THAT SAME NIGHT
there occurred, among the countless events which take place in any huge city, three events worth remarking, for they were linked to each other as in a play the characters are linked—even if the characters don't know each other, and even though one of them may be a simple drunk.

At the old Chichín, the bar on Almirante Brown at the corner of Pinzón, the owner was beginning to close up, and he said to the sole remaining customer at the bar,

"Drink up, Loco, time to close."

Natalicio Barragán finished off his glass of *aguardiente* and stumbled out the door. Outside, he once again performed with cool and unruffled placidity the small daily miracle of crossing the avenue, which at that hour of the night was a racetrack of mad automobiles and buses. And then, as though he were walking the rolling deck of a ship in a heavy sea, he made his unsteady way down Brandsen toward Dársena Sur.

When he came to Pedro de Mendoza, the water of the Riachuelo where it reflected the lights of the boats looked as though it were tinged with blood. Something made Barragán raise his eyes, until he saw, above the masts, a fiery monster spread out all across the sky, all the way down to the mouth of the Riachuelo, where the end of its huge scaly tail dipped out of sight.

He caught at the tin wall, closed his eyes, and did not move; he was terrified. After a few moments of confused reflection, his thoughts trying clumsily to find a path through a brain clogged with weeds and rubble, he opened his eyes again. But again, and now even more plainly, he saw the dragon covering the midnight firmament—a furious serpent glowing hot and blood-red against the abyss of India ink.

He was terrified.

Somebody, thank god, was coming. A sailor.

"Excuse me . . ." Barragán stopped him, his voice trembling.

4

"What's up?" the man asked in that tone of bonhomie that good-hearted people use with drunks.

"There."

The man turned his eyes in the direction Loco Barragán was pointing.

"What?" he asked again, looking attentively.

"That!"

After carefully studying that region of the sky a good while, the sailor continued on, smiling kindly. Loco stood looking after him, and then he turned and leaned against the tin wall again, closed his eyes, and pondered with shaky concentration. When once again he looked, his horror grew: the monster was now spewing fire from the mouths of its seven heads. Barragán fainted. When he came to again, still lying on the sidewalk, it was morning. The first workers were coming to work. Groggily, for the moment not remembering the vision, he got up and walked to his room in the boardinghouse.

The second event concerns a young man named Nacho Izaguirre. From the darkness lent by the trees along the Avenida del Libertador, he watched a big Chevy Sport pull up and stop; out of it stepped two people—a man named Rubén Pérez Nassif, president of Perenas Real Estate, and Nacho's sister Agustina Izaguirre. It was almost two o'clock in the morning. They went into one of the apartment houses. Nacho remained at his vantage point until four, approximately, and then he walked off toward Belgrano, in all probability going home. His shoulders were drooping and his head was bowed, and he walked with his hands in the pockets of his faded jeans.

Meanwhile, in the sordid basement of a police station just outside the city, Marcelo Carranza, twenty-three years old, accused of being a member of a guerrilla group, after days of torture, and finally dumped into a sack and beaten until he burst, was dying.

WITNESS, IMPOTENT WITNESS,
Bruno was saying to himself as he stopped at that point on the Costanera Sur road where fifteen years ago Martín had said, "We were here with Alejandra." As though this same sky filled with stormy clouds and this same summer heat had brought him all uncon-

5

sciously, secretly to this place he had not set eyes on since that day. As though there were emotions deep within him trying to come out once again, to make their way up out of some deep region of his spirit, and in order to do it they were using places, landmarks of his past, making him feel like visiting these spots again, though without any very clear understanding of what was at stake. Yet is it not true that nothing can return again as it used to be? he inwardly grieved. For we are no longer what we were then—new dwellings have been erected on the rubble of those ancient places destroyed by fire and battle, or on those abandoned relics worn away by time, whose in-habitants are now but confused memories, or legend, and then the memories themselves snuffed out, buried under new passions and miseries: the tragic luck of kids like Nacho, the torture and death of innocents like Marcelo.

Leaning against the low wall, listening to the rhythmic beating of the river behind him, he looked through the smog, as he had looked many times before, at Buenos Aires, the silhouette of its sky-scrapers against the evening sky.

Seagulls came and went, as they always did, with the atrocious indifference of natural forces. And it was even possible that while Martín had been talking to him that day about his love for Alejandra, the baby in its stroller that Bruno remembered noticing being pushed down the sidewalk by its nanny had been Marcelo himself. And now, while the shy, helpless boy's body, or the remains of his body, lay inside some block of cement or were simply ashes on the floor of some kiln, the same seagulls in an identical sky performed the same ancestral wheels. And thus it was that all things passed, all things were forgotten, as the water of the river went on beating rhythmi-cally against the shores of the anonymous city.

Write, at least, eternalize something: a love, an act of heroism like Marcelo's, a moment of ecstasy. Approach the absolute. Or maybe (he thought, that characteristic doubt of his asserting itself, that excess of integrity which made him waver, and therefore made him so ineffective), maybe writing was a necessity for people like him, people incapable of such absolute acts of passion and heroism. Because that kid that had set himself afire one day in the middle of a square in Prague, and Ché Guevara, and Marcelo Carranza—none of them had needed to write. For a moment he contemplated the

6

idea that writing might be what the powerless of the world turned to instead of action, the last resort of the impotent. Mightn't those young people that repudiated literature be right? He didn't know, it was all very complex, because then, as Sabato said, one would have to repudiate music and almost all poetry too, since neither music nor poetry did a thing, really, to further that Revolution that the young people hungered for. And besides, no real character was some mere simulacrum erected out of words—real characters were made out of blood, out of dreams and hopes and fears and real anxieties, and in some obscure way they seemed to make it possible for us, in the midst of this confused and troubled life, to find a meaning for existence, or at least a far-off glimpse of it.

He felt once again, as he had before in his long life, that he needed to write, though he couldn't have known that the need sprang from that sight of Sabato on the corner of Junín and Guido. But at the same time he experienced that chronic impotence of his in the face of the immensity of it. The universe was so vast. Catastrophes and tragedies, loves and partings, missed chances, hopes and deaths, all seemed to him so enormous, so out of all bounds. What should he write about? Out of all those infinite events, which ones were essential? Someone had told Martín that there might be a cataclysm in some distant country and yet that cataclysm mean nothing to someone here: to that boy over there, to Alejandra, even to himself. Yet suddenly the simple song of a bird, some man's expression as he walks by, the arrival of a letter become things which truly, actually exist, which for one particular person have an importance that an epidemic of cholera in India doesn't have. No, it wasn't indifference to the world, it wasn't egotism, at least it wasn't for him: it was something more subtle. What a strange condition, the human condition, if such a staggering event were not real. This minute, he told himself, innocent children are dying in Vietnam, incinerated by napalm bombs: was it not despicable triviality to write about a handful of people in one corner of the world? Heartsick, he watched the seagulls in the sky again. But no, he corrected himself. Any life, any story of the hopes and disappointments of a single man, of a simple unknown kid, could take in all humanity, and might serve to uncover a meaning for existence, or even somehow to console that Vietnamese mother weeping for her incinerated child. Of course, it

7

was only honest to admit (to fear) that what he himself would be capable of writing would never achieve those heights. But the miracle was possible, at least, and other people might accomplish what he himself didn't feel capable of achieving. Or maybe he did, you never knew. Write about certain teenagers—they were the people who suffered the most in this implacable world, the people who most deserved for somebody to describe the drama of their suffering and the meaning of it all—if indeed any of it had meaning. Nacho, Agustina, Marcelo. But what did he know about them? He could barely make out, through murky shadows, a few significant episodes in his own life, his own blurred memories of childhood and adolescence, the melancholy path his own affections had taken.

What, after all, did he really *know*—not necessarily about Marcelo Carranza or Nacho Izaguirre but even about Sabato, for instance, who had been one of Bruno's closest friends for fifty years or more? Infinitely much, yet infinitely little. Sometimes he felt as though Sabato were a part of his own spirit, his own self, and he could almost perfectly imagine what S. had felt at certain moments, at certain events. But suddenly it would all turn dark, and it would only be thanks to some fleeting spark in the other man's eye that he would be given the chance to suspect what was going on deep inside the other man's soul. It would always be supposition, though, that very risky supposition which we so assuredly cast over all the secret universe of others. What did he know, for example, about the real relationship between Sabato and that angry, violent young man Nacho Izaguirre, and above all between Sabato and Nacho's enigmatic sister? Insofar as Sabato's relationship with Marcelo, he knew, of course, how Marcelo had appeared in his life, that train of episodes which seemed casual and coincidental but which, as Sabato himself always said, were only apparently so. Bruno could even, finally, imagine that Sabato's collapse and the tortured death of poor Marcelo, and Nacho's savage, angry vomit (so to speak) spewed over his sister were events not only linked but linked by some principle so powerful that it formed the secret design of one of those tragedies that come to act as a metaphor for what may happen to all humanity in times such as these, that sort of tragedy that sums everything up.

A novel about that search for the absolute, that madness suffered by adolescents, of course, but also by mature adults, mature men

8

and women who will not or cannot stop being human: men and women mired in mud and shit who scream screams of desperation, or who die throwing bombs in some corner of the world. A story about kids like Marcelo and Nacho and about an artist who in some hidden redoubt of his soul feels something stir—those creatures (in part glimpsed outside himself, in part roiling in the deepest depths of his heart) who demand Eternity, the Absolute. So that the martyrdom of some will not be lost in the shouting and tumult and chaos but will reach the heart of other men, to shake them and save them. Somebody perhaps like Sabato standing in front of that class full of implacable teenagers, dominating it not only because of his own hunger for the absolute but because of the demons which from the dark caves within himself oppress him, because of the characters that once appeared in his books yet still feel betrayed by the clumsiness or cowardice of the intermediary; and Sabato himself ashamed of having outlived those creatures capable of dying, or of having murdered them out of hatred or love or because of their obsession with uncovering the key to existence. And ashamed not only of having survived them but of having done so meanly, with lukewarm repayments of their deaths. The disgust and sadness of success.

Yes, if only his friend were to die and he, Bruno, were to write the story. If only he were not what he unfortunately was: a weakling, a man without will, a man of pure but failed intentions.

Once again he looked up at the seagulls in the decaying sky. The dark silhouettes of the skyscrapers against the violet splendors, the cathedrals of smoke, and little by little the melancholy purples that precede the funereal weeds of the night. The whole city was dying, a man who had been grossly and noisily alive was now dying in dramatic silence, alone, withdrawn, pensive. The silence deepened as the night came on; it was the way the day always greeted the heralds of the shadows.

And thus ended another day in Buenos Aires, now forever irrecoverable, and taking him just that much closer to his own end.

CONFESSIONS, DIALOGUES, AND A FEW DREAMS WHICH OCCURRED BEFORE THOSE EVENTS, AND WHICH COULD BE THEIR ANTECEDENTS, THOUGH NOT ALWAYS CLEAR AND UNEQUIVOCAL. THE MAIN PART TAKES PLACE BETWEEN THE BEGINNING AND END OF 1972. THERE ARE ALSO, HOWEVER, OLDER EPISODES, WHICH OCCURRED IN LA PLATA, IN PRE-WAR PARIS, IN ROJAS, AND IN CAPITÁN OLMOS (THESE LAST, CITIES WITHIN THE PROVINCE OF BUENOS AIRES).

SOME CONFIDENCES MADE TO BRUNO

I PUBLISHED THE NOVEL AGAINST MY WILL. Events (not publishing events but others, more ambiguous) later confirmed my instinctive misgivings. I must have suffered under the curse for years. Years of torture. What forces worked against me, I can't explain to you very clearly at all, but there is no doubt that they were forces out of that territory governed by the Blind, and that for these ten years they have made my life a hell to which I've had to deliver myself, bound hand and foot, every morning, as I wake up, as though it were some inside-out nightmare, felt and borne with the lucidity of a man fully awake and with the desperation of a man who knows that there is nothing he can do to escape it. And who, to add insult to injury, has to keep the horrors to himself. It's not hard to understand how Madame Normand could write me in a panic from Paris, the moment she read the translation, *"Que vous avez touché un sujet dangereux! J'espère, pour vous, que vous n'y toucherez jamais!"*

How stupid I was, how weak.

In May of 1961 Jacobo Muchnik came to my house to wrest from me (there's no other word for it) my promise of the originals. I was clutching those pages, in large part written in fear, as though some instinct were warning me of the dangers I'd be exposing myself to if they were published. Even more than that—and this you know yourself—I don't know how many times I had told myself I ought to destroy the "Report on the Blind," just as on certain occasions I'd burned fragments of it and even whole books prefiguring it. Why? I've never understood why. I have always believed, and this is the reason I've publicly given, always believed that I had a certain tendency toward self-destruction, which is the same tendency that throughout my life has led me to burn the greatest part of what I've

13

written. I'm talking about fiction. I have only published two novels, and of the two only *The Tunnel* with full intention, either because at the time I was still to a certain degree naive about certain things or because my instinct for self-preservation was not intense enough, or perhaps because in that book I still hadn't penetrated to the heart of that forbidden continent: there was only one enigmatic character (enigmatic to me, I mean) that almost imperceptibly touched on the subject, the way somebody in a café can be saying something that could well be absolutely essential, but that gets lost in the noise or in other apparently more important pieces of the conversation.

At any rate, I didn't give Muchnik the originals that day, a day I remember very clearly because of what I'll tell you in a moment about my birthday. So that day he didn't manage to get his hands on the novel, but he did carry away my promise, which I made in front of certain friends who had taken his side, to turn it in a month later, when I'd had a chance to rework certain passages. It was a way of gaining some time, a chance to keep the novel from starting through the inexorable machinery of publication.

On June 24 Muchnik telephoned me to remind me of my promise. I was embarrassed to go back on my word, or maybe it was that my conscious mind won out over my instinct, whose misgivings seemed absurd. So, giving in to his friendly pressure—almost like making excuses to myself, as though I were saying "you see (who was I talking to?), I'm not altogether responsible for this"—I told him I'd be over that very day to take him the manuscript. The minute she heard this, M. asked me if I'd forgotten that it was my birthday, that some friends were coming over, as they always did. My birthday! That was what should have finally warned me off completely! But I didn't say a word. My mother had been ill when I was born, so my birth was only registered on the third of July, as though they really couldn't bring themselves to do it before. So I never found out with any certainty whether I'd been born on June 23 or 24. And then one day I was trying to make my mother remember, and she confessed that it had been just at sunset, and that there had been people outside lighting bonfires.

"Then there's no doubt—it was the twenty-fourth, the day of the feast of San Juan. It had to be," I said.

Mother shook her head.

14

"Some places they light bonfires on the night before."

That uncertainty always troubled me; it was that uncertainty that had kept me from ever having an exact horoscope. And I questioned her about it more than once, too, because I suspected she was keeping something from me. How could it be that a mother didn't remember the day her son was born?

I would look deep into her eyes, but she always answered me doubtfully.

Some years passed after her death before I discovered, as I was reading one of those books on the occult, that the twenty-fourth of June was a day of ill omen, because it's one of the days on which the witches gather. Consciously or unconsciously, my mother had tried to deny that date, though she couldn't deny the fact of the hour of sunset—an ominous hour.

That was not the only unlucky omen connected with my birth. My brother immediately older than I had just recently died, at two years of age. And I was given the same name! All my life I've been obsessed by the death of that child who had the same name as mine and who, as though that weren't enough, was always remembered with respect bordering on the sacred—because according to both my mother and doña Eulogia Carranza, who was my mother's best friend and a relative of don Pancho Sierra, "that child could not live." Why not? They always answered me vaguely, they would talk about his eyes, the way they looked, or about his portentous intelligence. Apparently, he was born with some mark. All right, but why then had they been so stupid as to give me the same name? As though the surname weren't enough, derived as it is from Saturn, the angel of solitude in the cabala, the Spirit of Evil for certain believers in the occult, the Sabbath of the witches.

"No," I lied to M. "I didn't forget my birthday. I'll be back early."

Later that afternoon, something happened which to a certain extent put my mind at ease. I had bound the novel, which was a bit unwieldy as a manuscript, into a series of folders, and as I handed the folders to Muchnik I told him I was going to keep the last one so I could make some final corrections to it. He got very angry; don't be ridiculous, he said. He argued that I'd never publish anything as long as I lived if I acted like that, I'd wind up totally sterile. All right, I finally agreed, but I asked him if he would mind if I corrected

15

some pages there and then. He could hardly object to that. And so, on one of the proofreader's desks, I randomly opened the last folder to the part where Danel is about to strip the flesh from Lavalle's body. I began scratching out adjectives and adverbs. Adjectives modify nouns and adverbs modify adjectives—modifiers of modifiers, I thought half sarcastically, half in melancholy, recalling some distant grammar class I'd taken somewhere. So much trouble to give just the right color to a horse, a tree, a dead man, and then to wipe out all those qualifiers, to leave those horses and trees and dead men as desolately naked, as harsh and hard-edged, as plain and unadorned as if the adjectives and adverbs were shameful disguises to alter or hide them. I did the work without conviction—one page meant no more to me than any other, they were all imperfect, clumsy, no doubt because when I write fiction there are some forces operating within me to make me do it, to push me on, and there are others that make me stumble and hold me back. Where do all these rough edges, these rocky places, which any educated reader can plainly see, these chipped and broken fragments come from?

Tired, discouraged, I closed the folder and handed it to the proofreader.

I left. It was a cold, miserably sad day. There was drizzling rain.

I still had some time, so it occurred to me to walk down Juan de Garay toward the Parque de los Patricios. I hadn't seen the place since I was a boy, when I first came to Buenos Aires from the little town I'd been born in. And suddenly I recalled that that first night I had slept in a house on Calle Echagüe, a street named after that same Echagüe that figures in Lavalle's Legion. Was it not significant in some obscure way that I should recall this just now, when I'd just finished correcting a page about the Legion, when I was walking just steps from that neighborhood I hadn't visited since that remote time of my childhood?

I came to the park and I decided to go in and walk through the trees. When the drizzle turned to pouring rain I took shelter inside a little kiosk, a newsstand there in the park, and while I was waiting for it to stop raining I watched the owner drinking *mate* out of a little clay pot. He was a man who must have been powerful in his youth.

"Ugly weather," he said, gesturing outside with the *mate*.

16

His broad back had grown stooped with the years. His hair was white, but his eyes were those of a child. Above a little window, written in clumsy hand-drawn letters, was a sign:

C. SALERNO
NEWSPAPERS AND CIGARRETS

Squeezed inside the newsstand there were also a child eight or nine years old and one of those caramel-colored stray dogs with white spots. In return, I suppose, for the man's modest friendliness, I asked him if the boy was his son or grandson.

"No, sir," he answered, "that boy there is a friend of mine. 'S name's Nacho. He gives me a hand now an' then."

The boy looked so much like the Van Gogh with his ear cut off that he could have been his son, and he looked at me with those same enigmatic greenish eyes. The boy in a way reminded me of Martín, too, but a rebellious, violent Martín, a child who might grow up to blow up a bank or a whorehouse one day. The somber gravity of his expression was all the more striking because he was so young.

[Freeze time in childhood, thought Bruno. He saw them standing in a huddle on some street corner, carrying on one of those hermetic conversations meaningless to adults. What were they playing? It wasn't tops, or marbles, or tag. Where were those trading cards he remembered? It was all different now, though maybe it was the same underneath. They would grow up, have their dreams, fall in love, carry on fierce arguments over the meaning of life; their wives would get heavy and turn vulgar, they themselves would wander back to the old café or the old bar to have a drink with their old friends (now gray-headed, fat, bald, skeptical), and then their children too would marry, and then would come the moment of death, that solitary instant at which they would depart this muddled world—all alone, every one of them. Someone (Pavese, was it?) had said that it was terribly sad to grow old and come to know the world. Among those men, among the old, there might be one like him, like Bruno, and everything would start over again—the same observations, the same thoughts, the selfsame melancholy, that staring at children playing on the sidewalk so innocently—one child perhaps like Nacho, who was now observing this stranger gravely and mysteriously

17

from the back of a newsstand, as though some premature and terrible experience had already jerked him out of that world of childhood and made him, grudgingly, contemplate the world of adults. Yes, he felt that he had to stop the course of time. HALT! he cried, ingenuously, as though he were trying to invoke some magical spell, some absurd charm. Then *Halt, O time!* he now almost whispered, as though a more poetic command might achieve what simpler words could not. Leave those children there forever on that sidewalk, in that enchanted universe! Don't let men and their baseness hurt them, break them. Stop life right there. . . .]

The rain had begun to let up, [Sabato was continuing,] and although I had felt inexplicably compelled to talk to the child—not knowing that one day he would reappear in my life (an understatement, that!)—I waved good-bye and ran to where I'd parked my car. I took the first cross-street toward the center of town. I was driving so absentmindedly—first from having turned in the manuscript and then from the impression the young boy's eyes had left on me—that I don't know how, but I wound up on a dead-end street. It was dark by now, and I had to turn my headlights on the street sign before I could read it. I was stunned: ALEJANDRO DANEL.

For a while I couldn't manage to do a thing. I could never have imagined running across that secondary figure from our past, never have imagined that a street named after him existed. And even if I had known, how was I to attribute to chance the fact that I should come upon it unwittingly in a city thirty miles across and immediately after having corrected the part of the novel in which Alejandro Danel strips the flesh off Lavalle's body? When I told this story, later on, to M., she assured me with that invincible optimism of hers that I ought to take it as a good omen. That calmed me, at least for the moment. Because it was only much later that I realized that the sign might have been ominous in the opposite sense than she imagined. Still, at the time her interpretation of the "coincidence" gave me tranquility, a tranquility that actually became euphoria in the months that followed the book's publication, first in Argentina and then in Europe. That euphoria made me forget the intuitions which for years had counseled me to keep absolute silence. The least that one can call this is myopia. We never see far enough, that's all.

Later there occurred, little by little, but with insidious persistence, the events which were to unsettle the last years of my life. Although sometimes, virtually always, really, it would be an error to call them "events"; they were more like those almost imperceptible but disturbing creaks we hear at night when we're lying in bed unable to sleep.

Once again I began to withdraw into myself, and for almost ten years I'd have nothing to do with fiction. Until, that is, two or three things happened that began to give me some hope, weak though it was—occurrences like the tiniest kind of winking lights that a lone aviator who's fought terrible storms, and who's almost out of fuel, begins to see (or to think he sees) far off, through the darkness, and which may be a sign of the coast where he can land, at last.

Yes, I managed to land, though the spot was inhospitable and uncharted, though the guttering lights that had drawn me there and wakened in me that trembling hope might be the bonfires of cannibals.

And so I once again became able to feel myself at home with people, and to walk on my own, just when I thought I might never be able to again.

But I wonder how long, and under what conditions.

HE WASN'T SURE HOW GILBERTO HAD TURNED UP,
who had brought him or sent him. They had needed somebody to fix a door. But how had he come to be there? Later, in moments of suspicion, S. tried to find out, but it turned out that no one was quite sure. At first Sabato's wife didn't like him very much—he seemed to be going around in circles, he was slow, lumbering, dim, he "wandered." His face was enigmatic, but that didn't mean much, since the Indian blood in him accounted for that. Then he began to work, slowly but efficiently, with that artful, perhaps even cunning silence that certain *criollos* have about them. Through him came the others. And now Sabato saw that nothing was casual, that they had been watching him for who knew how long. Little by little the man entered into Sabato's world. In conversations with Sabato's wife, Gilberto suggested that "they" knew his situation and were ready to help Sabato, to help him combat those "entities" that kept him immobilized. Señor Aronoff, he explained, was determined that Señor

19

Sabato should go on with his book at all costs. Maybe they thought it was some sort of masterpiece on the side of the Good, Sabato thought. And that suspicion began to make him feel like a con man, like a man pulling a fast one on the rubes. But what if they were right? They were, after all, seers; he'd heard about some of their little demonstrations of their power. And what if he did, albeit unknowingly, intend to defend the Good, take the side of the powers of light? He examined himself, but he simply could not see how that was possible—he couldn't see from what point of view, in return for what recompense it was that his inward being could be seen to manifest itself in benevolent works. Still, or perhaps for that very reason, those people's plea moved him. And so when Gilberto with his characteristic discretion asked him "how *it*, you know," was going, he told him it was going better, he was beginning to feel a little optimistic about it all, he was sure he'd be able to go back to the book soon, very soon. Gilberto nodded silently, his expression a mixture of humble respect and cunning, and assured Sabato that "they" would keep fighting, keep struggling, but that he "had to help."

One day Gilberto was going down into the basement, he had to check some pipes, he said. S. went down with him, not sure why. Gilberto looked around at everything, he seemed to be taking the most delicate sort of inventory, his eyes rested for a long while on the abandoned piano and on the portrait of Jorge Federico. When he returned a few days later, he asked S. certain questions, he asked for facts about "something that happened in 1949," about a person who looked such and such a way and acted such and such, a foreigner. Schneider, thought Sabato.

"That picture of your son . . ." queried Gilberto.

What about it? Nothing, just that he wondered who'd painted it. Señor Aronoff had said something about Holland. "Bob Gesinus!" thought Sabato, shocked. But no, they had to be wrong about that, Gesinus was the painter, all right, and he was Dutch, but he couldn't be "that person that looked like this and this and this, that foreigner" supposedly guiding the powers. They were mistaken, the image wasn't clear; both Bob and Schneider were foreigners and S. had known them both around the same time.

It would be surprising, he thought (it would be terrifying), if Bob were an agent of the powers of darkness.

20

But why then did they insist on having the séance in the basement? Of course it was true that Valle had turned it almost into an apartment. Don Federico Valle! For the first time the name occurred to him in connection with all this—a foreigner, a man of a certain age. But he never wore a hat. Or was this a detail they'd made some mistake about, from the muddiness the visions so often presented? And though Valle couldn't possibly have been an agent of the negative powers, it was strangely significant that he had always had an inclination for caves and tunnels, from the time he'd worked with Méliès underground in Paris to the time that shelter had been built (excavated) inside the mountain in Córdoba, a shelter he himself had called a "cave." And afterward, when he'd rented out the house in Santos Lugares, hadn't he kept the basement to live in himself? Be that as it might, Aronoff insisted on having the séance in the basement. In the same place they kept the piano that Jorge Federico had played when he was a boy. A piano closed up since then, ruined by the dampness. And on top of it the portrait that Bob had made of him in 1949. Now he realized that that was the date mentioned by Gilberto! But it was absurd, there had been nothing at the time to make him think that Bob was a member of the Sect, even indirectly.

The most startling thing was when the blond girl went into a trance and Aronoff, his voice imperious, ordered her to let a sign come through to them from the past. The young woman struggled and resisted, she whimpered, she wrung her hands, she sweated, she stammered that she couldn't, she couldn't, it was impossible. But Señor Aronoff repeated the order, more imperatively—she must bring a message to Señor Sabato through the piano, a proof that the malign forces were being forced to begin their retreat. While the blond girl went on crying and wringing her hands, the man, enormous yet rendered impotent by his amputated leg and his crutch, whirled about toward the other women in their various levels of trance and toward the boy Daniel, who was now in convulsions, his eyes wild and lost-looking, screaming that something horrible was moving inside him, in his belly. Yes, yes, Señor Aronoff said to him, extending his right hand over his head, yes, yes, you must expel it, expel it. The boy writhed, he looked as though at any moment he might vomit, and then he did; he had to be cleaned up, the floor mopped.

21

Meanwhile, the blond girl had opened the piano and with closed fists, clumsily, stiffly, begun to bang on the keys, whimpering that it was impossible, she couldn't do it. But Señor Aronoff moved his extended arm over her and in that somber, powerful voice he once again commanded her to bring a message to Señor Sabato. The woman called Esther, meanwhile, was breathing deeper and deeper, more and more audibly, and her face was covered with perspiration. Speak! speak! Aronoff ordered her. You are seized by the Entity that has set its power against Señor Sabato. Speak, tell us what you have to say! But she went on rocking, breathing with loud, harsh gasps, until at last she burst into frenzied hysteria and two people had to hold her down to keep her from breaking everything within reach. When she had calmed down a bit, Aronoff once again repeated his command to the blond woman: You must play the piano! he said in his grave, commanding voice, you must bring the message which Señor Sabato needs. But although the young woman tried desperately to revive her numbed and paralyzed fingers, they remained clutched tight, held by a force superior to her will. She banged at the keys, but the sounds she produced were cacophonous, harsh, discordant, like the notes banged out by a young child. Do it! Aronoff commanded. (Sabato could not help being surprised by the fact that the man spoke like a Spaniard.) You can and must do it! You must make the effort which in the name of God I ask you, I command you to make! Sabato felt sorry for the girl, he saw how she whimpered and moaned, saw her frantic, lost eyes, saw how she violently shook her head and tried to open her stiff fingers. But then he saw Betty stand up, with her arms outspread as though she had been crucified. Her face was turned up to the ceiling and her eyes were tightly closed, and she was mumbling unintelligibly. Yes, yes, yes! exclaimed Aronoff, swinging his great body over to her and shifting his crutch so that he could place his outstretched right hand on the woman's forehead. Yes, Betty, yes! That's it! Tell me what you have to say! Tell Señor Sabato what he needs to know! But she went on mumbling incomprehensible sounds.

And then, suddenly, chords erupted from the piano, and both Aronoff and Sabato whirled about. The blond girl, little by little, as her fingers loosened, was playing "In der Nacht," by Schumann. It was one of the pieces that Jorge Federico had played back then! Yes!

22

yes! cried Aronoff, exultant. Play, play! Let Señor Sabato receive that message of light! And he placed his right hand, filled with fluid, on Silvia's head; she played with more assurance, more precision every moment, until at last she was producing sounds more beautiful than could ever have been expected from a piano abandoned for twenty years in a damp basement.

Sabato involuntarily closed his eyes, and he felt his body shaken, rocked. He had to be supported, he had to be held up to keep from falling.

THE REAPPEARANCE OF SCHNEIDER?

THE NEXT DAY HE AWOKE as though he had bathed in a clear mountain stream after slogging for centuries through a swamp infested with snakes. He was sure he had emerged at last, he wrote letters he'd never gotten around to, he told Forrester he'd accept the invitation from that American university, he kept appointments and did reports he'd been putting off. And he felt that as soon as those secondary chores had been gotten out of the way he'd be able to attack the novel again.

He left the Radio Nacional building and was walking euphorically down Ayacucho when he thought he saw Dr. Schneider down the street, almost at the corner of Las Heras. But he had slipped quickly into the café there at the corner. Had he seen Sabato? Had he been waiting for him? Was it really Schneider, or someone who looked like him? At that distance it was easy to be mistaken, especially when one tends to superimpose obsessive images even onto mannequins, as Sabato did so often.

He approached the corner slowly, torn between what he did and didn't want to do. But when he had come to within a few steps of the place, he stopped and turned and walked straight away. He almost ran. That's the expression. Fled. If the man had come back to Buenos Aires—even if, say, it was just that he would sometimes stay for brief periods in Buenos Aires on trips, whatever those trips might be—wasn't he known by enough people who also knew S. that it would be impossible for S. never to have heard one word about him, even indirectly?

Or could it actually be possible that his reappearance was linked

23

to Señor Aronoff's séance and those people? It seemed a little far-fetched to think so. On the other hand, if he'd been invisible for so many years, or invisible at least to Sabato, and all of a sudden dropped into sight again, perhaps even letting himself be seen (or glimpsed, anyway) on purpose, wasn't it a deliberate sign? A warning?

All these thoughts went quickly through his mind, but then, thinking about it further, he told himself that there was no way he could be sure that the heavyset person he'd seen had actually been Schneider.

There was only one way to find out for sure. Conquering his fear, he turned back to the café, but just as he was about to enter he wavered again—he stopped, and then, crossing the avenue, he stood under a plane tree to watch the corner. He stood there for an hour or more, until he saw Nene Costa arrive—his cartilaginous body like some newborn's that had grown, mushroomlike, into a huge, spongy, flabby *thing*, its bones not developing at the same rate as its flesh, so that at last the bones could not support it—or to put it in positive terms, as though the bones had remained soft and quasi-cartilaginous. One always had the impression (not the fear, for no one liked him) that if he didn't lean or rest on something, a wall, a chair, he might simply collapse, like a soufflé or a meringue too heavy to support its own weight. Although the truth was, as S. had reflected more than once, that his weight, his actual weight could not be that great. The sponginess of the stuff the man was made of, the high percentage of liquid or gas in the flesh, the porousness of it all—his intestines, his stomach, his lungs, every cavity or organ of his body—saw to that. The impression of gelatinous enormity that one drew from the man was accentuated by his baby face, as though someone had taken one of those fat blond *putti* with white, white skin and eyes of celestial blue—a baby in a Flemish nativity, for example—and dressed it in men's clothes and stood the creature unsteadily on its feet and then looked at it through a magnifying glass. In S.'s opinion, only one detail betrayed the terrible error: the expression on his face. It was not a baby's expression but rather that of a perverse, clever, encyclopedic, and cynical old man who had gone straight from the cradle to spiritual old age without ever knowing faith, youth, enthusiasm, frankness. Unless, of course, he had

24

been born perverse, clever, and cynical, in virtue of who knew what teratological transmigration, so that from the first moment he turned to his mother's breast he looked up at her with those blue eyes filled with ancient, perverse, and calculating cynicism.

S. watched him go into the café with that unmistakable walk of his—twisted slightly to the side, his blond head bowed somewhat and looking sideways, as though for Nene Costa reality stood never in front of him but somewhere off to the left, and a little down. As he went inside, there flashed through Sabato's mind the memory of Costa's relationship with Hedwig: one of those relationships the man always had—more or less sexual, and apparently determined by the man's infinite snobbery, a snobbery so powerful, so fervent (perhaps the only fervent thing in his entire soul) that it could actually enable him to carry out the sexual act—because it was simply not possible to imagine a woman in bed with that lump of doughy flesh. Although, S. mused, you never know—the heart of man is inexhaustibly strange and unknown, and the power of the soul over the flesh, miraculous. Be that as it might, in those relationships with women that always wound up with a marriage shattered, it couldn't be the body that had triumphed, but the spirit; there was some perversity at work, some sadism, some diabolism that, whatever it was, could only be characterized as a spiritual phenomenon. But even granted that those traits could attract a sophisticated woman, it was still difficult to conceive how they could attract Hedwig, who was neither sophisticated nor frivolous, and who was hardly the sort to invite personal problems. Only one explanation remained: she had to be a tool (but please, that word had to be put between quotation marks) of Dr. Schneider. Nene Costa's snobbery, his Germanophilia, and his anti-Semitism strengthened, or encouraged, the enigmatic relationship.

DEEP THOUGHTS, A DIALOGUE

HE RETURNED TO HIS HOUSE IN A STATE OF PROFOUND DEPRESSION. But he refused to allow himself to be beaten so easily, so he decided to go ahead with his plans for the novel. He'd no sooner opened the drawer of the file cabinet and begun to rummage through his papers, however, than he asked himself, with sarcastic skepticism, *what*

25

novel? He leafed through the hundreds of pages—outlines, outlines of outlines, variations on outlines—all as contradictory and incoherent as his own soul. Dozens of characters were waiting there, like reptiles sleeping, catatonic, through the cold months of the year, the life in them imperceptible, silent, secret, latent, though they might be ready to sting, inject their venom the moment warmth restored them to their fuller existence.

As always when he performed this inspection, he came at last to the folder with the newspaper clippings about that gang of Calsen Paz's. Once more he gazed in fascination at the Dostoyevskian face. What moved that person? He remembered similar instants, similar scrutinies and discouragements, fifteen years earlier, when he had felt that intellectual, criminal gaze waking ambiguous monsters within him, beasts growling in the mud and darkness. Something had whispered to him even then that this face was the black herald of a monarch of the shadows. But when Fernando Vidal Olmos had arrived, this small-time crook—that voice's annunciatory mission apparently accomplished—had crawled back into the file from which it had slithered one day.

And now what? He contemplated that face of icy passions and tried to figure out what the link was between it and the novel he was so stumblingly trying to construct. Stumblingly, like always: everything inside him would be confused and obscure, things would come together and fall apart again, he could somehow never quite see what it was he wanted or where he was headed. The outlines of his characters would grow gradually more defined, would emerge little by little from the shadows, would become clear and cleanly demarcated, and then they would simply vanish, return to the realm of darkness from which they had come. What was he trying to say with his fiction? Almost ten years after publishing *On Heroes and Tombs* students, intensely curious ladies, clerks in government offices, kids doing their dissertations at Michigan or in Florence, typists, would ask him that. And navy officers going into the Officers Club now looked with intrigued suspicion at that old Blind Man dressed like an English gentleman, older and more stooped each day, who sold his trinkets at the door—until one day he disappeared. Forever? Was he dead? In what dark den had he died? Yes, those sailors too wanted to know what that famous "Report on the Blind"

26

meant. And when he told them that he could add nothing more to what he had already written there, they would grow insistent, then angry, frustrated, resentful, and they would look at him as though he were some sort of charlatan, and the whole thing a hoax. Because how could the author himself not know things? It was futile to try to explain to these people that some facts, some realities, some *things* can only be explained with mute and inexplicable symbols, just as the man dreaming does not always understand what his nightmares mean.

He went through his files, and felt how ridiculous all this meticulousness was: he was like some mad watchmaker working with painstaking patience on a watch that turns out to say that it's 3:12 P.M. at noon. Once again he pored over the yellowing clippings, the photos, the tortuous statements, the mutual accusations: one said it was Calsen himself who ran the stake through the heart of the bound boy and then twisted it; another said it was Godas under Calsen's orders; one said eighteen-year-old Dora Forte was Calsen's lover, another said she wasn't; one said Calsen was homosexual, the other that he wasn't. However it all was, Dora was to seduce Sale, the young Turkish boy, take him to Calsen, initiate him into the gang, and finally they would fake (or so Sale thought) the kidnapping to get money out of the old man. And it was only when they tied him up and stuffed a rag in his mouth that he realized that they were actually going to murder him. His eyes horrified, he watched the nightmarish scene and heard Calsen's curt order to dig the grave in the lot in back. Then he signed the letter they'd had ready.

Sabato wondered why Sale hadn't already signed the letter, if he thought the kidnapping was being faked; and why he would sign it at that point, when he must have realized that they were going to kill him one way or another. But maybe real crimes always have these rough edges and incoherences. Two details to illustrate Calsen's sardonic sadism: he had kept the letter hidden behind a print of Millet's *Angelus* until the moment of its signing, and the money was to be left in the porch of the Church of Our Lady of Mercy. Good lord. He looked at the photo again and though the two faces had virtually nothing in common thought of Nene Costa.

While he was rereading the testimony, his mind began to wander: the features of the faces in the pictures began to change, slowly but inevitably they began to form other faces that he was obsessed by, and particularly the hated face of R., who appeared to sit in judgment, like some perverse expert witness, on the errors of those small-time criminals.

R. always behind the scenes, in the darkness. And he, Sabato, always obsessed by the idea of exorcising him, writing a novel in which R. would be the main character. A novel set in the Paris of 1938, when R. made his reappearance, and Sabato's life had gone awry. That aborted project, "The Memoirs of a Stranger," that Sabato had tried to write. He'd never had the courage to tell M. about R., he'd always talked about such and such a character, a reactionary anarchist type, a man he would call Patricio Duggan. The piece of fiction he was "working on" was supposed to take Calsen's crime as its point of departure, but it all became distorted, changed, twisted about, little by little, until it was no longer recognizable: Dora Forte was no longer a poor little beauty from the slums but rather a so-phisticated young woman. And Patricio was the leader of the gang, but S. cast him first as the girl's lover and then as her brother (but maybe her lover too). It had petered out. Years later, still haunted by R., he had written *On Heroes and Tombs*, in which Patricio had been transformed into Fernando Vidal Olmos and the girl trans-formed first into his sister and then into his natural daughter—and that book still had nothing to do with the Calsen gang or with that yellowing crime.

And now, once again, he found himself half lost in that fetid labyrinth of incest and crime, slowly sinking once more into the swampy muck from which he had thought he had escaped once and for all, thanks to those naive exorcisms carried out by seamstresses and plumbers. He could see something beckoning to him from the shadows, beckoning him sarcastically with its claws, and once again he felt himself drowning in confusion and discouragement, in guilty fantasies, in the secret vice of imagining diabolical passions. The old monsters had returned—with that same nightmarish vagueness and imprecision they always had, but with the same terrible power too, and at their head the old ambiguous figure watching him from the shadows, its green eyes, which could see through the depths of the night like some nocturnal bird of prey's, glowing in the darkness. Hypnotized by the reappearance of this old nightmare, Sabato slowly

28

sank into sleep on the breast of that foreboding family, as though under the effects of some malign drug. And when, hours later, he returned to consciousness, he was no longer the man who a few days earlier had waked with optimism.

He began to pace, he looked for some way to distract himself, he leafed through a magazine. And there, if one could believe it, was the face of that creature, that animal, that insect—that smile of the perfectly innocent man who had nothing to hide, the man always ready to help and understand, the open, kindly eyes; but underneath those frank features Sabato saw, with the eyes of the patient technician deciphering the real message in a coded despatch, the true marks of an ignoble old whore, a lying, scheming, hypocritical whore. What was it he had to say about the Municipal Prize?

How disgusting, and how sad. He felt shame: he, after all, belonged to the same abominable race that man did.

He lay down and once again played with one of his favorite old fantasies, giving up literature and setting himself up in a little shop in some unknown neighborhood in Buenos Aires. An unknown neighborhood in Buenos Aires? He had to be kidding, what a dead end that would be. And on top of everything, he was in a foul mood because he'd spoken his mind at the Alliance. He had suffered for two hours, and then he'd had to suffer all night long, as though he'd taken off all his clothes in public and shown his scabs, and just to make the embarrassment worse, done it in the presence of stupid, frivolous people he had no patience for.

Everything started to look bleak again, and the novel, that famous novel of his, looked every minute more futile and depressing. What sense was there in writing one more novel? He had written novels at two crucial moments in his life, or at least they were the only two novels he'd ever allowed published, and he wasn't altogether sure why. But now he felt he needed something different, something like fiction squared. Something was pushing at him, all right. But what? So he turned again, almost grudgingly, to those contradictory pages, those pages that somehow wouldn't come together, those pages that were not, apparently, what he needed.

And then there was that rending gap between his rational, conceptual world and his subterranean world. He'd left science to write fiction, like some nice housewife that suddenly decides to go into drugs and prostitution. What had led him to invent those stories? And what was it they actually were?

Generally speaking, fiction was considered a kind of mystification, a not altogether serious undertaking. Professor Houssay, the Nobel Prize winner, had refused to shake hands with Sabato when he heard of his decision.

Without realizing that he had come there, Sabato found himself walking down the street alongside the wall of the cemetery on Recoleta. Those flophouses on Vicente López depressed him, and especially the idea that R. could live in some filthy room someplace around there, in some building with clothes hanging out the window to dry.

And Schneider—what did he have to do with this novel? And who was this "Entity" that kept Sabato from completing it?

He suspected that Schneider was one of those powers, and that from some secret place he was exerting his force on him, continuing to do so even though he'd disappeared for several years, forced to retreat for a while, perhaps, or withdraw, but always stalking Sabato, even from a distance—and now he had apparently come back to Buenos Aires.

The other presence, he already knew about that one.

And suddenly he realized that his preoccupation with Sartre was not the result of chance but rather of those same powers, or forces, which had been hounding and harassing him. It was the problem of the gaze, the eyes, wasn't it?

The eyes. Victor Brauner. Brauner's paintings full of eyes. Brauner's own eye, blinded by Domínguez.

As he continued walking, aimlessly, Sabato began to doubt every word of it, every fact, every event. Spies that were dropped off at some spot in England, speaking English perfectly, dressing and stammering like any graduate of Oxford. How could one distinguish one's enemies, then? That kid selling the ice cream, for example—S. had to keep his eye on him. He bought a chocolate ice cream and walked off, or pretended he was going to walk off, but suddenly he whirled and looked into the young man's eyes. The young man was startled. But his surprise could be either the proof of his innocence or of his deep subtlety. It was an infinite task: that guy carrying the ladder,

30

that typist, that salesgirl, that seven-year-old playing—or *pretending* to play. Didn't totalitarian regimes use children?

He found himself standing before the door of the Carranzas' apartment, though he didn't remember intending to go there.

He sank into the couch; somebody was saying something about Pipina. What, what? The lecture at the Alliance Française. The Alliance and Pipina? What in the world were they talking about?

Beba laughed. "No, you goose, we were talking about Sartre."

But hadn't he heard somebody say something about Pipina?

No, no, we were talking about Sartre.

All right, but then what did you say?

I was asking whether you'd criticized Sartre.

Discouraged, Sabato took off his glasses, ran his hand over his forehead, rubbed his eyes. Then, as Beba turned her inquisitorial eyes on him, he studied the parquet for defects. Her mother, looking (as she always did) like she'd just gotten out of bed, her hair tangled and frowsy, was muttering something about the tributaries of the Ganges, cephalopods, and pronouns.

Schneider, he thought, still looking down at the floor.

"When did he first come to Buenos Aires?"

"Who?" Beba asked, startled.

"Schneider."

"Schneider? Why on earth would you suddenly be interested in that charlatan after all these years?"

"But when did he come?"

"When the war was over. How do I know."

"What about Hedwig?"

"Her too, I guess."

"But I wonder if they met each other over there, in Hungary."

"I believe I heard that they met in some bar in Zurich."

Irritating; it was all so irritating—*I think, I believe, I think I heard.* Always the same ambiguities. Beba looked at him, puzzled. "That clown," she said. "All he needed was a snake and one of those all-purpose gadgets for threading needles, peeling potatoes, and cutting glass. And all those old ladies always following him around!"

It was true, he looked like, or really he *was* like a snake-oil salesman, some carnival shill. So what.

31

"What do you mean 'So what'?"

So far as S. was concerned Beba's anger was a by-product of that Cartesian mentality of hers. She might argue with Dr. Arrambide, but basically they both had the same kind of mind. He didn't feel like explaining anything.

"What do you mean, 'So what'?" she persisted.

Sabato looked at her tiredly. Baudelaire, all that stuff about the devil.

"Baudelaire?"

But he refused to explain, it all felt so futile. The worst villainy: making people believe that you don't exist. Schneider was grotesque yet somber, loud and raucous yet shadowy and secret. His guffaws hid a base, cunning, secretive soul, much the way the caricatured mask of comedy may hide the hard, scheming, and impassive visage of the inferno. Like a person planning a cold and ruthless crime telling jokes to his future victim. Maruja was asking something about coelenterates, five letters. Sabato imagined the gang's silken threads spinning and spinning out of the darkness, weaving its secret web. But what was he thinking about? Patricio and the Christensens were imaginary—how could Schneider, a real man, direct Sabato's fancies? Gustavo Christensen. Sabato thought once more that Nene Costa might be the perfect Gustavo Christensen. Why not? He'd seen him as thin, while Costa was fat and disgusting, but after all, why not?

"And that Nene Costa," he said.

Beba's eyes went fiery. What about that pig?

"I saw him. He was going into a café on Las Heras and Ayacucho."

What did she care? He knew she couldn't care less about Nene Costa. She'd closed the files on that case years ago.

"I tell you."

"I really couldn't care less, and you know it."

"I'm telling you because I think he was going inside to see Schneider."

"What are you talking about? Schneider's in Brazil. He has been for I don't know how long."

"I think he went into that café. And they were friends."

"Who?"

"Schneider and Nene Costa. Weren't they?"

32

Beba laughed—the idea of Nene Costa being friends with anybody!

"I mean they saw a lot of each other back then."

"I wonder who screwed who."

"They don't have to have been *friends*. They could have been conspiring with each other."

Beba looked at him questioningly, but Sabato had nothing to add to that. After a while, looking into his glass, he asked:

"So in your opinion Schneider went to Brazil?"

"That's what Mabel told me. Everybody knew. He went with Hedwig."

Still studying his glass, Sabato asked her whether Quique was still seeing Nene Costa.

"I imagine so. I hardly see how he could deny himself that pleasure. A jewel, you might say."

"But anytime recently—he hasn't said anything about Schneider recently? Hasn't mentioned whether he's come back from Brazil, whether he sees Nene? Quique'd be sure to know."

No, he'd never mentioned anything about him. And besides, Quique knew perfectly well that she didn't like to be reminded of Nene Costa. Sabato now was more tormented than before, because all this only proved that if the man had returned from Brazil—or wherever else he might have been—the return was not public but circumspect. Could, then, his contacts with Costa be linked to the problem that was bedeviling Sabato? It seemed at first glance absurd that the ridiculous Costa might be in on such a conspiracy, but it didn't seem so farfetched when one considered it from a demoniacal angle. But then in that case, why would they be seen in a bar in the middle of the city? Although he for one never went there. It might have been a coincidence. But such a telling coincidence? No, he had to discard that possibility. On the contrary, he probably ought to think that Schneider had somehow found out, somehow *known*, that he, Sabato, was going to Radio Nacional, and waited on the street for him until he had seen (or glimpsed) him coming out, and then turned into the bar. But what was it all for? To intimidate him? Once again, the question: who was hounding whom?

He tried to recall, but everything was all mixed up. Yes, Mabel had introduced him to André Téleki, and Téleki had introduced him to Schneider. *The Tunnel* had just come out in Spanish, so that must have been 1948, say. At the time he'd paid no real attention to the question Schneider had asked him about Allende— Why blind? It seemed an innocent enough question.

"A cuckold, and blind to boot," he had laughed vulgarly.

What had he been doing all those years between '48 and '62? Wasn't it significant that he should have reappeared in 1962, just as *On Heroes and Tombs* was being published? In an infinite city years can pass without one's running into a single acquaintance. Why had he chanced to run across him just as his new novel had come out?

He tried to remember the exact words of that meeting—something about Fernando Vidal Olmos.

So wasn't he ever going to answer her question?

"Huh?"

Had he said terrible things about Sartre, or not? Yes or no.

Beba, with that constant habit she had of jumping from one subject to another, with that eternal whisky of hers in her hand, with her blazing, inquisitorial eyes.

Criticized Sartre? Who'd been saying such idiotic things?

She couldn't remember. Somebody.

Somebody, somebody! Always those faceless enemies! He wondered why he still spoke in public.

He did it because he wanted to.

Would she please not talk such rubbish. He spoke out of weakness, he spoke because some friend asked him to, he spoke because he didn't like to seem arrogant, because it was for the poor guys in some night school in Villa Soldati or Mataderos, he spoke, in a word, because he couldn't say no—kids working during the daytime as electricians and going to school to try to figure Marx out at night.

Oh come on! The Alliance wasn't in Villa Soldati, dozens of perfectly well-fed society ladies went there.

"All right. I spoke for those well-fed society ladies, you guessed it. That's all I've ever done my whole life. Now will you leave me alone with my whisky, please, which is what I came in for."

"You two stop yelling, let me think. River in Asia, four letters."

"So the only thing this person told you was that I said dreadful things about Sartre."

He stood up, walked across the living room and into the library;

34

he examined the old cavalry swords, read some titles unseeingly. He was furious with everyone, and with himself. Caustic, ironic thoughts about roundtables, lectures, the Alliance Française ran through his mind, along with childhood memories, the realization of how thin Beba had gotten the last few months, amazement at the titles of some novels (*Á l'ombre des jeunes filles en fleurs!* Was that real?); ideas about dust and bookbinding. At last he went back to the couch, into which he sank as though he weighed two or three times himself.

"Something between Kenya and Ethiopia that looks like a zebu but that isn't a zebu—seven letters."

"Did you attack Sartre, yes or no?"

Sabato exploded. Beba, stiffly, said he might give some details, instead of screaming. He wasn't acting much like an intellectual, more like a madman it seemed to her.

"But who is the cretin that came to you with this tale?"

"The person is not a cretin."

"I thought you just told me you didn't recall who it was."

"Yes but now I do."

"So who was it?"

"I'm not going to tell you. You'll just want to know more."

"Of course, of course, why tell me."

He slumped back into a black silence. Sartre. Quite the contrary, he had always defended Sartre. How telling, that one always had to defend the truly authentic minds. Back at the time of the rebellion in Hungary, when the Stalinists accused Sartre of being a petit-bourgeois-counterrevolutionary-in-the-service-of-Yankee-imperial-ism. Then afterward, against the McCarthyites that were accusing him of being a tool-of-international-communism. And not to mention of being homosexual, of course, since they weren't able to drag in his Jewish parentage.

"But come, admit it—don't you think it would be better to tell me what you said than it is to throw this tantrum?"

"To what purpose?"

"Oh, I'm not worth telling."

"If you were so interested, you ought to have gone to the lecture."

"I've got Pipina with diarrhea."

"All right, then, there you are."

35

"What does that mean—there you are? I *am* interested in the problem of Sartre."

"And you want me, in twenty words or less, to explain to you what I patiently laid out for two hours. And *you* talk about frivolous people!"

"I'm not asking you to tell me every word you said. Give me an idea. The basic idea. And furthermore, you must admit that I've got more in my head than those fat ladies that push so hard to get in to hear you that they sweat for the next two hours."

"Oh come on. It was full of students."

"Unless my memory fails me, one day you told me that all philosophy is the working out of one central intuition, or perhaps of one metaphor: *panta rhei*, the Heraclitean river, the sphere of Parmenides. True or false?"

"True."

"And now you come out with this story about how your theory on Sartre needs two hours. Do you mean to tell me it's more important than the philosophy of Parmenides?"

Nothing.

"Eh?"

"That article Sartre wrote on *La Nausée*."

"Article? What article?"

That thing that had come out some time ago. No doubt the product of his guilt feelings.

"Guilt feelings?"

"Of course, there are children dying of hunger out there. And to write that novel . . ."

"*Whose* child is dying of hunger?"

"No, mother . . . All right, so then?"

"I began there."

"And you think that's a mistake?"

"Don't start all over again, now."

"But then?"

"But then, what? Will you be so kind as to tell me when a novel, not necessarily *La Nausée*, any novel, the finest novel in the world, *Don Quixote*, *Ulysses*, *The Trial*, any novel, has been any good whatsoever at keeping even one child from dying? If one weren't convinced of Sartre's integrity, one would have to think that they were

36

the words of a demagogue. I'll go even further: how, when, in exactly what way does a Bach chorale or a Van Gogh painting keep a child from dying of hunger? Are we to renounce literature entirely—all literature, all music, all painting?"

"A while back, there was this TV show on India, and I saw some children, little more than babies they were, starving in the street."

"Yes, mother."

"You saw that show?"

"No, mother."

"And I read this book, too, by some French writer, Jules Romains . . . no, wait . . . Romain Rolland, could that be it? I always get mixed up with last names, I'm hopeless about last names . . . anyway, something on that."

"On what, mother?"

"On this poor little thing that was starving to death. What was that name?"

"Of who?"

"That writer."

"I have no idea, mother. They're two different writers. And I've never read either one of them."

"You might read a little more, instead of arguing all the time and drinking so much whisky. And you, Ernesto, you don't know either?"

"No, Maruja."

"So you think Sartre was wrong. You see, the person that told me about all this was right. True or false?"

"For God's sake, that's not attacking Sartre, you idiot. It's virtually defending him against a charge of weakness. Defending the best Sartre, I mean."

"So the Sartre who grieves over the death of a child is a bad Sartre?"

"That is a sophism as big as the side of a house. Let's not lower the level of the conversation, if you please, quite so abysmally."

"All right, let's get back to your argument. You mean to say that Sartre reasons badly. That he is not capable of rigorous thought."

"I didn't say that. It isn't that he reasons badly, it's that he feels guilty."

"Guilty? Why?"

"That combination of demon-ridden and Protestant that he was."

"What of it?"

"Nothing. But maybe one indicator of that is that last name, Schweitzer. The other indicator is ugliness."

"Ugliness. What does that have to do with the article?"

"An ugly child, a frog. Have you read *Les Mots*?"

"Yes. Why?"

"He was terrified of people looking at him."

"So?"

"What is it of you that can be seen? Your body, of course. Hell is other people looking at you. Being looked at is being petrified, enslaved. Aren't those the themes of Sartre's entire philosophy and of his entire literary production?"

"You're so arbitrary. You're going to reduce all of Sartre's thought to those twenty words or less."

"Not five minutes ago, correct me if I'm wrong, you demanded that I do just that. *Panta rhei.*"

"Maybe so, but now you're going to turn a psychosis, or call it a complex, into the basis for a philosophy. If the Bolshies catch you . . ."

"Shame is not trivial. Especially shame over a child. It can come to have tremendous existential dimensions. I am ashamed, therefore I am. From that, all else proceeds."

"Everything? Don't you think you're pushing this just the slightest bit too far?"

"Why? The essence of a creator's work comes out of some child-hood obsession. Think of Sartre's fiction. Is there a single character that appears naked?"

"You assume that all I do is remember characters out of Sartre, how they're dressed or undressed. I haven't read Sartre for years and years."

"I ask you because you've been torturing me. A man has a desire to look down on other men, he feels omnipotent that way. Or a woman wants to be able to observe her friend without being seen. Some guy takes great delight in imagining himself invisible, and one of his secret pleasures is spying through a keyhole. Another man pictures hell as a look which pierces everything. In one novel, hell is a woman's glance, a glance which on top of everything men must suffer through all eternity."

"All right, enough. Where does it all end. But philosophy . . ."

"I think you've been reading novels very superficially. Otherwise you'd remember the invisibility, the hovering, the way they pop up, every so often. Page after page about the body, the gaze, shame."

At which juncture Quique came in and said, "Maruja, you're cuter every day, *et tout et tout.*" And then, turning to Sabato, he said, "Good afternoon, Maestro." Sabato thus realized that he was, in what he presumed would be Quique's words, *de trop*, and so he took his leave.

The moment he was out the door Beba turned on Quique indignantly.

"I warned you not to provoke him, at least in my presence!"

"I couldn't help it, my love. Ever since he made me work so hard in that novel of his, relieving some of its tediousness for him, you know. The bore, the boor, the dreadful leaden little man. One day when I have time I'm going to tell you a couple of stories that will . . . well, my dear. And all of it, let it be clearly understood, I have on the very highest of authorities."

"I don't see why instead of behaving so unpleasantly you didn't tell him one of your jokes."

"Sabato? A joke? Really!"

"Of course."

"Of course, she says. And have my very words turn up in one of his novels years later, darling? In that novel he's supposedly been working on for twenty years? Spare me!"

QUIQUE WAS GLUM.
Forbidding him to say terrible things about people was, Beba knew, tantamount to forbidding Galileo his celebrated riposte. But the arrival of Silvina with her girlfriends from school reanimated him instantaneously; they told him they'd seen the Molina kid on a motor scooter, with a leather jacket.

"Wonderful! The priest in his new habit! How delightful! Priests in shorts, nuns in bikinis. And forget about masses in Latin, when there is a language as universal as soap-opera Mexican Spanish, which thanks to television and advertising and the taste of the masses (we *were* speaking of masses, weren't we?) has now supplanted even ecclesiastical Latin as the *lingua franca* of the Church. I assure you, ladies, that Catholicism one day will be as popular as canasta, especially among the dispossessed classes. These Leninist priests, who'd rather spout *bons mots* from Marx and Lenin than quote Saint Thomas any day. *Après tout,* Christianity has always taken the yellow brick road to popularity. I mean if you don't see what I mean, girls, think of baptism—with water! It's the cheapest thing, isn't it? So there you are. Unless they get the brilliant idea of catechizing people in the Sahara. Remember that brilliant idea of baptizing people with the blood of a bull. What kind of cult could survive such extravagance—imagine having to kill a bull every time you have to turn a poor heathen child into a Christian! A cult for oligarchic Romans and Greek tycoons. And here it would be reserved for the babes in arms of the Anchorenas and the other noble families of Buenos Aires, or maybe one or two of the parvenu Italians like Bevilacqua."

"What's this about Bevilacqua?" Maruja asked, raising her head from her crossword puzzle. "Did he buy a bull, you say?"

"But for one such as oneself, you know, the distinguished poor, what is there but the Holy Mother Roman and Apostolic Catholic Church? At least it's a supermarket religion, dear."

"Enough, Quique. Tell us about Losuar, will you? We've been waiting."

Quique threw his enormous arms wide and raised them to heaven, then lifted his eyes, too, as though in an invocation.

"Women!" he cried.

"Get on with it."

"Well, then, you girls know that as a chronicler employed by a most specialized and prestigious periodical publication (because I'll have you know that I am now one of the pillars of *Radiolandia,* one of the electronic brains of that fascinating hebdomadal review), I feel obliged to follow the movements of the stars—not astrologically, mind you, but the stars of the great silver screen. Although, fortunately, I don't have to go to the Lorraine or that whole series of Biographs, as they were called in the olden days, that that shyster uses to milk culture with, those temples of entertainment, those

40

once-brilliant palaces of the motion picture arts which he has converted now into simply one more in a list of disasters perpetrated upon this city already plagued by potholes, broken water mains, and lumpy sidewalks. Anyway, after the Lorraine the Loire was begotten, after of course a survey of the in-people of Buenos Aires. A survey, by the way, of extreme subtlety, because the name had to be Franssh, *mes amies*, and had to begin with Lo. How very, very precious, don't you agree? But in fact there was a certain method in the modishness—the poor dupe running his finger down the list of movies in the newspaper might not fall into the snare of the Lorraine, but he'd have to skirt the Loire if he didn't, he'd have to tiptoe through a veritable minefield of Lo's before reaching the safety of the enemy's box office, how's that for a ruse for the rubes, babes? And this is how it all came about—after the Lorraine, all the *habitués*, especially those who go to the Alliance, strained their sweet little noggins going through the history, geography, and numismatics of La Belle France until at last somebody came up with the jewel of the Loire, a true *tour de force* even for connoisseurs like I, who never but never would have thought of such a *coup*. Because I mean who'd ever think of something so utterly obvious? As though you just blurted out 'the Seine, the Seine!' Please! For lives there a girl with heart so dead who never to herself has said, 'the castles along the Loire'? And so, as I was saying, that was the beginning of the dynastic series of movie palaces beginning with Lo—first the Lorraine, then the Loire, and now, after utterly *exhausting* every possible ounce of historical and geographical reference available, comes the Losuar, which for those of you who are not quite so with it as the with-its, is a kind of centaur formed of the head of the Lorraine and the loins, so to speak, of the Loire. But rivers or centaurs, what we must not lose sight of here, my dear ladies, is that the cunning gentleman has them packed full night and day, running for the nine hundred forty-fifth time *The Battleship Potemkin*, that virtuoso Marxist exercise in shipbuilding, as that naughty boy Charlie says, which ejaculates cannon shells that render the dens of the filthy bourgeois dust while taking the life of not a single poor innocent child. And as the snobbery of our peers is infinite, there's plenty of fodder for a good while yet. A good while! There's fodder for a lifetime, because every day there's a new trend to follow. First Italian neorealism, in which the wops

41

yell at each other as though they were haggling in a bazaar, which of course is taken to be the very *height* of art, until the groundlings tire of that, you know, and then it's back to Frahnce, which needless to say always holds the keys to our hearts, and we have to swallow all those kitschy scenes from Duvivier, which *cinéastes* around the world consider the apex of refined cinematographic style. And when we begin to be sated with the French, since (as I have heard peasants say) one cannot bathe twice in the same river, we move along to Svädish fälms, always a great success, because be we who we be, we *never* tire of seeing a blond damsel tupped on the screen, especially if the tupper is a brigand, or a brigand of a brother of the damsel better yet, with all the complexes and metaphysical soul-searching, as Maestro Sabato would say, which such an act of incestuous outlawry implies, with the result that all the moviegoers of our metropolis believe that in Sweden all anybody does all day, and all night too, be it added, is the old in-and-out, the old tickle-and-coo, you know, and between incest and the abortions of young unmarried women when the *fait accompli* obliges them to opt for heroic, so to speak, measures, the patrons of those motion picture establishments dream of going to the land of free sex and the home of the great chicks, as the Americans might put it, not knowing—the movie patrons I mean, *pauvres enfants*—that there's no sunshine for four months a year so you spend half your life with your teeth chattering too hard to, you know, *do it*, curled up beside or on top of or better yet *inside* a stove, so that when you finally come out, which is exactly August twenty-seventh by the clock on the wall, it's a national holiday, and *tout le monde* runs out onto the sidewalks to catch a few rays, the very friendly, super-nice king included, or take a trip to the country, where Bergman is filming *A Summer with Monica* and where all sorts of wonderful uninhabited high jinks can be committed *al fresco* in the hills, dales, and meadows of the country, and perhaps even in the gardens of the royal palace. *But*—because there is always a but, ladies—that is the only day of sun. So our own aborigine arrives on the twenty-eighth of August, the good times have gone for another year, and he finds his ass is frozen into a Svädish maitböll."

Silvina begged for a rest. When things had calmed down, Quique went on:

42

"Well, one day I get the urge to go to one of those dens of culture where the minute you walk in the front door you're washed in music from Albinoni and during the intermissions people sit around reading Marcuse, so as not to waste a single minute, as though you spent your life eating vitamins and breathing pure oxygen, right? And as I'm walking in the door, who should I not be able to avoid seeing but the most dispiriting sight, I assure you, in the world. Miss Coca Rivero. And to make matters worse, it hadn't been long since I'd gone to see her, so I could hardly pretend I didn't recognize her, you know. And you know how Coca is, even that library of hers—a hardbound copy of *The Inferno* by Barbusse, *The Disenchanted* by somebody else, *A World without God* by some Anabaptist from Minneapolis, and as though all that macabre bookbinding weren't enough, a paperback of *The Frigid Woman* by Steckel—I mean you see all that stuff and you run for a window for a little sunshine! And of course I had been dying to tell her all about the latest mess her sister had gotten herself into, but what with that funeral home of a library I got so depressed I was ready for embalming *myself*. Anyway, *noblesse oblige*, you know, so instead of spilling my guts, as I was panting to do, over Panucha's latest affair, I sat down and started telling Coca about all the funerals, divorces, tumors, hepatitises, and other disasters I could think of, and how expensive everything had gotten with the new exchange rates don't you know. When in Rome, you see, and also to pick Coca up a bit. After all, the only sun she ever sees is the black sun of Nerval. You could wither from gloom in her very living room!"

"But what did you do when you saw her in the Losuar?"

"What could I do? We went to La Paz for coffee, sat between two guys in beards and three cleaning women from one of the art galleries, and I began to unfurl my theodicy."

"Theodicy?" echoed Silvina, as she stopped laughing long enough for the question. "A Roman empress?"

"Please, Silvina! You just listen and paint, dear—at least you have some talent for that. . . . I explained to Coca that the world was like a symphony, but that God plays by ear. Though why be a monist? No, Silvina, that's not a specialist in money, it's something very different. I mean who says there aren't all sorts of possible explanations for all this. The Big Guy (and please, note, linotypist, it's capital-B-Big capital-G-Guy, you never know, so just in case make it with capitals, like that friend of Baudelaire's that was going to put his cigarette out on the belly of some statue of an African idol, but Bo says *Watch out! he could be the real one!)*—but as I was saying before I interrupted myself, the Big Guy likes his practical jokes once in a while, so the world is, as someone once said, *un mot pour rire*, a great, universal, cosmic cackle one quadrillion light-years long by two and a half billion light-years wide. Or it might be a score by a bad musician, somebody, say, that composes dreadful stuff after a big meal, like Rossini, whose stuff came out like canneloni (after he'd invented canneloni, I mean), and him taking a little nap, about half asleep, just a little nod, you know. Homer sleeps sometimes, so why not? Or it could be that the universe that we know is just a fraction of all creation, and we got the short end of the stick so to speak, like the society pages of the newspaper, for instance, no?, while other places got the sports section or at least the political pages instead of this shitty, if you'll forgive me the *gros mot*, part we're supposed to sing. Or read. Or whatever that metaphor was. Or maybe the Big Guy went to sleep and his nightmares—say he'd had himself a big bowl of spaghetti with homemade tomato sauce, lots of garlic—turned out to be our reality, and your sainted mother dies, a woman who's never done an evil deed in her whole life, everybody says how can God let such a thing happen, poor old lady dying like that, and it turns out the Big Guy's not responsible, he was snoozing at the time, your sweet mother's death is the nightmare which is the by-product of *le grand bouffe*. So that's how it goes, and now I'm off, as I have certain professional obligations to attend to."

"No, Quique, no! Tell us some more about Coca!"

"What can I tell you about that poor dear thing? All I can say is that just as our physics professors would pull out that electrostatic machine to teach us about electricity—you remember that?—well, Professor Heidegger had Coca on retainer so he could bring her out and show her whenever he talked about Angst. And if Raskovsky'd ever gotten ahold of her, he'd have dashed off a twelve-volume work on the traumas and complexes of Coca. Oh, and by the way, I've always wondered why there are so many psychoanalysts in Argentina, which is second only to the United States, I'll have you know. Amazing! There must be some *raison d'être*, as Leibniz would say.

44

Half a million Jews in Buenos Aires, if I'm not mistaken? And yet there's something wrong here, something psychoanalytical even before the arrival of the Odessa Russkies. I mean just think of our famous Argentine mixed grill, a true genitourinary, polymorphous perversity—tripes, udder, blood sausage, testicles."

"But I thought testicles were like oysters."

"That's why I told you to stick to painting. . . . There you have material for a case study in the cathedral of Dr. Goldberg. Not to mention the tango. Just listen again to Rivero singing about living with Momma! How touching! That cross between Freud and Sciammarella, Oedipus in two-four time. And so true to life as we know it in our dear Argentina! And therefore so beautiful, because *rien n'est beau que le vrai*. From which derives the entire industry on which those clever boys live. Not for nothing am I a solid card-carrying member of the Communist Fellow-Travelers, I'll tell you. All that added value in the hands of those exploiters of humanity. Because you aren't going to tell me that there are no wretched masses in Russia. It's just that over there psychoanalysis is nationalized, there's a Ministry of Angst, with a Commissar for Oedipal Relations. And although centralization brings with it its inevitable bureaucracy, as Alvaro so sagely notes, at least they don't exploit you. I can just imagine guys going into the army, and the sergeant yelling ALL YOU SHITHEADS WITH OEDIPALS, UP FRONT! And the minute the poor jerks step forward, they're marched off for work therapy in Siberia!"

Silvina couldn't breathe again. "Oh, please, I beg you," she said, "time out." So Quique stood up to go, adding that he was planning to send a press release about this to the Argentine Psychoanalytical Society—an organization, he affirmed, as large as the Hebraic Society. And with practically the same members.

THERE ARE FEW SOLITUDES LIKE THE SOLITUDE OF AN
ELEVATOR
(thought Bruno), an elevator and its mirror, that silent but implacable confessor, that fleeting confessional of the desanctified world, the world of Plastic and the Computer. He could imagine S. looking pitilessly at his own face. On it—slowly but inexorably—marks had been left, the marks of his emotions, his passions, his attachments

45

and his animosities, his faith, his hopes and disappointments, the deaths he'd experienced or had presentiments of, the cold seasons that had saddened and discouraged him, the loves he'd been enchanted by, the ghosts that visited him or haunted him in his dreams and in his fiction. On those eyes that cried in pain, on those eyes that closed in sleep but in shame, modesty, and cunning as well, on those lips taut with stubbornness, but with cruelty as well, on those eyebrows knitted in disquiet or puzzlement or raised in query and doubt, in those veins that knotted and swelled in rage, or in sensuality, there had been drawn the mobile geography that the soul sooner or later impresses on the subtle, malleable flesh of the face. And so the soul itself is at last revealed, the fate which belongs to it alone—for destiny can only exist in the flesh; the soul is revealed in that matter which is at once its prison and its only hope of existence.

Yes, there it was: that face through which the soul of S. looked out on (and suffered) the Universe, like a man sentenced to death looking out between the bars.

He walked toward La Recoleta.
What on earth were all the discussions, the arguments, the lectures good for—they were nothing but one long dreadful misunderstanding
that idiot, what's-his-name, explaining religion as added value
I'd like to see how he'd explain workers in New York backing Nixon
     against the demonstrating students
Sartre torn apart by passions and vices
but arguing for social justice
Roquentin and his cracks about the Autodidact and socialist
     humanism!
He sat down on a bench.
He was noticed. A young man whispered something to the girl he was walking with, pointing out S. with a gesture that he no doubt thought was imperceptible but which S. caught, the way birds can distinguish between people just walking along and people stalking them. He remembered with a tinge of melancholy when he had been like that kid, when he could go to the park to read a book, anony-

mously, without anyone's trying to control him or wanting to touch him.

Socrates and Sartre. Both ugly, both hating their bodies, feeling repugnance for their flesh, yearning for a world transparent and eternal. Who could have invented Platonism but a man with his guts full of shit?

We create that which we do not have, that which we most anxiously need.

All right, they weren't all fat society ladies, and not all the ladies were fat, don't exaggerate. There were students, too, a lot of them, people sincerely interested.

People sincerely interested! Come on!

He had to take hold of himself, lock himself up in that famous little study of his.

But no, no! That was cowardly, a desertion, a retreat in the face of those bastards!

That Negro in *La Nausée*, in that filthy little room, that summer in New York. Saved forever by the eternal melody of his blues. Eternity reached by way of garbage. He walked toward the cemetery. REQUIESCAT IN PACE, he read once more, as though looking once more at that object in the shop window that fascinates us and in spite of whose price we know we will have to buy one day.

He walked along beside the high wall of Vicente López, and then stopped to peer into the interior of a boardinghouse—clothes hung out to dry, stray dogs, dirty kids. Typical of R., he thought. Living in some grimy rented room like this, up there someplace.

M.'s dreams.

Trapped in a glass bell jar, trying with his hands to find some weak place in that transparent but unyielding wall, a little man, a homunculus no more than six or eight inches high, the miniature of an Englishman she'd seen in some American movie—thin, wearing a tweed jacket and one of those homburgs or whatever they were called, like people only wore in England anymore. He moved about violently, back and forth, angrily, but then suddenly he stopped and stood quietly and looked up, up to where M. was watching him. And then he screamed something, which naturally she couldn't hear, because everything was happening as though this were a silent film.

47

But she was appalled by that frightening, inaudible scream, and by the expression on his face. "A terrifying expression," she explained.

What did that word mean? He asked her this question offhandedly, as though the dream were of no particular importance, trying to dissimulate the disquiet he felt. She didn't know, she couldn't quite explain it. The only thing she was sure of was his terrifying expression.

"It was that man you were asking me about. Patricio. I'm sure of it," she added. She went on looking at him, as though waiting for something.

"Uh-huh, uh-huh, I'll attend to that."

But he spoke these words without conviction, because it was impossible to explain to her the forces that were holding him back. She knew only the most outward ones: slander, gossip, untrue rumors, that sort of thing. What she did not know was that all those things were provoked by the most subtle, and therefore all the more fearsome, power.

And months passed. And then one day M. told him another of her dreams: Ricardo was supposed to operate on somebody. The person was stretched out on the operating table, under the blinding spotlights of the operating room. Ricardo pulled back the sheet, and suddenly M. had seen that the person was wrapped from head to foot in bandages, like a mummy. Ricardo made an incision through the ancient, dusty cloth, and then through the parchmentlike skin, all down the chest and abdomen. The wound bled not one drop of blood. When the incision was spread, in place of the internal organs there was a large black worm in the abdomen, the full length of the gaping cut. The worm was a foot long, or longer, and it began to wriggle and put out pseudopods, which then turned into frantically waving extremities. In a matter of seconds the worm had metamorphosed into a small black demon that leapt out straight at M.'s face.

M. declared that *that* certainly had something to do with Patricio.

Sabato stood there looking at her, perplexed, because he knew she was sometimes a seer. He felt darkly, vaguely disturbed.

He was standing at the door of La Biela.

He sat down in a far corner of the café and began to take stock, meanwhile imagining that he was being observed, thinking that peo-

48

ple thought they knew him (such an arrogant, deceptive verb), that they could follow all the vagaries of his life through the news (according to that fantasy of the modern world which presumes that a man can be revealed in an hour of conversation ill-transcribed for an "interview"). But all that was nothing. Underneath, he (like everyone) lived a life of dreams, of secret vices which few or none suspected. Below, in the subterranean depths—the grotesque throng, the wicked, evil piling up of darkness. Above, one went to the French Embassy, where one politely delivered and received the lies and commonplaces which can and must be spoken in an embassy. All affable manners, understanding and compassion, courtesy. One might even be brilliant, inspired. Because afterward, when one was pulling off one's pants to go to bed, it was inevitable that one remembered Kierkegaard doing the same thing, and saying, "I subjugated the audience but when I found myself alone, in my room, I wanted to shoot myself."

Until he saw the two kids.

A RECKONING

HE HAD SAT IN A CORNER, LIKE ALWAYS, and from his table he could observe the two occupants of that little table in the window, overlooking the avenue. He could see the girl perfectly; she was facing him, and the afternoon light fell across her face. But the boy had his back to him, though from his movements S. could catch fleeting glimpses of his profile.

This was the first time he'd ever seen them. He was sure of that, because the girl's face was unforgettable. Why was that? At first he couldn't quite figure it out.

Her hair was very short, and the color of dark bronze, dull bronze. Her eyes at first looked dark, too, but then he saw that they were green. Her face was bony, strong, with a square jaw and one of those mouths which seemed to jut forward—the result, surely, of forward-pushing teeth. From that mouth he intuited the obstinacy of a person capable of holding a secret even under torture. Nineteen years old, he'd say. No, twenty. She hardly spoke, listening instead to the boy with a profound, distant look on her face—almost abstracted, one might say—and the look was memorable. What was there in that look? He thought there must be some slight deviation of her eyes.

No, he'd never seen her. Yet he had the sensation of seeing someone familiar, somehow. Had he one time met her sister? Her mother? This "déjà vu," as always, made him uncomfortable, uneasy, and the sensation was accentuated by the certainty that they were talking about him. That sad feeling that only writers can have, and that only writers can understand, he thought bitterly. Because for one to experience that twinge of unease, it wasn't enough to be well known (like an actor, or a politician)—one had to be a writer of fiction, a person on trial not only for the things that all public persons are judged by, but for all the things one's characters do, and are, and even suggest.

On yes, they were talking about him. Or rather, it was obvious that the boy was. He'd even looked this way out of the corner of his eye, a moment that gave S. the chance to study his profile better— the same mouth as the girl's (bulging a bit forward), the identical hair the color of unpolished bronze, the same bony, slightly aquiline nose, the same large mouth, the thick fleshy lips.

They were sister and brother, no doubt of that. And the boy was a year, perhaps two, younger than the girl. His expression was sarcastic, and his hands were very long and bony; they clenched and unclenched with tremendous strength. There was something dissonant about him; his movements were abrupt, sudden, and clumsy.

As time passed, S.'s uneasiness grew. And he was getting distinctly ill-humored when at least one of the nagging puzzles was cleared up: it was Van Gogh with his ear cut off. The difference of sex, age, bandage, leather cap, pipe had gotten in the way. But there was the same oddly focused gaze, the same abstractedly gloomy way of looking at the world. Now he realized why he'd had that first impression of dark eyes, when in fact they were green.

The discovery shook him, and his anxiety over what they were arguing about deepened.

Did other writers feel what he felt when they met someone who'd read their books, he wondered. That mixture of embarrassment, curiosity, and fear? Sometimes, like now, it would be some youngster, a student whose troubles, whose tribulations and bitterness you could see immediately, and at those times S. would try to imagine why he read his books, which pages might help him through his bad times and which ones, on the other hand, only served to feed them, which parts he would mark with fury or ferocity or delight, as proof of his grudge against the universe or as confirmation of his suspicions about love or loneliness. But sometimes it would be an older man, a housewife, or a woman of the world. What was most astounding was the variety of people who could read the same book as though it were many, even infinite different books—a single, unique text which nonetheless permitted innumerable different and even opposed interpretations of life and death, of the meaning of existence. Because otherwise it would be incomprehensible that the book could impassion a young man thinking about robbing a bank and at the same time an entrepreneur who had reaped a fortune in business. "Message in a bottle," it had been called. But the bottle contained an equivocal message, which might be interpreted in so many ways that it would be a miracle if the shipwrecked man could ever be found. It was more like some vast kingdom, with its castle perfectly visible, but containing complicated outbuildings for ser- vants and vassals as well (in some of which outbuildings, perhaps, the most important servant of all might be found), well-cared-for parks, but thick woods, too, and ponds and swamps with dark caves—so that each visitor would feel drawn to a different part of the vast and complex realm; some visitors would be fascinated by the gloomy grottoes and disgusted by the broad lawns and parks while others would travel with fearful rage through the dank swamps filled with snakes, and yet others would listen to frivolities in gold-leafed salons.

At one point what the boy was saying seemed to disturb his sister, who in a low voice seemed to be trying to reason with him. He, then, half-stood; but she grabbed his arm and forced him to sit down again. S. noted in that gesture that she, too, had strong, bony hands, and that there was great strength in her muscles. The argu- ment went on, or rather *he* went on arguing while she kept opposing whatever it was he was arguing for. Then suddenly the young man stood up brusquely, and before she could stop him he walked over to Sabato.

In cafés S. had often witnessed the hesitations and vacillations of some student who at last would get up the courage to approach

51

him. From that long experience, he calculated that something very unpleasant was about to happen.

The boy was tall for his age, taller than normal, and his movements confirmed Sabato's first impression of him when he had been seated: he was severe, brusque, violent, and his whole attitude radiated anger. Not only against Sabato—against the entire world.

The young man towered over S., and in a voice much too loud for what he was saying, almost a shout, he said:

"We saw a picture of you in that magazine *Gente*."

His face when he spoke the words "that magazine" was the face some people make when they have to walk past excrement on the sidewalk.

Sabato looked at him as though asking him what he meant by that.

"And not long ago there was an article in it about you," the young man added in a tone of accusation.

"Yes, that's true," Sabato admitted, pretending not to notice the boy's tone.

"And now, in the last issue, I saw you at the opening of a boutique on Alvear."

Sabato was on the verge of exploding. He made one last effort, though, to restrain himself:

"Yes, a young woman who's a friend of mine, a painter, just opened that boutique."

"Friends that own boutiques," the boy sneered.

At that, Sabato did explode. He stood up.

"And who are you to judge me, or to judge my friends?" he shouted.

"Who am I? I have a lot more right than a person like you could imagine."

Before he realized what he was doing, Sabato suddenly found himself slapping the boy so hard he almost knocked him down.

"Snot-nosed little brat!" he shouted, as people rushed between them and someone dragged the boy by his arm back to his table. The sister had gotten up, too, and run over to Sabato's table, but then Sabato saw her back at their own table, talking to her brother in a low, urgent, severe voice. Then suddenly, with that abrupt violence that seemed so much a part of him, the boy threw back his chair and ran out of the café. Sabato was left depressed and ashamed of himself. Everyone was looking at him, and there were three or four women whispering over at one table. He paid and walked out without looking around.

He began to walk along Recoleta, trying to regain his composure. He felt infinitely angry, but the curious thing about it was that the anger wasn't directed against the boy so much as against himself and the entire world. "The world"! What world? Which of the many worlds that existed? The worst world of all, perhaps, the most superficially human: the world of boutiques and paparazzi magazines. He felt disgust for himself, but indignation too at the spectacular but facile attitude the boy had taken. The disgust for himself apparently reached the boy, entered him, sullied him in some way that at the moment S. could not quite fully comprehend, and then bounced off the boy to hit himself again, full in the face, violently, humiliatingly.

He sat on a circular bench that embraced a grand old rubber tree.

The park was growing dim with the shadows of evening. He closed his eyes, and had begun to meditate over his life when he heard a woman's voice timidly calling him. When he opened his eyes he saw her standing before him, hesitant and perhaps guilty. He stood up.

The girl looked at him for a few seconds with that expression like Van Gogh's portrait, and then at last seemed to take courage:

"Nacho's attitude doesn't express the whole truth."

Sabato stood looking at her, and then sarcastically spoke.

"Well, thank goodness."

She pursed her lips and for one second realized how unhappy her phrase had been. She tried to qualify it:

"Oh, I didn't really want to say that either. You see, we all make mistakes, we say things that don't really express what we want to say very clearly, very exactly. . . . I mean . . ."

S. felt clumsy, especially because she continued to look at him with that inscrutable expression. This was becoming a little absurd, and then she said:

"Anyway, I'm very sorry . . . I . . . Nacho . . . Good-bye!"

And she walked away.

Then suddenly she stopped again, hesitated, and finally turned and added:

"Oh, Señor Sabato," her voice was tremulous, "I want to tell you . . . my brother and I . . . those characters of yours . . . Castel, I mean, Alejandra . . ."

She stopped, and they stood looking at each other for a moment. Then she went on, still almost stammering:

"Don't get the wrong idea . . . Those *absolute* sort of characters . . . You understand . . . you . . . those articles . . . that kind of magazine . . ."

She fell silent.

And then without transition she cried, as her brother would surely have done as well, "It's so horrible!" and turned and ran. Sabato stood paralyzed at these words of hers, her whole attitude, her somber, harsh beauty. Then, mechanically, he walked off through the park, taking the path alongside the high wall of the asylum.

As NIGHT FELL,

thought Bruno, with the statues looking down on him in his unbearable melancholy from their heights, there began to steal over S. the same feeling of helplessness and incomprehension that Castel had sometimes felt as he walked along this same path. And yet those young people who could understand *that* forlorn and helpless wretch were incapable of understanding the same helplessness and dejection in Sabato; they simply couldn't see that the same solitude, the same loneliness, the same sense of the absolute must have had a home in some corner of S. as well, must be somewhere in him, somehow, perhaps hiding from or struggling against other beings— horrible, swinish beings—that lived down deep inside there too, fighting for a place for themselves, demanding pity or understanding, no matter what their fate might be in his novels, while S.'s heart continued to bear this troubled, obscure, and superficial existence which fools and dullards call "the world."

NACHO WENT INTO HIS ROOM,

found the photo of Sabato at the French Embassy, cut it out of the magazine, and put it up with thumbtacks on the wall, alongside two others: one of Anouilh in a white dinner jacket going into a church, his daughter in a white wedding gown on his arm, and a caption, like in the comic strips, written in red indelible marker across the bottom: THE BASTARD CREON. The other was of Flaubert, with a tiny Nacho beside him shouting BUT SHE COMMITTED SUICIDE, YOU PIG!

With the same red marker, Nacho drew a little bubble coming out of the mouth of one of the spectators standing around Sabato, and inside it a single word: SWINE! A single word, but it was doubly meaningful because it belonged to that famous gentleman's arsenal of invective. Then Nacho stood back a little, as though to judge a painting in an exhibit. His lips pressed tight, the corners of his mouth turned down, his expression was at once of scorn and bitter repugnance. Finally he spat, cleaned his mouth off with the back of his hand, and sprawling across the bed lay pensive, staring at the ceiling.

Near midnight he heard Agustina's steps in the hall, and then the sound of the key in the lock. He got up and turned on the overhead light.

"Turn that light off," she said as she came in. "You know I can't bear it."

Her tone, at once imperative and anguished, alarmed him. In the light of the bedside lamp he couldn't make out her expression very clearly, though he knew that face and could trace every feature of it, like a burro making its way at night along the edge of terrible precipices without falling into the abyss. Still dressed, Agustina lay down on the bed, her face turned toward the wall. Nacho left.

As he walked he tried to calm himself, telling himself that the scene he'd made in La Biela had irritated her, that she no doubt thought the things he'd said to Sabato had been grotesque and melodramatic, that he'd made a spectacle of himself, and that he'd covered himself with ridicule; no doubt she felt embarrassed.

But, he wondered suddenly (and that fleeting thought was no more than a slight scent of danger in the darkness), would she have been so embarrassed and irritated if it had been another person?

He walked for a long time, down the barely lighted streets that bordered the main avenue, and then he went back home. Far from being calmer, he found that dwelling on the details of the scene had made him even more upset, especially one word which she had said (which she had cried out!) back when they were reading his novel together.

When he went into the apartment, he saw that Agustina had fallen asleep still dressed exactly as she had been when she came in, and without turning off the bedside lamp. Now, though, she was turned toward the light.

He sat on the floor beside her, and he looked at her. Her sleep was restless, and then suddenly she murmured something and furrowed her brow, seeming to find it hard to breathe. Carefully, fervently, and in fear of the unknown, Nacho reached his hand out toward her face, and with the tips of his fingers traced her large full lips. She shuddered, just a bit, murmured something else, and then turned over to face the wall again and went on with her solitary night journey.

He wanted to kiss her. But who would he be kissing? Her body was at that moment abandoned by her soul. And to what remote lands had her soul traveled?

Oh Elektra! he said, *forget neither Apollo,*
   King of Crisia, fertile in flocks,
Nor the black monarch of the obscure Acheron!

DR. LUDWIG SCHNEIDER
I THINK I'VE TOLD YOU HOW I MET THAT PARTICULAR INDIVIDUAL for the first time, just a short while after *The Tunnel* was first published in Spanish, in 1948. Do you know what the only thing he asked me was? He asked me about Allende's blindness.

I wouldn't have given the question a second thought if it hadn't been that after so many years of not seeing him, I mean we'd never crossed paths again, and then in 1962 more or less, imagine . . . "Crossed" . . . These half-conscious words we use in our ordinary lives, you know. Because I don't think that people "run across each other" in the usual way that expression is taken. The man *was looking for me.* Do you understand? More, even: he had followed me from a distance, who knows for how long. How do I know that he was following me? It's something you smell, it's an instinct that never deceives me. And he had been following me since he read my first novel, probably. "Probably," nothing. Think, just think a bit about what he said to me back then, about Castel's description of the blind:

"So their skin is cold, eh?"

He laughed when he said it, of course. But later, as the years went on, that laugh took on a sinister significance. I tell you, the man laughed the way a cripple dances.

Twelve years later he crossed my path again to say something to me. To say *what* to me? Something about Fernando Vidal Olmos. Do you see? But first I want to explain how I met him.

The human beings that love us the most can be used by the forces of evil to trick us, to harm us. So if you think about it for a minute, it will all be clear. It was through Mabel, Beba's sister, that I met Dr. Schneider. And I say "doctor" because that's how he was introduced to me, though no one ever managed to find out what kind of doctorate he had or where he'd gotten it. Actually, it wasn't Mabel directly, it was through one of the members of what we called Mabel's Foreign Legion: an army of Hungarians, Czechs, Poles, Germans, and Serbs (or Croats—how ironic, here we can't tell them apart, and over there, they cut each other's throats over the differences). Anyway, that whole multitude of people that dropped upon Buenos Aires like parachutists during or immediately after World War II. Adventurers, real and apocryphal counts, actresses and baronesses that dabbled in espionage (volunteer or forced), Rumanian professors, collaborationists, Nazis, et cetera. And among these there were some wonderful people, too, of course, blown in on the storm. But that very mixture of nice people, good people, you know, with adventurers was what made the situation so dangerous.

One of the people in the Foreign Legion—who later disappeared, they say, in the jungles of Matto Grosso—was a Hungarian man who undertook (and that is the right word) to introduce Dr. Schneider to me. As I told you, my novel had just come out, so that must have been sometime in '48. And one of the things that came to my mind years later, when *On Heroes and Tombs* came out, and that troubled me, was that a foreigner with no interest whatsoever in Argentine literature would have told Mabel's friend that he was "extremely interested" in meeting the author of *The Tunnel*.

We met in the Zur Post. I took him for one of those "types" from the Middle East, one of those people that could as well be a Sephardic Jew as an Armenian or a Syrian. He was very corpulent, all shoulders, a great deal of flesh across his upper back, to the point that he looked halfway hunchbacked. He was broad across the back, and he had powerful arms and hairy hands—very black hairs on the backs of his hands. In fact, with the exception of his shaved face—though his beard looked like it started sprouting again before the razor had been put away—thick curly black hairs emerged from every part of his body. From his ears, for example. He had large, heavy eyebrows, almost joined, like a balcony with dirty weeds growing out of it, and large, dark, almond-shaped eyes. His lips were what one would expect from that ensemble—if they hadn't been so gross and sensual one would have thought the man was a fraud. When he laughed, you could see that his teeth were a greenish color, no doubt owing to the permanent cigarette he smoked. His nose was aquiline but very broad. In short, all he lacked was the wingéd bull. One of those Oriental satraps from Malet's history. Or a member of some troupe of jugglers—the Armenian Baron, that sort of thing.

He drank beer avidly, voraciously, and with a pleasure proportional to his lips, his enormous nose, and his sensuous velvety eyes.

After wiping the back of one of his hairy hands across his lips—to clean off the froth from the half-liter of beer he had just downed in one long draught—he started asking me questions about *The Tunnel*. Why had I made María's husband blind? Did that have some special significance? His mysterious black eyes studied me from behind the shrubbery of his eyebrows, like wild beasts lurking among the lianas of the jungle. And what about their cold skin?

At the time I gave his questions no importance. I was so naive! A little later, with that laugh which was to a laugh of delight what love is to pleasure taken with a prostitute, he remarked:

"A cuckold and blind to boot!"

Many years were to pass before I went back to that apparent wisecrack in such bad taste, before I deduced that that was the way

58

he had used to try to erase any uneasiness his questions might have caused in me.

I forgot to mention that he made that last remark in front of a woman that had just come over to us—Hedwig Rosenberg. I took in her features with intrigued curiosity; they were beautiful but worn, somehow, and I thought at the time that it was as though by looking at the face stamped on a gold coin that has been in circulation for centuries one could make out what its original splendor must have been. And when Schneider, with that gross burst of laughter of his, said what he said about the blind cuckold, I saw that she almost winced. The remark distressed her, there was no doubt about that. Hardly had that unpleasantness passed when the man asked me to excuse him for a moment, there was a small matter he had to discuss with the Hungarian. The two of them went off to another table, leaving me alone with the woman. Later I saw that this maneuver had not been casual.

I asked her how long she'd been in the country.

"I arrived in 1944. I fled Hungary when the Russian troops entered."

I was taken a little aback, though I reflected that probably many rich Jews fled out of fear of communism even if they'd managed to hide themselves from the Nazis.

"Does that surprise you?" she asked.

"When the Russians entered?"

"Yes."

I sat looking at her.

"I'd have thought you'd have escaped before that," I said.

"When?"

"When Hitler's troops moved in."

She fixed her glance on her glass, and then after a moment she said:

"We were never Nazis, but they left us alone."

I must have looked surprised again.

"Why, does that seem so strange to you? We weren't the only case. Perhaps they thought they could use us."

"Use you? *Who* could use you?"

"Hitler. He always sought the support of certain families. You understand."

59

"Support from a Jewish family?"

She reddened.

"Oh, I'm sorry, I had no intention of offending you. For me that's no cause for embarrassment," I quickly said.

"Nor for me. But that isn't it."

After another moment of doubt she added:

"I am not Jewish."

Just at that moment Schneider returned with the Hungarian, who said his good-byes and left.

Schneider had heard the woman's last words, and with that vulgar laugh of his he explained to me that she was the Countess Hedwig von Rosenberg.

I was upset. In spite of my discomfort, though, I noted a curious phenomenon, which gradually became even clearer to me in later encounters: Schneider's presence made the Hedwig woman another person. And though it never went so far as to appear to be a case of the stage hypnotist and the subject he manipulates, I felt that something very like that was transpiring in her spirit. Later, on other occasions, I confirmed this impression, as I've said—it was an impression not only disagreeable but actually almost repugnant to me, perhaps because one felt one was witnessing the subjugation of a creature of extreme delicacy by a man vulgar to the ends of his fingers. What was the secret of that bond?

Many years later, when this same man reappeared upon my path, as it were, in 1962, I observed the phenomenon once again, and even managed to see more deeply into it; I arrived at the conclusion that between the two of them there could only be the relationship of the master to the medium. A silent sign from Schneider was all it took for her to carry out his wishes, to obey his will. What was curious was that he showed none of those traits supposed to be exhibited by people with "mental powers"—the penetrating eyes, the furrowed brow, the strained, tight mouth. His manner was invariably grossly ironic, and his thick lips always half-open. Let us not even mention the word love. Whatever the relations between them were, it was obvious that Schneider loved no one. The word "tool" was the best word to describe Hedwig. But a tool is a tool for some purpose, and I asked myself (at that last encounter, in 1962) to what end Schneider was employing the countess. At first I couldn't even imagine. To get money out of certain people? I inclined rather to the idea of the sort of link that exists between the chief of some espionage agency and one of his agents. But what sort of espionage? And on behalf of what country? It was inconceivable that in that case the chief would allow such a waste of time as was occurring with someone like myself, whom they could have no possible interest in, at least from the point of view of war. Yet it was obvious that he not only permitted, but actually encouraged her relations with me. That first time, I thought a great deal about the problem, and I decided there were only two possibilities: either there was no such espionage work, but rather some twisted sort of vice, or else there did exist the espionage but it was not in the interests of war but rather for something different, in which case it was probable that I was being enmeshed in some subtle but powerful web.

The second encounter with Schneider occurred in 1962, as I've said, a few months after *On Heroes and Tombs* appeared in the bookstores. And this time it was through Hedwig. It was a tremendous surprise to me, because I'd never seen her again after that first introduction, so I had assumed that she like so many other immigrants had returned to Europe. And indeed she had been abroad, she told me. She'd spent several years in New York, where some cousins of hers lived. This second encounter took place in a café where I never go, so at first it looked like a chance meeting. But afterward I reflected that this "coincidence" was altogether too pat: it was obvious that I was being stalked. A while later Schneider came in, and he, as I told you, talked to me about my novel. When he first brought up the subject he didn't ask me about the "Report on the Blind"; it wasn't until after talking about all sorts of other things—Lavalle, for instance. And then, as though he were noting something curious, he asked me about Vidal Olmos.

"Apparently you're obsessed with the Blind," he said, laughing grossly.

"Vidal Olmos is a paranoid," I shot back. "Surely you aren't so naive as to attribute to *me* what *that* man thinks and does."

He laughed again. Hedwig's was the face of a somnambulist.

"Come now, friend Sabato," he chided me, "you've read Chestov, haven't you?"

"Chestov?" I was dumbstruck that he should be familiar with an author so nearly unknown. "Yes, of course," I admitted sheepishly.

He took a long draught of his beer and dried his mouth with the back of his hand.

When he raised his eyes to me again, I thought there was a certain gleam that I'd never seen in them before. But it was for only a fraction of a second, I suppose, because at once they became laughing, waggish, vulgar again.

"Of course, of course," he nodded, enigmatically.

I felt suddenly sick. I invented an engagement, I asked what time it was, and I stood up to leave—but with the promise (which I had no intention of keeping) that we'd all meet again. When I said goodbye to Hedwig I thought I caught just the slightest look of pleading in her expression. What could she be begging of me? I may have been wrong, but it was because of that fleeting expression that I did meet her again. I asked her for her telephone number.

"There you are, there you are," Schneider muttered in a tone that sounded to me little less than sarcastic, "give him your telephone."

I'd no more than left the café when I rushed into a bookstore to consult the Gotha: if they'd lied to me about Hedwig's real identity I would have all the more reason to be on my guard. The family appeared in the second part: Catholics, descendants of Conrad ab dem Rosenberg, 1322. A list followed of the family's barons, counts, ladies of Lower Austria, princes of the Holy Roman Empire, etc. Among the last of the line, Countess Hedwig-Marie-Henriette-Gabrielle von Rosenberg, born in Budapest in 1922.

These references calmed me, but only for a moment. Almost immediately I reflected that Schneider couldn't be so stupid as to try to trick me with a "fact" so easily verifiable. Yes, she was truly Countess Hedwig von Rosenberg. But so what? What did that prove, after all? At any rate, when we met again, the first thing I did was reproach her for not having told me her real identity from the beginning.

"Why? What could it possible have mattered?" she argued.

Obviously I couldn't confess what it meant to me to be absolutely certain about the people with whom I had contact.

"And as for the comment about Jews," she went on, smiling, "it's true that Rosenberg is often a Jewish name. But besides that, one of my kinsmen, Count Erwin, married an American woman, Cathleen Wolff, around the turn of the century. This Mrs. Wolff had been divorced from one Mr. Spotswood, and both of them were Jewish."

I lived for months obsessed by the hypothesis I had invented. It was frightful to know that I was kept under constant watch by a man like Schneider, so frightful in fact that the possibility of vice seemed somehow preferable. Drugs? Could he be the leader of a group of drug smugglers, for example, and the countess a tool? I preferred that. But the relief was only relative, because if that was what it was, what did they want with me? Schneider disturbed me because of what he could do to me in my sleep, in the dreams he might somehow bring on. I believe in the separation of the body and the soul, because otherwise there's no explanation for premonitions. (I have written an essay on this; you've read it, I'm sure.) Or for reminiscence. Years ago, in Bethlehem, an old man with a white beard, wearing a burnoose, came up to me, and I had the confused but absolutely certain sense that I had lived that moment before sometime, though I had never been there before. During my childhood I used sometimes to feel suddenly that I was moving and talking as though I were another person, or as though *it* were another person moving and talking. There are people with the power to bring on the separation of the soul and the body in others, and especially in those, such as myself, who are prone to undergo that experience spontaneously. When I looked at Schneider I felt sure that he had that power. It's true that unless a person knew what to look for, Schneider would appear to be a sideshow charlatan. But for me that was simply all the more reason for precaution.

What led me to think that he had such powers, that he was a member of some dangerous sect? It was a few apparently innocuous words he said, but above all, what he didn't say. And looks, too, fleeting glances, gestures. One day I abruptly asked him if he knew Haushofer. He looked at me quizzically, then at Hedwig.

"Haushofer?" He seemed to be trying to recall. Then he turned to Hedwig:

"Wasn't he that philosophy professor in Zurich?"

Hedwig's face, too, had an expression of surprise. Because they didn't know him, or because I had caught them unawares with some fundamental piece of knowledge?

Schneider asked me whether I was talking about the philosophy professor.

"No," I said, "somebody else. I thought you or Hedwig had mentioned him once."

They looked at one another like partners at cards, and then he said:

"I don't believe so. In fact, come to think of it I don't believe that philosophy professor in Zurich was named Haushofer, either."

I told him it didn't matter, I'd asked because I was interested in knowing something about a general by that name.

He turned to call the waiter for another beer, while his friend burrowed in her purse for something. Neither piece of behavior looked natural to me.

Dr. Arrambide belongs to the school that sees Schneider as a joke. He says Schneider ought to be taken to those spiritualist sessions Memé Varela hosts, and I know Arrambide laughs at me behind my back. That drugstore Descartes will never see that in order to unmask these agents, you have to be a believer like I am, not a skeptic like him. (And I just called him a drugstore Descartes, but I should have said drugstore Anatole France—I'm certain that France is one of Arrambide's favorite writers.) And I don't mean unmask Schneider in the sense that Arrambide uses the words, of course, but rather unmask him in the opposite sense, in the only, and most appalling, most frightening way: by proving that he is *not* a sideshow hocus-pocus man, a carnival mystifier of some kind, but rather that he is truly linked to the powers of darkness.

His name could be false—who would doubt that it is? And even if it's real, there's no reason he has to be a Jew, no matter what his appearance is. There are thousands of Swiss and Alsatians with that name. But in the case that he is a Jew, one might wonder at the fact that a Jew should be so closely associated with a countess who happened to be the daughter of one of the generals in Hitler's armies. I see no problem there, myself. There are cases of Jews more anti-Semitic than the Germans themselves, and in many ways it is psychologically possible. Hasn't it been claimed that Torquemada was

a Jew? Even Hitler himself had a Jewish grandfather or grand-
mother. Everything about Schneider was ambiguous, hazy, equivocal—
beginning with the fact that I could never discover where he lived.
Every time I followed him I wound up losing him. At one time I
believed he lived in Belgrano R. Then I inferred that it must be
Olivos, instead, since from time to time he took the number 60 bus.

From the moment I began to harbor suspicions about Schneider,
I read everything I could find on lodges and secret societies and
sects under the Nazis, especially after I saw how he reacted to the
name Haushofer. The gestures of the two of them, the glance they
exchanged, made me suspect that they knew perfectly well who he
was. I think that was where Schneider tipped his hand. Because a
truly astute person would have taken the bull by the horns and said
of course he knew the name though he'd never had occasion to meet
the man. Because who could believe that a man such as Schneider
could be completely ignorant of a person as important as Haushofer?
It was that stumble that alarmed me more than anything, and that
induced me to probe in that direction.

Haushofer had spent periods of time in Asia, and he'd surely
been in contact with secret societies. During World War I he attracted attention for the first time with certain predictions which
came true. Then he devoted himself to geopolitics and to the study
of Schopenhauer and Ignatius Loyola. It is known that around that
time he founded a lodge in Germany and introduced the ancient
symbol of the swastika.

Be that as it may, it is curious and intriguing that several high
officials of the Nazi regime, beginning with Hitler himself, joined
occult lodges and maintained contact with people, like Haushofer,
who belonged to the Sect of the Left Hand. Hitler became linked to
Haushofer when he was no more than a little sergeant, Hitler I mean,
through an ex-assistant to Haushofer named Rudolf Hess. Remember
that Hess is one of the most hermetic figures of Hitlerism: for decades in prison he maintained the most ironbound secrecy about
his thoughts, his ideas, his intentions, his destiny. To me, he is
perhaps the most impressive of all those Nazi leaders, then. While
Goering belongs to the clownish side of this Schneider, Hess belongs
to the tragic, stoic side.

Haushofer is another of the enigmatic pieces in that demonic puzzle, and all I have been able to find out about him are a few fragmentary pieces of information. One is the poem found in the pocket of the jacket worn by Albrecht, Haushofer's son, when Albrecht was executed for his participation in the generals' plot against Hitler. It was written, almost certainly, moments before his execution, as one infers from the jerky, nervous, spiky hand:

Fate had spoken through my father.
Upon him depended once again
locking the Devil in his dungeon.
My father broke the Seal.
He did not feel the breath of the Evil One,
and he left him free in the world.

When the general learned of the death of his son, he committed hara-kiri, first though killing his wife. All this is fact. The possible interpretations are several, and contradictory. I have examined them, and I think I can summarize them as follows:

1. *"Upon him depended once again locking the Devil in his dungeon"*: This verse is very ambiguous. If Haushofer was a simple agent of the forces of Evil, he couldn't have the power to drive back the Devil, nor to "lock him up"; he would have to obey him. This verse reveals, however, that he drove him back one or several times (*"upon him depended once again"*), which proves that Haushofer possessed great powers. But drive whom back? I don't think that the son was talking about the true Devil, but rather about Hitler, who was one of the Devil's agents.

2. If this were a question of the real Devil, and if Haushofer possessed powers strong enough to drive him back, and even to lock him into a dungeon, it would be obvious that he could not belong to the Sect of the Left Hand, but would rather belong to the Sect of the Right Hand, or the Path of Goodness. This hypothesis collapses if we consider that Haushofer might have had an agent like Hitler.

3. It is, however, probable that he suffered some sort of internal drama toward the end of his life, culminating in the execution of his son. What that would mean is that he was not a pure agent of Evil but rather a man of flesh and blood, fallible, vacillating.

4. The other possibility, which we may infer from the same verse

66

(the driving back or defeat of the Demon) and one of the following verses (*"he did not feel the breath of the Evil One, and he left him free in the world"*), might be as follows: Haushofer actually belonged to the Path of Goodness, being descended from the Aryans who managed to escape the atomic explosion set off by the sectarians in the caverns. Warned in time by some positive power, they escaped to the regions of northern Europe, either long before the explosion or equipped with asbestos suits and oxygen tanks. The men of the Left Hand, however, took their perverse vengeance on those of the Right Hand by leading Hitler to them and presenting him to them in the not at all unpleasant light of race and tradition. The subsequent actions of Hitler would show the men of the Right Hand their horrific error, and members of the sect would kidnap Haushofer's son and try to murder that agent of the Devil, whom the father "had left free in the world."

It is legitimate to ask oneself, however, why an initiate (and seer) such as Haushofer could be tricked by such a childish ruse when Hess brought him that unknown army sergeant. And how he could be incapable of seeing the road his bloody future would take.

I am inclined, then, to believe that Haushofer was in fact a tool of the Devil and that Hitler was his medium, simply but horribly his medium. The occult sciences teach us that after the forces of Evil have been called together and have joined hands in a pact, the members of a group may act through a Magus, who in turn acts through a medium. Was Hitler the medium for that dark sect?

If General Haushofer was not a *Black* Magus, rather than an agent for the Light, why would he take such a subject to be his medium? It is not credible that he would not see, or foresee, his diabolical character. Or that, once having seen it, he would not have been able to control it.

Once Hitler's power was in collapse, the members of this secret society dispersed throughout the world. Not only Haushofer's sect, but others as well, like the sect whose head was Colonel Sieves. These were orders linked together through some secret superhierarchy, though it is also possible, of course, that internecine struggles might have occurred from time to time between these groups. Why does the power of Evil have to be monist? Dispersed, then, after the war, many of these men came in submarines to the coasts of Patagonia, as in the cases of Eichmann and Mengele—we do not know, naturally, of more mysterious instances. It well may be, then, that Schneider was one of those, in which case the countess might be his medium. Though her father was executed by the Nazis, let us not forget that Haushofer's son was, too. As I just said, one need not try to find too much coherence in diabolical power, since coherence, unity, is an aspect of the enlightened way, and in particular of its highest expression, mathematics. Diabolical power, in contrast, is in my opinion pluralistic and ambiguous.

That is the most terrible thing about it, Bruno.

About That Poster

ALL MARCELO SAW WAS THE NAME OF HIS FATHER, even though it wasn't written in the same glaring letters as the names of the bank's other lawyers, Krieger Vasena and the others. In fact it was almost lost among the other names. But all he could see was DR. JUAN BAUTISTA CARRANZA PAZ.

He turned and walked toward home, but it was hard going—he had to make his way through a thick swamp, under a load of lead and dung, with photographs of his first communion and strips torn from the flag of Argentina hung all over him. His mind worked as he walked, but it was as though it were groping in the darkness through rubbish, piles of garbage. He managed one idea: perhaps this terrible, hard task was just the task of living. (Later he would wonder "just"?)

He took a short rest when he drew near the Grand Bourg Plaza. He lay down on the grass, looked across at General San Martín's house, and once again saw that picture that was in every school-book—the general old, pensive, sitting in a chair somewhere in France. From his head there issued some sort of smoke cloud in which there was painted the crossing of the Andes, the battles.

Beyond and above the Automobile Club there was a sense of languor, of faintness in the air, as though something were about to expire at any moment. The day was beginning to decline, and it was as though the end of the world, not catastrophic but peaceful, though total and planetary, were at hand. It was as though the people all around were nothing but a crowd of imminent corpses, anxious men and women in the waiting room of some world-renowned cancer specialist, sitting in mutually distrustful silence, with no great hope though still alive, still holding to that small breath of existence left them yet.

Then he began his difficult walk home again. When he reached the house, he took the service elevator upstairs and went through the back door to his room. As he sat on the edge of his bed, he could hear the sounds of the party. When was his mother's birthday? Suddenly, without knowing why, he thought of her, thought with tenderness about those crossword puzzles of hers, that sweet head full of the rivers of Asia Minor, four-letter coelenterates, and love (however scatterbrained and distracted) for her children. He saw his mother talking sweetly to Beba as though she were Silvina, and petting Silvina's shoulder as though she were Mabel. And those confusions of names and jobs.

Why was he thinking about his mother and not his father?

His bedroom was virtually in darkness now. He could barely make out the photo of Miguel Hernández on the wall in front of him, Rilke's death mask, Trakl in that absurd military uniform of his, the portrait of Machado, Ché Guevara half naked, his head hanging down to the side, his open eyes staring out at all humanity, Michelangelo's *Pietà* with the dead body of Christ on His mother's lap, His head hanging down like Ché's.

He looked again at Rilke's death mask—*that reactionary*, Araujo would say contemptuously. Was he? Marcelo's soul was muddled, or at least that was what Araujo said. Was it possible to admire Miguel Hernández and Rilke at the same time?

He looked about distractedly at his boyhood library: Jules Verne, *Journey to the Center of the Earth, 20,000 Leagues Under the Sea.* He felt a terrible pain in his chest, and he had to lie down.

A COCKTAIL PARTY

DR. CARRANZA LOOKED TOWARD THE DOOR. He was waiting for Marcelo with a mixture of anxiety and sadness. Meanwhile, Beba wouldn't let the subject of the Hope diamond go:

"Two million."

"And what did you say the name of this woman was?"

"McLean, Evelyn McLean. Are you people deaf?"

"So they found her rotting body in the bathroom?"

"Uh-huh, neighbors. Worried because she hadn't used the car."

"So American, dying in the bathroom."

"No signs of violence, no trace of sleeping pills, or of martinis. An unfailingly peaceful life—until the diamond. And even so, when she got to the United States she had it blessed."

"Had what blessed, Beba?" Dr. Arrambide asked, moved by his constant *a priori* skepticism, as he got himself a ham and cheese sandwich.

"The diamond, obviously."

"Bless a diamond. Were they all mad?"

"Mad? Didn't I say she knew it was famous for its bad luck?"

"But why, then, had the idiotic woman bought the thing?"

"Ah, who knows. Texas craziness."

"But what's that? Hadn't we decided she was from the best Washington society?"

"Yes, so what? A person from Washington can have a ranch in Texas. . . . Yes or no? Or do we always have to ask you the question twice, like they do on television?"

"All right then, she was sane, blessing a diamond. But those priests!"

"Oh, I forgot—she had bought it because according to her, to this McLean woman, things that brought bad luck to other people were good luck for her. Have you seen those people that live on the thirteenth floor, on purpose?"

"But then," objected the implacable Arrambide, "why did she bother to bless it?"

What an unpleasant man.

They talked about blessings and curses, about exorcisms.

"All right then," insisted Dr. Arrambide, with that stereotypical expression of surprise he always put on, and which made him look as though he were always witnessing the most startling events, "but what happened to the hysterical American woman?"

"You mean you don't think it's enough for her to have died like that?"

"Oh, come now, we all die, without the necessity of bringing in diamonds under a mortal curse."

"No, you idiot. She died *mysteriously.*"

"Mysteriously?" asked Dr. Arrambide, picking up another sandwich.

"Didn't I just tell you they found her naked in the bathroom? And with no traces of poison?"

"So according to you, people die fully clothed of poisoning."

"Come now, must you stoop to cheap shots? This is a famous case, and very very strange. Isn't it all very strange?"

"All? What is *all?*"

"There was no poison, there were no traces of alcohol or tranquilizers, no marks of violence. Isn't that enough? Plus, the first child, a young man, dead in a car wreck, after she bought the diamond."

"How long afterward?" the doctor inquired coldly.

"How long afterward? Eight years."

"Good lord, the curse seems to take its time about working. And why attribute that accident to the jewel? Right here in Buenos Aires, thousands of people who do not possess the Hope diamond die every year in automobile accidents. Not to mention the poor who don't even have an automobile. The ones modestly run over and squashed by other people's automobiles."

Beba radiated fury. That was not all!

"What else then?"

"Her husband was committed to a mental institution."

"Listen, Beba. If my wife were capable of spending two million dollars on a diamond, and a cursed diamond to boot, I'd have to be carried off to an insane asylum myself. Besides, if you ever go to a mental hospital, you'll see seven thousand patients who have never so much as glimpsed the Hope diamond. And let it be noted, by the way—that is a very curious name for a stone which only produces car wrecks and attacks of schizophrenia."

"Just let me go on with my story if you don't mind. The other daughter died of an overdose of sleeping pills."

"But dying that way is virtually a natural death in the United States. As widespread as baseball."

71

Beba was sputtering and giving off sparks like an overcharged Leyden jar. She enumerated the calamities, disasters, and mishaps brought about by the stone in the past: Prince Kanitovitsky assassinated, Sultan Abdul Hamid losing his throne, plus his favorite . . .

"Abdul what?" He asked as though the complete name made some decisive difference—one of his little jokes.

"Hamid. Abdul Hamid."

"Who lost what?"

"His throne and his favorite."

"Oh please, no need to pile disaster upon disaster, as though that were further proof. Losing his throne is quite enough."

"But that's why his favorite left him, don't you see?"

And the list went on: the Zubayaba woman was murdered, Simon Montharides died with his wife and their son when their horses bolted . . .

"Where did you read that? How do you know all this is true?"

"There are very well-known people involved. And then there was the matter of Tavernier."

"Tavernier? Who might that gentleman have been?"

"Everyone knows that. The man who stole the stone in 1612 from the eye of an Indian idol. Everyone knows that. Yes or no?"

He, Arrambide, was a part of that "everyone" but he hadn't the slightest idea what she was talking about. There they could see how such stories were fabricated. And as for Tavernier, Arrambide had never so much as heard the name. How could she be so sure he'd even existed?

"He was a French adventurer so famous that even servants knew about him. It's simply that you only read those gastroenterology books . . . And what happened to Tavernier. Dreadful."

"What?"

"Devoured by a pack of starving dogs on the steppes of Russia."

Dr. Arrambide stood there suspended, with a piece of sandwich in his hand and his mouth half open, like one of those snapshots published by the weekly news magazines. No, please, that was too much—starving dogs, Russian steppes, troikas, Indian idols.

MARCELO, SILVINA SAID, COME DOWN, AND HER FACE WAS A PLEA.

"All right, all right, of course."

He came into the living room clumsily. He was still weighed down by that large, heavy load, that feeling of helplessness and incapacity. He kissed his mother's cheek and then took refuge in a corner of the crowd, not knowing what to do. His eyes were on the rug. Little by little, trying not to call attention to himself, he slipped out.

Dr. Carranza wanted to go after him, catch him, say something to him. But all he could do was silently watch him slip away through the noise and the people. There was a lump in Dr. Carranza's throat, and he remembered the times he would get up at dawn to study with Marcelo for his entrance examinations.

At last he, too, left and locked himself in his bedroom.

OUT OF SHEER WEAKNESS, THOUGHT SABATO,

who was irritated even before the thing got started, depressed, feeling guilty again for practically everything: for doing things and for not doing things. Oh yes, of course, Beba would say to him, make yourself "interesting," don't go to parties, play the part of the inaccessible man of mystery. Oh yes, of course. So sometimes he had to go. And besides, poor Maruja.

Sabato would look around at those groups that Maruja brought together in the most mindless naiveté—she would, utterly unconsciously, assemble the people one most hated, and then inconsequentially defend them.

"It's that you don't know so-and-so," she would argue.

It was futile to explain to her that he detested the person in question because in fact he *did* know him. But she would go on thinking that wars were fought because people didn't know each other, and it was useless to remind her of the unparalleled ferocity of civil wars, mothers-in-law, and the brothers Karamazov, so he wound up drinking his whisky off in a corner, while Dr. Arrambide looked about with that expression of his of invariable surprise (eyes very wide, eyebrows raised, forehead ridged in great horizontal ridges), as though at that very moment the Nobel Prize had been

73

awarded to a midget. And then suddenly, without being sure exactly why, Sabato found himself in the midst of an argument, because someone said that life was grand and Margot, with her look of a woman constantly grief-stricken, her brows circumflex, mentioned on the other hand cancer and muggings, drugs, leukemia.

"But science always progresses," Arrambide objected. "In the past, hundreds of thousands of people died of plagues like yellow fever."

Sabato was waiting for an appropriate moment to leave without hurting Maruja's feelings, but at those words he could not control his temper, and so he found himself doing what he had sworn never to do—arguing with Arrambide. Of course, he said, fortunately all that was now in the past, so that now in place of cholera precedence was given to Asian flu, cancer, heart attacks. To which, with an ironic smile, Dr. Arrambide was about to respond, when someone began an inventory of concentration camp horrors. Examples were cited.

One woman recalled that *The Tunnel* had talked about the case of a pianist who had been forced to eat a live rat.

"How disgusting," a lady gasped.

"Disgusting perhaps, but it's the only good thing about that novel," added the woman who had brought the matter up, assuming the author was somewhere else. Or assuming that he was right there.

At that point "the person" broke in. It seemed to Sabato that the man had been introduced to him before as a professor of something or other in the philosophy department.

"Did you happen to read that article by Gollancz that appeared in *Sur*?"

"Don't mention Victoria* to me," said the woman who had praised the novel's sole merit.

"But I'm not talking about Victoria," the professor tried to explain, "I'm talking about an article by Victor Gollancz."

"Uh-huh, and what about him?"

"He tells about the napalm bombs that were used in Korea."

"What kind of bombs?"

"Napalm."

---

*A reference to Victoria Ocampo, director of the famous literary magazine *Sur*, which published all of the important literary figures of Argentina. [E.S.]

74

"Napalm bombs," Dr. Arrambide put in, "were not used in Korea alone. Now they're used everywhere."

"Uh-huh, and what is it that happened?" asked the lady who had mentioned the rat. Her tone was hardly encouraging, and surely she was not likely to find anything interesting in an article which was in no way linked to Victoria.

"He says that out in front of them there was a strange figure standing there leaning forward a little, with its legs spread and its arms out wide, so as not to touch its sides. Something like the beginning of one of those gymnastics exercises. It had no eyes. It was half-covered with burned rags. The body, which was largely exposed, was covered with a thick black crust, or a scab, dotted with yellow spots. Pus."

"Ugh! How dreadful!" the woman who had talked about the rat exclaimed.

"Why was it like that—holding its arms out like that?" asked the woman who held no affection for Victoria Ocampo.

"Because it couldn't bear to touch any part of its body. It would break off at anything, at any contact."

"What is it that would break off?" she asked incredulously.

"Its skin, its flesh. Don't you understand? Napalm makes a crisp, crackling scab, a very fragile crust. The victim can't lie down, or sit. He has to stand up forever, with his arms outstretched."

"What a horror!" exclaimed the woman who always seemed shocked.

But the Victoria Ocampo woman commented, "Not lie down? Or sit? So what do they do when they get tired?"

"Madam," the professor replied, "I hardly think that the worst thing about it would be getting tired."

And then he continued: "The bomb is made of jellied petroleum. When it explodes, the petroleum adheres so tightly to the body, to the skin, that man and petroleum burn as one. So. As I was saying. Gollancz cites another example: he saw two lizards, horrible things, crawling slowly along, groaning like monsters. There were more, behind them. For a few moments, Gollancz was paralyzed with disgust and terror. Where could those nightmarish reptiles have come from? As the light increased somewhat, the enigma was cleared up: they were human beings flayed alive by the fire and heat, their flesh

75

ripped off them wherever they had come in contact with something hard. After a few moments he saw something that resembled a line of baked turkeys coming along the road, beside the river. Some were begging for water, in a hoarse, harsh, barely audible voice. They were naked, skinned. The skin of their hands had been stripped down from the wrists and was hanging from their fingers, just behind their fingernails, like a glove turned inside out. In the uncertain light of the dusk it seemed to him that he saw, besides all that, many children in a yard, in the same condition."

Various exclamations of horror were uttered. Some ladies went off other places, visibly disgusted by the demonstration of bad taste on the part of that person who, to cap it all, seemed delighted by the impression made by his story.

His delight was barely perceptible, but it was certainly there. Sabato observed him carefully; there was something disagreeable about him. The look of him intrigued Sabato, though, and he asked one of the people nearby, lowering his voice, what that man's name was.

"I think he's an engineer, Gatti, or Prati, something like that."

"What? Didn't someone say he was a professor in the philosophy department?"

"No, no. I think he's an Italian engineer."

Now they were back to the German concentration camps.

"You have to separate what's true from what's Allied propaganda," one man known for his nationalistic politics commented.

"It would have been best if they had frankly admitted it," the lady who had spoken about the rat replied, "at least they would be consistent with their doctrine."

"What this gentleman has told us about," the man of nationalistic sympathies responded, nodding toward the engineer or professor, "did not occur in German concentration camps, it was horrors produced by democratic American bombs. And what do you have to say to me, madam, about the tortures committed by French paratroopers in Algeria?"

The conversation became confused and violent. Until at last someone said, "All right, barbarity. There have always been barbarities, since man's first existence. Remember Mohammed II, Bajazet, the Assyrians, the Romans. Mohammed II had prisoners sawed in

76

half, alive. Lengthwise. And what about the thousands of people crucified along the Via Appia, during the Spartacan uprising? What about the pyramids of heads piled up by the Assyrians? And the papering of entire walls with the skins flayed off their prisoners, alive?"

Several means of torture were enumerated. For example, the classic Chinese torture of seating a naked victim on top of an iron cauldron which has an enormous, starving rat inside. As the cauldron is heated over the fire, the rat eats his way out through the victim's body.

There were renewed exclamations of disgust and horror, and several people said things were getting awfully ugly, but no one moved this time—apparently they were waiting for more examples. A survey was taken. The engineer or professor named the best-known tortures—slivers under the fingernails, impaling, quartering.

Lulú, who had just arrived but who had been in time to hear some of the last-mentioned atrocities, became truly angry.

"I don't know why we have to look at just the ugly things," she protested. "Life has its lovely moments, too—children, friends, working together for common ideals, moments of tenderness, happiness, joy . . ."

"That may be the most perverse thing about existence," argued the engineer or professor. "Perhaps if we lived our lives in perpetual horror, cruelty, shock, disgust, we would come at last to get used to them."

"Do you mean to say that those moments of happiness only exist to accentuate the horror of wars, tortures, plagues, catastrophes?"

The engineer smiled and raised his eyebrows in that way that means "Obviously."

"But then life would be a true hell!" Lulú almost shrieked.

"And how could you doubt it?" the engineer asked.

"The famous vale of tears."

"That is precisely it."

"No, not 'precisely' at all," the engineer broke in, as though he had been misinterpreted.

"Pardon?"

"It's something else," mysteriously replied the engineer, raising a hand.

"What 'something else'?" shot back the woman who was dying of curiosity. But she was interrupted by Lulú, who, undaunted, stated, "It may be true, what this gentleman says, though to my mind, life has beautiful things in it."

"But no one denies that it has beautiful things in it," the engineer interrupted.

"All right, all right, all right, whatever you say. But even if this life were altogether horrible, which it isn't, there will always exist the consolation of a paradise for those who are capable of bearing their earthly existence with kindness and charity, with faith, with hope."

In the professor or engineer's little eyes there appeared a gleam of sarcasm.

"It appears that you doubt that," Lulú commented bitterly.

"It's that there is another possibility, you see," the man responded sweetly.

"What other possibility?"

"That we are already dead and damned. That this is the hell to which we are condemned for all eternity."

"But we're *alive*," put in a man who had never opened his mouth until now.

"So you think. So you all think. I mean to say—what you all *must* think in the case that my hypothesis is correct. Do you understand?"

"No, we don't understand a thing. At least I don't."

"That illusion of being alive. That hope which lies in death. Although it sounds like a joke to talk about a hope that lies in death. That illusion, that hope would also be part of the hellish farce."

"Seems to me pretty farfetched to imagine we're not alive," Dr. Arrambide commented. "And what about the dead, then? The mortuary business?"

On the engineer's face, which for his smug pomposity was beginning to take on an unwelcome aspect in everyone's eyes, there appeared a shadow of contempt.

"That is a spectacular argument, but weak," he replied. "In dreams too, there are people who die, and there are funerals. And funeral parlors." There was a silence. The engineer then went on, "Think—for an omnipotent being it would cost nothing to organize

78

a comedy like this one, so that we would go on believing in the possibility of a death and, therefore, of an eternal rest. What would it cost him to pretend to have deaths and burials? What would it cost him to feign the death of a dead man? Make a cadaver go out at one door, so to speak, and make it come in at another, in another wing of the hell, to begin the comedy all over again with a newborn corpse? With a cradle this time in place of a casket? The Hindus, who were a little less uncouth than we are, had suspected something of the sort when they declared that in each existence the sins of the previous existence are purged. Something like that. Not exactly. But the poor buggers got very close."

"Well," breathed the lady indisposed toward Victoria Ocampo, "but even if that were true, what difference does it make whether this is reality or illusion? When all's said and done, if we are not in the least aware of any of that, if we have no memory of our previous life, it's all the same, then—it's as though we actually were born and died. What would kill all hope would be the full awareness of the diabolic comedy. It's as though one were dreaming a pretty dream and never awoke."

There was a certain relief among those people who were content with what in philosophy is known as naive realism.

The adherents of that accredited school of philosophy cast on the Italian engineer or professor a look of malevolent satisfaction. He could see that the gathering had by now become openly hostile. He coughed, consulted his watch, and showed signs of gathering himself to leave. As he was turning away, though, he added, with a slightly scornful expression on his face, "It is precisely, madam, precisely as you say. But it could be that the person who is organizing this sinister simulacrum of reality might from time to time send someone to wake people up, to make them see that they are dreaming. Might that not be possible?"

ALL THAT NIGHT MARCELO WALKED AIMLESSLY.
He went into cafés, turned down anonymous streets, sat on benches in hushed and deserted parks. It was morning by the time he returned to his room and lay down to sleep. When he awoke, in the afternoon, he had an idea—his great-uncle Amancio. While he

walked to his great-uncle's house, Marcelo reflected that the gentleman might be surprised by his visit, show too much interest, ask too many questions, and that he himself in turn might find himself unable to make the right replies, unable to not tell his uncle the truth, unable to cause him worry. Marcelo thought about saying that it was other reasons that led him to ask the favor—a desire to live a more quiet life, think about himself a little more, other people too maybe, the old man knew how these things were . . .

He made his way with contradictory thoughts up the old stairs, wondering once again how the poor old man had managed to resign himself to a life like this, almost sandwiched between two walls, living in one tiny room in an old turn-of-the-century two-story house now cut up into sordid apartments. He found his great-uncle wrapped in shawls, mufflers, and sweaters. Even his old frayed overcoat with the greenish velvet collar. Another old gentleman was also in the room, don Edelmiro Lagos, Amancio's lifelong friend.

Gesturing toward the window, Amancio said, "If this wind stops, Marcelo, there'll be a frost tonight. The fruit trees will all freeze."

Marcelo looked out, as though down there in the street there were orchards. His courtesy overpowered his logic. Then, enigmatically, don Edelmiro spoke: "The pampas wind will be the pampas wind."

With his black suit, his high stiff collar, his starched cuffs, don Edelmiro looked as though he were sitting in his notary office (ca. 1915), ready for the signing of some deed. And the way his left hand rested on the silver handle of his walking stick made him look like some sleepy Argentine totem, with its eyes half-closed. His face, which seemed made of clods, was a great geographical expanse with moles as mountain peaks and odd clumps of hair appearing among geological anfractuosities. His famous silence was broken from time to time by those aphorisms which, in Amancio's opinion, made him a "man of good counsel."

"Neither one extreme nor the other: the middle road."

"Time erases all things."

"One must never lose faith in the Nation."

These sententious pronouncements did not come forth unexpectedly; they were preceded, rather, by signs which were almost imperceptible but which would not escape a person watching closely. It was as though some dark and silent totem should suddenly begin to reveal a sign of life making itself manifest at last in a slight shudder, the slightest trembling of the enormous hands and a quiver, perhaps, in the great nose. Then it would speak, and after the aphorism it would return once more to ceremonious silence.

With difficulty, Amancio began to stand, but Marcelo would not allow it. The things for the *mate*, that was what he wanted.

"My knee's acting up," he explained, settling back into his chair again.

He prepared the *mate* with delicate, precise gestures, meanwhile commenting:

"I tell you, Edelmiro. This climate has never agreed with me."

After some minutes of silence, he expressed amazement at what a fellow had had to pay for a little piece of land in Punta del Indio. Some fellow named Fischer, he believed it was.

Gosen, the Turk, had told him about it.

Edelmiro half raised his eyelids, his curiosity piqued, apparently.

"That Turk that had the store on Magdalena."

But that land was underwater half the time. Pure swamp. Oh, but they were going to plant some kind of trees or other, some sort of imported trees. Big important business, no? Anyway, that was how he'd heard it told. Big Business. Imagine.

Looking out toward the street, he shook his head.

And then there passed ten or fifteen minutes of silence. All that was heard were the soft sounds of the silver *mate* implements, the sipping. Finally, musing, Amancio asked:

"Do you remember that young Jacinto Insaurralde boy, Edelmiro?"

Edelmiro's eyelids fluttered half-open again.

"You know," Amancio insisted, "Jacinto Insaurralde. That dandy sort of fellow. Very spiffy dresser, he always was."

His friend closed his eyes, perhaps to rummage through his memories.

"He's dying of cancer. Of the liver, to make matters worse."

Don Edelmiro Lagos opened his eyes halfway and sat there an instant, perhaps having finally remembered Jacinto Insaurralde, perhaps surprised at the news. Though there was no means of telling from that silent, deserted landscape of his face. Still, after a moment, he spoke:

"Cancer is the scourge of civilization."

Then he took from the pocket of his vest the gold Longines he carried on the end of a heavy gold chain, opened the case and consulted the dial as though it were some delicately scribed legal document, snapped the case closed again, slipped the watch carefully back into his pocket, and rose to leave.

It was growing dark.

"Uncle Amancio," Marcelo found himself blurting out, as though someone had shoved him.

"What is it, son?"

Marcelo felt a wave of blood rush into his face, and he realized that he would never be able to speak to the old man about that empty back room.

Amancio awaited Marcelo's words with solicitude and surprise, as though in a region famed for its droughts a sudden hail of fat raindrops had begun to fall.

"No . . . I mean . . . it may freeze, like you say . . ."

The old man continued to look at him, intrigued, and while he repeated, almost mechanically, "I tell you, it's the pampas wind," he was thinking "What's got into Marcelito?"

Marcelo at the same time was thinking, "Uncle Amancio and that threadbare overcoat of his, that genteel poverty of his, that faded noble generosity of his, that sweet, gentlemanly tactfulness of his."

Moved by that tact, Amancio was already trying to change the subject; pointing to *La Prensa*, he asked Marcelo whether he'd read the editorial on the atomic bomb. No, Marcelo hadn't read it. "And the delicate way he has of handling things," he thought tenderly. As though the old man were asking him whether he'd read Belisario Roldán's speeches lately. The old man's head shook heavily.

"It all depends . . . I mean, Uncle Amancio . . ."

The old man looked at him, curious to see what came next.

Marcelo made a grand effort, and at last brought out:

"I mean . . . maybe one day it can be used for something good . . ."

"Something good?"

82

"I don't know . . . I mean . . . a desert, for example . . ."

"A desert?"

"Uh-huh . . . to change the climate . . ."

"And would that be good, Marcelo?"

The boy was growing more and more red-faced, more and more uncomfortable, more and more ill at ease. He hated to give the impression that he knew more than other people, hated to give lessons, explain things. He considered it vulgar, especially with someone as defenseless as Amancio. But it was too late to go back.

"I think . . . maybe . . . in countries where there's so much hunger . . . I read once . . . those places where it hardly ever rains . . . on the Ethiopian border, for example . . . at least that's what I think . . ."

Amancio turned his eyes once more to the newspaper, as though he might find there the key to this vast problem.

"Of course, of course. I'm an ignorant old man," he muttered.

"No, no, no, Uncle! I'm not saying that!" Marcelo cried, shame-faced. "I didn't mean that. . . ."

Amancio looked at him, but Marcelo no longer knew how to go on.

After a few moments things grew calmer, and the old man went back to gazing out the window at the street.

"Fischer. I remember now," he said all at once.

"What's that, Uncle?"

"The fellow who's buying that land. German fellow. Fischer, something like that. Those people that came after the last war . . . Hardworking people, plenty of ideas . . ."

Pensive, he considered the trees along the street.

"Those people know what they're about. Progress, indubitably."

Then after a moment he added:

"But still, those were lovely times . . . There was not so much science, I suppose, but there was more kindness . . . Nobody was in a hurry . . . We had time for drinking *mate* and watching the evening get dark, out on the veranda. There weren't as many ways to distract yourself then, to entertain yourself, you know—there were no moving pictures, we'd never heard of this television. But there were other pretty things: christenings, harvest days, somebody's birthday . . ."

A long silence fell.

"People didn't know as much then as they do now. But they were more disinterested. Disinterested. People thought about one another. In the country, people were poor, especially where we lived, the Magdalene coast. But things were grand, noble. The city was different, too. People were polite, helpful, respectful of a man."

As the darkness fell in the room, the silences grew longer and more profound. Marcelo studied the old man's silhouette against the softening light from the window. What did he think about during those long nights he spent alone?

"The world has grown full of lies, Marcelo. No one trusts anyone anymore. When we went with my father to Uruguay—I was just a boy, you know, it was when Uncle Saturnino died—we didn't need any papers to travel with. Today . . ."

His voice fell quiet again. Then, slapping the newspaper with the palm of his hand, he went on:

"Today, with these bombardments . . . those creatures in Vietnam . . . And you, Marcelo, what do you think about all this?"

"I . . . I think maybe one day . . . things will change . . ."

The old man awaited Marcelo's words with melancholy, polite attention. Then, as though he were speaking for his own benefit alone, he said:

"Anything is possible, Marcelo . . . But I don't believe the country will ever be what it was again. There were lakes, and pink geese, and wild ducks. . . ."

It was night.

THE CLOWN

HE IMITATED QUIQUE COMMENTING ON THE OBITUARIES, he told jokes, he recalled old stories about the time he taught math in a boys' school. They thought he seemed better than ever, full of life and energy.

And suddenly he had the sense that the thing was about to begin—with unconquerable force, for nothing could hold it back once the process had commenced. It was not to be anything horrendous, there would not be any monsters. Yet inside him he could begin to feel that terror that comes only in certain dreams. Little by little he was being possessed by the sense that people were becoming

84

strange to him, and far away, the way he might feel peeking through a window at a party, seeing the people laughing, talking, dancing in silence, and unconscious of the fact that they were being watched. But that was not exactly it, either. It was more as though people were separated from him not by glass panes or simple distance, which one could always bridge by opening a door, or by merely drawing closer, but rather by some *unbridgeable* dimension. Like a fantasy in which living persons can be seen and heard while they cannot see or hear us. But it wasn't that, either. It wasn't that he alone could hear them; they could hear him, too, and talk to him. Other people never experienced the least sense of strangeness or wonder; they were totally unconscious of the fact that the man having this conversation with them was not S. but some sort of substitute, some sort of usurping clown. While the other S., the real one, slowly and in awe-filled fear grew more and more isolated, more and more distant and withdrawn. And though he might die of terror, like a man watching the last ship, the one that might have rescued him, lift anchor and sail away, he was incapable of making the least sign of desperation, of giving the least indication of his growing distance and solitude. And so, as the ship pulled away from the island, he began to tell a funny story about his student days, once when they'd invented a Hungarian poet, the protégé of an equally nonexistent princess. It seems they were up to here with Rilke and all that Rilkean snobbery. The more confident they got, the more daring they became; they published two or three poems (in French!) in *Theseus*, published excerpts from his memoirs, and finally leaked the news that he had leprosy. The idea was to trick Guillermo de Torre into publishing a piece on him in *La Nación*.

Everyone died laughing, including the clown, while the other watched the ship grow smaller and smaller on the horizon.

THE SUDDEN BURSTING-FORTH OF THE BROTHER AND SISTER through the smoke of lies and of flames, through ecstasy and vomit, made his life more and more muddled, the great cocktail party more and more filled with anguish. Where had all the absolutes gone? The rebels inside him were pushing to break free, they wanted to act, say ultimate words, fight, die, murder before they got all tangled

85

and involved in the carnival themselves. The insolent Nachos, the harsh Agustinas. *And what about Alejandra?* They badgered him: *Had she actually lived, and where—in that house there, in another one, in that mirador?* They went to the newspaper archives, they wanted to know—how eager these people in the circus were for the absolute, how insatiably thirsty. *Was that news report true?* As though it weren't the most apocryphal things of all that were boxed up in the archives. But no matter: the questions went on—*Had those characters actually lived, and what were their lives like, where did they live them?* Not seeing that they had never died, that from their subterranean lairs they stalked him anew, sought him out, found him, and insulted him. Or maybe it was the other way around—maybe he was the one who needed them if he were to live on and survive. And it was in this state of mind that he waited for Agustina, anxiously awaited her reappearance.

The mask of the lecturer that speaks before ladies' groups, that smiles and does impressions
of good upbringing
of a gentleman correct in all his manners,
of a well-dressed, adequately nourished man.
Not to fear, ladies and gentlemen,
this wild beast has been tamed,
his teeth filed down,
pulled—riddled with cavities they were,
and weakened from eating little snacks, tidbits of this and that, *hors d'oeuvres.*
He's no longer the beast in the jungle that eats raw meat,
that leaps and kills.
He has lost his majestic savagery.
Step up, ladies and gentlemen.
A spectacle for every member of the family,
ladies and gentlemen, boys and girls.
Bring your mother on Mother's Day,
your father on Father's Day.
Here you may have yourselves a look at him.
Turn a bit to the right, there,
hop!
Wave to the Honorable Folks.

86

That's it,
wonderful,
here's a sugar cube for you.
Ladies and gentlemen,
boys and girls,
families—
this powerful king of the jungle, this fierce lion,
will perform for you: dream,
docilely do your prettily choreographed
little pirouettes,
with secret, smiling irony.
—Poor things, the truth is
that there are kids out there that love me,
there I go, around the ring, leap through the hoop,
one two hop!
Excellent!
and I dream of the jungle
of its ancient evening shadows
while I distractedly do my tricks
neatly and politely jumping through the ring of fire
perching on a chair
roaring absentmindedly
and remembering the pale lagoons
on the plains
to which one day I will return
to live forever
(I know this, I believe it, I need it),
devouring a lion tamer
(a title symbolic)
as my farewell
in an act of madness
the newspapers say
unexpectedly his head disappeared between the salivating jaws
dripping blood, oh horror!
panic reigned
while for the moment
I dream
of that violent but innocent land

the proud principality
the ceremonies of hurricanes and death
a fugitive from shame
de-born from the filth of the pig
to the chasteness of the bird and the rain
to the pride of solitude.
Step up, ladies and gentlemen,
this wild beast has been tamed.
For every member of the family
to see—hop!
—I wave to the Honorable Audience
while I dream of the hard but beautiful jungle,
of its moonlit nights
of my mother.

THERE WAS A PARTY WHEN T.B.'S BOOK OF POEMS ON DEATH AND SOLITUDE CAME OUT.

In the photographs that appeared in the magazine one saw a multitude of people drinking wine, eating little sandwiches, and laughing. One could make out the same faces as always, including T.B.'s mortal enemies—people who before, after, and even during the cocktail party made jokes about his poems behind his back.

Nietzsche, he thought.

He needed to talk to somebody literate, breathe some fresh, pure air, do something with his hands—make a table, repair some little girl's tricycle, Erika's for example. Do something humble, useful. Clean.

He turned off the light.

As it had at other moments of disgust and sadness for mankind (and for himself), that memory returned. Why? What was there about it that made it so basic to his life? He was carrying his calculus assignment to Dr. Grinfeld, through the twilit evening. The silvery cupola of the observatory had begun to glimmer and stand out, with serene mystery, like a silent link to cosmic space, against the softly falling darkness. He was walking along the paths between the introverted trees in the La Plata Forest Reserve. The harmonious universe of the stars in their ecliptics. The precise theorems of celestial mechanics.

HE FELT THE NEED TO RETURN TO LA PLATA,
to the house no longer his—to spy on it, like some intruder, like
some thief of memories. And once again he recalled that summer
evening when he'd come to the house and silently entered, and there
seen her sitting, with her back to him, at that great solitary table in
the dining room, staring into space, staring into emptiness (into her
memories, that is), there in the half-darkness of the room with its
closed blinds, her only company the tick-tock of the old wall clock.

In those happy times we would have her birthday dinners
and I would be happy and nobody was dead

and everybody would sit around the enormous Chippendale dining
table, with those great sideboards and silver carving tools we used
to have, with the father at the head of the table and the mother at
the foot, and the laughing when Pepe told those stories of his, the
innocent lies of that family folklore

and me surviving myself
like a match blown out
the table set with more places, with better china, with finer crystal

"How are you, mother," he had said.
"I was thinking," was the reply. And her eyes seemed to blur.
Yes, of course.
"About that saying, 'life is a dream,' son."
He had looked at her in silence. What could he say to soften it
all? She was looking back on ninety years of phantasmagoria.
Then she went to rummage through those wardrobes that were
always locked up tight, looking for something, opening them with
the jumble of jealously guarded keys.
"This ring, here, when I die . . . I've kept it for you."
"Yes, mother."
"It was my great-grandmother's. María San Marco."

89

It was small, gold, with an enameled seal—an *M* crossed with an *S*.

Then for a while they sat face to face but did not talk. Once in a while she would say something, remember something—*Fortunato, do you remember him? Don Guillermo Boer's ranch. Your Uncle Pablo, and his gout.*

He had to go.

Oh, did he really have to? Her eyes blurred again with tears. But she was stoic, she came from a family of soldiers—even if she wouldn't admit it, even if she denied it, in fact.

He still remembered how she had stood in the door, waving good-bye vaguely, feebly with her right hand—*who would ever think, such a thing to happen* . . . When he reached the end of the walk, he turned his head: she was alone, once more.

Stop, my heart
do not think.

On Third the trees were beginning to spread the enigmatic silence of their evening gloom.

He turned his head once more. Once more she repeated with her hand, timidly almost, her good-bye.

THE ENCOUNTER

THE TWO DOWN-AT-HEELS OLD LADIES came in tired from the heat, and perhaps from the wait at Recoleta. They sat down and ordered tea and cakes.

"Poor Julio," one of them sighed, still a bit out of breath, "imagine, dying in February, when there's not a soul in Buenos Aires." It was all such rot, making your peace with the world, and all in the name of Art. You felt the pain and anguish, of course you did. But take an *absolute* sort of person, like R. was, for example—a black, terrible sort of person. They just keep living, keep coming to La Biela, and it worked, because vomiting always works, you know, you need to vomit so you can get rid of the bad things, and I'll tell you, if R. should ever manage to become a writer, he'd no doubt wind up going to the French Embassy, too, giving lectures and what have

90

you. All things come to him who waits, that was a fact. What could those kids do. Spit on them, kill one another, prostitute themselves. If there's no God, after all, everything's allowed.

He had not stopped thinking about her, though finally he had virtually lost hope of ever chancing to see her again. But now that need to see her, to talk to her, became unbearable. He left the café and walked up a little slope and sat down on one of the benches near the statue of Falcón.

And he saw her, walking along the sidewalk. Her steps were wary, as though the ground were unsteady, or dangerous, or might give way.

He hesitated for a second, but then he made up his mind to speak to her. All those months he had been thinking that it would be she who sought him out, and in a certain sense this coincidence proved it: one could hardly deny that he often walked through this neighborhood, crossed this park, had coffee in La Biela, sat on a bench and meditated. He was pretty sure her shyness, that strange reticence of hers, would never allow her to walk into the café, that she would much rather have it this way—stroll through the park, turn their meeting into a casual coincidence, or the appearance of one.

He approached her, came up beside her, but since she continued walking, taking no notice of him, at last he took her arm. She looked at him in silence, though with no surprise, and that confirmed his theory that she'd been looking for him.

"Do you live around here?" he asked her.

"No," she replied, turning her eyes away. "We live in Belgrano R."

"And what are you doing in Recoleta, then?"

Though he had spoken the words almost carelessly, immediately he was sorry he had asked the question: it was as though he were trying to force her to admit that she'd wanted to find him.

"Anybody can walk down the sidewalk," she answered.

This upset him. They were standing face to face, in this ridiculous situation, and she was staring at the ground.

"I'm sorry," she said. "That was rude."

"Forget it."

She raised her eyes, looked at him fixedly, and clenched her

91

jaw. She blushed. And then, softly, she confessed: "Not just rude. A lie, too."

"I know, but forget it."

"What do you mean, you know?"

He didn't know what to say to her without hurting her. He took her arm and guided her over to the bench and they sat there for a long while. The girl, angry, seemed to want to study the grass, until at last she broke her silence.

"It's that you know that I've wanted to see you, isn't it? That I've been wandering around here for weeks hoping to run into you?"

He didn't answer; there was no need to. Both of them knew that their meeting had been inevitable. And that things would have been all the worse had it not occurred.

IT WAS AFTER DARK WHEN AGUSTINA RETURNED.

She came in crestfallen, distant, no longer the hard Agustina of before. From what painful, sad land had she returned? Nacho raised his right hand with his open palm toward her, turning his face away, as though protecting his gaze from some pitiful, moving sight.

"What new calamity has fallen upon this house? I seem to see Elektra, striding in great mourning."

Agustina fell into her bed.

"Take that record off," she curtly said. "I'm sick of Bob Dylan."

Her brother lowered his arm, studied her a moment, and then, falling to his knees before the record player sitting on the floor among piles of books, old newspapers, and dirty plates, he turned off the record. Then once again, still on his knees, he studied his sister. His face was pained. Tenderly and almost timidly, he murmured, "I am Orestes. Seek not a better friend than I."

Then, walking on his knees, he shuffled to the edge of Agustina's bed, like some pilgrim to the shrine of Lourdes, or Guadalupe.

"You see. I have come on my knees to this sacred place for you. It is a sacred promise I have made."

He took her hands and held them to his breast.

"You forget, O Elektra, that I was the most beloved of men to you. Those were the words you spoke to our father at the catafalque that shelters his remains. When we poured out the propitiatory li-

92

bations. When you invoked Hermes, the messenger of the gods, both those above and those below. When the demons heard your supplications, the demons that watch over the paternal dwelling."

"Stop it, Nacho. I'm dead, can't you see? Fuck off."

"O Zeus! Behold, look down upon this offspring of the race of eagles, bereft of father and now held in the suffocating clutches of the horrendous serpent! Look at us, children without father, exiled from the paternal home!"

"Stop it, I told you. I'm really beat."

His voice suddenly grating, vulgar, Nacho still went on:

"That whore! I saw her in Pérez Nassif's car."

"Uh-huh."

"You seem not to care." Nacho studied her face. Then growing more and more furious, he screamed at her, asked her whether she wasn't ashamed that that whore had gotten her her job in that asshole's office.

"Oh sure, Nacho, then we can live on welfare. Or panhandle in the street."

Throwing himself on her, he cried that he was serious.

"Stop yelling. That's enough." Agustina's face had grown stiff. "You're so stupid, Nacho. I guess I'll have to draw you a picture. Can't you see that I never showed more contempt for her than when I took that job? So don't mention the woman to me again."

Sarcastically, her brother reminded her that "that woman" was their mother, and that nobody was issued more than one. Then he stood up, went off into the corner, and produced a little package wrapped in flowered paper with a red ribbon.

"What kind of joke is this, now?" Agustina asked tiredly.

"Have you forgotten Mother's Day?"

It was a very small package. His sister raised her eyes to his face.

"You know what I'm giving her?" His face radiated twisted happiness. "A condom."

Then he went back into his corner, lay down on his bed, and smiled silently for a moment.

"I want you to make me a promise," he said.

"Will you stop bugging me with these promises of yours?"

"Come on. It's just a little promise. Just one."

Agustina didn't reply.

93

"A micropromise. A tiny midget-sized promise."

"A promise to what?"

"It's a test."

"What kind of test?"

"I know what kind," Nacho responded evasively.

"All right. Shoot. It's the only way I'll ever get to sleep, I'm sure. And in case you've forgotten, I'm exhausted, Nacho."

Nacho beamed, then got up and handed her a record album with a photo of John Lennon and Yoko Ono on the cover. "I want you to promise never to listen to this record again."

"Why not?"

"You see, you see! That's the test! You still don't understand a thing! You're totally out of it!" he cried, grabbing the album and slapping her face with it.

Agustina stared at him angrily.

"Don't you see? It's all her fault. That shit woman!" Then, dispirited, he sat down beside his sister on the edge of the bed, muttering things like "that cunt, that contagious fetal miscarriage, that bitch" to himself. Then he returned to the attack.

"Will you?"

"Okay, okay. Will you just let me sleep?"

He threw the album to the floor, stomped on it, and then in a rage picked it up and twisted the record viciously until he had broken it into pieces. When he had finished, he looked into his sister's eyes, as though seeking some sign, some emotion. Then he went back to his bed, flopped onto it, and turned off his bedside lamp. After a while, in a voice which through the dimness of the room seemed to take secret paths which they had once known but which now were littered with obstacles and mined with hidden traps set by some perverse invader, he whispered, weakly, "Something's happened, Agustina."

There was no reply. She simply turned off her lamp. With a shock that turned slowly into despair, Nacho realized that she had turned off the light *to hide her nakedness*. In the unsure light from the window, he could see that she was removing her clothes.

He took his clothes off, too, and got into bed. He watched her for a long time, there was no way to measure for how long (for there was a whole childhood there, dogs, hiding places in Parque de Los

Patricios, candy, solitary afternoon naps, nights of tears and embraces), and he felt that she, too, was still awake, thinking, troubled; her breathing did not sound like the breathing of sleep. Trembling, with effort, he asked her if she was asleep.

"No, I'm not asleep."

"Can I?" he asked almost fearfully.

She did not answer.

After a moment of hesitation, Nacho got up and went over to the other bed. He sat on it and caressed his sister's face, touching with his fingers the tears under her eyes.

"No," she said softly and almost sweetly, but in a voice which he'd never heard before. And then she went on:

"I'd rather you didn't."

Nacho didn't know how to feel, sitting there beside that body which his hands softly brushed yet which lay at some unreachable distance from him.

He got up, little by little, and went back to his own bed and collapsed into it.

> *Your body and the ribbon of rough silk that leads*
> *to the plantations*
> *along the coast*
> *the sweat of your hair burned by the clouds*
> *at those unforgettable instants*
> *moving so many times, so often, like a nomad*
> *or a rebel gone underground,*
> *so many homages to a savage beauty*
> *homages which demand disorder*
> *all the ramps of changing life*
> *the speed of love*
> *the magic philtre of excommunication*
> *the starving light of the unmingling of our veins*
> *of scourge*
> *and the solitary frenzy of the palm trees*
> *when in your absence*
> *growing toward my breast*
> *the bottom of the sea gives me back again, suddenly,*
> *all our caresses*

the furious knot of passion
in the black iron chain links of time
that furniture of robberies and of rains
the light of breasts in the water
and its seagulls and its songs
on an altar of disunion, with great fascinating moons
no meadows but your eyes
incorruptible land
narcotic land
with alcoholic laughter on the wind
and your hair across my face.

JORGE LEDESMA'S FIRST COMMUNICATION

THE WORLD'S STILL GOING TO HELL IN A HANDBASKET. All the more reason for optimism, of course, since we're past the point of being surprised by anything.

And my success rate is still laughably low. I was born a dolt, and all of a sudden I don't know what to do. Just take the latest example of my doings—I climbed a lamppost, naked, on the corner of Corrientes and Suipacha. Picture it: Saturday afternoon at five o'clock. I was in the clink for several months.

I'm going to confess something to you, my friend Sabato—it wasn't my idea to come into this world, I never showed the least desire. I was so comfortable and warm, in fact, that when it came time for me to make my entrance, I came in ass-first. But they dragged me in anyway—and I do mean dragged. I've always been dragged, in fact, and always in the name of "what's best for me." For that reason alone, I soon figured out that this world was ass-backward. Surely you've made a similar discovery. We've lost the game, I know we have. We're whipped. Beaten. Rolled over. Struck out. But we're supposed to take it like men. Stoically. Stiff upper lip. Not a whimper. Well, to hell with that. We're two of a kind, and we're going to tell it like it is, as the Americans, I am told, say. Two of a kind? Yes, two poor wretches. Of course, I've got you beat in the ignorance department.

I'm writing to tell you that in anticipation of my death, I have

96

decided to make you my heir. I don't want what happened to Marconi to happen to me—that after I'm dead nobody can figure out what it was all about. I've informed my family.

Donne: "No man sleeps in the cart that carries him to the scaffold." You were the one who reminded me of that. Tremendous. For some time now I've been looking into the famous Aristotelian enigma: we must find the Principle; all else will follow from that. Sabato—*I have found the principle.* I know how and why we were made. Do you realize what I'm saying? I want to be calm and controlled about this, and not embroider anything. A theory must be pitiless, cruel, and it will turn against its own creator if the creator doesn't treat himself with cruelty. The fear that some unforeseen event will make me carry this incredible discovery to Potter's Field has led me to write you. I must foresee all, calculate all the odds, aside from any petty concern for vanity. And I do not delude myself. Voltaire called Rousseau an energumen, and Carrel called Freud a dangerous and harmful mind. Ignored, unknown, sad, panoramically alone, I care about nothing but humanity—only that humanity not lose the end of this ball of tangled twine that it has cost me so much to find. And that truth, like a fire in the forest, illuminate the spectacle of the lion and the gazelle saving each other from the flames.

I know why and for what we were put into this madhouse of a brothel, and the reason for our subsequent annihilation. As you can understand, this assumes that one has the Pattern by which to measure all human activities. God was a necessary stage—which will make students laugh in a hundred years or so, exactly the way Ptolemy makes *us* laugh now. If Kant says this can't be, it's because he never struggled, as we have, to get inside himself. The asinine (I mean, of course, mulish) regularity with which he strolled at the same hour down the same streets proves his respect for the establishment. He was so comfy with chaos that he *explained* it, instead of solving it. How can one be content with having been placed involuntarily on this planet and, in due time, when one is disgustingly old, being forcibly expelled from it in the midst of horrible pains, and never receiving a word of explanation or apology? And should we be afraid of this guy just because he happened to have been born in Germany? Meanwhile, for millions of years, and in spite of Kant,

all science, the splitting of the atom, and every other calamity, man—
like the fly or the turtle—has continued to suffer and die without
knowing why. Sabato—they can't do that to me.

I punched a little hole in the wall and I put my eye to it. And I
now invite every fearless person to peek through and behold the
hair-raising spectacle.

If my limitations make you laugh, consider that Farraday learned
everything he knew from the books he bound. I have written to you
because I saw you up on the mountain, mad, cold, frozen. But if you
should come down one day and start thinking like these geese down
here, you'll have become, so far as I'm concerned, just another Sainte-
Beuve, and you'll have earned my unending contempt.

You have proof of my courage, because I'm the man that dared
to climb up a lamppost, naked, to punish myself for being a coward
and to prove to myself that I was strong enough to laugh at the
people that came and laughed at me. The difference being that I was
laughing from a higher position than they.

Do me the favor not to die until at least 1973, which is when I
will be sending you the final manuscript with my researches. We
are on the threshold of a new age. We will suffer all manner of
arbitrary discriminations, crimes, and injustices. There will be new
bonfires for the heretics. Vain effort. The Age of Moral Technology
has begun. As happened millions of years ago, new eyes are opening
new apertures out through our skulls. What a vantage point, Sabato!
And how wonderful the future will be for those whose nervous systems can take it!

If the forces of the antiworld destroy me, you must put in order
and publish everything that comes into your hands.

HE AWOKE SCREAMING,
for he'd just seen her coming toward him through the fire, her long
black hair stirring in the furious flames of the Mirador, like some
hallucinatory living torch. She seemed to be running toward him,
crying for help. And suddenly he felt the fire on his own body, he
heard it crackle, heard his flesh sputter in it, and heard Alejandra's
body moving beneath his own. The sharp pain and a wave of terrible
anxiety woke him.

The prophecy was being repeated.

But it was not the Alejandra that some people with such melancholy imagined, nor the Alejandra that Bruno believed he could sense through his will-less, contemplative spirit, but rather an Alejandra of dream, of fire, the victim and executioner of her father. And once again Sabato asked himself why Alejandra's reappearance seemed to remind him of his duty as a writer, seemed to remind him that he had to write, even in the face of all the potencies and powers that opposed him. As though he had to try once more to break those codes which grew more and more fiendish by the day. As though on that complex and doubt-filled frenzy depended not only the salvation of that young woman's soul but, indeed, his own as well.

But salvation from what? he almost screamed in the silence of his room.

YOUNG MUZZIO

maintained, as the saying goes, monkish silence. The large leather armchairs, the wait, the importance of Señor Rubén Pérez Nassif, the clerks' soft, timid way of walking produced in him a mixture of fear, shame, and resentment, and also brought to his mind phrases and bits of phrases like the following:

CONSUMER SOCIETY

CAPITALISM, BOURGEOIS PIGS

STRUCTURAL CHANGES, etc.,

behind which, and through the cracks, he thought he could make out the disagreeable, mockingly inquisitive face of Nacho Izaguirre, that petty-bourgeois counterrevolutionary, that putrescent reactionary.

He tried to push aside the unpleasant apparition, he mentally blew it to atoms with polished phrases: The structures must be changed! Rebelling against one person in particular, such as Pérez Nassif, made no more difference than giving alms to a beggar in the street! Social Revolution or nothing!

But Nacho's face would re-form before him after every broadside and, on top of that, there would be more sarcasm in its smile each time.

He made an effort to push aside the apparition; he concentrated on Benjamin Franklin's "Advice to a Young Man Going into Business":

Remember, that time is money.

Remember, that credit is money. If a man lets his money lie in my hands after it is due, he gives me the interest, or so much as I can make of it during that time. This amounts to a considerable sum where a man has good and large credit, and makes good use of it.

Remember, that money is of the prolific, generating nature. Money can beget money, and its offspring can beget more, and so on. Five shillings turned is 6, turned again it is 7 and threepence, and so on till it becomes an hundred pounds. The more there is of it, the more it produces every turning, so that the profits rise quicker and quicker. He that kills a breeding sow, destroys all her offspring to the thousandth generation. He that murders a crown, destroys all that it might have produced, even scores of pounds.

The most trifling actions that affect a man's credit are to be regarded. The sound of your hammer at 5 in the morning, or 9 at night, heard by a creditor, makes him easy 6 mos. longer; but, if he sees you at a billiard-table, or hears your voice at a tavern, when you should be at work, he sends for his money the next day; demands it, before he can receive it, in a lump.

Keep an exact account both of your expenses and your income. If you take the pains at first to mention particulars, it will have this good effect: you will discover how wonderfully small, trifling expenses mount up to large sums, and will discern what might have been, and may for the future be saved, without occasioning any great inconvenience.

Remember, that 6 pounds a year is but a groat a day. For this little sum (which may be daily wasted either in time or expense unperceived) a man of credit may, on his own security, have the constant possession and use of an hundred pounds.

SOME INTERESTING EXCERPTS FROM THE INTERVIEW

AGE, SEÑOR PÉREZ NASSIF?

Forty-two, married.

Children?

Yes, three, aged 15, 12, and 2. The first, a boy, Rubén, after his father. The second, Monica Patricia. The third, another girl, Claudia Fabiana, born somewhat unexpectedly, after Señor Pérez Nassif and his wife had grown perfectly content with the size of their little family.

How had be begun his career?

It was well-known, almost notorious, that he had begun as an office boy at Saniper, and he was rightly proud of those modest beginnings. Argentina had, thank God, that wonderful quality which allowed young persons to achieve high positions through perseverance and faith in their own bright future. As one more—if one will—*telling* detail, he would confess (though he'd prefer that this be strictly off the record) that Señor Lambruschini had chosen him from among six boys because that eminent gentleman had seen something in his face that told him *this one would have a future.* Quoting from Señor Lambruschini himself. He had ever afterward remembered the faith that Señor Lambruschini had reposed in his modest self from that first moment.

Who would ever have imagined that one day he would be so far above even that high niche which Señor Lambruschini had occupied!

He had to marvel, young Muzzio. Life was truly amazing. One had to admit, though, that Señor Lambruschini had always been the most conspicuous and shining example of that honesty and the solid work ethic that the company had always recognized in its dealings with its employees and its clients alike. It was by recognizing and promoting men of the caliber and temper of Señor Lambruschini that Saniper had managed to reach the position of leadership that it commanded today. And although he no longer belonged to the Board of that organization, as he had decided to reap the fruits of his long years of work in a much-deserved retirement, his much-remembered and we might even say patriarchal figure was ever-present in those offices. It gave one great pleasure to recall him now, to praise his self-denial, his total and unsullied honesty, his many sacrifices, and his love for the great family of Saniper. Why, Señor Pérez Nassif himself had had to personally order Señor Lambruschini to miss a day's work once, one day out of thirty years of uninterrupted service, so that that gentleman would go for a much-needed checkup when his health began to fail. That was the kind of man that made Argentina great. And indeed, recently Señor Lambruschini's mother had died, and as Señor Pérez Nassif attended the interment of that saintly lady he was glad to see that in spite of the bereavement of Señor Lambruschini he still held himself with the strict uprightness and fortitude that he had shown in his finest days.

In what other businesses did Señor Pérez Nassif take an active part?

Apart from Saniper, of course, he was on the Board of Directors of various enterprises. He was President of Perenas Real Estate, and Vice-President in charge of public relations for Propart. Great responsibilities, as one of course might understand, but not so great as to prevent him from taking part in work somewhat distinct from business, strictly speaking, but which redounded to the good of the community, did one follow? Of course, it didn't do to exaggerate their importance, either. That sort of thing is an obligation which we all share, particularly those who had had the good fortune to reach positions of ease. The Lions Club might be one example, in Lomas, of which he had been a member since 1965.

Señor Pérez Nassif was then asked whether there were any foundation for those rumors currently circulating that mentioned a potentially important expansion of his business into other areas. Concretely, one heard that there might be a merger of Saniper with a sanitary-fixtures company.

Señor Pérez Nassif believed that it was still too early to comment on that possibility, though he could not deny that such a transaction might be in the offing for his company, and that this possibility might be brought up during the next stockholders meeting. No, please, there was no reason to apologize, it was a perfectly legitimate question, and he did not think he had committed any sort of breach of trust whatever in giving the qualified answer he had given. The problem, one saw, was not at all simple, for such a step could only be taken after adequate marketing studies and the like, and taking into account the difficult moment in which the entire national man-

102

ufacturing community in general and the bath-fixtures industry in particular found themselves.

And what were the reasons for these difficulties?

It was difficult to say. They were many, and very complex. And of course this was no time to go into detail. When the time came, he would be happy to expand on his statements of today. But there was one factor he could point to even now: unbridled competition and general uncertainty in the face of the national policy with respect to industry. He was one of those who had faith in the nation's future, but the current political situation obliged one to adopt something of a wait-and-see attitude.

Did the current political circumstances of the country enter into the discouraging picture Señor Pérez Nassif painted for industry? That attitude that he had called "uncertainty" over the outcome?

Without a doubt. A prompt emergence from the current political atmosphere was essential, always within the limits of the respect for institutions that had traditionally characterized Argentina, of course. It was needless for Señor Pérez Nassif to underscore the obvious desire of us all that our national character should remain proof against any foreign influence, against any attempt to involve our country in ideologies which do not coincide with our own temperament and traditions. What has traditionally been called Western Christian ideals should be the basis for the Argentina of the future. He had given a speech on that very topic at a recent meeting of the Lions Club chapter of which he was a member.

Etc.

DEAR, DISTANT YOUNG MAN:

You ask me for advice, but I can hardly give it to you in a simple letter, nor even with the ideas in my essays, which correspond not so much to what I am as to what I *wish* I were, were I not so firmly incarnated in this rotting (or about to rot) carrion which is my body. I can't help you with those nothing-but-ideas that bob about in my fiction like so many buoys anchored off the coast and shaken by the fury of the blast. I could help you rather more (and perhaps I have) with that hodgepodge of ideas and vociferating (or silent) ghosts which emerged from somewhere inside me and got into my novels,

characters that hate each other or love each other, support one another or destroy one another—and support and destroy me at the
same time.

I don't mean to shirk, to avoid giving you the hand you ask of
me from so far away. But what I can tell you in a letter is really not
worth very much, sometimes less than the encouragement you'd find
in a look, in a cup of coffee we might drink together, in a walk
through the labyrinth of Buenos Aires.

You're discouraged by something or other that somebody or
other said to you. But that friend, or acquaintance (deceiving word!),
is too close to judge you, probably feels that because you eat like he
does, the same things that he does, the two of you are equals. Or
that since he can "put you down" he's superior to you. It's an understandable temptation: if one has dinner with a man that climbed
the Himalayas, and watches closely enough how he holds his knife
and fork, one runs the risk of being tempted to think oneself his
equal or superior, forgetting (or trying to forget) that what's at stake
is the Himalayas, not table manners.

There'll be a million times that you'll have to forgive that sort
of presumption, that sort of insolence.

You will only receive real justice at the hands of exceptional
people, the sort of people blessed with modesty and sensitivity, lucidity and a generous dose of understanding. When that resentful
wretch Sainte-Beuve declared that "that clown" Stendhal would never
be able to write a masterpiece, Balzac objected. But that's only natural—Balzac had written *La Comédie Humaine*, while the other gentleman had written one little novel whose name I can't seem to
recall. People on the order of Sainte-Beuve laughed at Brahms—how
was that great fat thing ever going to write immortal music? Hugo
Wolf said of the premiere of the Fourth Symphony, "Never before
in a work were the trivial, the vacuous, and the deceitful more in
evidence. The art of composition without ideas or inspiration has
found in Brahms its worthy representative." Schumann, on the other
hand, marvelous Schumann, most terribly ill-fortuned Schumann,
declared that the musician of the century had been born. You see,
greatness is necessary for admiration, although that may seem paradoxical. And that is why the true creator is so seldom recognized
by his contemporaries—it is almost always posterity that accords

104

recognition, or perhaps that sort of contemporary posterity that can be found in a foreign country, a foreign reader. Somebody far away. Somebody who can't see how you drink your coffee or how you dress. If such a thing happened to Stendhal and to Brahms, how can you be discouraged by what a simple acquaintance says, the man that lives next door? When the first volume of Proust appeared (after Gide had thrown the manuscripts in the trash), a certain Henri Ghéon wrote that this author had "flown in the face of the world by producing precisely the opposite of a work of art—the inventory of his sensations, a census of his knowledge, in a portrait purely successive, never unified, never whole, of the movement of landscapes and souls." That is to say, the presumptuous fool criticized what we see as the very essence of Proustian genius. At what Bench of Universal Justice will Brahms be repaid for the pain he felt, inevitably must have felt, that night when he himself played the piano for his First Concerto for Piano and Orchestra? When his audience booed and whistled and threw garbage at him? Not just Brahms—underneath a single modest song by Discépolo—how much pain there is, how much stored-up sadness, how much desolation.

All I needed to do was see one of your stories. Yes, I think that one day you may do something great. But are you willing to undergo all these horrors? You tell me you're lost, you don't know what to do, you tell me it's my duty to speak one word to you.

One word! I would have to *not* speak, which of course you could interpret as cruel indifference, or would have to talk to you for days, or live with you for years, sometimes talking and sometimes not talking, or we would simply have to go walking together, not necessarily saying a word, the way a friend does for us when someone we love very much has died and we realize that words are laughable, or clumsily ineffectual. Only the art of other artists saves you at those moments, consoles you, helps you. The only thing useful to you (Horrors!) is the suffering of the great souls who have preceded you to that calvary.

That is the moment when, over and above talent, or even genius, you will need something else—you will need certain qualities of the spirit: the courage to tell your own truth, and the tenacity to go on with your work, plus that strange combination of faith in what you have to say mixed with constant disbelief in your own powers, not to mention the other difficult combination of modesty before the giants and arrogance before the imbeciles; you will need affection, tenderness, love, and the toughness to be alone, to refuse the temptations (and the dangers) of cliques and sycophants and other halls of mirrors. At those moments you should call on the memory of those who wrote alone: Melville, on a boat; Hemingway, in a jungle; Faulkner, alone and actually mistrusted in a small town. If you are willing to suffer, to be ripped to pieces, to face pettiness and even malevolence, misunderstanding and stupidity, resentment and infinite loneliness, then yes, my dear B., you're ready to give your testimony. But the worst of it is that no one can guarantee the future, a future that is sad no matter what its outcome may be: sad if you fail, because failure is always painful—and in the artist, tragic; sad if you succeed because success is always one kind of vulgarity, the sum of a series of misunderstandings, and turns into a pawing sort of thing in which you become that disgusting creature The Public Man, and any kid (just like you were at the beginning) turns out to have the right (the right?) to spit on you. But you must tolerate that injustice as well, put your shoulder to the wheel and go on producing your work, like a man raising a statue in a pigsty. Read Pavese: "To have drained yourself totally out of yourself—because you have poured out not only everything you know of yourself but also everything you suspect and assume as well, your passions and fears, your ghosts, your unconscious life. And to have done that under sustained weariness and tension, with care and trembling, with discoveries and failures. To have done it so well that all of life is concentrated in that one tiny point, and to have seen that all of that is nothing if it is not embraced and given warmth by some sign of humanity, some word, some presence. And then to die of cold, speaking words in the desert, being alone night and day like a dead man."

But yes, soon you will hear that word—as now, wherever Pavese may be, he hears ours—you will feel that yearned-for presence, the long-awaited sign of a man or woman who, far away on another island, hears your cries, a man or woman who will understand your gesturings, who will be able to find the key and decipher your code. And then you will find strength to go on—for an instant you won't

106

hear the grunting of the pigs. Even if only for one fleeting moment, you will glimpse eternity.

I don't know when, at what moment Brahms's disillusion became translated into those melancholy trumpets we hear in the first bars of his First Symphony. Perhaps he lost faith in the answers, because it took him thirteen years (thirteen!) to go back to that work. He must surely have lost all hope, have been spat on by someone, have heard sniggering laughter behind his back, have thought he saw people looking at him strangely. But that call from the trumpets has crossed time, and suddenly you and I, whipped and beaten down by the heaviness of things, hear them, and we see that out of duty to that poor unfortunate artist we must respond with some sign of recognition, some indication that we do understand.

I don't feel too well now. Tomorrow, or soon, I'll pick this up again.

MONDAY MORNING

I WAS OUT IN THE GARDEN, and the sky started to turn light. The early-morning silence is so good for me—the kindly companionship of the cypresses, the Norfolk pines, though suddenly it saddens me to see that giant there, like some great lion in its cage, when it ought to be up on some mountain in Patagonia, on the noble, solitary border of Chile. I've reread what I wrote you, and the pathos of it embarrasses me a bit. But that's how it came out of me, so I'll leave it. I've reread the letters you sent me in that interval, too, the cries for help. "I just can't see very clearly what it is I want." And who can, beforehand? Or even afterward. Delacroix said that art resembles mystical contemplation, which moves from a confused supplication before an invisible God to the clear, precise vision of the theopathic moment.

You assume there is some global vision, but one really doesn't know what it is one wants until one is done, and sometimes not even then. By the light of your premise, theme or subject precedes form. But as you make some progress with the writing, you'll see how the expression enriches, or reciprocally creates, the subject, until in the end it becomes impossible to separate them. And when

107

you try, you get either "social" literature or Byzantine literature. Both disastrous. What sense does it make to separate the form from the essence of *Hamlet*? Shakespeare borrowed his plots from third-rate writers. What are their contents? The plots of his miserable predecessors? Look what happens with dreams: When we wake up, what we grossly remember is the "plot," a thing as utterly different from the real dream as the plot stolen from that poor devil of a hack is from the play by Shakespeare. Which leads to the failure of certain psychoanalysts, who try to untangle the enigmatic myth of the night from the babbling of their patients. Imagine trying to understand the secrets of Sophocles' soul from the report of some member of the audience of his plays. Hölderlin summed it up: we are gods when we dream and beggars when we awake.

It's to this same problem that are owed the failures of certain adaptations (sinister word) of essentially literary works to film. Did you see *Sanctuary*? All that was left was a sort of outline of the plot, what's often called the "theme" of the novel. And I say what's called the theme because truly the theme is everything—the richness and splendor, the recondite implications, the infinite echoes of its words, sounds, and colors, not just those famous "events," the "what-happened."

There are no such things as "grand" themes and "small" themes, "sublime" subjects and "trivial" subjects. It is men that are small, grand, sublime, or trivial. The "same" story of a poor student that kills an old woman who lends money at usurious rates may be fodder for the police blotter or the central action of *Crime and Punishment*.

As you will observe, quotation marks are frequent and almost inevitable in this sort of false problem. And they show that that's all they are—*false* problems. The truth of the matter is that as existence grows more and more complex, and language more and more hypocritical or hollow, we will have to be using them all the time.

That you aren't able, as you tell me, to write "about just anything" is a good sign, not cause for discouragement. You mustn't believe in those who can write about anything at all. Obsessions have very deep roots, and the deeper one goes the fewer obsessions one finds. Thus the deepest of all is perhaps the most obscure but at the same time the sole, unique, and all-powerful root of all the rest, the Obsession, if you will, that appears throughout *all* the works of a true creator. Because I'm not talking about story-makers, or those "marvelously fertile" spinners of soap operas or best-sellers written to order, those prostitutes of art. Of course they can choose any old topic. But when one is serious about writing, and writes seriously, it's the other way around—the subject chooses *you*. You should not write a single line that doesn't address the obsession which haunts you, the obsession which pursues you from the deepest and darkest regions of your being—and sometimes for years on end. Resist, wait, test every temptation—don't let yourself be tempted into facileness. That is the one temptation you must at all costs not give in to. A writer may have what is called "facility" in writing, just as a painter may have it in painting. Be careful not to give in to it. Write when you can't stand not to anymore, when you feel that it may drive you mad. And then write "the same thing"—by which I mean to say dig in again, go at it again—by another path, perhaps, and with more powerful resources behind you, with greater experience and desperation, but go at the same thing again. Because it is just as Proust said—the work of art is one ill-fated love which inevitably presages others. The phantoms which rise out of our underground caverns sooner or later appear again, and they will demand a job suited to their qualifications. Abandoned plans, aborted outlines, half-done pieces will return, to find a less fatally flawed embodiment.

And don't worry that the "clever" men and women, those who pass themselves off as the "intelligentsia," may say that you always write about the same thing. Of course you do! That's exactly what Van Gogh and Kafka did, and everyone else that matters, too, the strict (but loving) parents who watch over your soul. Your successive works, your *oeuvre*, to give it a fine-sounding name, turn out to be something like those cities raised over the ruins of others—though they are new, they incarnate a certain kind of immortality, an immortality assured by ancient legends, men of the same tribe who go on living, similar dawns and sunsets, eyes and faces that recur, again and again, and that reflect the ancestral visage.

That is why what we so often think about the characters of fiction is so stupid. One ought, once and for all, to be able to say, and say in all arrogance, *"Madame Bovary, c'est moi."* But that has not been possible so far, and it won't be possible for you either. Every day somebody will turn up to question you, to make discreet inquiries, to ask whether you took such and such a character from this place or that, this person or that one, whether it isn't a portrait of that woman, or whether you yourself aren't "represented" by that lonely spectator of the action. This is all part of that pawing I mentioned awhile back, of that infinite and almost labyrinthine misunderstanding that every work of fiction calls forth.

The characters! One autumn day in 1962, in all the eagerness and anxiety that might have been felt by some callow youth, I went looking for the spot upon which Madame Bovary had "lived." That a boy would go looking for the places where literary characters had lived is pretty amazing in and of itself, but that a *novelist* should do so, a person who, one would think, *knows* to what extent those creatures have never lived, save in the imagination, the soul of their creator—this shows that art is more powerful than this much-bruited reality.

And so when I stood atop that hill in Normandy and at last glimpsed the church at Ry, my heart fell: through the enigmatic power of creation, that village had achieved the pinnacle of human passions and likewise its darkest and most tenebrous abysses. In that village had lived and suffered a person who, had she not been animated by the powerful and tormented spirit of an artist, would have passed from oblivion to oblivion, like so many others, in just the same way an insignificant medium, in the moment of falling into the trance, is possessed by spirits greater than she, and can speak words and be convulsed by passions that her little soul would otherwise have been incapable of feeling.

They say that Flaubert did go to that little village, see the people who lived there, go into the pharmacy where his protagonist would later buy the poison. I can imagine how many times he must have sat on one of the hilltops around there, perhaps on the same hilltop where I sat to look for my first time upon that insignificant hamlet, and meditated on life and death—meditations inspired by that creature who was destined to embody many of his own cares and tribulations. That bittersweet voluptuousness of imagining a new life, a new destiny: *what if* he had been a woman; *what if* he had been dispossessed of other qualities (a certain bitter cynicism, a certain

110

fierce lucidity); *what if*, that is, he had been not a novelist but rather condemned to live and die a provincial petit-bourgeois?

Pascal declared that life was a gaming table on which fate bet our births, our characters, our circumstances, which we may not escape. Only the creator may make another bet, at least in the spectral world of the novel. Not able to be a madman or a suicide or a criminal in the life he is given to live, he can be those things at least within the intense simulacra of his novels.

How many of his own anxieties, his own yearnings must Flaubert have incarnated in the body of that poor romantic village woman! Imagine for one moment his gloomy childhood in that Hôtel-Dieu, in that hospital in Rouen. I observed it carefully, attentively, with trembling minuteness. The surgical amphitheater opened onto the garden of the wing of the building in which his family lived. Climbing up to the grilled windows and hanging onto the bars with his sisters, Gustave, fascinated, looked down on the rotting cadavers. There, at that moment, there must have caught fire in his soul that anguish over the passing of time that he would suffer forever; there must have been planted in the most macabre and sordid way the *mal metaphysique* which moves virtually every great creator to rescue himself through art, for art it seems is the only power that can save us from transitoriness and inevitable death: *que j'ai gardé la forme et l'essence divine de mes amours décomposés . . .*

It was from that grilled window, perhaps, looking down on corruption, that Gustave became that shy, withdrawn child that he is said to have been: distant, ironic, arrogant, with the consciousness of precariousness but at the same time of power. Read his best works, not those sample cases packed with epithets and aphorisms, not the boring jewelry boxes full of words, but the hardest, toughest pages of that pitiless novel, and you will see that it is that child at once sensitive and totally without illusions who describes the cruelty of existence, who employs that tone of angry and resentful pleasure. Melancholy and sadness form the backdrop of that stage. The world is repugnant to him; it wounds him, it offends him, it *bothers* him. Arrogantly, he decides to create another one, in his own image. He will not compete with the State as, with frank injustice to his own genius, Balzac had tried to do, but rather with God Himself. Why create if we are satisfied by this reality we are given? God doesn't

111

write fiction, fiction arises out of our imperfections, out of the flawed world in which we are obliged to live. I didn't ask to be born, I was forcibly made to be.

And don't think Flaubert wrote the story of that poor wretched woman because somebody asked him to. He wrote it because he was seized with the sudden blinding sense that in that story from one line in a police report he might be able to write his own, secret police report, ridiculing himself with all the cruelty that only a great neurotic can muster against himself, against his own ego, caricaturing himself in that insignificant provincial neurotic *woman* who loved, as he did, distant lands and remote, romantic spots. Reread chapter 6, and you will see Flaubert himself in that taste for other times and places, for journeys, post chaises, inns, for kidnappings, elopements, exotic seas. The romantic dream in all its purity, just as that boy peering with fascination through the barred window felt it, forever. The subject of his novel is thus his own life, his own existence, the every-day-greater distance between his real life and his fantasies. Dreams become clumsy realities, sublime loves transfigured into laughable clichés. What could the poor thing do but kill herself? And with the sacrifice of that poor deluded woman, that poor helpless woman, that poor absurdly romantic provincial woman, Flaubert (sadly) is saved.

Saved . . . Just an expression, just a somewhat hurried way of summing things up, like we always do when we aren't watching out too carefully. I know, on the other hand, what my mother, with tears in her eyes, would have murmured—thinking not about Emma, no, but about him, about that sad survivor Flaubert: "May God help him!"

The collision of the romantic soul with the world thus gives off that sarcastic, dissonant clang, ringing with sadistic fury. In order to destroy or ridicule his own dreams and illusions, he paints the scene of the fair, that caricature of bourgeois existence: down there below, the city officials give their speeches; up above, at the window of the sordid hotel room, we hear that other rhetoric, Rodolphe's rhetoric, the rhetoric that seduces Emma with clichés. That monstrous dialectic of the trivial with which Flaubert, the romantic, winking disgustedly, mocks and makes fun of false romanticism—like a religious

112

man might come to vomit in a church filled with the blessèd! There you have Flaubert. The patron saint of objectivists!

And I beg you, by the way, not ever to mention that word again. It's like talking about the subjectivity of science. You must be proud to belong to a continent which in countries as tiny and helpless as Nicaragua and Peru has produced such giants of poetry as Darío and Vallejo. Once and for all, let's be ourselves! Why should we allow Monsieur Robbe-Grillet to tell us how to make a novel? Leave us be! And why, above all, should young people with talent, like you, listen with beatific respect to what some cross between a Byzantine politician-priest and a terrorist insists that we do? The barbarians produced such great creators precisely because they were thousands of miles from the preciosity of those courts full of exquisite gentle-men and ladies—think of the Russians, the Scandinavians, the Americans. Forget about dictates and commandments from Paris, then—manifestos smelling of perfume and the houses of couture.

Objectivity in art! Science can and ought to be carried on with-out the I, but art cannot be, and it's absurd and futile to propose it as an obligation, or a goal. Art's "impotence" is precisely its great virtue. Give or take a word, Fichte said that *objets d'art* were the creations of the spirit, and Baudelaire believed that art was a magic which interwove the creator and his world. Those mysterious caves and grottos inhabited by the creatures drawn by Leonardo, those bluish, enigmatic dolomites, figures that we can barely make out, as though they receded deep into some submarine background, behind the ambiguous faces—what are those if not the expression of Leon-ardo's spirit?

Weary of pure emotion and fascinated by science, these "objec-tivists" wanted the novelist to describe the life of men and women as a zoologist would describe the habits of ants. But a profound writer can't merely *describe* the life of some man on the street. The minute the writer drops his guard (and he always does, sooner or later), that little man he's wound up and set going begins to feel and to think, like an emissary from some dark, heart-torn place deep within the creator. Only mediocre writers can give a simple chron-icle, describe faithfully (such a hypocritical word!) the external re-ality of a time or a nation. The power of great writers is so overwhelming that they can't do this, couldn't even if they wanted to. We are told that Van Gogh tried to copy the paintings of Millet. He couldn't do it, of course—his own terrible suns and trees emerged, suns and trees which are precisely the outward manifestation of his hallucination-ridden spirit. It doesn't matter what Flaubert said about the necessity of being objective. Somewhere in his correspondence he also says, on the other hand, that he was walking through a wood one autumn day and that he felt he was a woman and her lover, the horse and the leaves it walked through, the wind and the very words those lovers spoke. My characters haunt me, pursue me—he said—or rather, I myself am inside them.

They spring up out of the very bottommost part of our being, they are a hypostasis which both figures forth the creator and betrays him, because they can surpass him in both kindness and iniquity, in both generosity and miserliness. They are surprising creatures even to their own creator, who observes their passions and vices in perplexity. In fact these vices and passions may turn out to be exactly the opposite of those that the little semipowerful god is prey to in his own daily life: if he is a religious man, he will see rise up before him a raving atheist; if he is known for his kindness or for his generosity, he will see in some of his characters the most extreme attitudes of pettiness and meanness and even evil. And even more staggering, it is entirely probable that he will feel a sort of twisted satisfaction at these visions.

Madame Bovary, c'était lui, of course. But so was Rodolphe, with his cynical incapacity to withstand his lover's romanticism. And poor M. Bovary, and that M. Homais, too, that drugstore atheist—because by Flaubert's having himself been a desperate romantic, by having himself sought the absolute without ever finding it, he of all people should understand that atheism, should understand that sort of atheism of love that the bounder Rodolphe professes.

Contemporaries of Balzac's tell us (with that smug complacency by which little men feel themselves enlarged by discovering the pettinesses of giants) that the "real" Balzac was vulgar and vain—as though they wanted us to believe that his grand creatures are the simple fantasies of a mythomaniac. But they aren't—they are the most genuine emanations of his spirit, for good and ill. And even the castles and landscapes that he chooses for his fiction are symbols

114

of his obsessions. Stephen Dedalus, in the *Portrait*, tells us that the artist, like the god of creation, stands behind his work, indifferent, paring his nails. Irish leg-pulling! From what we know of that particular genius, both the *Portrait* and *Ulysses* are nothing but the projection of Joyce himself into the world—his passions, his drama, his personal tragicomedy, his ideas.

The creator is in everything, not just in his characters. He chooses the plot, the setting, the landscape. In *The Republic*, Plato asserts that God created the archetype of the table, the carpenter creates a copy of that archetype, and the painter a copy of the copy. That is the only possibility for imitative art—shadows cubed. But great art is an invigoration, a *giving* of life, not the reduction of it, not the carpenter's clumsy imitation but the discovery of a reality by the soul of the artist.

So when, in the fall of 1962, I stood on the top of a hill in Normandy with my heart in my throat and looked down on that little church in Ry, when I walked, wordless and trembling, into what had been M. Homais's pharmacy, when I looked at the spot where Emma, pathetic, yearning for something more, took the coach which carried her to Rouen, what I saw was not a church, not a pharmacy, not a village street in Ry—it was the fragments of an immortal spirit that I was seeing, feeling through those mere objects of the external world.

MONDAY EVENING

I'VE SPENT A BAD DAY, MY DEAR B. Things are happening to me that I can't explain. But meanwhile—and for that very reason—I try to keep a tight grip on this well-lighted world of ideas. The temptations of the Platonic universe! The greater the tumult inside, and the more intolerable the pressures that torment us, the more we feel inclined to seek order in ideas. I have always found that to be true—but what I ought to say is that that's always true. Just look at those famous harmonious Greeks our heads were filled with in high school—they are an invention of the eighteenth century, part of the arsenal of clichés in which you'll also find the phlegm of the British and the measured spirit of the French. The fatal, anguish-filled tragedies of the Greeks would be enough to blast that absurd idea to kingdom come had we not more philosophical proofs, particularly the invention of Platonism. Because each man looks for, or invents, what he doesn't have—so if Socrates seeks Reason it's precisely because he urgently needs it to oppose his passions—all his vices could be read in his face, remember? Socrates invented Reason because he was rash, and Plato repudiated Art because he was a poet. Nice forefathers for these worshippers of the Spirit of Contradiction! As you see, logic doesn't work even for its inventors.

How well I know that temptation toward Platonism, and not simply because people have told me about it. I first felt it when I was a teenager, when I was alone, masturbating in a filthy, perverse reality. Then, like a man who's dragged himself through a dungheap to find a lake of transparent water in which he can bathe, I discovered that Platonic paradise. And many years later, in Brussels, when I thought the world was going to end, when I didn't believe it could go on, when I heard the stories that young Frenchman who would later die at the hands of the Gestapo told me about the horrors of Stalinism—I fled to Paris, where I was not only hungry and cold in the winter of 1934 but desolate and lonely as well, until I met that doorman at the École Normale on the rue d'Ulm who let me sleep in his bed. Every night I had to climb in a window. That was when I stole a calculus textbook from a bookstore, and I still remember the moment I opened it. I was drinking a cup of wonderfully hot coffee, and with trembling hands I opened the book, like a dirty, hungry man who's just escaped some city devastated and overrun by barbarians would silently, tremblingly take sanctuary in a cathedral. The theorems in that book seemed to pick me up and gently carry me away, like delicate nurses pick up and carry the body of a man whose spine may have been broken. And little by little, through the rents in my crushed and torn spirit, I began to catch glimpses of grave and beautiful towers.

I remained in that realm of silence for a long time. And then one day I caught myself listening to (not hearing, but listening to, anxiously listening to) the sound of people, outside. I began to feel a certain nostalgia for blood and noise, confusion and dirtiness, because that is the only way we can feel life. And what can replace life, even with all life's pain and finiteness? Who, how many people, committed suicide in the concentration camps?

116

That is the way we are made, swinging from one extreme to the other. And in these bitter final years of my life, several times I have found myself tempted again by that realm of the absolute—I have never been able to pass by an observatory without feeling that *other* nostalgia—for order, for purity. And though I have never deserted from this battle with my monsters, although I have never given in to the temptation to go back to the observatory, like a soldier into a convent, I have sometimes, shamefacedly, taken refuge in ideas about fiction—halfway between the blood and the convent.

SATURDAY

YOU MENTION THAT THING THAT CAME OUT IN THE COLOMBIAN MAGAZINE. That's the sort of horror that one day will make you want to let your pen fall from your fingers in discouragement or scream in indignation. It was the debris left over from an interview, scraps and pieces of it, the *parings* of an interview, with the most important part of my ideas left out; it neither had, nor has, any relation to me. You know what we did once, my friend Itzigsohn and I, when we were students? We concocted a refutation of Marx using quotations from Marx.

From what I can see, you're going through a crisis over certain things happening in Latin American literature today. And since you ask me, I might as well correct those almost comic statements I seem to be stammering out in that so-called interview. I have always said that formal innovation or novelty is not essential for an artistically revolutionary work, as is amply shown by the example of Kafka. Nor is formal novelty sufficient, as is demonstrated by so many travesties of art perpetrated by manipulators of punctuation marks and bookbinding techniques. Perhaps it isn't altogether off base to compare a literary work with chess: using the same old, stale pieces, a genius can renovate the game. It is *the entire corpus* of Kafka's work that constitutes the new language, not his classical vocabulary and his suave syntax.

Have you read Janouch's book? You should, because in times of charlatanism like ours it's a good idea to look again at saints like Van Gogh or K.—they will never trick you, never fool you, never cheat you. Quite the opposite: they will help you put your road

117

straight again, they will force you (morally) to return to seriousness. In one of their conversations, K. was talking to Janouch about the virtuoso, who levitates himself above the subject with the facility of a prestidigitator. But the true work of art, he points out, is not an act of virtuosity, but rather of giving birth. And how can anyone talk about a pregnant woman's giving birth with virtuosity? That is a genius for comedians, who begin at the point at which the true artist stops. That type, K. says, do parlor tricks with words, while a great poet will not stoop to traffic with emotions—he suffers the visionary tension (the tuning of a string, I mean) of a man confronting his fate.

These caveats are even more important to us Spaniards and Latin Americans, who are so constantly tempted by wordplay and verbal virtuosity, the brilliant lie. You remember when Mairena made so much fun of lines like "those quotidian happenings that transpired every day on the boulevard." Now that sort of blather seems to be reappearing in the writings of the vanguard. Borges, who can never be suspected of contempt for the language, says of Lugones that "his genius was eminently verbal," and the context reveals the pejorative sense of that formulation. And of Quevedo he says that "he was the greatest artificer of the language," only to add "but Cervantes . . ."— just that way, with three melancholy dots. If you bear in mind that Borges (as he himself admitted) had spent three days looking for the perfect epithet, then you must share my conclusion that in those confutations there is a great deal of painful self-criticism, at least of the preciosity that lived in him beside his virtues—tendencies which are precisely those praised (and caricatured) by his imitators, when he himself is denigrating them in those lamenting asides. A great writer, you see, is not an artificer of the word but rather a great man who writes, and Borges knows it. Otherwise how could he have preferred the vulgar barbarian Cervantes to the virtuoso Quevedo?

Machado in his time admired Darío, whom he called an incomparable master of form, though years later he called him a "great poet and great corrupter" because of the unhealthy influence he had had on the poetasters who merely showed up, and multiplied, his defects. And sometimes even arrived at verbal frenzy, grotesque turgidity, caricature—which is the punishment the gods of literature

118

save for such schoolboys. Think of Vargas Vila, think of his delirious phonorrhea—the feeble-minded heir of a founder of dynasties.

There is an ongoing dialectic between life and art, between reality and artifice. One manifestation of that enantiodromia noted by Heraclitus, that everything tends toward its opposite in the world of spirit. And when literature turns dangerously literary, when the great creators are supplanted by manipulators of words, when the high magic becomes music-hall legerdemain, suddenly there comes a life-impulse which saves it from death. Every time Byzantium threatens to strangle art with excess of sophistication, the barbarians rush in to save it—barbarians from the periphery, like Hemingway, or the autochthonous creators, like Céline—riding in like the cavalry, or like knights of the olden age with bloody lances, storming the salons in which marquesses in powdered wigs dance the minuet.

No. How could I have made those very precarious statements that appeared in that article? I did not deny the renovation of art, I said that we must be on guard against several fallacies, and especially against that adjective "new," which probably leads us into more semantic errors than any other single word. In art, there is no progress in the sense that there is progress in science. Our mathematics is superior to Pythagoras', but our sculpture is neither "better" nor "worse" than the sculpture of Ramses II. Proust caricatures a woman who out of pure avant-gardism said that she thought that Debussy was better than Beethoven, since he'd come later. In art there is not so much progress as there are cycles—cycles responding to changing conceptions of the world and of life. The Egyptians didn't sculpt those monumental geometric statues because they were unable to sculpt "naturalistic" figures, as the figures of slaves found in the tombs prove. It was rather because for them the "true reality" lay in the beyond, where time does not exist, and what most resembled eternity was that hieratic geometry. Picture to yourself the moment at which Piero della Francesca introduced proportion and perspective into art: it was not "progress" with respect to religious art, it was no more than the manifestation of the spirit of the bourgeoisie, for which the "true reality" is the reality of this world; this is the spirit of men who believe more in an IOU than in a mass, put their trust more in an engineer than in a theologian.

119

And thence comes the danger of the word "vanguard" in art, especially as it is applied to strict problems of form. What sense does it make to say that the naturalistic sculpture of the Greeks represents an advance over the geometric statues of the Egyptians? On the contrary, in art it's often the case that "the old" suddenly turns out to be revolutionary, as we saw in hypercivilized Europe with Negro and Polynesian art. Be careful, then, about that adjective "new." Each culture has its own sense of reality, and within that cultural sphere, each artist. The new for Kafka is not what John Dos Passos thought of as new. Each creator must look for and find his own instrument, the tool that will allow the artist to speak his *own* truth, portray his *own* vision of the world. And although every art is inevitably constructed on the shoulders, so to speak, of the art which preceded it, if the creator is authentic, genuine, he will do what is natural to himself, sometimes with a stubbornness almost ridiculous to those who follow fashions. Don't let yourself be confused—fashions are fine for clothes or hairdos, but not for novels and cathedrals. It so happens, too, that it is easy to see the new, or novel, in the outward aspect of the thing, which is why John Dos Passos was more striking than Kafka. But as I said, it is the entire *oeuvre* of Kafka that constitutes a new language. During the age of German Romanticism there lived a theologian named Schleiermacher, who believed that the sense of the whole should precede the examination of the parts, which is more or less what the structuralists are saying now. It is the totality which confers a newness on each sentence, each phrase, even each word. Someone noted that when Baudelaire writes "Somewhere very far from here," a word like "here" escapes its own triviality and "rises," we might say, into Baudelaire's own very particular perspective on the earthly condition of man; the empty sign, apparently void of all poetic resonance, is given value by the stylistic aura of the entire work. And as for K., it should be enough to think of the infinite metaphysical and theological reverberations that he produces from a word as worn, as clichéd, as trivialized by the legal profession as the word "trial" . . .

And so it isn't that I refuse to accept newness, novelty, "the latest"—call it what you will. It's that I refuse to allow myself to be *taken in* by it, which is not at all the same thing. And I grow less tolerant every day of frivolity in art, especially when that frivolity is

120

mixed with Revolution. (Observe, by the way, that many words are at first capitalized, then sad experience reduces them to lower case, only at last, after more, and sadder, experience, to wind up between quotation marks.) That a woman be fashionable is only natural; that an artist be fashionable is an abomination.

Look what happens in the plastic arts. With dramatic exceptions, they have become an art of the élite in the worst sense of the word—an ironic rococo similar to the rococo which dominated the salons of the seventeenth century. Far, that is, from being avant-garde, they have become rear-guard. And as always under these conditions, minor: the plastic arts serve to entertain, divert, produce conversation, and often amid the winking of those who are in on the joke. In the salons of the seventeenth century there came together men and women sick of life, people who loved gossip and who took nothing seriously. Ingenious acrostics were invented, epigrams and *jeux de mots*, parodies of the *Aeneid*. People suggested themes and then sonnets were written on them, to measure. Once twenty-seven sonnets were written on the (hypothetical) death of a parrot. This activity is to great art what fireworks are to the burning of an orphanage. *Musique de table*, nothing to upset the digestion. Seriousness, gravity was ridiculed; ingenuity supplanted genius (which is in bad taste in any age). But so long as the poor continue to die of hunger or be tortured in dungeons, an art of that nature can only be considered a perversity of the spirit, a putrescent decadence. One must say, however, in defense of the seventeenth-century decadents who produced it, that they did not consider themselves champions of the Revolution to come. They even showed a certain good taste in that, which cannot be said of those who produce the same sort of art today. We don't have to go far for examples—right here in Buenos Aires young people who consider themselves revolutionaries (or who considered themselves revolutionaries last week—it's quite possible that by now they've gotten good jobs and have even honorably contracted matrimony) receive with great acclaim the announcement of a new novel which can be read both backward and forward. They talk about the masses and about the disadvantaged, the poverty of our people, but just like those marquesses, they are rotten, decaying *exquises*. At the last Venice Biennial somebody exhibited a mongoloid sitting in a chair

121

up on a platform. When things reach that extreme, you can see that all of civilization is threatened with imminent collapse.

You see, then, what sort of novelty I was railing against in that interview. The interviewer thought I was a reactionary because I felt like vomiting. But it's when you stand before that Academy of the Anti-Academy that you will probably need to find in yourself the courage that I've been talking to you about from the beginning. You must strengthen yourself by remembering the great unfortunates of art, like Van Gogh—men who suffered the punishment of solitude and loneliness for their rebelliousness while pseudo-rebels were lionized by specialized magazines and journals, were treated like kings, lived royally—at the expense of the poor bourgeois whom they insulted—and were encouraged, cheered on by the very consumer society which they pretended to fight against but for which they wound up being the interior decorators.

And people will laugh at you. But you must remain firm and remember that *"ce qui paraîtra bientôt le plus vieux c'est qui d'abord aura paru le plus moderne."*

Of course, you may never be a writer of your own little stretch of time, but you *will* be an artist of your Time, a witness to the apocalypse that in some way, to save your soul, you will have to chronicle. The novel now lies somewhere between the beginning of modern times and their end; it runs parallel to the growing profa-nation (what a significant word!) of the human animal, parallel to this terrifying process of the demythification of the world. And that is why attempts to judge the novel of today in strictly formal terms are sterile—one must see the novel as located within this terrible, total crisis of humanity, on the long arc which began with Christi-anity. Because without Christianity the unquiet conscience would never have existed; without the technology that characterizes mod-ern times there would be neither desacralization nor cosmic inse-curity nor solitude nor loneliness nor alienation. Europe gave to the legendary tale and the simple epic adventure this psychological and metaphysical disquiet that we see and experience now, and a new genre came out of it (and now we are justified in using that adjective "new"!). This genre's fate will be to reveal a fantastic territory: the conscience of man.

Jaspers has said that the great Greek playwrights offered tragic knowledge which not only filled their audiences with emotion but which actually transformed them, thereby turning the playwrights into the educators of their people. But later, Jaspers argues, that tragic knowledge was transmuted into an *aesthetic* phenomenon, and both the poet and his audience abandoned their serious original attitude in order to be witness to bloodless images. This is not true in any total way, however, because a work like *The Trial* is no less serious, no less grave than *Oedipus Rex*. But it is true for that art which undergoes a process of greater and greater refinement until it becomes at last a mere manifestation of aestheticism and byzantinism. It is by the light of that doctrine that you should judge the literature of our continent.

THESE DREAMS WILL DRIVE ME MAD,
she said to him, looking at him fixedly, as though trying to make out his silent plans. "All right, all right," he answered, "I'll look into them, don't be afraid."

The homunculus looked out at her from his bottle, a terrifying expression on his face. Should she let him out? But then what about the black worm, the black demon that jumped out of that belly straight at M.'s face when Ricardo was operating on that strange patient?

Both alternatives—letting the creature out, or leaving it there inside—were horrible, and S.'s vacillations seemed to go on for an eternity. Meanwhile, pieces of papers from R. kept appearing mysteriously, like black sarcasms peeking out of deep-buried hiding places. He "left" them in the most unexpected places, but places that sooner or later S. would have to visit or look into. There they would be, right there, for example, those brief, poisonous words written in R.'s irregular, almost unreadable handwriting: "Why don't you go off and join that Sartre–de Beauvoir *ménage*? Such nice people."

OTHER SORTS OF DIFFICULTIES

HE WOULD START WRITING THE NEXT DAY. It was a firm, well-reasoned decision, and a certain degree of animation accompanied it. He went out for a walk in very good spirits, and although over in the west he caught a glimpse of a cloud which for some unknown reason made him uneasy again, he brushed the incident aside, and once in the center of the city he strolled down Uruguay, near the Courts Building, looking into the shop windows. Shop windows always attracted him, and he examined these with interest, perhaps because of childhood memories. Very minutely, trying not to miss a single detail, he studied the things in the windows—one by one, as it was easy to get lost in the jumble of objects: colored pencils, all sorts of glue, Scotch tape in various sizes and colors, compasses, Japanese staplers, magnifying glasses. There were several stationery stores along here, and the walk produced almost euphoria in him, which he judged to be a good sign for the work he was to recommence the next day. He had coffee in El Foro, bought *La Razón*, and systematically read the news, beginning at the last page of the newspaper, since as he had proved to himself over and over again throughout his life, newspapers and magazines are built backward, and the most interesting things are always on the last pages.

That night he went to sleep with an emotion that was if not exactly happiness at least something not too far off: the same relation as one might find between the color of a particular geranium and the recollection of it. When he woke up he had a terrible pain in his left arm, which kept him from using it. Impossible to do anything on the typewriter.

After a little over a week, the pain became unbearable, but then arrived Professor Doktor Gustav Siebenmann from the University of Erlangen.

When the professor left, so much correspondence had piled up that he decided to dedicate two or three days to answering it, so he wouldn't have any interruptions when he began writing. And just as he was finishing that chore, he received a letter from Dr. Wolfgang Luchting detailing the latest problems with Frau Dr. Schlüter over the translation. What should he do? Personally, he, Luchting, thinks they should get another translator.

124

It wasn't so much getting all these problems straightened out, the letters he had to write Luchting and Dr. Schlüter to smooth out the situation, as the sense that some perverse thing had once again gotten in the way of his project. And so at last, although with some effort, he sat down to write. But just then Noemí Lagos called to tell him that Alfredo had told her that somebody had said that G. had said (where? what? huh?) that he, Sabato, had said something or other, which made Noemí think that he ought to straighten the matter out (but with whom? when? how?), make it clear that *that* version is not quite what happened.

He fell into a depression that lasted for several days, during which time he thought that: (a) it wasn't worthwhile explaining to G. something that he hadn't said anyway; (b) it wasn't worthwhile explaining anything past, present, or future to anybody; (c) the best thing was not to be a public figure at all; and (d) better yet would be never to have been born, period. But this program was so vast and so difficult to carry out, especially the part about never being born, that the minute he formulated it he sank even deeper into the depression that had begun to herald its arrival with the pain in his arm.

But things didn't end there, as he might have foreseen from long experience that they wouldn't.

After countless trials and failures, fits and starts, approaches and retreats, Mr. Ralph Morris had finally been selected as the English translator of *On Heroes and Tombs* for the United Kingdom, but after almost ten years of conflict with Heinemann in London over this, it turned out that the approved trial translation had not in fact been done by Morris at all, as was proved by the chapters he was sending in. He had to be gotten rid of. But what about the contract with Holt, Rinehart? The Heinemann affair had held up the publication of the book in English for ten years, and now this new threat to its publication in New York. While he brooded over the possibility that all this had something to do with the Blind (one of those who took part in the selection of the English translator—as enthusiastic reader of Morris's submission, in fact—was named Augen!), countless letters were sent:

from Sabato to Morris

from Morris to Holt

from Holt to Morris and Sabato

from Morris to Sabato and Holt.

And at last, the murky, troubled and troublesome, irritating, sad negotiations concluded with the retention, and promised friendship, of Mr. Morris, with the promise of an English version to be produced within a length of time which could not be calculated, and with the confidence from the editors at Holt, Rinehart and Winston to Sabato that they now tended toward the opinion that *no one* will *ever* be able to translate the novel into English.

In the course of all this, Professor Egon Pavelic confirmed that the Serbo-Croat translation by Dr. Schwarz had gross, and in many cases devastating, defects. Sabato communicated the greater part of Egon Pavelic's comments to the publishing house of Ateneum, Ateneum communicated the comments to Stefan Andric, and Stefan Andric immediately set in motion a powerful machinery of letters to critics, journalists, professors, and friends, setting forth the literary and personal merits of his own version, his sacrifices and dedication to the work, and the moral, intellectual, and physical defects of Ernesto Sabato.

At virtually the same time, Dr. Luchting sent a new ultimatum to the publishing house, threatening to throw over the translation of the essays if Limes didn't give in to his demands. Consequent letters from Sabato to Luchting and Dr. Schlüter, clarifications, bilateral and trilateral recriminations—between Dr. Luchting and the publishers, the publishers and the author, the author and Dr. Luchting, Dr. Luchting and the publishers—over the course of several weeks, which are complicated for Sabato by the death and burial of K.; a meeting in Besaldúa's house during which P. claims that Sabato has totally and significantly forgotten about his friends; a terrible argument stemming from something that H. said that G. said about a clarification that Sabato refused to make; a letter sent to the Bogotá magazine *Razón y Fábula* rectifying the grossly distorted statements made in an interview that S. had agreed to give a certain individual with charming manners; and finally an attack of gout which lasted a couple of weeks, at the end of which he promised himself that no matter what happened, come what might, he was going to get back to his novel.

126

But just at that moment a student, Richard Ferguson, arrived. Ferguson was at Washington University writing his doctoral dissertation on Sabato's work.

And no sooner had this event occurred than Sabato had to undertake the revision of his complete works for Losada and give at least a courteous glance at the cryptogram sent him by one Ahmed Moussa—the Arabic translation of *The Tunnel*. Meanwhile he was asked to write or sign declarations concerning:
the state of Jews in Russia
torture
political prisoners
Argentine television
Peronism
Anti-Peronism
events taking place in Paris, Prague, Caracas, Ceylon
the Palestine problem.

At the same time, he was forced to begin extremely difficult correspondence over the Hebrew translation of his work, in which the translator proposed by the publishers was considered, accepted, and then at last, after hard choices were made, rejected.

At which point there arrived from McGill University in Montreal a professor who gave courses in Latin American literature there and who wanted to tape-record a conversation with the author of *The Tunnel.*

While in the meantime there had piled up another huge stack of mail, obliging Sabato to refuse invitations, without giving offense, from:
the University of Santiago, in Chile
a writers' conference in Caracas
the Jewish Rosary Society
the Cooperative Commission of Industrial School No. 3, in Córdoba
the Committee for the Preservation of Jerusalem
the Club of Rome
the Catholic University of Salta
a magazine published by the Popular Library, a division of Almafuerte Publishers
the Alumni Association of Lincoln (in the province of Buenos Aires)
the Mariano Moreno de Belle Ville Faculty Institute

the Institute of Letters of the University of Cuyo
the Writers' Society of Río Cuarto
the Festival at Manizales, Colombia.

For some of these, he pleaded a nonexistent attack of gout, which in fact materialized the minute it was invoked. This attack lasted some fifteen or twenty days, and Sabato took advantage of his immobility to read the *Quixote* from cover to cover, promising himself at the same time that the second the attack subsided he would sit down to write.

This promise, however, had to be postponed due to the occurrence of an event which came like a bolt from the blue: *someone* wanted to talk to him, urgently, about *something*, but it was very very personal, please, not on the telephone. The voice underscored this condition. Something? The unidentified caller hemmed and hawed forever, until finally the reason for the interview came out: it had something to do with what Sabato had written about the Blind. Oh goodness, he was so sorry, he wouldn't be able to meet the Unknown Caller to discuss that particular subject, for many reasons but mainly because he could hardly be held responsible for what one of his characters said or did. The Unknown Caller seemed to accept this argument, but within a few days he called again, to insist upon the urgency of his request, and he spoke for many minutes with the maid. Then two times more he tried to speak with Señor Sabato, who refused to come to the phone. But because of these telephone calls, Sabato once again put off his intention to write.

All he did was sit in his study for hours, staring into a corner of the room.

HIS RUN OF BAD LUCK WAS NOT OVER, OBVIOUSLY ENOUGH.
But there was no turning back, so he sank into an armchair, swearing to himself that no matter what happened he wouldn't let himself get involved. Beba's eyes shot laser rays.

"That's the last straw!" she cried. "Now you deny the fact of clairvoyance!"

To which Dr. Arrambide, tightening the knot in his tie and pulling down the cuffs of his blue shirt, his face bearing that constant

128

expression of surprise, replied that what he was asking for were facts, not generalities. "*Facts*, my friends." It all depended, moreover, on what one understood by the word "clairvoyance": a radiologist who discovered a tumor by means of X rays, for example, certainly saw things that other people could not see. Beba's little eyes flashed with acid irony:

"You're one of those people that have an orgasm from just seeing a photograph of the Wright brothers," she fumed, "and now you bring in that old chestnut about X rays."

"Only an example. As I said. Perhaps certain subjects emit rays that we still do not understand."

Oh, of course. Typical. Going over to Arrambide and waving her glass of whisky at him threateningly, she demanded that he answer her: Did he believe in Saleme, yes or no? Arrambide adjusted the knot in his tie again, pulled down the cuffs of his shirt, and answered:

"That Turkish fellow? . . . I don't know . . . If you say so. . . ."

It wasn't a question of her saying so, or of his cheap irony, either! She didn't say so, all of Buenos Aires did! But all he believed in were tibias and fibulas and metacarpals, which is what he called facts, and everything else was poppycock. And what was more, he had that habit of denying everything but what he PERSONALLY (and she screamed the word, practically in the doctor's face) had seen. So to be consistent, he ought to deny the existence of Kansas City, since he'd never been there. Yes or no?

Dr. Arrambide stepped back a bit, since he could hardly talk for Beba's glass in his face.

"I don't see why you make me out to be a contemporary of the Wright brothers."

As though this reflection confirmed her assumptions, and in accord with Beba's private logic, she concluded:

"So you don't believe in clairvoyance, then."

Arrambide turned to S., who was staring down at the floor. "You are a witness," he announced. "Tell this drunken bacchante whether I have denied the possibility of clairvoyance."

S., without raising his head, said that he had not.

"There you are. I neither believe nor do not believe. If some gentleman or lady proves to me with *facts* that he or she is able to

129

see what's going on in the next room, how can I not admit it? I am a scientist, and it is my habit to admit those things that I am proved."

"Of course, of course! That's what you've always said, you have to see everything with your own eyes. Even if other people saw it, Dr. Arrambide *personally* did not, so he doubts it. There're a lot of people that have had the experience of clairvoyance. Did you hear what I said—*seen it for themselves!*"

"One would have to examine those famous witnesses in a spirit of scientific examination. Almost every one of them is a charlatan or con man or trickster, or some poor wretch who's willing to believe what he's told."

"Oh, of course, Richet was a charlatan or one of those geese you mention, right? Not two minutes ago you mentioned X rays. I suppose you're going to tell me now that Crookes was a charlatan too."

"Crookes? Why?"

"What do you mean 'why'? Didn't you know that he studied these phenomena?"

"How old was he at the time?"

"How old? What difference does that make? And how should I know anyway?"

"His age is very important. At twenty-five, Pascal turned mystic. And you're not going to swear to any gobbledygook he pronounces at the age of thirty-five just because at the age of twelve he made important advances in mathematics. If old man Rockefeller tells me I ought to invest in a flying-saucer business, I'm not going to follow his advice just because at the age of thirty he was a fox at making money."

"Let's just stop going off on tangents—I want you to tell me whether you've ever heard about Saleme, yes or no."

"It is impossible to live in Buenos Aires without having heard about that individual."

"You've no doubt heard certain things in particular, then."

"Nothing very precise."

"Ah. So that story about Etcheverry doesn't seem very precise to you."

"That story about Etcheverry?"

"Yes, that . . . about Etcheverry's death, I mean."

"What—Etcheverry is dead?"

"Oh, come now. Don't pretend you live on the moon."

"All right. What is it that the gentleman predicted, then?"

"I just told you—Etcheverry's death. There were lots of people. I'm not sure exactly how it all happened, but . . ."

"There we go. No one *ever* knows exactly how it all happened."

"Let me talk, if you don't mind. At one point Etcheverry made some sarcastic comment about Saleme. I don't know whether Saleme heard him or not. . . ."

"If he's clairvoyant he'd hardly have needed to hear him."

"Exactly. So the Turk, Saleme I mean, of course, Saleme turned absolutely livid, and he turned to somebody sitting beside him and said . . ."

"Somebody, somebody, somebody . . . It's always the same, always the same imprecision. And then people talk about the facts. Or repeat generalities, or tell things all tangled and twisted, and then everybody tries to straighten things out, with that curious propensity for helpfulness that people always have when they try to justify those charlatans. They mention a gray armoire. And then it turns out not to have been an armoire at all, but rather a poster, and then 'something' that's not quite a poster but that looks a bit like one. But no, on second thought it was a chest of drawers, and it wasn't gray at all, it was mahogany. Et cetera. But everybody's very excited because the seer has hit the mark, and they get extremely resentful about your humble servant who casts doubt on the superman. Everybody rushes to defend *him*. And in the end it was neither an armoire nor a chest of drawers nor a poster nor was it gray or green or mahogany—it was an old linotype machine, or a Ming vase. . . ."

One might almost have thought that Dr. Arrambide was angry. He pulled down the cuffs of his shirt and straightened his tie.

"You just listen, maybe if you'd just learn to listen, since you claim to be so scientific—Saleme turned livid and said to the person sitting beside him . . ."

" 'The person sitting beside him'! Who, pray, might that have *been*? What was the name of this key gentleman? Precise facts, if you please. Names, numbers, dates. Generalities will not do, I tell you."

"How am I supposed to know who it was that was sitting next to him just then? But there are several people who could tell us—Lalo Palacios, Ernesto himself was there at the time, weren't you?"

"Yes," Sabato admitted, still staring down at the floor.

"All right, then, we will allow that first vague 'fact.' So what did Saleme say to this indefinite person with the uncertain name?"

"He told him that Lalo wouldn't have long to laugh at him, because before long he'd be dying in an auto accident—that very afternoon, in fact."

Beba gave Dr. Arrambide a telling look, but her interlocutor seemed to be waiting for her to go on. With visible sarcasm, Beba added:

"I suppose you've at least heard that much. That Lalo was killed that very afternoon by a car. Yes or no?"

"Lalo Palacios was killed by a car?"

"Are you mad! There's no way to talk to you, you are a person of utter and absolute bad faith. Lalo Etcheverry, for god's sake. Who are we talking about?"

"I thought I heard you say Lalo Palacios, not a second ago."

"Then you admit it."

"Admit what?"

"I'm telling you that Saleme foretold that that very afternoon, Etcheverry would be killed as he left Lou's house. In an auto accident."

"All right, I admit that Etcheverry died in an auto accident. But how can we be sure that his death was foretold?"

"Am I not saying that there were witnesses?"

"I believe that I have just been informed that Saleme did give out that piece of mortuary news, in what I must suppose to be a voice sufficient unto the case, not shouting that is, to a person who up to the present time has wished to remain anonymous. And who appears to be the only real witness, is that not true?"

"I wouldn't know. I don't know whether what Saleme said was heard by other people or not, but I do know that after the accident everybody was talking about it."

"After Etcheverry died? I am acquainted with that sort of boasting from supposed clairvoyants."

"But what about the other man, the one who heard him?"

132

"The other man? So far he's so mysterious that you haven't even been able to tell me his name. And who's to say he's not that charlatan's shill, an accomplice to the hoax, or at least one of those people that are always ready to come to the aid of the presumed seer? Who knows but that Saleme said something like 'What a horror the way people are being killed by cars in the streets these days.' "

"If you keep talking in such bad faith, Carlitos, we might as well change the subject. I'm getting a little fed up with this. I tell you there were people there, a lot of people. Even Ernesto was there."

"All right, go on. You're going to have an attack of nerves, you're going to somaticize and then it'll be me that has to deal with your eczema. Go ahead."

"The people that heard what Saleme said were stunned, so some of them decided to go with Lalo, at least until he got across the avenue."

"Just a moment."

"What now?"

"One of two things: if that little Turk is a fortune-teller and said Etcheverry was going to die, how were they supposed to avoid what was going to happen? And if he isn't, what was the rush to protect Etcheverry?"

"Just listen, for heaven's sake. These friends of Lalo's left with him without saying a word, of course. That black man, Echagüe, and the Hungarian went with him, they crossed the avenue with him to get his car. Then they came back."

"I have no desire to offend that interesting group of friends of yours, but you have to admit they are hardly overwhelming in their combined intelligence."

"Why do you say that?"

"Saleme had predicted that he was going to die that afternoon in an auto accident, not that he was going to be run over as he crossed the street."

"Exactly right. They'd no more than turned their backs on Lalo when they remembered Saleme's exact words, so they climbed in a car and started following him. They caught up with him in about ten minutes, and Peque began blowing the horn to get his attention and pull him over. Lalo probably thought some idiot wanted to pass him, so he didn't turn around to look. Until finally they pulled up beside him and yelled at him to stop. Lalo got scared and started yelling at them, they were talking back and forth at the top of their lungs, and since he had his head turned to look over at them he didn't look where he was going and he ran into a post. What do you say to that?"

"Hardly a convincing proof."

"Oh? You think that's nothing, huh?"

"There are several explanations."

"Such as?"

"First, that this Saleme has a certain influence on weak or suggestible persons. He wanted to have his revenge for Lalo's laughing at him, so he sent him to his death."

"According to that theory, seers don't predict the future, they create it."

"Certainly that is a possibility. But there are other possibilities. Such as that that idiot Peque—because you can't deny that Peque is mentally retarded and that there was no need to start yelling like a pack of fools to scare a man going at least seventy miles an hour, that the idiot Peque, as I was saying, may have been the only true cause of the death. It may be that if so many geniuses hadn't gone out to try to save Lalo, he'd have arrived safe and sound at San Isidro."

"Listen to me—whether you like it or not, Saleme said that Lalo was going to die, and he did. Whether the instrument of that death was an idiot or a genius makes absolutely no difference. You want Einstein to be used for these things? You're asking for facts. Lalo's death is a fact. Yes or no?"

"Well, yes."

"I don't know, then, why you insist on denying the fact of clairvoyance."

"I don't insist on anything. I demand proof, not humbug. Besides, I never said I didn't believe in clairvoyance. What I said was that so far I've never seen any convincing proof. It is possible that someone might see what's happening in another room. But the future . . . What happens is that many times people see the present as the future."

"What's that?"

"Very simple. When it was predicted that your sister would get the chair at the university, for example."

"So? Didn't she get it?"

"Oh yes, but it had *already* been granted her. Don't you see?"

"What do you mean 'already'?"

"When that fortune-teller told your sister about the chair, the decision had already been made—in some administrator's head, for example. And so far as the case of Lalo is concerned, I don't consider the proof convincing. I tend rather to think that Saleme took his vengeance by placing the idea of an auto accident in the heads of Peque and the rest, so that they'd go after Lalo and run him off the road."

"So every time somebody yells at you, you die."

"I think you can let it go now, Beba dear."

"But tell me one thing—do you want to talk to Saleme, yes or no?"

"No. How can I have any interest in talking to a person that is capable of telling you that that very afternoon you're going to die in an auto accident?"

"What sort of scientist are you if you're afraid to talk to somebody that might make you change your mind?"

"I'm not afraid of changes of mind, I just try to avoid people I don't like."

Arrambide stood up, pulled down his shirt cuffs, straightened his tie, poured himself another glass of wine, and said:

"And you, Ernesto, you haven't said a word about this."

Wrinkling his forehead, Sabato replied very softly:

"I said that I was there when Saleme foretold the death."

"No, I meant about the problem in general."

"Good or bad, my opinions are pretty well known. I've even published an essay about it. A theory."

"A theory? How interesting. Accepting the fact of premonitions, I suppose."

"That's right."

"Very strange, you a physicist and all."

"An ex-physicist."

"In this case it's the same thing. You spent years studying relativity, epistemology."

135

"And what is it that's so strange?"

"I don't know . . . Your silence, your attitude. You give the impression of disagreeing with me very strongly. Have you renounced your mathematical studies?"

"I'm not sure what you mean by 'renounce.' And besides, I didn't study mathematics because I had the same mentality as people who only believe in galvanometers and numbers and the like. I studied mathematics and physics for other reasons."

"Other reasons?"

Sabato did not reply.

"Perhaps you think that parapsychology is a science and that that sort of phenomenon will at last be explained. Is that it?" the doctor asked.

"No."

"Good lord. We're all people of a certain intellectual level here. I don't think it would be too much to ask you to answer a serious question in a serious manner. My question is, after all, strictly intellectual. Isn't it?"

Sabato responded grudgingly:

"If you are talking about science in the sense that a creature of the laboratory talks about it, I do deny that. The sort of phenomenon you're talking about has nothing to do with *laboratory* phenomena. That's as naive an idea as the eighteenth-century notion of the soul."

"The soul?"

"Yes, that the soul is located in a gland. But they are of two essentially different orders of being."

Dr. Arrambide pulled down his cuffs and straightened his tie. An expression of irony had appeared on his face.

"Two orders of being?"

"Yes. Two orders totally distinct from one another. Or better put, *essentially* distinct. The world of matter and the world of spirit. Scientists want the world of spirit to be ruled by the laws of causality. And therein lies the error."

"So you believe in the separate existence of the spirit? From that to spiritualism, voodoo, *espiritismo*—it's a very short step, don't you think?"

"You say spiritualism and it all turns into a joke. You somehow reduce me to the level of Tibor Gordon and Mother María. A cheap shot, doctor."

"Don't be angry. What I meant was that the idea of pure spirit, with no flesh to contain or support it, seems a bit difficult to sustain."

"I didn't say the separate *life* of the spirit. I only said that they are of two orders of being essentially different from one another. An aviator and an airplane are united, but they belong to two totally different spheres. But I said I didn't want to argue. Why should two people who know beforehand that they aren't about to be convinced argue over these things in private?"

"So I'm nobody!" piped up Beba.

"You already know what I think about all this."

"All you've ever told me is bits and pieces. I spend my whole life begging you to explain relativity to me."

"Precisely," Arrambide interrupted. "I think that if premonitions are ever to have any explanation, it will come from a discussion of the fourth dimension."

Sabato began to study the floor again, holding his peace.

"I should think you might condescend to us enough for a reply."

"There's no point, I said. We hold two irreconcilable positions."

"But I have just tried to build a bridge. The fourth dimension."

"Yes, a lot of people come up with that one. But matter and spirit do not obey the same laws. Relativity rules the physical universe. It has nothing to do with the other. Explaining things of the spirit by using geodesic figures is like wanting to get rid of Angst by pulling it out with a dentist's forceps."

"Do you think so?" Arrambide asked snidely.

"I do."

"Sometimes anguish is the result of hepatic dysfunction."

"I've heard that theory, doctor."

Arrambide stood up.

"My patients."

No sooner had he got out the door than Beba turned on Sabato in fury.

"If you don't take the cake, Ernesto! Carlitos is the best pediatrician in Buenos Aires!"

"Who says he's not? A person can be the best doctor in the world at curing diarrhea and still think that William Blake was just some poor madman."

"Oh, you're so clever, and you argue in such bad faith. When it's convenient for you, you argue one side. And when it's not, you argue the other."

"That's what *you* say. You've never heard me explain premonitions by using relativity. It's that the minute a person starts talking about space-time, that sort of dilettante—and they always consider themselves so clever—thinks you're using Einstein's theory."

"And you're not?"

"You see how pointless it is to try to discuss this? No, I'm not. You just heard me answer our distinguished friend—I told him that matter and spirit do not obey the same laws. Relativity governs the physical universe. It has nothing to do with the other. Didn't you hear me say that?"

"What?"

"Say that explaining, or trying to explain facts of the spiritual world by using geodesic figures was like trying to pull out Angst with dentist's pliers?"

"Yes. All right, then, but how did your theory go?"

"You can read it if you want to."

"I don't have time."

"Patience, nobody's going to die."

"Come on, don't be nasty."

Sabato sighed.

"It's based on the possibility that the soul can be separated from the body."

"Oh, is that *all*?"

"That's all. But that is the only way, as I see it, that premonitions, clairvoyance, all that sort of thing, can be explained. Read Frazer, for instance: all primitive peoples believe that during sleep the soul escapes the body."

"Oh no, Ernesto! That's too much! Now it appears that the best proof of a theory is what Hottentots believe! That's the epitome of irresponsibility, and of obscurantism, as well. The Bolshies are right, buddy. It's just one short step from that to taking money from the U.S. embassy."

138

"So now Lévi-Strauss is a CIA agent. Go find what he says about the so-called primitive cultures."

"All right, then, we'll let the CIA go for the moment. What next?"

"When the soul is separated from the body, it is also separated from the categories of space and time, which govern only matter, and it can observe a pure present. If this is true, then dreams will not only bear meaningful traces of the past but visions or symbols of the future as well. Visions not always clear, of course. Almost never univocal or literal."

"Why not?"

"Because in those regions the past, with its pains and memories, with its passions, appears mixed with the future, muddying it in a way, ruffling the waters, distorting it in the transmitter, which is the soul now semi-incarnated at the moment we begin to awake. Do you see? It begins to enter the body, and therefore causal and rational categories begin to dominate. Still, it brings a recollection of that mystery, though in an earthly sense it is a dark, confused, and murky recollection, ambiguous at its best. I'll go even further: since the death of our body lies in our future, dreams may bring us, sometimes, visions from beyond our life. Nightmares would then be visions of the Hell that awaits us. That's perfectly clear, isn't it?"

"Yes, clear as a bell. Of course, it all depends on the Hottentots' knowing more than we do. Go on, get out of here, get on over to the embassy, I need a few dollars."

"Wait, that's just the first part of my theory. What the ordinary man experiences in his dreams, extraordinary men live in a state of trance: seers, madmen, artists, mystics."

"Hold on, I'm calling the head of the Communist Party."

"During an access of madness, the soul undergoes a process similar, if not identical, to the process that every man undergoes as he falls asleep: he leaves his body and enters another reality. Haven't you ever thought about that expression 'to be beside yourself'? They used to call psychiatrists 'alienists,' did you know that? What *is* alienation but to be outside yourself? I have never seen one of those furious, ranting madmen without having the frightening sense that the poor devil was experiencing the torments of Hell. But now I see that his soul is *already* in its Hell. The frantic movements, the suffering face and body, the gesturing, the look of a trapped beast, the

139

terror on the face, the delirium—what could that be but the direct and immediate experience of Hell. Awake, they are experiencing what we suffer in our worst nightmares. In some cases, that descent into the bowels of Hell may be only temporary. That is the case of the possessed, for example. Look at the intuitions of those ancient forms of wisdom."

"The Hottentots?"

"Beings who only after complex manipulations or operations, which only certain initiates have the knowledge to carry out, return to normal life, as though they were awakening from some horrible nightmare."

"I don't see why, though, if your theory is correct, there are not people who also see Paradise."

"But there are. Haven't you ever had beatific dreams? And what about insane asylums—haven't you ever seen those peaceful madmen, smiling and serene, who wouldn't harm a fly? . . . Now pay attention to what I'm about to tell you. This so-called alienation can also be called forth voluntarily. Mystics. Poets: *'Je dis qu'il faut être voyant, se faire voyant!'* "

"And if the head of the Communist Party isn't in, maybe I'll try to get in touch with an exorcist."

"Right. Descend to the lowest rung on the ladder of positivism. And you laugh at poor Arrambide. Basically, I think you're both cut from the same cloth."

He was irritated, and he rose to leave.

"No, don't go. Don't leave me in suspense."

"All right, but *listen* to me then. I am telling you that some people have been able voluntarily to achieve that alienation, or separation. You can aid it with zeal and fasting, the tenacity of your purpose, plus, of course, your native faculties or abilities, divine or diabolic inspiration. It's what mystics achieve. Ecstasy. You see how language only fools a fool? Ex-tasis. To put oneself out of oneself, to escape one's own body, to be located in pure eternity. Yogis, for example, in that death of the self which is to be reborn into another region, to be liberated from the temporal prison. And artists. Plato says no more than what had been thought by the ancients: the poet, inspired by demons, repeats words that he would never have said in his sane mind, describes visions of supernatural places, just as

140

the mystic does. In that state, as I told you, the soul enjoys a perception distinct from normal modes of perception, the boundaries between the object and the subject, between the real and the imaginary, between the past and the future become blurred. And thus it is that ignorant men and women have undergone visions and have spoken words in languages they could never have known, how a girl such as Emily Brontë, who had led such an innocent life, could have written such a terror-filled book. How otherwise could she have described a soul such as Heathcliff's, under the sway of infernal powers? That disincarnation of the soul of the artist at the instant of inspiration would also explain the prophetic character she achieves at some moments, though in the enigmatic, symbolic, or ambiguous guise of dreams. In part enigmatic et cetera due to the obscure nature of that continent our soul probably sees as though through a glass darkly because of the imperfect disincarnation of our soul. And in part no doubt because our rational consciousness is not suited to describing a universe not governed by the logic of every day, not ruled by the principle of causality. And also because man appears unable to bear hellish visions. The instinct of self-preservation at work, that's all."

"Whose?"

"The body's. I told you that neither in dreams nor in inspiration are we totally disincarnated. And the body's instinct of self-preservation protects us with masks, like those asbestos suits worn by men who have to walk through fire. It protects us with masks and symbols."

Beba looked at him. Was she looking at him with irony or tenderness? Perhaps with that mixture of irony and tenderness that mothers use to look at their daydreaming children who are playing at pirates, or romping with invisible dogs.

"What are you thinking about?" S. asked mistrustfully.

"Nothing, silly. Just thinking," she replied, her expression unchanging.

"Well, shall I go on? Theologians have argued over Hell, and sometimes have even proved its existence as easily as you'd prove a theorem in geometry. But only the great poets have revealed the truth to us, have spoken what they have seen. Do you understand? What they have truly seen. Think: Blake, Milton, Dante, Rimbaud,

141

Lautréamont, de Sade, Strindberg, Dostoyevski, Hölderlin, Kafka. What man is so arrogant that he dares call into question the witness of those martyrs?"

He looked at her almost sternly, as though demanding that she accede to his vision of all this.

"Those are the men who dream for the rest of us. They are damned, do you understand, *damned*," he almost shouted, "to reveal their hells."

He was quiet then, and silence fell over them. Then, as though talking to himself, he added:

"I don't remember where it was that I read that Dante had done nothing but translate the ideas and feelings of his age, the theological prejudices then in vogue, the superstitions that were 'in the air.' In other words, he had quite simply described, or transcribed, the conscious and unconscious mind of the culture. There might be some truth in that, too. But not in the sense that those sociologists of horror think. I believe that Dante *saw*. Like all great poets, he saw what lesser men feel much less precisely. People watching him walk down the streets of Ravenna, this thin, silent man, muttered to each other in sacred fear and mistrust: *There goes the man that saw Hell.* Did you know that? Their very words. It was not a metaphor to them—those people believed that Dante had been in Hell. And they were right. The ones who are wrong are these slick types, these people who pretend to be so intelligent."

He fell silent and began looking at the floor once more, thoughtfully.

Beba watched him with tears in her eyes. When S. raised his head he asked her what was wrong.

"Nothing, silly. It's just that in spite of everything I'm incurably feminine. I'm going to go give Pipina her bath."

NACHO FOLLOWED HIS SISTER
from far down the street, to the corner of Cabildo and Echeverría. Agustina crossed Cabildo and continued down Echeverría, and when she came to the plaza she slowed down. She began to walk very slowly, still with those long strides of hers but now deliberately, as though the ground under her were mined. What most saddened

142

Nacho, though, was that every few seconds she would stop and look all around her, as though she had lost someone. Then, after a while, she sat down on a bench in front of the church. Nacho could see her in the light of the streetlamp; she was lost in thought, looking sometimes down at her feet, sometimes off to one side or the other.

That was when he saw S. approach. Agustina stood up rapidly and Sabato took her arm with decision; the two of them went off along Echeverría, toward Arco.

Leaning against a tree, in the darkness, Nacho stood for a long time with his eyes closed. When he recovered his strength, he walked off toward home, never once looking back.

ON POOR MEN AND CIRCUSES

LYING SOMBERLY ON HIS BED, NACHO GAZED AT THE GIRAFFES on the plains of Kenya grazing peacefully, in utter freedom, on the tree limbs. He didn't want to go on thinking about it. He didn't want to be seventeen years old. He was seven, and he looked up at the sky in Parque de los Patricios.

"Look, Carlucho," he was saying, "that cloud up there is a camel."

Still sipping at his little cup of *mate*, Carlucho raised his eyes and nodded, grunting.

It was dusk, and there was a wonderful peacefulness about the park.

Nacho loved this time of day with his friend; they had such important conversations. After a long stretch of silence, he asked:

"Carlucho, I want you to tell me the truth. Do you believe in the Three Wise Men?"

"The Three Wise Men?"

He didn't like that question, and as he always did when he got worried or upset, he began to straighten the candy bars and mints.

"Come on, Carlucho, tell me."

"The Three Wise Men, you say?"

"Uh-huh. Tell me."

Still not looking at the boy, he answered him in a murmur:

"How'm I supposed to know stuff like that, Nacho? I ain't no-body to be asking that sort of thing. I never went to school, never learned nothing, I'm just who I am. I ain't no good for questions,

143

never was good for anything but working. Yard work, field work, stevedoring, getting in the corn, that kind of thing. How'm I supposed to know 'bout the Three Wise Men?"

"Come on, Carlucho. I want to know whether you believe in them."

Carlos began to be angry.

"What bug's bit you, young man! I'm telling you I don't know about them things!"

Out of the corner of his eye, he saw the boy bow his head, and he realized he had hurt his feelings.

"Listen, Nacho, I'm sorry. I'm sorry. I'm your friend, it's just that you know I've got this awful temper. . . . "

He played at setting a row of candy bars straight again, but finally he turned and said:

"Awright, Nacho. You're seven years old, so I guess you might's well be told, once and for all. *There ain't no such things as the Three Wise Men.* There. It's just a story, Nacho, nothing but fooling. Not a word of truth in it. A lie. Life's sad enough, Nacho, without us fooling ourselves about such things as the Three Wise Men. And it's your friend Carlos Américo Salerno telling you that."

"But what about the toys?" Nacho's voice was almost despairing.

"The toys?"

"Uh-huh. The toys they bring you."

"It's a story, Nacho. No better than a lie. Didn't you ever notice that the Three Wise Men go to certain little children's houses? When I was little the Three Wise Men never came anywhere near where we lived, I'll tell you. They never went anywhere but to the houses of the rich children. You see what I'm telling you, Nacho? It's as plain as the nose on your face, child—the Three Wise Men are your poppa and momma."

Nacho bowed his head and started drawing little circles in the dirt between the stepping stones of the path. Then he picked up a stone and threw it half-heartedly at a tree. Carlucho, as he made himself up another *mate*, watched the boy closely.

"Well, who knows how things really are," he finally said. "It's just one man's opinion. The world's a myst'ry, as my old friend Zaneta, may he rest in peace, used to always say. He was prob'ly right."

144

A customer came along then and bought a pack of cigarettes. After a long while, Carlucho, sibylline, remarked:

"Son of a bitch! We oughtta have anárchism."

Nacho looked at him quizzically.

"Archism?"

"That's right, Nacho, anárchism."

"What *is* that, Carlucho?"

Carlucho sat down on his tiny chair and smiled softly, his eyes meditative and nostalgic. It was obvious he was thinking about something very faraway and beautiful.

"Ludwig'd have to be here," he said.

"Ludwig?"

"Uh-huh, Ludwig."

"But who's Ludwig?"

At certain momentous times, when Carlos was about to launch himself into one of the subjects he felt most deeply about, he would take his time, change the leaves in his little cup of *mate*, prepare for what he was about to say with long silences, somewhat the way the statues in the plazas of the city would be placed at the center of grand spaces to make the statues stand out in all the more grandeur and beauty.

"Who was Ludwig . . ." he murmured, his eyes still soft. He sat down again on the tiny chair at the back of the kiosk—the same chair his father had sat in—and then he began:

"I told you that in '18, when the war was over, I went to work as a hand on the Don Jacinto, doña María Unzué de Alvear's ranch. Me and Custodio Medina. And that was when Ludwig came along. You've heard tell of tramps?"

"Tramps?"

"They'd come from way off somewhere with their bundles on their backs. Some folks called 'em bindlestiffs for that, though we always just called 'em tramps. But we didn't mean nothing by it. Nothing bad, I mean. They'd walk in on the railroad tracks, or along the highways. They'd come to the ranch and there'd always be a cot and something to eat for the tramps, that's for sure."

"Then they were hands like you and Medina."

Carlos waggled his finger.

"Nossir. They was not hands. Tramps was tramps, not hands. It was us that was the hands, it was us that was the ones that had to work for our living."

"You mean the tramps didn't work?"

"Of course they worked, I didn't say that. They just didn't work to earn a living. Nobody *made* them work."

Nacho didn't understand. Carlucho looked at him, furrowed his brow, made a great effort to pin down the distinction in his mind, and then tried to explain:

"Tramps was as free as a bird. They'd come to the ranch, do some little piece of work that had to be done, and then they'd move on as free as they'd come. I can see it as clear as if it was yesterday, Ludwig had got all his stuff together and tied up his bundle to leave. Don Bustos, that was the foreman, the boss you might say, told him, he said, If you want to stay on, friend Ludwig, why there'll always be work for you if you want it. But Ludwig said, No, don Bustos, I thank you but I got to get on."

"Get on? Where to?"

"What do you mean, 'where to?' Didn't I just get through telling you that the tramps was like the birds, just that free? Where do you suppose the birds goes? Do *you* know?"

"No."

"There you are, then." He sat there, thoughtfully, missing the old days.

"I can almost see 'im," he said. "Tall . . . and skinny as a rail, with a beard that was almost red-colored. And he had blue eyes. With his bundle slung over his shoulder. We all watched him walk off through the casuarina trees down to the road, and then off down the highway. Lord only knew where to."

Carlucho looked into the park, as though he were watching Ludwig walk off through the trees into infinity.

"And you never saw him again?"

"Never. I 'spect he's dead by now."

"That's a funny name, Ludwig. Isn't it."

"Some kind of foreign name. He was German or Italian or something . . . But then I don't know, 'cause he wasn't Italian like my poppa was Italian. He said he came from someplace with a funny name, but I misremember now. Ludwig . . . He came in one day, did

146

some mechaniclike work, fixed some motors that wasn't working, something or other with a thresher. He knew how to do all kinds of things. And at night in the barracks where we all stayed, he explained all about anárchism."

"Archism?"

"I told you, anárchism. He'd read this little book he had that explained it."

"But what *is* anárchism, Carlucho?"

"I'm no good for questions, I told you. What do you expect, you expect me to explain it the way Ludwig did?"

"No, but . . . but tell me something about it. Was it a story like that story you told me about Charleymaine?"

"No, you goose. I'm talking about something else. This was *real*."

He freshened his *mate* again and concentrated deeply.

"I'm going to ask you a question, Nacho. Think hard."

"All right."

"Who made the earth, and all the trees, and the rivers, and the clouds, and the sun?"

"God."

"That's right. And that means they're for everybody, isn't that right, everybody got a right to have the trees and the sun and all? Tell me, does the birds got to ask somebody's permission to fly?"

"No."

"They can fly around and enjoy the air and come and go as they please, can't they?, and make their nests and lay their eggs and all and raise their little chicks, isn't that right?"

"Of course that's right."

"And when they get hungry or when it's time to feed their little chicks they can go out and get something to eat, some seed or some little something, and bring it home with them. That's so, isn't it?"

"Why, yes, I guess so."

"You guess so. Well I know so. And people ought to be able to be exactly like the birds, the way Ludwig explained it. Come and go as they please, and if they feel like flying, why then fly. And if they feel like making them a nest, why making a nest. Because a seed or a piece of grass or hay or something to make a nest with, and water to wash yourself in or to drink—God made all those things, and God made 'em for everybody in the world. And every bird and creature. You see what I'm telling you, Nacho? If you don't understand this so far, we can't go any farther."

"I understand."

"Awright, then. So can you tell me why just a handful of people, no more than a few men in the whole wide world, have to go and take over the land and the rest of us have got to work and be hands? Where'd they get those ranches of theirs? Did they *make* 'em?"

After thinking a moment, Nacho said no.

"Very good. So then they must've stole 'em."

Nacho was shocked. You mean robbers didn't go to jail? Carlucho smiled bitterly.

"Hold your horses, young man, hold your horses. I'm telling you they stole all that land."

"But who'd they steal it from, Carlucho?"

"Why, how should I know? From the Indians, I 'spect, the people that was here first. I already told you I'm no good for questions . . . but Ludwig knew. He knew all about that. Anyway, think for a minute. Let's s'pose, and it's just to s'pose, that tomorrow morning all the hands had gone and disappeared. Would you tell me what'd happen then?"

"There wouldn't be anybody to work in the fields."

"Exactly right. And if nobody worked in the fields or on the ranches or anything, there wouldn't be no wheat, let's say, and if there wasn't no wheat there wouldn't be no bread, and if there wasn't no bread, there wouldn't be nothing to eat in all the wide world, for nobody. For *nobody*, Nacho. Not even for the bosses, nor the big ranchers. Where you going to get bread, I'd like to know? So now pay attention, because we're about to go one step farther here. Let's s'pose that the people that makes shoes was to disappear too. What would happen then, do you think?"

"There wouldn't be any shoes."

"That's exactly right. And now let's s'pose there wasn't any more carpenters. What then?"

"There wouldn't be any houses?"

"Right again. And now I want to know what would happen if we all woke up tomorrow morning and all the bosses and ranchers and owners of everything was to have disappeared overnight. They don't

148

plant any wheat or corn, they don't make nobody no shoes, they don't build nobody no houses, they don't go out and get the crops in on time. Can you tell me what would happen if all of those people just up and disappeared tomorrow morning?"

Nacho looked at him dumbly. Carlucho smiled in triumph.

"Come on, child, tell me what'd happen if tomorrow morning all the big shots disappeared."

"N-nothing," Nacho replied, shocked at the enormity of what he was saying. "Nothing would happen, I guess."

"You guess. Well, child, I *know*. That is *exactly* what would happen—nothing at all. Not a blessèd thing. So now listen to how Ludwig would explain that—for shoemakers to make shoes, they need leather, and carpenters need wood, and hands need the land, and seeds need the plow. True?"

"Uh-huh."

"But who's got the leather and the wood and the land and the plows?"

"The bosses and owners and all."

"That's exactly right. Everything is in the hands of the bigshots. That's why us poor people are slaves. Because they've got everything, and we don't have nothing—except our hands to work with. But then there's one more big step, so pay attention."

Nacho nodded gravely.

"If us poor people took over the land and the machines in the factories and the leather and the sawmills, we could make shoes and houses, and we could plant and grow things ourselves. What are these hands of ours for, anyway? And there wouldn't be no slavery nor no poverty either. Nor no being sick. And we could all go to school."

Nacho was looking at him in amazement.

Carlucho straightened the magazines and cigarettes, but his mind was still running along the iron rails of his argument. He was making great mental efforts, but his voice lacked any sign of stress or of anger; he spoke serenely, sweetly to the boy.

"Listen, Nacho," he said, "it's simple. Ludwig explained it all with that little book he had. He'd set things in a certain way on the floor—this little rock here is the factory, this *mate* is a machine, these little beans here will be us hands. And I tell you, he explained how

149

there wouldn't be any more being sick, or having the cough, or being poor, or any what he called explotation, something like that. Everybody would have a job. And if you didn't work, you'd have no right to any food or anything. I mean healthy men and women, not children and sick people and old people. On the contrary, Ludwig said that everybody that worked had a duty to keep up the invalids and the children and old folks and all of those that couldn't fend for themselves. So one person would make shoes, and another person would grind up the wheat into flour, and the next person would make bread, and one person would get in the crops. And everything that was made would be put into a big warehouse, where there'd be some of everything—food and clothes and schoolbooks and everything. Anything you can imagine. Even toys and candy bars for the children, because those things are just as needful to children as horses and hats are to us grown-up people. And at the front door of this warehouse there'd be a man that worked there, a man that took care of the things for everybody to use. I'd go up to him and I'd say Give me a pair of shoes size so-and-so, and you'd go up and say I'd like a pound of chicken, please, and a little boy would go up and ask for a candy bar, and one man would want a new suit because the elbows had wore out of his old one. Everybody what they needed. But no more than what they needed, now."

"And what about if a rich man wanted something, could he go up and buy it?"

Carlucho, surprised, looked at the child with severity.

"A rich man, you say?"

"Uh-huh."

"What are you talking to me about a rich man for? Didn't I just explain to you how there'd be no more rich men?"

"But how come, Carlucho?"

"Because there'd be no more money, you goose."

"But what if he had some from before?"

Carlucho smiled and shook his head.

"If he kept a pile of money in the closet or somewhere, he was just fooling himself, Nacho, because it ain't any good anymore. What do you want money for, when you can get anything you want out of that warehouse? Money's just a piece of paper, child. And it's dirty and covered with cooties besides." He smiled. "You know what a cooty is?"

Nacho nodded.

"Well then. That's it for money. We don't care if some dumb rich man keeps a whole houseful of it—it ain't worth a thing. He can keep all he wants. He just can't spend it!"

"But what if you wanted another pair of shoes, and you went to the warehouse to get some?"

"What do you mean, 'another pair of shoes'? I don't know what you're talking about. You can go get some shoes if you need them."

"But I mean if you want three or four pairs."

Carlucho stopped in mid-sip, astonished.

"Three or four pairs of shoes?"

"Uh-huh, three or four pairs."

Carlucho laughed uproariously.

"What in the world do you need three or four pairs of shoes for? All you got is two feet!"

That was true. Nacho had never thought of it that way.

"But what if somebody goes to the warehouse and steals stuff?"

"Steals stuff? What for? If you need something you just go and ask for it, and they'll give it to you. What are you talking about?"

"Then there wouldn't be any police anymore."

Slowly and seriously, Carlucho shook his head.

"There wouldn't be any police anymore for sure. The police are the worst of all, Nacho. I'm telling you from experience."

"What experience, Carlucho?"

Carlucho suddenly seemed to retreat into himself; in a low voice he repeated the word as though he had no desire to expand on it, or as though he could no longer remember whatever it was that had happened to him.

"Experience, that's all," he said.

"But what if somebody didn't want to work?"

"Why you wouldn't have to work if you didn't want to. But we'll see if you don't change your mind when you get hungry."

"But what if the government doesn't like it that way?"

"Gover'ment! What in the world would we need a gover'ment for? When I was little and we was put out into the street, starving

151

to death, my poppa survived because don Pancho Sierra helped him start up a butcher shop. When I went off to be a hand on the ranches, we didn't have no need of the gover'ment. Much less when I joined the circus. And when I went to work in Berisso's grocery store, the only thing the gover'ment was good for was to send the police in during the strike so they could torture us."

"Torture you? What's torture, Carlucho?"

Carlucho looked at him sadly.

"Nothing, child. That just slipped out. That's not a word for a child to use, now. And besides, I told you I'm no good for questions."

Carlucho fell silent, and Nacho realized that he wouldn't talk about anárchism any more that day. A customer came up then and bought cigarettes and matches. When he walked away, Carlucho sat down on the tiny chair and sipped his *mate* in silence. Nacho looked up and watched the clouds; he was thinking. After a while he said:

"You know what, Carlucho? There's a circus over in that lot at Chiclana."

"Chiclana?"

"Uh-huh. They were passing out flyers today. Could we go?"

"I don't know, Nacho. To be frank with you, these circuses nowadays can't compare. The days of the grand circuses are gone. . . ."

Holding his *mate*, he grew distant, thoughtful, dreamy.

"Many years ago . . ."

Then, coming back to earth, he added:

"Probably trashy folk."

"But when you were little they had little circuses like that, too. You told me about that one circus. . . ."

Carlucho smiled tenderly.

"Why of course there were, child . . . Fernández's circus . . . But those grand circuses in my day, there aren't any more of them left. All gone . . . The nickelodeon killed 'em."

"Nickelodeum? What's a nickelodeum?"

"Nickelodeon, Nacho. What they call the movies nowadays. That's what did 'em in."

"But why, Carlucho?"

"That's a pretty complicated subject for a boy, Nacho. But I give you my word on it—the nickelodeon came and good-bye, circus."

He refreshed his *mate* and returned to his own thoughts. In his

152

face one could see the trace of a smile, but a smile tinged with sadness.

"In '18, the Toni Lobandi circus came. . . . It covered the whole Plaza España. . . ."

"But tell me about that little circus of Fernandez's."

Carlucho sucked deeply at his *mate*, as though the sucking at the straw showed how deeply he was thinking.

"From the day the locusts came . . . Well . . . My poppa worked on a little farm that belonged to don Pancho Sierra, between Cano and Basualdo. A good man, don Pancho was. He was a fine doctor, he knew how to cure people, and not only that but he took good care of all the poor people, too. He had a long, white beard, came all the way down to here. 'Bout half witchy, too. Whenever my momma had another child, she'd take 'em before they christened 'em, and he'd tell her This one is going to live, or This one is not going to live. There were thirteen of us, I told you that. And don Pancho told my mother that three of us were not going to live—Norma, nor Juana, nor Fortunata."

"And did they really die?" Nacho asked, fascinated.

"Why of course they did," Carlucho answered simply. "Didn't I say he was about half witchy? That way Momma would resign herself to it from the beginning, because don Pancho would tell her Listen now, doña Feliciana, don't cry now, you just resign yourself, because it's the will of God. Of course Momma would cry and take care of the baby anyway, but it always died. That's the way life is, Nacho."

"Now tell about why you left the farm, Carlucho."

"My poppa was Italian. About '16 or thereabouts he lost the last cent he had in the world. I'll tell you the truth, there's not a more amazing sight anywhere than a plague of locusts. The whole sky gets black and us children would run out and bang old kerosene drums. But it didn't make any difference. Nobody can do anything against a plague of locusts. As my momma would say, you just have to pray they pass over, that's all you can do. If they light, it's good-night, Irene . . . I remember it sort of like a dream, running outside when I was about six years old and banging on a kerosene can as hard as I could. For us children it was practically like a party, you know, but Momma, oh how she cried when she saw that they were going

153

to light. And in the end, kerosene can or no kerosene can, there was nothing that anybody could do. That was when my poppa said I've had enough, goddammit, enough, and he told Panchito and Nicolás to stop running around like that, to be still . . . My poppa stood there like his mind was way off somewhere, and it scared us, because he sat down in this tiny little chair like a person deaf and dumb. That was the chair he sat in to drink his *mate*. It was in under the eaves of the house, and he just sat there like a half-wit or something and watched those locusts eat everything. He didn't move a muscle, and for I don't know how many days he didn't speak a word. Then all of a sudden one day, he said Feliciana, we're leaving this place, we're going to the city, load everything up in the wagon, he said, so we all ran to do what he said, because he was acting like he was crazy, although he never once raised his voice. And when we'd gotten everything loaded up in the wagon and we was all ready to leave, Momma didn't want to leave the house, but Poppa went up to her and he said 'Come on, now,' real calm he said it, 'come on, now, this is done and gone, what can we do here, we're poor folks, let's try our luck in town.' But Momma still wouldn't move out of the kitchen, she was crying, so finally my poppa took her by the arm and dragged her to the wagon. And when we left and shut the gate my poppa sat there for a long time, looking at that house we'd lived in, not saying a word, but I think he was about to cry, too, but finally he turned around and said Giddup, and that was the end of it. We went to town, with the whole pack of house dogs following us. I'm telling you, there wasn't so much as a flea left in that house."

For a while Carlucho said no more, sipping at his *mate*, looking down at the ground. Then he went on.

"So as I was saying, my poppa set himself up in a little butcher shop with some cows that don Pancho let him borrow, and we lived in the house that sat beside the stock pen, which also belonged to don Pancho."

"And that was when the circus came."

"Right. And my poppa rented out the horse lot for fifty *nacionales*."

"Fifty *nacionales*?"

"Fifty pesos. But I mean fifty pesos in money of those days. Back then that was a lot of money. So they set up that little bitty circus.

154

There was a ring about ten yards across, and they had shows Thursdays, Saturdays, and Sundays. Naturally, when there was people to see 'em. Sometimes there wouldn't be no more than five or ten people, and don Fernández would put out the lights in the carbide lanterns and turn sort of green-colored. He drank a good bit, and he'd hit doña Esperanza when he got bad. She was his wife and the balancing act. Then there was Marialuz, his daughter and the horseback rider. There was a clown, too, that was doña Esperanza's brother, but he never butted in when don Fernández would beat up doña Esperanza. Don Fernández did an act that was awfully dangerous, he was the knife thrower."

"And you worked there too, didn't you?"

"When my poppa wasn't looking. I'd light the lamps and carry things. I liked the circus, I wanted to go off with it."

"So you went off with don Fernández?"

"Why no, child, how was I going to go off with the circus when I wasn't but thirteen years old, I was born in '03 . . . And besides, don Fernández barely made his expenses. My poppa would give 'im a little meat and they'd buy some crackers and things, and they managed like that for a little while, but they just couldn't make it, they finally left. And when they pulled down the tent, they didn't have the fifty *nacionales* for the rent, so don Fernández offered to leave my poppa the rifle he used in the sharpshooting act, but poppa told him No, don Fernández, you keep your rifle, how can I take the rifle you need for your act? So anyway, they went off and we never saw them again. One time, when I was working in the Rivero Brothers' Circus, down in Pergamino, I heard they'd finally gone under, sold their tent and everything, the rifle and the wagon and the whole kit and caboodle, you know?, and that doña Esperanza had died of the pneumonia. Marialuz and her uncle had gone to work for the Fassio Circus, I heard, which was somewhere off in Chacabuco, and don Fernández was drinking, so they hadn't been able to do the knife-throwing act nor the sharpshooting act, either. . . ."

Carlucho's mind wandered off. Nacho tugged at him and asked him to tell him about the time he went off with the circus. A shy, dreamy smile played across Carlucho's features, and he began to talk again:

"What days those were, Nacho, what days those were . . . I'll tell

155

you the truth, it's the time in my life I still think about the most, the best time in my life. It was '22, I'd say, I was working as a hand on María Unzué de Alvear's ranch, but when I heard Toni Lobandi's circus had come to town, I was gone. Nelia Nelki was in it, and she was dressed like a man riding a white horse with the whitest tail you ever saw, and so long it reached the ground. And then Toni Lobandi came out. There was never anybody else like him, he'd jump up on that horse from behind and he'd strip off twenty-five different waistcoats of all different colors as that horse trotted around and around the ring. And Scarpini, the famous clown . . . Then there was an act with a cage that took up the size of the whole ring, with an African lion turned loose inside it, and the lion tamer and a horse as black as coal . . . And then came the famous Human Pyramid of the Lopresti brothers . . . When I saw that, I said to myself, I'm going off with this circus and the devil take the hindmost."

"And they put you in the Human Pyramid?"

"No, Nacho, how could they do that? I didn't know the first thing about the circus. What do you think a circus is? A circus is a serious thing, I'm telling you. I worked as a hand. I'd clean up after the horses and sweep out the tent, a little bit of everything, you know. But when there was a show and I got to put on that uniform with the gold braid on the shoulders and this little hat they had me wear, and they'd stand us in two lines along the entrance, sort of like a hall for the performers to go down, and all the acrobats and horses and trained dogs and clowns would run out. I'll tell you, Nacho, it was wonderful. Later on they saw I was getting the hang of things pretty good and I had a good build and all, they put me in the Pyramid. But that wasn't until three years later, when one of the Lopresti brothers got killed. We were in Pergamino, I remember it like it was yesterday, and Lobandi said to me Carlucho, this is your chance, and I almost died. I had to go off in a corner so nobody would see me crying. The biggest dream of my life. And that's how the most important years of my life got started."

Carlucho has risen to his feet and the evening light has begun to illuminate him. A magical glow emanates from him, from his tights as white as snow. There stand the five Lopresti brothers, strong, agile, and radiant in the colored spotlights. They leap gracefully, powerfully up onto Juan Lopresti's shoulders. And as the Human

156

Pyramid is being built upon his Herculean shoulders, the drumroll grows louder and louder. The tension builds, until it reaches its peak. Then, one after another, the men jump down from their precarious perches and the drum roll fades and dies away. There they are again, standing all in a line, smiling, waving gracefully at the audience applauding madly. Then the spotlights begin to fade, and the circus becomes once again the cigarette and candy stand and Carlos becomes once again the man bent by years and sadness, as though some strong coiled spring had broken somewhere inside him.

"Oh, Nacho . . . Those was wonderful days . . . But those grand circuses have all gone now, and they'll never be back."

Nacho looked lingeringly at him as the silence grew deeper and deeper. Then, though he knew the answer, once again he asked him why he had left the circus.

"We were in Córdoba when I hurt my backbone."

His voice broke, and he ducked his head and sipped at his *mate*.

"Lobandi said to me, Carlucho, you'll always have a job here, but I said Thank you, don Lobandi, but I better go. Because me work as a hand again, like somebody'd taken pity on me and kept me on, me just to be what they called a roustabout, I couldn't ever have done that, Nacho. So I came back to Argentina, but I didn't want nobody in my hometown to see me either, so Custodio Medina said Well then, come to work for me in the grocery store. . . ."

He straightened a few newspapers, tidied up a row of candy bars, and tried to keep Nacho from seeing his face. Neither of them spoke; they had both turned inward on their own thoughts.

It was almost completely dark now; the night had crept upon them on tiptoes.

THE DREAMS OF THE COMMUNITY

WHILE SABATO WAITED HIS TURN IN THE LINE for the telephone, a young man sitting at a table nearby kept looking at him. Finally he stood up and somewhat indecisively walked over. He wanted to say hello, just wanted to say hello.

"I've read your books," he said with a smile, stammering a bit. "My name is Bernardo Wainstein."

It was a long line, it looked like there was going to be quite a

157

wait, and the situation was uncomfortable. Both men were nervous, agitated somehow. Was he a student? No, he was working. The boy stood there looking at him.

"You have something you want to say to me."

Yes, of course, he had *so many* things to ask him. He repeated the words *so many*, stressing them slightly yet somehow anxiously. And then all of sudden, as though getting up the courage to say what was on his mind, he said, "The cruelty."

S. looked at him questioningly, and Wainstein once again grew nervous, mute.

"Go ahead, go ahead. Say whatever it is."

"You believe in social change."

Yes, of course he did; everyone knew that.

The dialogue looked to be on the verge of ending without ever having really got off the ground. The young man couldn't quite find a way to bring his two comments together, couldn't see how to establish a logical relationship between them. And although S. suspected how they were connected, he couldn't see his way out of the situation, either. He finally took pity on the young man.

"If I understand you, you want to tell me that my novels are absolutely full of cruelty, and even of pitiless, sadistic episodes, am I right?"

Wainstein stared at him.

"Certain comments by Castel and Vidal Olmos, for example, certain notions they had, isn't that right? That little schoolteacher in the 'Report on the Blind.' Is that it?"

Yes, that was it, but please, S. shouldn't take this the wrong way, he didn't intend, that is, how to explain. Who was he to . . .

The boy was very uncomfortable, and obviously he wasn't sure he wanted to go through with this. But making a gesture with his hand to sweep away the young man's objections, and also to put him more at ease, S. went on:

"And how is one supposed to reconcile that cruelty, those sarcastic views that Vidal Olmos expresses, his contempt for 'progress,' for a progressive agenda, with my own avowedly leftist position, right?"

Wainstein lowered his head, as though he himself were guilty of that contradiction.

158

"Yes, of course, but that's nothing to be ashamed of. You have asked an excellent question. I've asked myself that same question hundreds of times—I've often wondered, and I've even been embarrassed, I must confess, that I should be capable of conceiving such perverse ideas."

"Well, but there are other ideas, of course," the young man hurriedly put in. "Sergeant Sosa, Hortensia Paz, you know . . ."

S. stopped him with his hand.

"Oh yes, I know . . . But what I find truly interesting is that other side, the things you mention. It's a bit difficult to explain. We are all contradictory, of course, but perhaps novelists more than other people. Perhaps in fact it's that that makes us novelists. I have anguished, I tell you, over that duality, and it's only in the last few years that I believe I've been able to begin to understand it."

The woman using the telephone was asking how some girl (or woman) named Meneca was feeling, and also generally about the weather in Ciudadela. Then she remembered, brought up, analyzed in detail, and finally gave her firm personal opinion of an incident that had occurred between her, a neighbor, and a cat. The line stirred impatiently.

"Then when it's finally your turn," S. mused, "it either won't work or you get the wrong number or it swallows your coins and you can't make your call at all. . . . Did you ever read that story, one of the last stories Tolstoy wrote? A rich businessman takes advantage of this poor devil to pull off a great business coup. It's an autobiographical story, they've proved it to be. And do you know what he was writing at the same time?"

No, he didn't have any idea.

"That book on art. What art is. A morally committed book."

The woman on the telephone changed position and everyone imagined that the change prefigured the end of the conversation. It was so she could shift her weight to the other foot, though. The protests grew biting. But she was impervious to moral pressure. Now she had apparently entered into the crucial part of the conversation, something to do with a tumor.

"I mention the case of Tolstoy because it is a famous and very clear case. A sort of practical exercise."

"A practical exercise?"

Laughing, S. said, "Just a manner of speaking, don't pay me any mind."

Meanwhile, the woman appeared to be coming to the end of the conversation: a certain dying fall in her voice indicated as much, and everyone in the line began to feel a bit relieved. And although suddenly that tone (for some unknown reason, probably because of something the person on the other end of the line was saying from Ciudadela) grew animated again, and one overheard unexpected variations on the advantages and disadvantages of certain surgical procedures, it must be admitted that soon the woman's tone resumed that descending fall, there were a series of messages for persons known to one or the other speaker, and then at last the woman hung up and walked off regally, without a backward glance at a soul in the line behind her. The line advanced then with the slow, clumsy movement of an animal with all sorts of legs trying to scale a mountain hard to conquer, the difficulties further complicated by the unfortunate composition of the caterpillarlike creature: a different and totally independent nervous system for every segment.

Wainstein's perplexity could be seen in his eyes.

"You see, in these last few years I have been very troubled by this problem, and have anguished over it a great deal. They have done experiments on sleeping people, done encephalograms. At a U.S. university, of course. When a person dreams, the brain waves are different, so you can tell whether the subject is dreaming or not. So then every time the subject starts dreaming, they wake him up, and do you know what happens?"

Wainstein was looking at him like a man waiting for some final revelation.

"You can drive a man to madness, to utter psychosis."

Wainstein appeared not to understand.

"Don't you see? Fiction is very much like dreams—dreams can be cruel, heartless, sadistic, homicidal, even in normal people, people who during the daytime will give you the shirt off their backs. The dreams, then, may be something like discharges of electricity from overloaded circuits, or the jettisoning of excess cargo so that a ship can stay afloat. And the writer dreams for the community. A kind of collective dream. A community that forbade fiction would run grave risks."

160

The young man continued to stare at S., though his gaze was not quite the same as before.

"I don't know, it's just a hypothesis. I'm not sure about all this."

He had fallen into a bad mood again: that woman on the telephone, the conversation about cats and fibromas, uncles and aunts and the weather in Ciudadela. Life suddenly seemed so off the mark, somehow, so disorderly. The woman with the tumor was going to die, of course she was. But what was the meaning in all that hodgepodge of stuff? And the line, this creeping, restless, polycerebral caterpillar. Waiting. All of them. For what, for what. Sleep, and dreams.

When we sleep we close our eyes, and therefore *we become blind*. He stopped, shocked.

The soul casts off into the great nocturnal lake and begins its shadowy journey: *"cette aventure sinistre de tous les soirs."* Nightmares would then be the visions of that horrible universe. And how was one to express those visions? By means of signs inevitably ambiguous: there were no "wineglasses" nor "dear sirs" nor "pianos." There were winevaginaglasses, dearshit sirs, vagipianos, fuckglasses, dear cunts, pianoses, peeing sirs. "Analysis" of dreams, psychoanalysts, explanations of those symbols irreducible to any other language: don't make him laugh, his stomach hurt anyway. Ontophanies, period.

And how naive. The Blind remain eternally mute. When one tried to explain, everything was reduced to a mouthful of innocuous, deceiving, false words: like explaining relativity to a mongoloid child by gestures alone. Of course symbols can be constructed from words. Didn't Kafka do it? But those words taken by themselves weren't symbols. Good lord, what a stomachache.

A STRANGER

HE WAS A THIN, DARK-SKINNED, SEEDY-LOOKING MAN sitting thoughtful and remote before a wineglass. Part of his face was visible, an angular face that looked as though it had been hacked out of ironwood, with bitter lines around the mouth.

That man, thought Bruno, is utterly, absolutely alone.

He didn't know why the man looked so familiar to him, and he sat for a long time rummaging through his memory, trying to tie him to a photograph in some newspaper or magazine. On the other hand, it seemed almost shocking that a person in such threadbare clothes, a man who had sunk to such depths, could have achieved the notoriety of print. Unless, it suddenly occurred to Bruno, he'd been involved in some affair of a legal nature. After an hour, or perhaps a little more, the stranger got up and left. He looked about sixty years old; he was stoop-shouldered, though he was tall and thin. His face was hard, hard, and his clothes were little better than rags, yet there was some distinction in his features and in his way of carrying himself. He walked away somehow absentmindedly: it was obvious that he had nowhere in particular to go, that no one was expecting him, that everywhere was the same to him.

Bruno, who was used to sitting alone and studying people, contemplative and slothfully sedentary as he was, thought: "That man is either a criminal or an artist."

For several months that image remained, inexplicably and stubbornly, in his memory, until one day a thought occurred to him, he had a hunch. He searched through his files, which were the files of neither a philosopher nor a journalist nor a writer, but the files rather of a man for whom humanity presented a dolorous mystery.

Yes, there was the photo: the stranger was that Juan Pablo Castel who in 1947 had killed his lover.

"The absolute man," then thought Bruno Bassán, with serene and melancholy envy.

SECOND COMMUNICATION FROM JORGE LEDESMA

I'M VERY SORRY, BUT I HAVE TO TELL YOU SOMETHING that I'm afraid, or really that I'm sure, will burst your bubble, but then I did not create reality. I must tell you, distinguished author, that the Danube is not blue. It's dirty, brown water mixed with mud, oil, and sewage. Shit, in fact. Exactly like the Riachuelo, though this latter has so much less literary and musical prestige—but what can one do.

There are two ways to write. I got stuck with the second, my best stuff is no better than a rickety old run-down one-room shack. Worse. Because standing there with my pants in my hand, sometimes I can't even find where the bed is. I tack on a little bit of

162

everything, I'm a lazy good-for-nothing. And since I have such a tiny little brain, I have to wait for one idea to leave before another one can get in.

The hardest thing for me to explain—because it's with drawings and I'm no good at drawing—is the Law of Heads. Advanced Craniology. As you may well imagine, the Lord is not going to be simpleminded enough to leave to chance a matter so important to love as the selection of the Other (read: *continuation of slavery through the offspring*). When purely by chance there is born a genius, it's because everything was done backward, natural law was broken (violated, one might even say): thousands of retardates for one genius.

Schopenhauer was never loved by his mother, and if we are to believe legend, the Virgin Mary never really loved Jesus either. If you know of other cases, please let me know about them, as I want to expand this list. I, for example, was manufactured when my mother could no longer bear so much as to look at my father. I am not the result of love: I am a by-product of nausea. Because of incompatibility, the uterus rejects certain spermatozoa. When the starting gun went off, so to speak, and the race was on, and I, like an idiot, came in first, I did try to back out—but the womb had already closed behind me. With me inside! What a mess. Everything went wrong, right from the start. And there I was, all alone, helpless, in the middle of this dark, wet, unknown, cavernous place. Outside, trillions of my little brothers wriggling and writhing in asphyxia; they all died. This too is love, you poets who sing anthems to the crepuscular light—you might sometimes, it seems to me, sing just of pus. And that feeling still is with me, this icy wind which sometimes freezes one side of my face into a grimace of anguish. Infinite loneliness.

HE LOOKED AT THEM IN EXASPERATION AND
DISCOURAGEMENT.
What? You mean they had to go over all that ground again? He thought he had put all this to rest ten years ago. Those pseudo-Marxists that divided literature into the political on one side and the purely aesthetic on the other. And since *Ulysses* was neither a political book nor a purely aesthetic book, it ceased to exist. It was

some sort of teratological creature. Or it might belong to botany. Maybe it was a platypus. Do we have to go on wasting our time with this kind of nonsense?

"But there are kids that ask these things, that accuse you . . ."

He became furious. With that kind of argument you could accuse Béla Bartók of composing music, and T. S. Eliot of writing poetry.

"I have a lot to do and very little time to do it in. And I don't mean by the clock, I mean by the calendar."

"Yes, but you have an obligation."

This was a young man with a chiseled-looking face, a kind of short, thin-lipped Gregory Peck.

"Who exactly are you? What's your name?"

"Araujo."

"I wrote about all this ten years ago."

"We've all read it," put in a girl in a yellow polo shirt and faded jeans. "It's not us, what we want to do is record this and publish it."

"I'm sick and tired of tapes and interviews!"

BRUNO WANTED TO LEAVE,

he felt uncomfortable. And now he saw S. over in that corner, taking off his glasses and rubbing his eyes and forehead with that tired, discouraged way he had, while those kids carried on the argument among themselves. Because not even the inquisitors themselves were in agreement, and what an absurd potpourri of types they were. (What was Marcelo doing there, for example, and that sullen, unspeaking friend of his? What crazy sort of rule of association did that bunch obey?) And that discord, that loud, violent, and ironic discord—it occurred to him that it was the sign of the crisis of the times, of the breakdown of all doctrine and dogma. They were throwing accusations at each other like mortal enemies, and yet they all belonged to what they would have called the Left—but each one of them appeared to have his own motives to consider, and to distrust the boy or girl beside him as though any one of them might have been subtly (or openly) linked to undercover agencies, to espionage services, the CIA, the powers of imperialism. He looked at their faces. How many different worlds were there behind those

164

façades, how many essentially different modes of being? Future Humanity. What canons, what schools, what sort of beings? The New Man. But how was this New Man to be built out of that hypocritical *arriviste*, out of that Puch fellow he could hear yammering over there, out of somebody like Marcelo? What attributes, what toenail of that climbing little leftist could be mixed into the recipe for this New Man? He contemplated Marcelo, in his worn-out windbreaker and wrinkled jeans; he had that barely perceptible presence which nevertheless impressed Sabato so strongly. Because, Sabato explained, he always felt so guilty when he talked to Marcelo, as he'd felt years ago with Arturo Sánchez Riva—and not because Marcelo was so fierce or wrathful, no, but quite the opposite, because he was so gentle, so kind, because he had such quiet reserve and delicacy. Sabato didn't think the young man's soul was serene; almost certainly it was tormented, in fact. But the torment was reserved, circumspect, even polite. It was strange to see in his face the same features one saw in Dr. Carranza Paz—the bony, prominent nose, the high, narrow forehead, those large velvety-looking eyes, often a little moist: one of those gentlemen at the funeral of the Count of Orgaz. Why such differences between them, then? Once more he realized how little the flesh and bone of a face counted toward the revelation of character. It was subtleties that expressed the differences—differences sometimes overwhelming. But things were distinguished by their similarities, as Aristotle had long ago discovered, the Proustian part of that polymath genius. And indeed it was what those eyes and that mouth and that bony, prominent nose had in common with the father's that revealed the chasm that loomed between father and son. A natural chasm, perhaps, yet one that grew wider and wider with the years. Almost imperceptible folds at the corners of the eyes, on the eyelids, at the corners of his mouth, the way one bent his head and folded his hands (in Marcelo, timidly, as though apologizing for having hands, for not knowing where to hide them) were things that sadly but definitely divided two beings who were paradoxically so close and even (he could almost swear) so necessary to each other.

sighed the girl in the yellow shirt. "The Critic, who is of course the Initiate, replaces the word 'history' with the word 'diachronism,' affirms that a synchronic description is irreconcilable with a diachronic description, decrees the universal validity of synchronic descriptions, and therefore can deny the possibility of finding any meaning in the historical narrative."

"What?!" cried a big lumbering kid with one of those Cossack faces. Sabato looked at the girl.

"What's your name?" thinking Silverstein, Greenberg, Edelman.

"Silvia."

"Silvia what?"

"Silvia Gentile."

Hah, so that was it. Hadn't Jorge Itzigsohn said he'd never in his life seen so many Jewish faces as in Italy? And anyway, she might be Saracen, those faces you see in Calabria, in Sicily. She carried her head a little forward, with that exploratory sort of look of a near-sighted person who might be standing, all unknown, before a mine shaft or a camel not three feet away.

His error made him gentler. It was all right, they didn't have to read his books, the best thing they could do, in fact. The boy named Puch blurted out that he'd already read them all.

"No kidding," Sabato murmured sarcastically, but paying him no further attention.

The young people went on arguing among themselves, denouncing each other over structuralism, Marcuse, imperialism, revolution, Chile, Cuba, Mao, Soviet bureaucracy, Borges.

"So?"

"So, what?"

What the Cossack, in a voice surprisingly high-pitched and insufficient, wanted to ask was whether one then had to stop writing.

"And who might you be?"

"Mauricio Sokolinski, with an i, no home address or telephone."

S. studied him for a moment. He didn't happen to write, did he?

"I confess."

And what exactly was it that he wrote?

"Aphorisms. Aphorisms by a barbarian. I'm pretty stupid, I'll have you know."

What sort of aphorisms were these?

"You told me they were very good ones."

"I did? When?"

"When I sent you the book. My picture on the back cover. Didn't make any great impression on you, obviously."

Why of course, of course. Sokolinski with an *i*, he remembered now.

"All right. So then?"

There were thousands of magazines in the stands all along Corrientes spitting out the same stuff, the same denunciations, the same declarations.

"What?"

"That literature no longer has any significance."

"Excuse me," broke in S., "but those guys, who are they? Construction workers, metallurgists?"

"No, of course not. They're writers, or at least they write magazines."

"And so?"

"And so, what?"

"Nothing," said Silvia, "except that the consistent thing to do would be to stop publishing those magazines. Which are not going to make the masses to the northeast rise in revolt anyway. Why don't they grab a rifle and join the guerrillas? That would be the consistent thing to do."

"But even allowing for their joining the guerrillas," S. went on, "that would speak well of the ones that made the decision to do so, but it would render invalid neither writings *á la* Marx and Bakunin nor literature in the strict sense of the word. That would be like the study of medicine being discarded because of the actions of Ché Guevara. And another thing: when did a Beethoven quartet ever serve to further the progress of the French Revolution? Shall we deny music because of its revolutionary inefficacity? And not only music—poetry as well, almost all of literature and all of art. And one more thing. Unless I have forgotten my Marxist dialectics, a society has not reached maturity until it is capable of seeing what is valuable, and therefore salvageable, in the society which it wishes to supplant. I believe Marx himself might even have said as much. Are these kids more Marxist than Marx? Conclusions, please."

167

"First," counted Silvia on her fingers, "those kids on Corrientes . . ."

"And you, where're you from!" shouted Araujo.

"Those kids on Corrientes mutually stirring each other up with their mirror-image magazines should put down their pens and pick up a gun. Second . . ."

"One moment," interrupted Sabato. "I don't read those magazines. But I insist that revolutions are not made with guns alone. And who's to say but that one of those magazines may not further the cause."

"Second, the arts, including literature, should be left in peace while the Revolution is being forged."

"Sure," cried the Cossack, "but the problem is that most of them are not going to go off and join the guerrillas, they're going to claim that their patriotic duty is to give it help from the trenches."

"Trenches? What trenches?"

"Literature."

"But how can that be? Didn't we decide that literature has no significance? That it made no practical difference? That it was never going to bring down this putrescent society?"

"Of course. But that's *this* literature."

"What literature are we talking about, if you don't mind?"

"The literature that Sabato just mentioned. Dante, Joyce, Proust, etc."

"Oh, you mean *all* literature."

"Naturally."

"But then," Sabato had to break in, "what in the world is the *other* one?"

"I'll try to explain it to you," Silvia replied. "These kids have chosen literature, they continue to act like writers, and they say, or pretend, that from that standpoint, from that Front, if you will, they can launch their attack on the Moncada Barracks. Thence your request for a statement of principles: the possibility of a sort of Revolutionary Book, the absolute model which resides in that heaven in which Plato holds up for our inspection, among other Ideal Objects, the Face of Fidel. And from that high place, these people decide which books—now in lowercase, mind you—attain to the level of that archetype, and which do not."

"Unless I've misunderstood you," said Sabato, "the *which do not* are the books that constitute all of literature."

"That is correct. And these revolutionaries put that literature, which is to say all literature, into the same big box they put charades and crossword puzzles in. Gratuitous games. Outside that big box Revolutionary Literature, with the power of a mortar shell, would still remain."

"The only drawback to that literature," Sabato observed, "is that it doesn't exist."

"You think not?" Araujo asked icily.

"Unless you want to call proclamations, soapbox orations, pamphlets, and ripping speeches revolutionary literature. Those Soviet plays where the medal-bedecked Tractor Driver marries the Prize-Winning Stakhanovite in order to conceive chemically pure Children of the Revolution. The same thing the French did in their time. There were plays (so we are told, because they're virtually apocryphal, they were so bad they simply disappeared) called things like *Virgin and Republican*."

Araujo and Silvia grappled with each other violently.

"But those terrorists of left-wing criticism," said Silvia, "can't see beyond the nose on their own faces—they still see a colonialist in every fantasy writer. And the funniest thing about it is, they themselves have the soul of a writer."

"Because they won't stop writing for even one second," put in the Cossack.

"Or let anybody else write, either."

But Sabato, what did he have to say about all this?

He had been listening to them: it was incredible to him that people were still arguing over some of these things. Had everybody forgotten that Marx could recite Shakespeare from memory?

He was telling *them*? said Silvia. "Shakespeare wrote that Revolutionary Book, and those kids on Corrientes don't know it."

All right, but they ought to let up on poor Karl Marx, who so far as S. could tell had been an incurable romantico-petit-bourgeois-counterrevolutionary-in-the-service-of-Yankee-imperialism.

"But then," unexpectedly asked the young man with the indigenous-looking features—unexpectedly because up to now he had maintained a hieratic silence—"other than joining the guerrillas, is there nothing that a person can do for the Revolution with books?"

"We're talking about fiction, poetry," burst out Sabato in irritation. "Of course there are a lot of things that can be done to further the Revolution with books—sociology books, criticism. That's what I began by saying. *The Communist Manifesto* is a book, not a machine gun, for heaven's sake. But we're talking about writers in the strictest sense of the word. It's not only *possible* for a person to help the Revolution with a manifesto, or with a criticism of social institutions, or with a book of reportage, or even of philosophy; it's what is most needed. And if one pretends to be a revolutionary, it's what one *must* write. The fatal error is to fail to distinguish the two planes. As though one were to claim that what is valuable in Picasso is that little dove of his, while his women in profile with the two eyes on one side of their heads is pure bourgeois rot. Which Soviet critics still manage to claim. Socialist realist storm troopers."

Somebody mentioned an exhibit of Picasso's work in Moscow. Really? When?

A confused argument ensued; there was much shouting back and forth.

"Let's not waste any more time on this pointless argument," Sabato said. "I don't know whether they finally had any Picasso exhibits or not. I'm talking about official doctrine, which is the serious issue. I don't think that little dove of Picasso's will have forestalled a single bombing in Vietnam, but at least it is legitimate. What's illegitimate is to affirm that that is *the only* art, that that sort of poster or billboard art is what a painter who wants to change the social order ought to do. What is illegitimate is to confuse the two planes, as I said: art and the poster. And moreover, sometimes you hear people argue that *at the present time*, in this troubled *now*, when the world is coming down about all our ears, art cannot afford itself the luxury of disinterestedness. But the world was falling apart in the time of the French Revolution, too, and an artist like Beethoven was a revolutionary—to the point of tearing up the dedication of the *Eroica* to Napoleon when Napoleon betrayed him. And yet Beethoven didn't write any little military marches. He wrote great, grand music. It wasn't Beethoven that wrote the 'Marseillaise.' "

"Right on!" Puch practically shouted.

170

BRUNO WAS FASCINATED BY THAT FACE,

and every servile remark that issued from it made him ashamed of the entire human race; he knew the young man was capable of becoming a police informer, or perhaps of rising to be an official in this, or even the opposing, regime. But then, with relief, he thought again of Carlos. Though it was a painful relief, because he knew how much the existence of maggots like Puch had cost men like Carlos. Wasn't that him again beside Marcelo? Because the spirit did come round again, now incarnated in virtually the same burning, concentrated face as the face of that Carlos of 1932, the face of a boy suffering some deep, deep pain which could not be revealed to anyone, not even to that Marcelo who was probably his best friend, the friendship forged in silence and action. With Carlos there came back to his mind the names of those times: Capablanca and Alekhine, Sandino, Al Jolson singing in that grotesque film, Sacco and Vanzetti. What a strange and melancholy assemblage! He could once again see Carlos, whose real last name they never discovered, sitting in that room on Calle Formosa, leaning over a desk, his temples resting on his clenched fists, moving his lips slowly, in silence, as he feverishly devoured the cheap editions of Marx and Engels in which, like a man painfully trying to find and then dig up a chest full of treasure, he would find the key to his ill-starred existence, his pain and miseries, the death of his mother in a tin-walled shack filled with hungry children. He had been a pure, religious spirit. How could he understand men in general? The incarnation, the fall? How could he understand the polluted condition of humankind? How could he ever have understood and accepted the existence of Communists like Blanco? Bruno saw his burning eyes set in that emaciated, worn, yet intensely concentrated face. He had suffered to the limits of all suffering, until he had become pure spirit, as though his flesh had been burned away by fever, as though his body, burned and tormented, had been reduced to the very minimum of flesh and bones, to a few hard muscles that bore up the weight of existence. He had almost never talked, like that one over there now, but his eyes had burned with the fire of indignation and his lips in that rigid face had squeezed tight together to protect his anguished secrets. And now he had returned in this second boy, this one likewise dark-skinned and emaciated, and who could not seem to understand why

171

he was here, in the midst of so many words to him incomprehensible. Perhaps out of his loyalty to Marcelo. And the curious fact was that this was a repetition of that other symbiosis. Because in Carlos' friendship with Max, so superficially inexplicable, the kindness and sweetness of Max (who was of course not really the model for Marcelo) was essential for calming Carlos' tenseness from time to time, like water was necessary to calm a man's thirst as he crossed the desert.

ALL RIGHT, ALL RIGHT THEN,
I'll admit that you have to be pretty stupid to throw out all of literature for the sake of the Revolution," Araujo said. "Neither Marx nor Engels did that. Not even Lenin himself. But I do think a certain kind of literature has to be questioned."

"And what type might that be?" Sabato asked.

"The literature of introspection, to begin with."

Sabato exploded in fury.

"I'm fed up to here with that kind of idiocy! Why don't we try to raise the philosophical level of this discussion? Naturally, the syllogism you have in mind, and a perfectly specious syllogism, by the way, is this: introspection means to retire into the self; the solitary self is an egoist that doesn't care a thing about the world, a counterrevolutionary that tries to make us believe that the problem lies within the soul, not in social organization, etc. But you overlook, or willfully ignore, one small detail—the solitary self does not exist. Man exists within a society, suffering, struggling, and sometimes even hiding within that society. To live is to live with others. The self, or I, and the world, we might say. And it is not simply a person's voluntary, waking acts and attitudes which are the result of that interaction—even a person's dreams and nightmares come out of that living together. Even a person's fits of madness. From that point of view, the most subjective novel in the world is social, and it may do so directly or in a very roundabout way, but in one way or another it does give witness to all of reality. There is no such thing as the novel of introspection and the social novel, my friend—there are great novels and small novels. There is good literature and bad

172

literature. So relax: the writer will always portray the world, even if his world is tiny, tiny, tiny like this."

Araujo had listened with mute, indrawn hardness.

"I don't think it's quite so neat as that," he argued. "There must have been some reason that Marx admired writers like Balzac. That kind of novel is a portrayal of society."

"The novels of Kafka don't deal with rail strikes in Prague, and yet they will always stand as one of the greatest and most profound portrayals of contemporary man. But following your argument, his entire *oeuvre* would have to be burned, as would Lautréamont's, and Malcolm Lowry's. Look, kids, I already told you I have very little time left, and I refuse to waste it on these purportedly philosophical puerilities."

"I think we're wasting time," Silvia remarked.

"So do I," said Sabato. "I've talked about this until I'm blue in the face, but I notice that people keep bringing up the same old arguments. And not just here. Look at the article by Asturias."

"On what?"

"On us, on certain selected Argentine writers. He explained that we were not representative of Latin America. An American critic said something similar a while ago: Argentina has no national literature. Naturally, the lack of strong local color confuses that sort of self-styled censor, because basically what they're after is a 'picturesqueness' before they'll grant us a license. For that sort of ontologist, a black man on a banana plantation is real, but a high-school student sitting in a plaza in Buenos Aires meditating on existential loneliness is an anemic entelechy. They even call that kind of superficiality *realism*. Because all this nationalism stuff is tied to the central and inevitably mistaken question of realism. That word, ugh . . . Oh how people play tricks with that word. If while I sleep I dream of dragons, should we infer, considering the absolute absence of dragons in Argentina, that my dreams are not patriotic? I think we should ask that American critic whether the nonexistence of metaphysical whales in American territory makes Melville a man without a country. Spare me! I tell you I'm up to here with these stupidities."

Sabato took off his glasses and wiped a hand over his forehead and eyes, while Silvia argued with the Cossack and Araujo. But Sa-

173

bato neither listened nor even heard them, because suddenly he was back in the fray:

"That kind of stupidity comes from assuming that the real mission of art consists of copying reality. But notice one thing: when those people talk about reality they mean *external reality*. The other reality, *internal* reality, as we all know, has had very bad press. That is, art is supposed to become some sort of photographic machine. But anyway, even for those who believe that realism consists of revealing or uncovering or portraying that exterior world, the growth of Argentina, its population increased by European immigrants, its powerful middle class, its industry, all militate for, or at least legitimize, a literature which has nothing to do with banana imperialism. But there are more worthy purposes for art, since art does not have that mission that people suppose. Only a very naive person would try to learn anything about the agriculture on the outskirts of Paris at the turn of the century by studying the paintings of Van Gogh. It's obvious that art is a language closer to dreams and myths than to statistics and the happenings chronicled in newspapers. Since myth and dream are ontophany . . ."

"Onto *what*?!" cried the Cossack in alarm.

"Ontophany. A revelation of reality. But a revelation of *all* reality, all right? *All* reality. Not just external reality but internal reality as well. Not just rational reality but irrational reality as well. Try to understand. This is infinitely complex. Because it does undoubtedly suffer strong penetration or impregnation from the objective world, but it maintains a very subtle, very complex relationship with that world. Maybe even a contradictory relationship. If society were decisive in this, the only thing that mattered, how could one explain the difference between a literature like Balzac's and a literature like that of his contemporary Lautréamont? Or between Claudel and Céline? There can be no doubt that all art is individual, because it is the vision of a reality by a unique, separate spirit."

"We're getting off the track," Araujo gruffly interrupted.

"You're the one that's getting off the track! And I haven't finished. I was saying that all art is individual, every work of art is individual, and that that is the great difference between it and scientific knowledge. In art, what is important is precisely that personal, unique scheme or pattern of vision, that concrete expression

174

of individuality. That is why there is style in art but there is no style in science. What would it mean to talk about the style of Pythagoras in the Pythagorean theorem? The language of science can and in a strict way *must* consist of abstract and universal signs. Science is reality seen by an essentially unnecessary subject. Art, on the other hand, is reality seen by an essentially *necessary* subject. The inability to do without the seeing subject, 'inability' in quotation marks, of course, is precisely the wealth of art. And that which allows art to portray the totality of human experience, to achieve that interaction between the self and the world, is the whole, entire, and integral reality of the man. From that point of view, it's absurd to accuse Borges of not being representative. Representative of what? Of *what*? He represents, as no one else possibly could, the Borges-world reality. There is no reason why that reality has to be a photographic reproduction of what you and I see as Argentina. That unique way of looking at the world, or *seeing* the world, is manifested in a language which is itself unique. There's no way out—we have to call it an idiolect. It's an ugly word, and probably it's a synonym for *style*. It seems proper, then, at this point in the evolution of our letters (and note that we aren't a hundred and fifty years old, ours is not a 'new' literature—we're a *thousand* years old, and we are as much descended from the poetry of *El Cid* and any inhabitant of Madrid as we are from the gauchos), at this point as I say in the evolution of our literature, it seems only proper that we put aside these absurd fallacies. And accept once and for all that there may exist among us—and with no problem of a guilty conscience, either—writers as distinct as Balzac and Latureamont."

He got up and was about to leave, but he was too overwrought. He stopped and added:

"These camp followers of Marx do him no favor by making him responsible for every stupidity that comes into their minds—like that direct and proportional relation between the owners of banana plantations and the literature of introspection. And the fact that Marx preferred Balzac is perfectly respectable, but I hope they're not going to tell me that Marx is the only man in the world that has a right to express his literary preferences. It seems we all have to prefer Balzac because Marx did. And then a poet like Lautréamont will be suspect because in his delirium he escaped, or fled from, the French reality

175

of his time, the high cost of potatoes. A sellout to capitalism. Using those criteria, when the French Revolution was bruited all over Europe, Beethoven ought to have written soul-stirring little military marches, or at least music like Tchaikovsky's *1812* Overture, instead of the quartets he was writing. I don't know where I read it, probably in one of those two-for-a-nickel broadsides, but I read somewhere that in France a man like Lautréamont could produce such literature, but that if we did it here, in the New World, we were imitators of European literature.

"Now then, if we keep in mind that an art like that has a great deal to do with dreams, then it must follow that one can only dream in France. We aren't allowed to dream here, and if we do we have to dream about wage increases and strikes by ironworkers. And not whisper a word if we have a dream about death. I don't remember which of those 'critics' it was that criticized me because I was concerned with the 'European theme' of death. Here, of course, no one dies. Here, of course, we are all immortal folklore types. Death is an issue linked suspiciously closely to Wall Street. Funerals in the service of capitalist imperialism. Enough, for god's sake! Enough of all this philosophical demagoguery!"

He stood up to leave.

"No, please, don't go," Silvia pleaded.

"Why not? There's no sense in these arguments."

"But please, there are a couple of things we'd really like to ask you about," she insisted.

"Like what?"

Bruno took his arm and urged him to calm down.

All right, but what was the point of it all, after all.

"The point is," he said when he'd calmed down a bit, "that that sort of person hasn't even understood Marxism. If literature were indeed an enemy of the Revolution, or even some sort of solipsistic masturbation, there would be no explanation for the fact that Marx admired Shakespeare. And the courtier and monarchist Goethe. Naturally, these minithinkers will jump up and argue that the situation is much more pressing now, especially in the Third World, and that therefore this is not the moment for Literature. But I'd like them to tell me, then, whether the time when Marx was going to the British Museum, when children seven years old were being cruelly and bar-

176

barously exploited in the coal mines, was the moment for poetry and novels. Because Dickens was not the only person writing at that moment. Tennyson and Browning and Rossetti were writing too. And at the height of the Industrial Revolution, one of the most inhuman historical periods ever to have transpired, there were writers of the stature of Shelley and Byron and Keats. Many of whom also read and admired Marx. So these people do Marx a pretty favor by attributing such absurdities to him! Not to mention that other false and superficial notion that art is the reflection of society, of the class to which it belongs. And not art alone—philosophy as well. Good lord, under those rules Marx himself couldn't have been a Marxist, since he was a bourgeois. Marxism would have to have been invented by a miner from Cardiff. I don't believe they even understand what dialectics is all about. I presume they'll have read Lenin's *What To Do?* All right then, the working class would of itself have been incapable of achieving socialism, it would never have passed beyond the yellow stage of guilds. Socialism was created by members of the bourgeoisie like Marx and Engels, aristocrats like Saint-Simon and Kropotkin, intellectuals like Lenin and Trotsky."

"And Ché Guevara."

"And what I said about thinkers goes for poets and writers too, but even more emphatically. Because fiction, like dreams, and for much the same reasons, is in general antagonistic to reality, not a mere passive reflex. That is the reason that it is often hostile to the society of its time. What we're talking about here, I should point out, is a dialectic more in the Kierkegaardian vein."

"What! What!" exclaimed Araujo in surprise.

"Yes, young man. You heard right. Kierkegaardian. I don't see why that ought to alarm you, or make you run off and disinfect yourself. After all, the reaction against that entelechy which enlightened thought defined man as being was not just the work of Marx but of Feuerbach as well, and of Kierkegaard. The defense of the concrete man. But as I was saying, art tends to be an act of antagonism. And, like dreams, often is opposed to reality, even aggressively so. Look at the United States. The epitome of alignment, and it has produced one of the most remarkable literatures of all times. And Czarist Russia. Look at the secret mechanism at the two peaks of it: one, Count Tolstoy, aristocrat to the marrow of his bones, who offers us one of the bleakest and most harrowing visions of the condition of man. And the other, that Czarist named Dostoyevsky."

"But proletarian art . . ." began Araujo.

"What's that? Where can I see some? Are you talking about those colored postcards with pictures of Stalin on horseback directing battles he was never at? Those kitschy postcards that he thought were the apex of revolutionary aesthetics but that were actually the epitome of the flattest sort of bourgeois naturalism? Curious, and worthy of thought: Revolutions seem always to prefer reactionary, superficial art. Those famous *pompiers* of the French Revolution. Notice where that famed theory of reflection leads. Delacroix is not the artist of the Revolution, David is, and others worse even than such an academician as he. And while Stalin swooned in ecstasy over those productions, he refused to allow great Western art."

"Yes, but that was right in the middle of the Revolution," Araujo insisted, "when nothing can be tolerated that hampers or endangers the Revolution. It's a war. And therefore it's a question of conquering or dying. And if a work of art gives arguments to the enemy, or even softens or distracts the combatant, one has the historical right to prohibit it."

"A counterrevolutionary art, in a word?" asked Sabato.

"That's right."

Even Silvia looked at him without saying a word.

Yet it was not Araujo's words or the girl's silence that most unsettled Sabato—it was the eyes of Marcelo's friend, which Sabato now found fixed upon him. He had felt uncomfortable the whole time in that powerful presence—powerful by reason of its simple purity, or because it reminded him of the expression on the face of that Carlos of 1932. This young man's eyes shone in silence from his austere, painfully withdrawn face, like two burning coals in an arid, dried-out, suffering land. Beside him, Marcelo was like some kind angel watching over a creature at once strong and defenseless in a world rotting and apocalyptic. Yes, he reminded Sabato of Carlos' tormented anguish, the same anguish that sooner or later this other young man would suffer as well, or perhaps already had. And all the words he had been saying, all those philosophical sparks flying, became suddenly cause for shame before the solitary reticence of this boy sprung up from who knew which woebegotten

178

provincial town, this person a victim of and witness to infinite injustices and humiliations. In a voice suddenly soft, almost as though he were talking to himself, and looking down at the floor, Sabato said:

"Yes . . . But be careful with that word, be careful of applying it with hatred, of using it lightly, because then men like Kafka . . ."

He was terribly torn. On the one hand he thought that anything he might say could wound or disillusion the boy. On the other, he felt the obligation to clarify, to explain. The obligation to prevent them, one of them the purest of them, from one day committing some great injustice, even though it might be a sacred injustice.

"The dilemma is not between social literature and individual literature, you all understand . . . The dilemma is between the serious and the frivolous. When innocent children die from bombs in Vietnam, when the purest men and women are tortured in three quarters of the world, when hunger and desperation dominate the globe, I understand that all of that cries out against a certain type of literature. . . . But against which type? Which type? I think one has all the right in the world to reject mere frivolous games, ingenuity, verbal entertainment . . . But one must be careful not to repudiate the great, heart-wrenching creators who are the most awesome and terrible witness man has. Because they too wage a struggle for dignity and salvation. Yes, it's true, by far the greatest number of them write for secondary reasons. Because they want fame, or money, or because they're good at it, because they cannot resist the vanity of seeing themselves in print, or because it's fun, or because just because. But there are still the others, the few who truly count, those who are serving out their dark sentence of giving word to their drama, their perplexity at this pain-wracked universe, their hopes in the midst of the horror, or of war, or of solitude . . . These are the great witnesses of their time, don't you see? These are creatures who write not with ease but with pain and suffering. They are men who somehow dream the collective dream, and who express not only their personal anxieties but the anxieties of all humanity . . . Those dreams may even be horrifying, as in Lautréamont or de Sade. But they are sacred. And they are valuable *because* they are horrifying."

"Catharsis," spoke Silvia.

Sabato looked at her, but said no more. He seemed very preoc-

179

cupied, very uneasy. He took off his glasses and pressed his fingers against his forehead, in the midst of a total silence. Then he muttered something that couldn't be caught, and left.

TO DIE FOR A CAUSE,
thought Bruno as he watched Marcelo walking away down Defensa with his friend. To die for Vietnam. Or maybe for Argentina, right here. And that sacrifice would be futile, naive, because the new order would be filled at last to overflowing with cynics and businessmen. Poor Bill volunteering for the RAF and going off to war—now burned, legless, looking pensively out the window down on Calle Morán—so that when it was over with, German businessmen, many of them Nazis or crypto-Nazis, could make juicy deals with their English counterparts, negotiating while they consumed exquisite meals and smiled lovely smiles. When it was over with? Why, in the bloody middle of the war hadn't ITT collaborated with Hitler? And General Motors surreptitiously sold him tank engines?

Of course. How could one not admire Ché Guevara. But softly, sadly, something whispered to him that in 1917 the Russian Revolution had been romantic, too, and that great poets had sung songs to it. Because every revolution, no matter how pure it may be, and especially if it *is* pure, is doomed to become a dirty police bureaucracy, while the best and brightest, as somebody called them, wound up in swamps or madhouses.

Oh yes, that was all bitterly true.

But the act of signing up in the RAF had been absolute, uncontaminated, and eternal: neither one nor one thousand canning magnates could strip Bill of that diamond. What difference did it make, then, what a revolution might turn out to be "one day"? And what was more (he thought with amazement, remembering Carlos tortured not by Christ or Marx but by Codovilla, the head of the Communist Party himself)—it didn't even matter whether the doctrine were true or not. Carlos' sacrifice was an absolute, the dignity of man had once again been saved by that one single act. In spite of his having been an incorrigible dreamer—in fact precisely for his having been one—Carlos rescued all of humanity from cynicism and

180

accommodationism, from baseness, from rot and corruption and putrescence. There the two of them went. Beside the shy aristocrat who renounced the privileges of his class walked that other boy, emaciated and humble. Perhaps to die for someone who one day would betray their lives or, worse, their faith.

There they went, down Defensa. To what terrible but wonderful fate? he wondered.

IT HAD BEEN MANY YEARS
since S. had walked through the Parque Lezama. He sat down in front of the statue of Ceres and brooded on his fate. Then he got up and went to a café on the corner of Brasil and Balcarce, where Alejandra had so many times, he thought, sat over a drink with Martín. He looked distractedly about him; there were arguments going on. *Panzeri's hysterical. No, sir, he's just a man that refuses to sell himself, that's all. All Panzeri can see is disasters,* Prode *has its good side, too, let's not kid ourselves.* A young man, almost a boy, apparently quite tall, was reading a newspaper that covered his face. The fact would never have attracted Sabato's attention if he hadn't noticed (because he lived on continual alert, and a good thing) that the young man kept peeking over the top of the paper. It might be nothing, naturally—one of those kids that always seemed to recognize him. From the little he could manage to see of the boy's face, it seemed to him he had seen him somewhere before, and more than once. But where? When?

HE'D NEVER SEEN HIM BEFORE
but he knew it was him, he'd have been able to pick him out of a crowd anywhere, and not just because of the photographs he'd seen of him but because his heart began thumping the moment he spotted him sitting over in that corner of the café—as though between himself and Sabato there existed a silent, secret signal that might set off that recognition anywhere in the world, even from among millions of people. But suddenly embarrassed by the possibility of being recognized by Sabato, Martín hid behind the newspaper he had just

bought, though he kept spying at him over the top of it, like a man committing some terrifying, forbidden act. He tried to make out the reason for that emotion, but it was hard, like reading the words of an immensely important letter rendered illegible by lack of light and the indecipherability of the handwriting—a consequence of the age of the paper, perhaps, the crinkled folds, the wearing-away of time. He concentrated intensely, trying to define that indefinable senti- ment, until at last he decided it might perhaps be something like the emotion of a boy who after long months of journeying through remote parts of the world returns to see the face of a man who he's told is his father, though he's never seen that face before in his life.

He tried to puzzle out what there was underneath that mask of bone and tired flesh, because Bruno had told him that flesh and bone were not enough to make a face, that it was something infi- nitely less physical than the rest of a man's body, the flesh qualified as it were by the moldings of the spirit, the face showing those subtle attributes by which the soul manifests itself, or tries to manifest itself. Which was the reason, Bruno had argued, that at the instant a person died his body became something somehow different, so different that in fact we say "he doesn't look like the same person," even though the body of course has the same bones, the same *stuff*, as it had a moment ago, one moment before the soul withdrew from the body and the body lay as dead as a house when those who lived in it, suffered in it, loved in it, packed up all their things and left it, forever.

Yes, thought Martín, the nuances of the lips, the little wrinkles around the eyes—those vague and imprecise glimpses of the internal inhabitants of a man, the strangers that peek out the windows of the eyes, the ambiguous, fugitive, almost translucent figures of the in- ternal ghosts of a man.

It was hard, it was almost impossible to discover all those things from a distance.

And so that man, that face, looked to Martín like barely more than the rumor of some distant conversation, rendered visible, would have looked—a conversation we knew to be infinitely important and which we almost desperately want to be able to understand.

I am an orphan, Martín told himself, sadly, and not quite sure why.

182

HE LEFT THE CAFÉ AND WENT BACK TO THE PARK.

There, steely and imperious, stood don Pedro de Mendoza, pointing with his saber down at the city that one day he had taken it in his head to found here: SANTA MARIA DE LOS BUENOS AYRES, 1536. What men!—those were the words that always came to Sabato's mind. And the women—Isabel de Guevara, Mari Sánchez, Elvira Pineda . . .

Those idiotic phrases mouthed by abstract humanism: all men are equal, all nations and peoples are equal. There were great men and dwarves, gigantic peoples and peoples as tiny as *that*.

The cruelty of the conquest. Those who demanded virtue from the pure state.

And the Conquest of the Americas for Gold!

How could one pretend that the gambler gambled for money and not out of passion.

Money was an instrument, a tool, not the end in itself.

He sat down on one of the benches, when he saw the girl in the yellow shirt coming timidly toward him.

What, had she followed him? His question was filled with irritation—he despised being followed, and feared it as well.

Yes, she had followed him, she had seen him go into the café, she had been waiting for him in the park, waiting for him to come out.

What for?

She now seemed even more nearsighted than she had at the meeting, and more reticent as well; she was not the brilliant girl of a few hours ago.

Was her name really Gentile?

It was.

But wasn't she Sephardic, something of the sort?

What did he mean, "something of the sort"? Her grandfather was from Naples.

"Napoli e poi morire," S. said, laughing at the cliché.

She seemed thinner now that he was close to her, with her sallow skin and aquiline nose.

"Your face looks Saracen."

She did not respond.

"And you're awfully nearsighted, aren't you?"

Yes, but how had he noticed?

183

He'd have to find a new job if he weren't at least that good an observer. Her way of looking at things, of walking, of holding her head forward.

Yes, when she was little she would even walk right into doors.

Then why didn't she wear glasses?

"Glasses?"

She seemed not to understand.

Yes, glasses. Eyeglasses.

It took her a long time to answer. Then she murmured; because she was ugly enough as it was.

Ugly? Who said so?

She said so. The mirror said so.

"This park was much prettier before. They've ruined it now," S. said. "And that statue they've parked over there. Did you see it?"

Yes, she'd seen it. Sort of a rocket ship to Mars on top of a truckbed.

"You're funny. I like your sense of humor. What you said about structuralism back there."

She did not respond.

Didn't she have a good sense of humor?

Uh-huh, in public.

What did that mean?

When she was alone with another person she was shy.

"Lord, that's the opposite of everybody else."

She knew.

And why had she followed him?

It wasn't the first time.

This alarmed Sabato. And for what purpose, he'd like to know.

"Don't be angry. I thought the meeting today had irritated you, disturbed you. We didn't want that. I, at least, didn't want that."

"So others might have, huh?"

Silence.

All right, that was clear enough, then. But why the devil did he have to go through that cross-examination in front of people like Araujo? He hadn't asked Araujo to read his books. He never said Araujo had to agree with him. Before Araujo had ever even been born, S. had already studied not only Marx but Hegel. Not in cafés,

184

though, mind you. He'd studied them while he was risking his life, for years.

Yes, she knew that.

So leave him alone, all of them. Life was hard enough without having to put up with that kind of young turk.

"Come on, let's walk awhile," he said to her with sudden affection, taking her arm. "I won't let you walk into the statues."

They stopped to contemplate two bronze lions.

"Can you see them?" he asked with that sadism sometimes provoked in him by people he liked.

Yes, more or less. *"The pensive lions,"* wasn't it?

"Yes, but I should have written 'sternly pensive.' The minute you're the least bit careless, you start writing by approximation, you botch it. *I* do, anyway. Look at their exact expression."

"Me?" she asked in ironic helplessness. "I'd have to get too close."

"Then you'll have to take my word for it—their expression is stern and pensive at the same time. Curious. I wonder what the sculptor had in mind."

"Alejandra," the girl murmured, her voice wavering.

"What?"

Was she alive? Had she ever lived?

S. answered her with a certain degree of sternness. Her too?

"Come over here, sit down. Not long ago, these benches were made of wood. A little more and we'll be sitting on plastic benches and chewing pills instead of food. Fortunately I won't live to see it. You notice, I take it, that I'm a reactionary? Or at least so you Marxists think me."

"Not all Marxists."

"Whew, thank goodness. All I have to do is say 'myth' or 'metaphysics,' and somebody accuses me of taking money from the U.S. embassy. And speaking of the United States, do you know something? Some guy from some U.S. university somewhere noticed, or I mean wrote in his dissertation, that my novel started out in front of the statue of Ceres. Right over there."

"So?"

"The goddess of fertility. Oedipus."

And had he done that on purpose?

185

"Are you serious?"

Of course she was.

"No, you goose. Back then there were lots and lots of statues here. I remember I had chosen Athena first. But I really didn't like it very much, I don't know why. So finally I wrote 'Ceres.' "

"So it's entirely possible that your unconscious led you to do it."

"Possible."

"*The Tunnel* also starts with an image of maternity."

"So I've been told. People writing dissertations discover everything. I mean they discover things you didn't know yourself."

"But then you agree."

"In a narrow sense, no. But I do think that if you write by abandoning yourself to your impulses, something happens like what happens when you dream. Your deepest obsessions begin coming out. My mother was a powerful woman, and she grabbed us, in a manner of speaking, the last two of us, Arturo and me—almost imprisoned us. You might almost say I saw the world through a window."

"The overprotective mother."

"Oh please, jargon. Yes, perhaps I've been unconsciously revolving around, orbiting around, beating around the bush of my mother. Another guy does a Jungian analysis, symbols and all that. No, not *one* guy; there are several of them doing it. Must be something to it, then. But sometimes it isn't what they think, or what some of them think, I mean—it isn't what you read. If that were true, you see, when we dreamed about undersea depths it would be because we'd been reading Jung. As though before Jung, that is, nobody dreamed about the bottom of the ocean. It's just the opposite, of course: Jung exists thanks to those dreams."

"You've often said that art and dreaming stem from the same root. Or more or less said that."

"Yes, of course, at least at first. At that moment when the artist submerges into his subconscious—like the moment at which one falls off to sleep. But then there comes a second moment, which is a moment of expression. Note carefully—*ex-pression*, a pressing outward. That is why art is liberating and dreams not—dreams don't come out. Art does, it's a language, an attempt to communicate with

186

others. You cry out your obsessions to other men and women, even though it be with symbols. But in that case, you are awake, and mixed in with those symbols there are things you've read, all sorts of ideas, the creative spirit or will, and the critical spirit. That is where art is radically distinct from dream. Do you see? But you can't seriously make art without that initial submersion into the unconscious. That's why what these fools suggest is so absurd—this obligation to produce national and popular art. As though before you went to bed you told yourself, Now we'll just dream ourselves a nice national, popular dream."

Silvia laughed.

"So you're descended from Neapolitans."

No, on her mother's side it was Spaniards.

"Oh, well, perfect. Italians, Spaniards, Moors, Jews—my theory of the new Argentina."

What theory?

"Argentina is the result of three great forces, three great peoples—the Spaniards, the Italians, and the Jews. If you think about it, you'll see that our virtues and our defects can be traced back to them. Of course there are also Basques and Frenchmen and Yugoslavs and Poles and Syrians and Germans. But the fundamental part comes from the Spaniards, the Italians, and the Jews. Three great peoples, but each with certain defects which . . . Need I be more specific? In Jerusalem, I was talking to an Israeli man who said to me, 'Isn't it a miracle? In the midst of a desert? Surrounded by trillions of Arabs? In spite of war?'

" 'Oh come on, man,' I said, 'it's *because* of all that, not *in spite* of it. The day this country is at peace, the day that Jehovah decides, this won't last a minute.' Can you imagine, Silvia, two million Jews without a war to fight? Two million presidents of the republic? Every one of them with his own ideas for housing, the army, education, language? Try running *that* country! The guy selling you a sandwich talks to you about Heidegger. And what about Spanish individualism? And Italian cynicism? Yes, three great peoples. But what a combination, my god! The only thing that could have saved us in Argentina was a good healthy national war, say fifty years ago."

"That sounds awfully pessimistic."

"It is."

"So why do you keep fighting, struggling the way you do, then? Why do you insist on staying here?"

"Don't ask *me*."

He looked at her warily.

"Do you belong to some Peronist organization?"

She hesitated.

"I mean some Marxist organization with Peronist tendencies."

"Yes . . . Or really, no . . . I don't know, I'm confused, I've got these friends . . . we'll have to see . . ."

"But you *are* a Marxist?"

"Oh, yes."

"Look. I do still believe, as I did back when I was a . . . how shall I put it . . . a catechumen, that Marx is perhaps the single most misleading philosopher of contemporary thought. But then I began to notice several things . . . Do you remember Marx's surprise, his perplexity at the Greek tragedies?"

"No."

"They made him think, so to speak, about how those ancient poets still have the power to stir us, in spite of the fact that the social structures out of which they arose had long disappeared. He would have had to admit that there were 'metahistorical' values in art, which admission would have cost him greatly. Abashed him, one might even say. Do you study philosophy?"

"No, literature," she admitted, as though such a thing were vaguely ridiculous.

"I'd have thought you'd be more interested in philosophy."

"I probably am. I read more philosophy than literature. But I've read very little, really, and very badly, I think."

"Don't worry. I haven't studied very much either. I'm little more than a writer that's been battling with the question of man for thirty years or so. The crisis of man, I mean to say. The little philosophy I know, I've learned by stumbling across it, by way of my personal quests in science, and surrealism, and in revolution. It isn't the product of a library but of my own agonies. I have huge lacunae, just as I do in literature, in everything. How can I explain it to you?"

He remained silent awhile, thinking.

"It's as though I were an explorer in search of a treasure hidden

188

deep in the jungle, and to find it I've had to climb dangerous mountains, cross swollen rivers, terrible deserts. I've been lost many times, not knowing where to turn. I think it was nothing but the instinct of life that saved me. And so—I know that road, I mean I have lived it, I didn't learn it out of a geography book. Yet there are infinite things that lie somewhere off to the side of that one road that I have no idea of. That I'm not even interested in. I've only been able to learn those things which I have felt passionately about, those things that were integral to the search for that treasure."

Silvia seemed to push her head even farther out than was her custom, scrutinizing him.

"Yes, I understand that," she said, her voice clipped.

S. looked at her tenderly.

"Wonderful," he said. "You've been saved from the professors of literature. Though actually, they could never do somebody like you any harm."

He stood up.

"Come, let's walk a little."

As they walked, he explained:

"At virtually the same time I got involved in physics I got involved in Marxism. So somehow I managed to live through, actually to be a part of, the two most unsettling experiences of our times. In 1951 I published what might be called the balance sheet of those two experiences: *Hombres y engranajes*. I was almost crucified for it."

His laughter was pained.

"Do you see? I talked about that other form of alienation, technology. And technolatry. And I was accused of being a reactionary because I had 'attacked' science. The inheritance of enlightened thought. And so it seems that in order to be on the side of social justice you have to fall to your knees before a nine-volt battery."

He bent over, picked up a small stone, and threw it into the pond. After a moment, he went on:

"Now it's not so dishonorable, after Marcuse and the rebellion by a generation of American hippies and the revolt of the students in Paris. But then I was only a poor South American scribbler."

His voice was bitter.

"But technological alienation comes from the *misuse* of the machine," Silvia said. "The machine itself is amoral, beyond ethical

189

values. It's like a rifle: it can be used in one direction or in the other. In a community whose highest value was the human life, that alienation would never occur."

"Up to now, there's no society that's proven what you've just asserted. In the great collectivist countries there's the same sort of roboticization as in the United States."

"That may be temporary. On the other hand, how are we supposed to solve the problems of humanity, the exponential increase in population, without producing food and objects in massive quantities? Mass production implies science and technology. Can you reject technology when three-fourths of the world is starving?"

"Poverty, social injustice of any kind, ought to be abolished. What I'm saying is that we ought not to go from the disasters of underdevelopment to the disasters of overdevelopment. From poverty to a consumer society. Look at young people in the United States. A more debilitating servitude than the servitude of poverty itself. I don't know but what hunger is preferable to drugs."

"But then what is it that you propose?"

"I'm not exactly sure. What I am sure of is that we should be aware of this terrible problem. Now that we're at the midpoint of development, we should not be so stupid as to repeat the catastrophic mistakes of overdevelopment."

"If poor countries don't develop themselves, though, they are simply helping to prolong their enslavement. Going to the mines in Bolivia to speak out against materialism—isn't that just one kind of *preciosité*?"

"I've never approved of exploitation, and you know it. What I've said time and time again, and will continue to say, although at the present time it's neither easy nor pleasant to say it, is that it's pointless to wage bloody revolutions if they're waged so that one day houses can be filled with useless knickknacks and so kids can be hypnotized into idiots by television. If we're going to judge by the results, there are very very poor countries that are better off than the United States. Vietnam. With what resources did it defeat the most technologically advanced country in the world? With faith, and the spirit of self-sacrifice, and love of one's country. Spiritual values."

"All right. But you don't explain how you propose to feed a

population that's increasing exponentially—because you were talking about useless *knickknacks*, not food."

"I don't know how. World population might have to be stabilized. But at any rate I know what I *don't* want to see. I don't want to see supercapitalism, or supersocialism either. I don't want superstates with robots. In Israel somebody was scornfully commenting on one particular kibbutz—it seemed they manufactured shoes, I think it was, three or four times more expensive than some factory or other in Tel Aviv. But who says the mission of a kibbutz is to manufacture cheap shoes? Its mission is to make men and women. Do you have the time?"

Silvia put her eye down to her watch. It was ten after seven. They were on the terrace of the old mansion. Leaning on the railing, S. told her that the river used to run right down there, where now there was nothing but madly racing cars. *Faded old park*, recited S., as though to himself.

"What?"

Nothing. He was just thinking.

"The great myth of Progress," he said aloud, at last. "The Industrial Revolution. With Bible in hand (because it's always a good idea to do your dirty work under honorable pretexts) whole civilizations were destroyed, colonizers waded into ancient African and Polynesian cultures with fire and bloody sword and razed them to the ground. *'They left not one stone upon another.'* And why? So they could load up the people they had just conquered with vulgarities made in Manchester, so they could ruthlessly and pitilessly exploit them. In the Belgian Congo the native people's hands would be cut off for stealing some trifle—cut off by men who'd stolen the whole country from the poor creatures. And they didn't just enslave them, they took their ancient myths away from them, their harmony with the cosmos, their innocent felicity. Technological barbarism, European arrogance. Now we are paying for that terrible sin. Kids addicted to drugs, a generation lost on the streets of London and New York are paying for it."

"Aren't you making romantic nostalgia out of leprosy and malnutrition and dysentery?"

S. looked at her with tender irony.

191

"Let's get off this subject, Silvia. I'd rather talk about something else, something that got left hanging back in the café. Of course Marxism goes right to the mark about many, many social and political wrongs in this society. But there are other facts that resist."

"Resist?" Silvia craned her neck toward him.

"Of course. Art. Dreams. Myth, the religious spirit."

Shyly (such contrast between the outspoken, contentious Silvia of the café, a woman full of irony and brilliance, and this woman in the park), she argued that Marxist atheism was more political than theological. Its object had not been the death of God but rather the destruction of capitalism. It had criticized religion insofar as religion constituted an obstacle to the revolution.

S. looked at her with peaceful incredulity.

He didn't agree?

"We know very well that the Church supported exploitation. I mentioned the Bible in Africa as an example of that very thing. But I'm talking about something else, I'm not talking about the political attitude of the Church but about its religious spirit. Marx was *a true atheist*, he honestly believed that religion was a fraud and a hoax. It was neither more nor less than worshippers of the spirit of science believed."

Then he laughed.

"Television is the opium of the people. *That* is the true aphorism. But don't get angry. I have great admiration for Marx. He, along with Kierkegaard, set in motion the vindication of concrete man. But I'm referring now to his faith in science, which, as you well know, has carried us into yet another form of alienation.

"That's where I diverge from his theory. As I do from the theories of neo-Marxists like Kosik. Underneath, they're rationalists."

"But dialectic thought is not the simple dialectics of yesterday."

"Dialectic thought or not, it's still abstract. And they want to rip the veil off everything, explain everything. I'm not, of course, talking about those people who 'explain' Shakespeare by reference to the primitive accumulation of capital. That's a joke."

He sat down and was silent, thoughtful for a while. Then he added:

"Look what happened with myth. Those guys that wrote the *Encyclopédie* just laughed—pure mystification, a hoax. And there you

192

have, by the way, the root of our current confusion: demystification becomes the same as demythification. The men of science split their sides. You've never known these people like I have; I've worked right next to them, Nobel Prize winners, at research centers. But there's one case I think of as particularly pathetic, and that's the case of Lévy-Bruhl. Do you know him?"

"No. I only go as far as Lévi-Strauss. Are they related?"

"Very funny. This one's with a *y*. He embarked on a work in which he proposed to *demonstrate* the ascent of primitive mind to scientific consciousness. You know what happened to the poor bugger? He got old trying. But he was honest, and finally he had to admit his defeat; at last he recognized that that much-bruited 'primitive' mentality is *not* an inferior state of mankind. And that in a man of today there still exist two mentalities. What a horror, don't you see? Observe that this sort of 'positive' mentality (the adjective makes me laugh, I can't help it) brought to the West the notion that scientific culture is superior to the culture of, say, the Polynesians. What do you think about that? And that science is superior to art, naturally. When I left physics, Professor Houssay declared he'd never speak to me ever again. Did you know that?"

"No."

"Enlightened thinking insists that mankind has progressed as it has grown further from the mythopoetic state. This was famously stated in 1820 by an illustrious cretin, Thomas Love Peacock, who said, 'a poet in our day is a barbarian in a civilized community.' What do you think of that?"

Silvia pondered.

"Poor Lévy-Bruhl's excavations revealed to just what degree that sort of pretension was a misapprehension, not to mention outrageous and arrogant. What had to happen happened: banished by thought, myth took refuge in art, which turned out to be a profanation of myth though at the same time its vindication. Which proves two things to you: first, that myth is unconquerable, that it is a deep need in man. And second, that art will save us from total alienation, from that brutal and mindless separation of magical thinking from logical thinking. Mankind is all things at once. That is why the novel, which has one foot on each side, is perhaps the single activity which best expresses the total being."

He bent down and arranged some stones into an R.

"Not long ago, a German critic asked me why we Latin Americans have great novelists but no great philosophers. Because we're barbarians, I told him, because we were saved, fortunately, from the great rationalist schism. As the Russians were saved, and the Scandinavians, and the Spaniards—those on the periphery of things, one might say. If you want our *Weltanschauung*, I told him, look to our novels, not to our pure thought."

He set the stones into a square.

"And I'm referring, of course, to the novels as a totality, not to simple plots and the like. Naturally people come to us from Europe and tell us that in novels there are no ideas. Objectivists. Great heaven! So long as mankind is at the center of all fiction (and there are no novels about tables or gastropods), that objection is idiotic. Ezra Pound said that we cannot afford the luxury of ignoring the philosophical and theological ideas of Dante, nor of overlooking those passages in his metaphysical novel or poem which best and most clearly express them. And it is not only ideas incarnate that are legitimate; pure Platonic ideas are legitimate as well. Was it not a man who reached those heights? You wouldn't be able to write a novel with Plato as a character, under those assumptions, unless you wiped out a good part of his spirit. The novel of today, at least in its most ambitious manifestations, should attempt the total description of mankind, from its deliriums to its logic. Is there some Mosaic commandment that forbids that? Who hands down the absolute Law of what a novel *ought* to be? '*Tous les éscarts lui appartiennent,*' said Valéry with reproachful disgust. He thought he was demolishing it, when he was actually praising it. Rationalist! And I say 'novel' because there's nothing else so hybrid. Actually, we would have to invent an art that mixed pure ideas with dance, cries and shouts with geometry. A thing, a 'work,' produced in a hermetic, sacred place, a ritual in which gestures and movements would be merged with the purest thought, and philosophic discourse with the dances of Zulu warriors. A combination of Kant and Hieronymus Bosch, Picasso and Einstein, Rilke and Genghis Khan. But so long as we are unable to produce a means of expression as beautifully integrated as that, let's at least defend the right to produce monstrous novels."

He moved the little stones about again, this time once more into the shape of an R.

"Only through art is reality revealed—*all* reality, I mean. And we're told that this mythification of art is reactionary, antiquated or outmoded, a relic of the eighteenth century, leftovers from the Romantics. Of course it is. The proto-Romantic genius Vico saw very clearly what many thinkers still couldn't see many years later. He began what Jung and, paradoxically—because they come at it from the side of science worship—Lévy-Bruhl and Freud were to do much later. The ideas of German Romanticism have been forgotten or deprecated by this pretentious culture. They have to be polished up and brought out onto the stage again. Schopenhauer said that there are moments when reaction is progress, just as sometimes progress is reactionary. Today, progress means recovering that old idea. The philosophers of German Romanticism were, after Vico, the first to see the thing clearly. Just as they intuited the idea of structure, a correct idea even though the scientists had rejected it. Look . . ."

He held up one of the little stones.

"The scientific mentality works like this: this stone is feldspar, and this feldspar is in turn composed of molecules, and those molecules of atoms of such and such a makeup. From the complex to the simple, from the whole to its parts. *Analysis*, de-composition. That has been the way of things."

Silvia looked at him.

"I'm not talking about technical progress. Of course when you talk about stones or atoms that all works very well. I'm talking about the calamity that ensues when a person presumes that the same method can be used for mankind. A man is not a stone, you can't break him down into liver, eyes, pancreas, metacarpals. Man is a whole, a structure, in which no part means anything, has any significance, without the whole, in which each organ influences all the others, and the others in turn influence it. Your liver goes bad, and your eyes turn yellow. How can there be eye specialists? Science cut everything into tiny pieces. And the most dangerous thing about that is that it cut the soul out of the body. In the past, if you didn't have a boil or you hadn't actually broken a leg, you weren't sick, you were *un malade imaginaire*."

195

He put the stone back in its place.

He stood up then and leaned on the railing.

"Down there you have the world we have come to, the product of science. Soon we'll have to live in glass cages. My lord, how can that be anyone's dream?"

Silvia was meditative. He turned and sat down again.

"Myth, like art, is a language. It expresses a certain type of reality in the only way that reality can be expressed, and it is *irreducible* to any other form of language. I'll give you a simple example: you go to a concert to hear a quartet by Béla Bartók, you leave the hall and somebody asks you to 'explain' it to him. No one would ever do such an idiotic thing, of course. Yet that is precisely what we do with a myth. Or with a work of literature. People are forever asking me to explain what the 'Report on the Blind' means. And the same thing happens with dreams. People want you to explain a nightmare to them. But that dream expresses a reality in the *only* way the reality can be expressed."

He stopped to think.

"It's strange," he finally said, "that a man like Kosik should allow art its revelatory role and yet deny that role to myth. That's where you see the remnants of the Enlightenment. But when he talks about myth he says—more or less, mind you—that thanks to dialectic logic we can go from simple opinion to science, from myth to truth. You see? Myth is a kind of lie, a mystification. One achieves 'progress' by moving from magical thought to rational thought. One sees the same thing in Freud, with all his genius. And by the way, I've always been struck by a duality in Freud. A Janus-faced genius: on one side, his intuition of the unconscious, of the dark, shadowy recesses of existence makes him a brother of the Romantics; on the other, his positivistic education and training make him another Dr. Arrambide."

"Arrambide?"

"Oh, you don't know him."

He remained thoughtful for a moment, and then once more spoke to her:

"Light versus darkness. It's futile, these men have got the idea stuck in their heads. They've always been convinced that mythological creations must have an intelligible meaning. And that if it's

196

hidden with fantastic and symbolic images, it must be 'unmasked.' It's strange what happens with Kosik . . . When you read his book, you'll see what a remarkable man he was. And yet . . . On the one hand he says that art is revolutionary, demythifying, since it leads up out of false ideas to reality itself. Yet he doesn't understand myth. A dream, for example, is always a pure truth. How can a dream lie? The same is true of art, when it is profound art. A principle of law may be a mystification, it may be the instrument or tool used by a privileged class to legally promote or eternalize itself. But how can the *Quixote* be a mystification?"

For the first time in a long while, during which she seemed to have turned inward on herself, thinking, Silvia commented:

"I agree. But I think there's some truth in Marxism, when one considers that art doesn't emerge from a void but rather out of a society. There is, in some sense, a relationship between art and society. A homologous relation."

"Of course there is *some* relationship between art and society, as there is *some* relationship between a nightmare and everyday life. But that word 'some' has to be very carefully examined, because that is where all the errors come from. *Because* Proust was a boy from a certain genteel level of society, his literature is the corrupt expression of an unjust society, you will be told. Do you see? There is a relationship, but there's no cause for it to be a *direct* relationship. It might be inverse, or antagonistic, a reaction or revolt. Not a reflection, that famous reflection. It's a *creative* act by which mankind enriches reality. Marx himself declared that it's mankind that produces mankind. Which is so diametrically opposed to that celebrated *reflection* that it might even be seen as a breaking of the mirror. And in this as in so many manifestations of Marxism, you have to take your hat off to Hegel and his idea of the self-creation of man. That being who creates himself does so out of everything that the subjective spirit is capable of creating—from locomotive to poems. Let's go have some coffee."

They walked toward Brasil and Defensa.

"I had neither the patience nor the desire to explain all this at that absurd kaffeeklatsch we were having. And besides, there's no call for me to have to answer to little pedants like Araujo, who discovered Marxism twenty-seven minutes ago in some little man-

197

ual. These revolutionary types see nothing but disguised class interests behind every work of art produced by a member of the privileged class. They do a great deal of damage, because then people come along who pretend to refute Marx by refuting these caricatures. Marx admired the monarchist Balzac but he laughed at a Communist named Vallès who'd written a book named, if I recall correctly, *L'Insurgé*. And he would have had contempt for the proletarian literature that Russia produces with so much blood, sweat, tears, and toil. Between those particular products and the works of that snob from the Sixth Arrondisement who swooned over dukes, there can be no choice—the writer who'll last will be the high-class child of gentility."

They walked past the lions again.

"It's that artistic creation comes out of the *whole* of the human being. Don't you see? The *whole* man, not simply the conscious part, the part that contains the ideas—which may of course be erroneous, and which generally are—even Aristotle made huge mistakes. Creation comes out of regions which are untouched by economics. There are still Oedipuses today, as there were in the time of Sophocles. Oedipuses have nothing to do with Greek economic or financial questions. Problems of life and death, finiteness and infinity, suffering and hope—limits of the human condition that have existed since man was first man. That is why the tragic Greeks continue to move us even though the social structures out of which their tragedies sprung have ceased to exist."

When they came to the café and Sabato saw that it was after eight, he told her he had to leave. One day, maybe, they'd have another talk.

When?

He didn't know.

But could she write him?

Yes.

Would he answer?

Yes.

198

A SORT OF IMMORTALITY OF THE SOUL,

thought Bruno, not a true immortality. Because that Alejandra who
lived on inside Martín's soul, who had been sheltered in the boy's
heart and memory, burning yet fragmentary, like glowing coals buried in the ashes, would go on living as long as Martín lived, and for
as long as he himself, Bruno, lived, and perhaps for as long as Marcos Molina lived, and even Bordenave and other men (magnanimous
or evil, distant or close-by) who had once felt the touch of her spirit,
some wonderful or terrible fragment of her spirit. But what would
happen then? Growing fainter and fainter through the years, turning
day by day less clear, more ambiguous, becoming with the passage
of time mere pieces, and the pieces themselves more and more jumbled and confused and distant, like the recollection of those countries we visited in our youth and which later were devastated by
storms and catastrophes, by war, by death and disillusions—great
regions of that recollection wiped out by the slow, gradual disap-
pearance of that which had once touched and been touched by Alejandra, her soul shrinking away faster and faster, growing older with
the aging years of her survivors, dying with the death of those who
had in one way or another taken part in that shared magic, in the
love or desire, in delicate sentiment or in ignoble prostitutions. And
then, little by little, the final death would overtake it. Not that body
which had once stood naked before a trembling Martín in that old
Mirador de Barracas, but now that spirit which still lived on, frag-
mentarily, in the soul of Martín and in his own, Bruno's, memory.
Not authentic immortality, then, but a sort of put off, postponed
mortality, a mortality shared out among those who reflected or re-
fracted Alejandra's spirit. And when they at last died (Martín and
Bruno, Marcos Molina, Bordenave, and even that Molinari who'd
made Martín vomit), and their confidants died as well, there would
fade away forever the last memory of a memory, and even those
reflections of recollections glimpsed by people farther off, and the
faint signs and portents, the glimmerings, the degradations, of purest
love and most depraved sex.

"What? What?" Bruno asked then, Martín answering that it was
early in the morning that he had felt somebody shaking him furiously by the shoulders. And had seen, thinking it was a dream, the
hallucinated face of Alejandra hovering above him, just when Martín

had reached the point of expecting nothing whatever from her. And in a grave, trembling voice, he told Bruno that she had said to him:

"I just wanted to see you. Or rather I *needed* to see you. Get dressed, I want to get out of here."

While Martín dressed, she lit a cigarette with trembling hand, and then went to make coffee. Fascinated, Martín could not take his eyes off her even as he went on dressing; she was wearing a fur coat, and she looked like she had come from some party, though she wore no makeup. She was thin, worn-looking, and she had bags under her eyes. But even more, she appeared to have dressed quickly and carelessly, like a person who has had to flee someplace without wasting a moment, from a fire, for instance, or an earthquake. He went to her and tried to put his arms around her, but she shouted at him not to touch her, and he froze. She had screamed with that sort of savage glare in the eyes which he knew so well; it broke forth when she was tense and coiled like a spring about to break. But then at once she apologized, and she dropped the cup she was holding.

"See?" she said, as though in explanation.

Her hands kept trembling, as though she had a high fever. Martín left the kitchen to go wash his hands, though mostly to put his thoughts in order. When he came back in, the coffee was ready and Alejandra was sitting pensively at the kitchen table. Martín knew it was best not to ask questions, so they drank their coffee in silence. Afterward, she asked for an aspirin and she chewed it, as she always did, and swallowed it without water. Then she had another cup of coffee. After a while she got up, as though revisited by that restlessness, and suggested they go out.

"Let's walk down along the river. Or better yet, go up on the bridge," she added on second thought.

A sailor turned his head and Martín thought, with pity, that the man must have taken her for a whore, with that fur coat and ravaged face, and at that hour of the night.

"Don't worry so much," she muttered in a dry, flat voice, intuiting what he was thinking. "He'll never guess it right."

They climbed up on the bridge and perched on the railing, halfway across, looking out toward the mouth of the river. Like they always did, like they had done back in those infinitely happier times, those times that at the moment (thought Bruno) must have seemed to Martín to belong to some previous lifetime, to some distant incarnation that one can only barely, dimly remember, like a dream. It was one of those cold August nights, cloudy, and the southwest wind blew across them. But Alejandra threw open her coat as though she wanted to freeze herself; she breathed anxiously, deeply. At last she buttoned up her coat, squeezed his arm, and turning her eyes downward, said:

"This is good for me—being with you, seeing a neighborhood like that, where people work, make simple, healthy, useful things like screws and wheels. I feel all of a sudden like I'd like to be a man, be one of them, have one of those small fates."

She fell silent, thinking, then lit a cigarette off the one she was just finishing.

"We used to have spiritual exercises, retreats."

Martín looked at her uncomprehendingly. She laughed that hard, almost macabre laugh of hers.

"Didn't you ever hear of Father Laburu? He had some descriptions of Hell that would terrify you. *The eternity of the punishment— a sphere the size of the earth, a drop of water dripping and wearing it away. And when that sphere is worn totally away, another one begins. And then another, and another, girls, millions of spheres the size of this entire planet. Infinite spheres. Imagine, girls. And all that time, you are burning in the flames of hell.* That all seems so innocent and almost sweet to me today. Hell is here."

She fell silent again, sucking eagerly at the cigarette.

Far off, downriver, some boat's horn sounded.

"How far away leaving Buenos Aires seems now!"

Martín reflected that Alejandra was not thinking about going on a trip, but about death.

"I'd like to die of cancer," she said, "and suffer terribly. One of those cancers that tortures you for a year, while you rot."

She laughed that hard laugh again, then fell silent for a good while. "Let's go," she finally said.

They walked toward Vuelta de la Rocha, not talking. When they came to Calle Australia she stopped, spun him around to face her, and looking straight at him with eyes like the eyes of a woman delirious with fever, asked him if he loved her.

201

"What an idiotic question," Martín answered in grief and desolation.

"Well, listen to what I'm about to tell you. It's a terrible mistake you make in loving me. And a much worse mistake I make in asking you to. But I need it, can you understand that? I need it. Even if I never see you again. I need to know that somewhere in this horrible filthy city, in some corner of this hell, you are there, and that you love me."

Like drops of water issuing from the dry, hard cracks in a burning stone—that was the way a few drops of tears came from her eyes and rolled down a face hard and wasted.

Between that Alejandra and the Alejandra whom he had met in a park in Buenos Aires a year or two ago, there had fallen an abyss of dark and gloomy centuries.

And suddenly, without saying good-bye, almost running, she was walking away down Australia in the direction of her house.

Bruno watched how Martín looked at him with that same interrogative look he almost always had, as though in Bruno Martín might find the key to that indecipherable hieroglyph which his relationship to Alejandra presented to him. But Bruno made no response to the mute interrogation, and in fact sat thinking about this return of Martín's, after fifteen years, to the places that reawoke those stubborn memories. Impelled by the solitude and loneliness of his adolescence, at the age of eighteen Martín had wandered all these paths in Parque Lezama, and now, at thirty-three, he was wandering them again, now a man, that is, but one who had never managed to free himself of that weight—a man who in some way Bruno saw clumsily but tenderly summed up in that white penknife he still carried and that he had played with so many times as he sat with Alejandra or with Bruno himself, opening and closing it mechanically, looking at it without seeing it, while his spirit stammered out words of love or desperation. The simple old paths of dirt and gravel had now been made hard with asphalt, the statues had been taken away (with the one miraculous exception of that copy of Ceres, at the feet of which the magic had all started), the wooden benches were gone now, out of that stupid Argentine propensity for leaving no trace of the small but for that very reason moving past, thought Bruno. No, it was no

202

longer the Parque Lezama of his teenage years, and his melancholy was no doubt helped by that abstract, frigid cement bench he sat on and from which he could view, from afar, that same statue which in 1953 had witnessed Alejandra's silent call. No, Martín didn't say that in so many words, of course he didn't. His reticence, or modesty, kept him from talking about anything as meaningful as time, or death. But Bruno could guess at them, because that boy (that man?) represented virtually his own past, and he could decipher his most secret thoughts from words as trivial as "gosh, what a shame, those concrete benches, those little asphalt paths, I don't know, I think," as he opened and closed his penknife in a way that seemed aimed at controlling the state of the workings of his thoughts. It was out of those kinds of trivia that Bruno reconstructed his true feelings, then, and he could picture the young man sitting that afternoon, contemplating the statue of Ceres for hours on end, until night fell, once again, over the solitary creatures that still sat in the park, brooding on their destinies, and over the lovers attempting their secret violence or receiving the modest magic of their love. And perhaps (or surely) he heard once more the muted horn of some distant boat, as he had in that not to be believed time of their first meeting. And perhaps (or surely) his clouded eyes absurdly, painfully sought her out among the shadows.

QUIQUE

"THAT SABATO MADE ME WORK IN HIS NOVEL WITHOUT PAYING ME. You people can tell him he'd have been better off writing a Report on Pigeons than that windy statement of his on the visually handicapped. Have you ever seen such a dirty, disgusting animal in your life? And all those people that go to the Plaza Mayo to feed the beasts little seeds and bread crumbs—poor little pigeon, the dove of peace, indeed. And that old pussycat Picasso, too, that *billionaire du communisme*. One Sunday when nobody in particular was around he started doodling, didn't know quite where to start, *l'embarras du choix*, you know, but at any rate he managed to put *hors de combat* several of those flying reptiles, who'll never be heard of again, thank god, before that is he began to be lionized by the mob."

203

"Quique, please—chemical element, essential to life, six letters."

"Sorry, Maruja. I can barely tell iron from bronze. My celebrated education, planned to the last detail by my mother, who wouldn't even let me cross the street. Example: since I was this very, well, *protected* child, and I never had the opportunity to see a cow live and direct as you might say, and since *ma mère* had taught me that one should never ever kill an animal, but had neglected to explain where steaks came from—which didn't mean that I wasn't going to think about that sort of dilemma, because one thing had to be said for me, I was a child with an inquisitive sort of soul—do you know what I wound up thinking?"

No, nobody could possibly imagine what Quique might have wound up thinking under those or any other circumstances.

"I wound up thinking that you got steak by peeling the crust off a breaded cutlet."

So when he finally realized, or when somebody told him—because there was always some perverse soul lurking, to tell one things—that you cut steak off a cow with a long knife, he was destroyed.

"And then later, when there was nothing to do for it but send me off to school, things did not significantly improve, in virtue of that pedagogical system which consists of explaining what the stomach is by telling you that it's like a bagpipe. The perfect example for kids from the green isles of Britain, but hardly the thing for little Argentine urchins like ourselves. Who'll probably never have need of much anatomy anyway."

"You sound exactly like yourself in Sabato's novel."

"There you go! There you go! If that's not the last straw! Ever since that much-admired gentleman stuck me in that novel of his, the whole world throws my own caricature up to me. Base and calumnious! There really ought to be a law against people like that. And he should thank heaven that my many duties in the Fourth Estate prevent me from producing literature, or else he'd have good reason, I assure you, to regret his attack on me. What a caricature I'd write! Or really not a caricature at all—all I'd have to do is describe him exactly the way he is. Ha!"

At which moment Sabato came in and Quique said:

"I've heard wonders about your appearance on TV, *mon cher.*"

To which the other man, looking at him mistrustfully and somewhat ambiguously, replied, "You don't say."

The conversation went on.

At last S. got up to leave.

"I said I needed to talk to you," Sabato said coldly to Beba.

He stalked out, and Beba ran after him, grabbing his arm. What a pain in the ass, why was he so full of himself?!

"It's not that I'm full of myself!" he shouted, when they were at the door. "I wanted to talk to you about Marcelo. I told you that."

"When did you tell me?"

"The minute I walked in. But you never hear a word a person says when that clown's around."

IT DID HIM GOOD TO BREATHE THE NIGHT AIR,
there was something in the freezing air that seemed to speak of purity
It is colder now
there are many stars
we are sailing, drifting.
I beg you (you who may read this note)
form with your lips the words that were our names.
I will tell you everything we have learned.
I will tell you everything.

HE WAS WALKING SLOWLY ALONG TOWARD THE PLAZA
BOULOGNE-SUR-MER
when he heard Beba behind him calling his name:

"Wait! Wait, dammit!"

No, Marcelo had left hours ago, quite awhile ago anyway.

No, nobody knew what was going on.

It was all so complicated, because Marcelo never talked to anybody, you know that.

She fell silent and stood looking at him, sadly: she was no longer the brilliant Beba of years gone by, or at least of other places. She was not the same Beba of just short minutes ago, in fact.

"I need to see him."

205

Well, she'd tell him when she saw him, or when he called.

No, she didn't know where he might be living, she hadn't known anything since he took all his things and left his room.

She was scared.

Scared? What was there to be scared of?

She didn't know, once somebody had come to his room.

Sabato recalled the boy at the café: was he short, stout-looking, and pretty badly dressed?

Yes, that was him.

Beba had a feeling, just a hunch, that was all it was.

What was that?

Beba had the impression the boy was a guerrilla.

Why?

Just a feeling, she said. Little things.

But Marcelo wasn't the person to be mixed up in some guerrilla group, Sabato tried to calm her. Could she imagine him killing somebody, carrying a gun?

No, of course not. But he could do other kinds of things.

Like what.

Helping somebody in danger, for example. Hiding people. That kind of thing.

SABATO HAD HARDLY LEFT
when Quique raised his eyes and his two arms to heaven, in a show of thanks.

"Go on, now, tell us some more about transplants."

"You people would kill for a good story, wouldn't you. Giddy creatures. But I am a person of large theories. Let me give you one didactic example:

"The young Negro man Jefferson Delano Smith kicks the bucket and his heart is transplanted into the chest of one John Schwarzer, a miner, whose name from that moment onward will either be Schwarzer-Smith or the science of jurisprudence will be pure bullshit. One might write the transplant donor's name in lowercase, you could do that I suppose, like this:

SCHWARZER-smith

206

in some proportion to the volume of the heart to the total volume of the rather robust miner's body that it now inhabits. But to continue: *En suite*, this cardiac centaur receives the transplanted kidneys of Miss Nancy Henderson, and his name then becomes Schwarzer-Smith-Henderson, with of course a slight change of gender, which might be indicated on documents as MASCULINE₁feminine₂. *Puis*, he receives the transplanted liver of an ape (leading to a slight change in his zoological categorization)."

"But Quique! . . ."

"Shut up. Our friend the miner then receives, in the following order:

a cornea from Mr. Nick Minelli, owner of the pizza-drugstore on Dallas Street in Toledo, Ohio (leading to a small change not only in name but also profession *e indirizzo*),

a yard and a half of small intestine from Ralph Cavanagh, butcher, of Trurox, Mass. (leading to yet a further change in *indirizzo* and profession),

a pancreas and spleen from a baseball player named Joe di Pietro, from Brooklyn,

a pituitary gland from ex-professor Sol Shapiro of the Dayan Memorial Hospital in New Jersey, AND

a metacarpal from Seymour Sullivan Jones, an executive of the Coca-Cola Corporation, in Cincinnati.

"Then the primitive miner Schwarzer, now known, for simplicity's sake, as Mr. John Schwarzer-Smith & Co., Inc. (or 'Inky,' to his friends), undergoes an ovarian transplant from Miss Geraldine Danielsen, of Buffalo, Oklahoma, this innovative procedure stemming from the sensational *découverte* by Professor Moshe Goldenberg of the University of California in Palo Alto, who has proven that the implantation of an ovary in the body of a man (or of a testicle in the body of a woman) is the only way, after a certain age (and the Schwarzer-Smith conglomerate has now reached one hundred seventy-two years of age) of returning the arterioles of the brain to their erstwhile flexibility without actually performing a brain transplant, which—at least for the moment—is not considered absolutely necessary in this case . . ."

"But listen—Quique . . ."

"*Cazzo di niente!* Due to the complications that this latest transplant begins to produce after the second year, The Schwarzer-Smith Co. starts to show signs of growing what for modesty's sake we will call a bust, so it decides (using the neuter personal pronoun only for convenience's sake, you understand), it decides I say, proof of the remarkable youthfulness brought on by the latest transplant, to initiate, so to speak, sentimental relations with one Mr., or rather the company of, DuPont, Inc., in Ohio. To which end, Schwarzer-Smith & Co. ardently desires, and finally demands, the incorporation into its own body of the vagina of Miss Christine Michelson, this lady having just perished as the result of a (failed) transplant of a dysfunctional adrenal gland.

"Upon the flat refusal of the Michelson family to meet its wishes, however, as that family professes strict and abiding belief in the doctrines of the New Baptist Church of the Third Day, the Schwarzer-Smith holding company takes over a plastic organ—one of a kind, of course—made to the rigorous specifications of Mr., or the firm of, DuPont, or just 'DuPont, Inc.' for short, by the prestigious Plastic-Opotherapic International Manufacturing Co. Performed with great success, the operation permits, at the end of three weeks' time, the merger of the two corporations, *mariage de raison* if you will, in a most impressive industrio-theological ceremony held in the Temple of Christian Science (Reformed) in the small town of Prague, Illinois, where the first-mentioned of the conglomerates has its main stock-holding in the Coca-Cola Co., the shares of which having been acquired from its part of an inheritance that came to it by way of a pancreas transplant from one Mr. D. D. Parkinson, the highly respected but ill-fated president of the bottling franchise for that company in the state of Illinois.

"So all this turned out for the best, not only from the point of view of the Progress of Science and Technology but as well, and most movingly, from the point of view of American Democracy, since it has allowed an old hayseed like the primitive miner John Schwarzer to rise—thanks to well-tuned viscera—to the presidency of one of the world's most respected companies, and to go from that most gross and exaggerated state of pure male animal to the subtle gender of Unisex and Publicly Held Corporation, a state which allows him (or it, depending on one's view of corporate law), if he (or it) wishes, to *épater*, so to speak, *les bourgeoises* on his corporate

208

team by one day wearing a smart little outfit designed by none other than Rudi Monokini Gernreich, fireworks starter *par excellence* among the upper crust, and the next day sporting a very macho design by Saville Road, which of course needs no introduction.

"Meanwhile, the most astute businessmen and speculators on the continent have rushed to create Organ Banks. I myself happen to have read the following want ads:

"Joe Feliciello, of Salt Lake City: duodenum, in good condition.

"Joshua Loth Marshall, of Truro, Massachusetts: two yards of small intestine and a ventricular valve.

"Sol Shapiro, Vice-President of Panoramic Movies, Inc.: urgent, liver.

"Thomas Jefferson Smith, construction worker, Rome, Arkansas: black nose, preferably aquiline.

"Mike Massuh, private eye, of Zion, Utah: right tear duct.

"Gene Loiacono, of Loiacono Pizzas, La Junta, Colorado: testicles.

"While under ORGANS: SALE OR TRADE, I've seen such ads as the following:

"Edison Weinberg, 40, musician, killed in auto accident in Brooklyn, NY, various abdominal organs in good working order.

"Father Junípero Villegas, of Missions of California, 37, r.i.p., heart attack: intestines, exc. cond.

"Cornelious Coghlan, 32, Paris, Iowa, killed in Caterpillar Co. explosion, all organs saved from fire.

"Rodney Munro, bricklayer, 25, killed in fall from scaffolding from 5th floor, vrs., gd. to exc. cond."

AND WHAT ABOUT THE IDEA OF FREEZING PEOPLE, QUIQUE?
"I already told you, how many times do I have to repeat myself? Are you people brain-dead yourselves?

"The first millionaire had the brilliant idea of crawling into the freezer so he could keep his cancer frozen until a cure was found. Then things started taking off, you know how *that* is. Not a month later the Kelvinator Cancer Co., Inc., was formed, under the leadership of H. B. Needham, chairman of the board of South-Kelvinator of East Hartford, Connecticut, and with the cooperation of Mr. William W. Sebeson, ex-president of Majestic Television Co. of New Jersey (cancer of the liver) and of Sam Kaplan, sales manager for Movies! Inc. of Los Angeles, California (throat cancer). Huge hangarlike buildings were constructed, warehouses in which specially constructed refrigerators were installed to keep the millionaires in, and from which they were taken periodically so that they could attend to various urgent matters that came up: they would be gently thawed in a double boiler, driven off to see to their business interests, then returned and quick-frozen and popped into their Antarctic doghouses again. Of course, since these men were extremely busy, and had to be punctual to a fault, soon freezers with alarm clocks were invented and on the market: wake me up at a quarter past February, please. Then, through a brainstorm brought to fruition by the Radio-Electronic Corporation of Toledo, Ohio, 'the frozen stiffs' (as they are called by the yellow press of the country) came to be able to maintain communication with the outside world via an amplifier system with intercoms at each end. Thus was opened the possibility that the merest whispers from the frozen millionaires could in the ordinary course of events reach their secretaries, and from the secretaries reach their boards of directors. An alternative, yet at the same time complementary, invention appeared, which was 'hibernation-with-secretary.' And if we were talking about cancer, all the better, since we could, if you'll pardon the expression, kill two birds with one stone, which, by the way, was what happened with the already-mentioned Sam Kaplan, who was quick-frozen along with his secretary, Lucille Nuremberg, aged twenty-seven, who was suffering from some sort of intestinal tumor. That is why it has become relatively common nowadays to read want ads that say things like WANTED: SECRETARY. MUST HAVE GERMAN, SPANISH, AND ENGLISH, BREAST CANCER, ATTRACTIVE APPEARANCE. SALARY COMMENSURATE WITH QUALIFICATIONS. This year in fact saw the First Congress of Frozen Executives, which was held in the Washington Hilton, and which saw as much infighting as backslapping, just as in any normal event of this kind. The convention was presided over by the Grand Cancer Noath H. Pedersen (spleen, pancreas, and stomach), who looked quite splendid on TV. He was accompanied by his personal, and favorite, secretary (he said, smiling), who had just a small uterine cyst, malign.

210

"And that's enough for now, if you don't mind, since duties of the Fourth Estate call."

HOW COULD MARCELO NOT ASK THE YOUNG MAN ANYTHING ABOUT HIMSELF?

It was *not* Marcelo, though, but he who brought up the issue, and the boy himself, who needed to talk, it seemed (that provincial accent of his), and who, in a voice filled with shame, said, "I lied to you; my name isn't Luis, it's Nepomuceno," and after a silence, Marcelo, blushing, muttered something that he no doubt meant to be heard as "You don't have to tell me anything." But they called him Scarecrow, maybe because he was not from the city, and had Indian features, like that other guy, that guy that sang on the radio, but especially because he was "like this, see?," pulling up his pants leg a little, shyly, with a little smile, almost apologetic, showing Marcelo his skeletal shins, the skin stretched across the bone, because though they had already been living in the same room for several days, he had always managed not to undress in front of Marcelo, or with the light on. There had been eight children, eight brothers and sisters that had lived together in that little house, and their mother, too, who went out to do laundry for people; the father he never mentioned, maybe he was dead, maybe he'd gone away to find work—and all this, thought Marcelo, to explain those skinny, ridiculous legs.

They were drinking their *mate* in silence.

"There are a lot of things I have to tell you, Marcelo, that I need you to know."

"I . . ."

"Ché, Ché Guevara, Comandante Guevara . . ."

Marcelo became even more nervous, he was almost embarrassed, he suddenly had an intuition of what he was about to hear, and he felt himself unworthy.

"I was there, I was there through the whole campaign. I managed to escape with Inti, but I was luckier than he was."

Then he stopped, and that afternoon they didn't talk any more.

Other places in the world call for the aid of my modest efforts.
I can do things which are denied to you, which your responsi-

211

*bility at the head of Cuba will not allow you, and so the hour
has come for us to be separated. Here I leave the purest of my
hopes for construction and the most loved of my loved ones. I
free Cuba of all responsibility save that which flows from its
example. If my last hour should come under other skies than
these, my last thoughts will be for this country and especially
for you, Fidel.*

Inti Peredo. Had Marcelo ever heard of him? No . . . well, actually, he had, really . . . He was ashamed to confess that he'd run
across Peredo's memoirs in some bookstore; it seemed so unfair to
talk about bookstores to somebody like Scarecrow, who was virtually
illiterate but who'd actually been there, suffered, lived through that
hell. Inti was a great person, he told Marcelo, Ché had loved him,
although it was hard to tell whether Ché really liked you or not,
though of course sometimes the men could tell. One day, he'd been
lying under a tree, resting, or thinking, actually. August had been so
hard, they'd been hungry, thirsty, some of his buddies had drunk
their own urine, though the Comandante had warned them about
that, it caused problems, naturally. And to top it all off Moro, who
was the only doctor, had had an attack of lumbago, he'd had terrible
pains all during the march, and there was no way to help, no way
to cure it, they didn't have anything to treat it with. Morale was low,
everybody was feeling the discouragement, and sometimes they were
even scared. Camba, for example. While they were sitting around
the fire that night, Ché talked to them, and his voice was quiet but
at the same time serious. This would be their test as men, he said.
And if there was anyone there that didn't feel up to what was to
come, Ché said, they should leave the war that very minute. The
men that stayed felt their love and admiration for the Comandante
grow and grow and grow, and they swore to win or die—*vencer o
morir.* Those were hard moments that night, because Joaquín's whole
group had been killed in an ambush, at a ford on the Yeso, on the
last day of August—they'd been betrayed by a bastard named Honorato Rojas, a campesino. Didn't Honorato come from the word
"honor"?

Yes, it came from the word "honor."

Well anyway, the army waited till this bastard led the men into

212

the trap, and as they were fording the river they murdered them all, gunned them down from behind, and a lot of men died there, including a girl named Tania, too, a very brave girl, and only twenty-two men were left. Some of them, like Moro, were in pretty bad shape, and others—you had to face it, even if you were ashamed to admit it—others were scared to death. So the Comandante started what he called orientation every night again, with lectures and bits of advice and things, and he would scold them, too, motherly you might almost say, but tough. And one of these nights Scarecrow had seen him sitting all alone, leaning back against the root of a tree, looking down at the ground. He didn't know why, but he had to go over to him. I was just thinking, Ché said, almost apologetically. Thinking about Celita, his daughter. He'd left her in Cuba.

Scarecrow fell silent again. He lit another cigarette, and in the darkness Marcelo watched how the glow at the tip of the cigarette illuminated the Scarecrow's face each time he dragged at it.

Dear parents—
Once again I feel beneath my spurs the noble ribcage of Rocinante, as I take the road again, with my shield on my arm. Just about ten years ago now, I was writing you another good-bye letter. As I recall, I said I regretted not being a better soldier and a better doctor. That latter title doesn't interest me much anymore, and I'm not such a bad soldier now . . . This may be it. Not that I'm looking for it, but it's certainly within the realm of possibility. If so, with this letter goes one last embrace. I have loved you both very much, I just haven't known how to express it. I'm so very very stiff that I think sometimes you didn't understand me. On the other hand, it couldn't have been easy to understand me anyway. Believe me, though, if only today.

"Yes, Marcelo, sometimes we could see it. When Benjamín died, for example—a kid even weaker than me," he laughed shyly, "but with an incredible will. We suffered so much, so much on those marches—from the very beginning it was hard, and by the last few days a lot of us didn't have any shoes, our clothes were just rags. Thickets of thorny bushes, brambles, I don't know what they were

213

called, and rocks, and fording the rivers. Ché's idea was to get to the Masicurí River, so we'd have a chance to get our first look at the soldiers, not to get into fighting yet. We'd been on the march for almost a month already, with the sick men, the mosquitoes, every kind of insect you can imagine, our packs weighing more every day, the weapons, and the exhaustion . . . By the end of the month we barely had anything to eat. At the Río Grande, Benjamín had problems with his pack—he was absolutely worn out. And like I was telling you, he was weak to begin with, you felt sorry for him dragging himself and his stuff along like that. We were going down along a shelf a few feet above the river, and Benjamín took a false step or something, I don't know what happened, something, and he fell into the river. The river was swollen, big, and the current was strong, so he didn't have the strength even to try to swim against it. Rolando jumped in, but he couldn't catch him—we never saw him again. We all loved Benjamín, he was a friend in the best sense of the word. The Comandante didn't say anything, but all that day he was quiet, he didn't talk, he walked along with his head down. Any time he called a halt, or any time we were sitting around eating, for instance, around a fire, he'd always talk to us, teach us things. That night he told us that the main weapons of the revolutionary army were its morale and its discipline. A guerrilla should never loot a town, he said, or mistreat the people in it, and especially not the women. But over and above that, you had to keep up your will to defeat your enemy, to fight to the death for the ideals that you had embraced. And discipline was essential to that—not the kind of discipline you get in the army, in training camp, the rules and so forth; what Ché was talking about, he said, was the discipline of men who know what they're fighting for and who know that what they're fighting for is noble and good. He didn't say a word about Benjamín, but his voice was different that night, and besides—we all could tell that what he was telling us had something to do with Benjamín, with the way he'd gritted his teeth, with the way he'd stood up to all the hardships. Because we'd seen Ché help Benjamín, lots of times, carry things for him, lighten his load—Ché always carried the heaviest load of all of us, and ran the worst risks, too. Even when he could barely breathe from asthma, because his medicine had run out. You know what asthma is like."

214

In the darkness, Marcelo saw the flare of the match when he lit another cigarette.

"Want one? Just one can't hurt you."

They were sitting in silence, each one looking at the ceiling, lying back to back in the bed.

"When I saw him for the first time, I couldn't believe it. It was late at night, out in the jungle. He looked like just another guerrilla . . . But then somehow, right away you could see there was a difference. . . ."

His voice trailed off as he puffed again.

"Not that he tried." He seemed to want to make this clear. "He never tried to seem different, that's not what I meant to say . . . What I meant to say was that you could feel it, without him even trying. He wasn't stiff, like you'd expect military commanders to be—it was something else. He'd joke around, he was funny sometimes. But then there'd be other things that he wouldn't stand for. He couldn't stand slovenliness, letting yourself go, for example. You know, when you're out in the jungle, in the middle of nowhere, you can let yourself go, little by little, and if you let yourself go, pretty soon you've got nothing but rags to wear, because your clothes get torn apart by those thorns, and you're marching, and there's the rain . . . And because it's hard to bathe, and sometimes you have to eat with your hands. And the minute you let yourself go like that, you're no better than an animal. I'll tell you, Ché wouldn't stand for it. You had to keep yourself clean, keep your clothes decent, you had to take care of your pack, your books. I very seldom heard him raise his voice, but when he did, he was right. Usually, he'd be almost *loving* when he set you straight, though firm and decided at the same time. We'd no more than get to the place he'd decided on for setting up our camp and he'd start directing what he called the public works—he'd have benches built, and an oven for baking bread, that sort of thing. And every so often, he'd have the camp cleaned from one end to the other and from top to bottom, even if the camp was just temporary. And every day, from four to six, we'd have classes. The ones with the most education would teach, and the others would learn. There'd be grammar, and arithmetic, and history and geography, and politics, and Quechua. There were even classes at night, but those were voluntary, for the ones that wanted to learn more, or the ones

215

that could take it all in. Ché himself gave a night class in French. 'It's not just shooting,' he'd say, 'it's not all guns. One day some of you will have to be leaders, if we win this war. The cadre can't just be brave, it has to be ideologically sound, it has to be educated, it has to be able to think quickly and to make fair decisions, it has to be capable of loyalty and discipline. But above all,' he said, 'it has to set an example—it has to be the model for the new man that we want in a fair and just society.' "

He paused again and smoked in silence.

"The new man," he murmured, as though thinking aloud. "He talked to us a lot about the new man. I can't tell you all of it, I can't explain it all, because I'm not an educated person. But while he talked to us and tried to explain all this to us, I would watch him, I'd never take my eyes off him, and all I could think was that this new man was him, this Comandante Ché Guevara. But he would talk as though it would be something else, something wonderful that he would find some day, or maybe build. But I always thought, and I think other people thought this way too, that this new man would have to be somebody like him, like Ché—with a spirit of selflessness, of sacrifice for other people, and brave, but *feeling* at the same time, compassionate, and . . ."

He seemed for a moment to hesitate, and also to be having some difficulty speaking, as though choked up by his memories, by sadness. But at last he nerved himself to say the word before which he had, almost embarrassed, halted:

"Loving."

Then he fell silent again, until he felt himself obliged to explain:

"Love, I don't know . . . I don't mean love like in romantic novels, you know . . . I don't want you to misunderstand what I mean . . . It was . . . He would say that you can't fight for a better world without it, without love for your fellow man, and that it was a sacred cause, that it wasn't just words, but that every day, every minute you had to prove it . . .

"I don't know how many times we saw him take soldiers that had been shooting at us, shooting to kill I mean, five minutes earlier, and treat those soldiers without one second's anger, or resentment, or . . . or anything. He would bandage them, and treat their wounds, he'd even use up the little medicine and supplies

216

that we had for ourselves. I told you, it wasn't long before his asthma medicine ran out, and it was terrible for him. Sometimes he'd go off and hide when it got really bad. But he'd always come back and we'd pick up the march again, and he'd get mad if any of us tried to help him or make things easier on him, or if the cook for example gave him something special to eat, or if we tried to change his guard duty so he'd have an easier hour."

He paused, and smoked in silence.

"The Ñancahuazú ambush, the first time we had to fight . . . We took quite a few prisoners, and one of them was this Major Plata. It was embarrassing to see how scared he was. His own soldiers wanted us to shoot him—they said he was merciless, heartless, terrible. We pulled out some clothes for the soldiers and gave them civilian clothes. We fixed up their wounds, and Inti Peredo explained what we were trying to do, our goals and aims, because Ché had to conceal the fact that he was in Bolivia. And we explained to them that we didn't kill enemy prisoners. I mean, we treated this man the way Ché had taught us to treat people—like a human being, with respect.

"Another case: Lieutenant Lardeo. They found a letter from his wife in his campaign log. A friend of theirs had asked her to ask him to bring home a guerrilla's scalp to decorate the living room with. That's exactly what it said: to decorate the living room with. And yet Ché decided that this second lieutenant's log—now that I remember, he was a second lieutenant—that we had to send this second lieutenant's log to his mother, since that was what this enemy officer had written that he wanted, there in the log. So Ché kept that diary in his pack till he could find a place to send it back to the man's mother. They found it still in Ché's pack when he was killed in the ambush at Yuro. And I'll tell you about another case. On the third of July we were still close to the gasoline supply road where we'd had the encounter with the army. Ché had ordered an ambush, and we were waiting for some trucks to come by. Pombo was supposed to give a signal with his handkerchief, he was up at a lookout post, a signal when the first truck was within firing range. After five and a half hours of waiting the first truck came by, but Ché, who was supposed to be the one to fire the first shot with his M-2, Ché didn't fire. The truck went by safe and sound. Do you know why?"

217

He seemed to be awaiting Marcelo's reply, though Marcelo said nothing.

"Did you hear me? Are you asleep?"

"I'm awake, Scarecrow. I'm listening to every word you say."

"Do you know why, then? Because in the back of this truck there were just two soldiers, and they were all wrapped up in blankets asleep, lying there next to some hogs they were transporting. Two poor soldiers, Ché said, and they were asleep . . . Do you think that was weakness, Marcelo?"

"I . . ."

"That night, sitting around the fire, he told us that a decision like that could be taken to be a sign of weakness, and that weaknesses like that might at any given moment turn out to be fatal to a guerrilla. But that's where the question of the new man came in again. Killing two poor helpless soldiers in their sleep, and not running the least risk to your own life, two soldiers that had probably never done anything to anybody, innocent I mean because all they were doing was following orders, was that really a weakness? Could you create this new man we were fighting to try to create on a foundation of atrocities? Could you achieve noble ends through ignoble means? It's hard. A lot of people criticized him later on for things like that."

"Who?"

"I, I don't know . . . revolutionaries tougher than he was, more realistic, pragmatic—is that the word? I've heard a lot of that kind of criticism of Ché—'petit-bourgeois idealist,' things like that. One time I had to break a guy's nose for saying that, criticizing Ché in just those words. I couldn't help myself, I just jumped. I wanted to kill him . . . I was the only person in that meeting that knew who the real Ché Guevara was, and it hurt me I tell you to hear such things, people that had never done the thousandth part of what Ché Guevara was capable of doing . . . But like I say, I don't know, I'm not an educated person . . . The person that said that was a Communist that knew Marx and Lenin backward and forward. 'That's not Marxism,' he said. What do you think, Marcelo? Is it?"

Marcelo, as always, did not immediately answer.

"I'm nobody to be giving lessons in Marxism or Leninism, Scarecrow . . . But I think Ché was right. . . ."

218

"I do too. And if we were out there fighting it was so there wouldn't be any more men ready to fire from ambush at two poor defenseless little soldiers asleep in the back of a truck that would have died without knowing why. In his diary . . . Did you read it?"

"Yes."

"In his diary he says he didn't have the courage to shoot them. But you know as well as I do that if there was one thing Ché had more than enough of, it was courage. He meant something else. And what happens, besides, is that when you're part of a guerrilla group out in the middle of the jungle, there are feelings, emotions that people in the city can't understand. When Tuma got shot in the stomach, we had to carry him to Piray, several miles farther ahead, so that Moro could operate on him. But Tuma's liver was completely destroyed, and his intestines were punctured in I don't know how many places. There was just nothing that could be done. It was a painful, terrible day for all of us, because Tuma was one of the cheerfullest, happiest men you'll ever meet, always ready to help out . . . Plus a brave man, a brave fighter. Ché loved him like a son, which is exactly what he says in his diary, so I imagine he suffered more than all the rest of us. Though like always, he did his best not to show it. Anyway, when Tuma fell, he thought he would die right there, so he gave us his watch to give to Ché. That was what we always did, because the Comandante would later on make sure the wife got it. Or the mother, as the case might be. Tuma had a son he'd never seen, because his wife had had the baby while we were still up in the mountains. He asked us to save it for his son so he'd have it when he grew up."

I have been on patrol for four days with the 1st Battalion of the Fourth Division, out in that primitive jungle full of snakes, and boas, and gigantic spiders, and jaguars. (From the story filed by Murray Sayle, war correspondent of the London Times.)

"September was worse than August. We had to make terrible marches, we lost men, we fought I don't know how many times, and we started running out of even the most essential supplies. And to top it all off, we realized that Joaquín's group was never coming back, that they'd been wiped out. Moro was in terrible pain, and Ché was worse every day—the medicine for his asthma had run out weeks before. Sometimes he'd go off somewhere and try to hide, so we wouldn't see him when the attacks were worst. Our next objective was La Higuera. But we already knew that the army knew our position. Coco found a telegram in the telegraph operator's house in Valle Grande—the subprefect was reporting the presence of guerrilla forces in the area. Sometime around noon on the twenty-sixth, our vanguard party left to try to make it to Jagüey. Half an hour later, when the center and rear groups were just about to march, we heard heavy firing from the direction of La Higuera. The Comandante immediately set up the defenses to wait for the vanguard to come back in, or what was left of the vanguard, because there was no doubt in anybody's mind that they'd run into an ambush. So we sat there and waited for news. First came Benigno, shot in the shoulder. The bullet had gone all the way through, though. This is what had happened, he said: first Coco had gotten wounded, then when Benigno had run out to try to rescue him, he'd just started dragging him back when they opened up on them with machine-gun fire—Coco was killed, and one of the bullets, after it went through Coco's body, had hit Benigno in the shoulder. The others were either dead or wounded. It was a terrible blow to Inti, because Coco was more than a brother to him—they'd been together in prison, and they'd fought together in the struggle, and they'd gone into the guerrillas together. One day, to give you an idea, some men were out in the jungle talking about Ricardo's death, about how his death had hit his brother Arturo. And Coco turned to Inti and said, 'I'd never want to see you dead, I don't know how I'd act. But thank goodness they'll get me first, I know it,' he said. Which is exactly what happened. Coco was a good friend, a generous, good man, a brave man, but he cried the day Ricardo was killed.

"Fortunately, Inti didn't see him die. He was not a man to cry, but from that day on he turned even more reserved than ever."

Scarecrow fell silent again. His voice had grown hoarser and hoarser as his story of misfortunes had gone on, as though his voice were going through the same increasingly harsh trials the small troop of condemned men had gone through.

At last he got out of bed and said, "I'm going to the bathroom."

220

He did this frequently, Marcelo knew; his kidneys were not those of a normal man. When he came back, he got into bed again and went on with his account:

"The ambush at La Higuera was the worst blow yet. It was the beginning of the end."

[Sept.] 27.—At four o'clock we started out again, trying to find a place where we could climb up, which we did about 7, except it was on the opposite side from what we had wanted; in front of us there was a bare hillside, innocent-enough looking. We climbed a little higher to get to a location out of sight of the planes, in a thinly wooded stand of trees, and that was when we discovered that there was a road on the hill, though nobody traveled it all day. Toward evening, a campesino and a soldier climbed about halfway up the hill and played around for a while, without seeing us. Aniceto had just scouted the hill, and had seen a good number of soldiers in a house nearby; that was the easiest road for us, but now it was cut off. About dawn we saw a column going up a hill not far off, their gear glittering in the sun, and then, about midday, we heard some isolated shots and a few bursts, and then later shouting—"There he is," "Come out of there," "Are you coming out or not?"—accompanied by gunfire. We don't know the man's fate, but we assume it was probably Camba. We crept out at nightfall to try to get down the other side to the water, and we stayed in some scrub a little thicker than the other; we had to go all the way down into the canyon to get the water, since the shelf kept us from doing it from above.

The radio brought us the news that we'd run into the Galindo Company, leaving three dead that were being taken to VG for identification. Apparently they haven't taken Camba and León prisoner. Our casualties have been high this time; the worst loss is Coco, but Miguel and Julio were magnificent fighters, and the human value of the three, simply immeasurable. León was a good painter.—Altitude: 5500 feet. (From the Diary of Ché Guevara.)

"The Comandante was looking for an area where the terrain would give us less disadvantage, until we could get reinforcements and food. But to do that, we'd have had to get through two perimeters: first, the roadblock directly in front of us, practically from here to there I mean, and the other a wide circle the army had laid down, which we knew about from the radio communications. During the last few days of September and the first part of October we tried to keep hidden during the day, though we scouted around for a retreat route in case it was necessary. To make matters worse, we didn't have any water. Just some foul-tasting water that we got only at tremendous risk, at night, and brushing out our trail behind us. We could hear soldiers passing by within feet of us, more and more of them as time went on, and very well equipped. Whenever we lighted a fire, we had to practically cover it with our raincapes to keep it from being seen."

It is believed that Commander Ernesto 'Ché' Guevara must fall at any moment, surrounded as he has been for several days by an iron circle. The terrain and insect bites in this country turn any human being's flesh into a cloak of torment. The thick fabric of dry vegetation covered with thorns, makes almost any change of location impossible, even during the day, unless it is by way of the riverbeds, and they are all under heavy surveillance. One simply cannot understand how the guerrillas can bear up under this siege of thirst, hunger, and horror. 'The man won't come out alive,' one officer told us. (From a war correspondent's report.)

"Things went on that way till the eighth of October. The previous afternoon had been the start of our eleventh month in the fighting. The morning was cold. The march was slow because it was too hard on Chino to move at night, Moro still had terrible pain in his leg, and the Comandante, with no medicine for his asthma, was suffering terribly. At two o'clock in the morning we stopped to rest. We went on at four. There were seventeen of us, moving along through the darkness and that pain-filled silence down the deep canyon of the Yuro. When the sun came out, the Comandante stopped to study the situation; he was looking for a hill to get to the San Lorenzo River by. But the hillsides were almost all bare, so

222

that way out looked to be practically impossible. So he decided to send out three pairs of men to explore: one to the right, one straight out ahead, and the other to the left. They came back soon enough—all the routes were cut off. And we couldn't go back now, either, because the path we had come down at night was impossible by day. The Comandante decided then that we should hide out in a little canyon running off to the side and try to hold off action as long as possible, since if the shooting started after three, he said, we might have a chance to hold out until the sun went down, and then we'd have a better chance to escape."

At eight o'clock in the morning, a farmer named Víctor came to the military post at La Higuera to report that unknown men were moving through the underbrush near his house. The officer gave the informant money and immediately began to transmit the information to the Ranger units which had been dispersed throughout the area. Major Miguel Ayoroa, commander of the two Ranger companies operating in the region, radioed orders to blockade the exits of all the canyons of the San Antonio, Yagüey, and Yuro rivers. Captain Prado took his detachment into the Yuro canyon, and his men made contact with the guerrillas about noon. Two soldiers were killed in the first skirmish. Exchange of fire continued sporadically for approximately three hours. Slowly, the Rangers gained ground, coming at last to within approximately 70 yards of the enemy. At 1530 hours, the guerrillas suffered their first visible casualty. (From the military report.)

"It was a shame that the attack started at noon, since like I said, Ché's hopes were that it would hold off until at least three. We started hearing the rattle of the machine guns, which were clearing the very same path we had come down during the night. It was obvious they thought we were farther back. That allowed us to gain some time on them. The Comandante divided us into three groups, and we decided on a place to meet after dark. But when my group got to the place we'd agreed on, there was nobody there. We just looked at each other, nobody said a word, and then we collapsed from the exhaustion and the grief—though we still had the hope that

223

Ché and his group, even if they hadn't been able to make it to where we were, would have tried to go on to the San Lorenzo."

Scarecrow stopped talking. Marcelo, lying with his back to Scarecrow, could feel his chest weighed down by his asthma. "By my asthma," he thought then, like a man surprised to find himself committing the meanest act of his entire life. After Scarecrow's long and terrible silence, he heard him go on in a voice barely audible:

"We didn't know that his whole group had been killed, or that Comandante Ernesto Ché Guevara had been wounded and taken prisoner, or that he would soon be killed in the most . . ." but Marcelo could not make out the last words. They talked no more that night.

> *We spread out in order to surround the guerrillas, and immediately launched our attack. The first rebel we saw was the man we later identified as Willy, followed by the man later identified as 'el Ché.' We immediately opened fire, wounding Ché with machine-gun fire. Willy and the others then tried to drag him away, while the fighting was going on. Another burst of machine-gun fire from our Rangers blew the Comandante's cap off and wounded him in the chest. While the others covered him, Willy managed to get his commander over to a hill, where four other Rangers were ready to engage them. Out of breath from the effort, Willy carried his commander on his back. And when he stopped to recover his strength and give some aid to Guevara, the soldiers who had been lying in wait ordered them to surrender. Before either man could fire, the Rangers fired first. Ché was seriously wounded, and his asthma prevented him from breathing. We transmitted the coded message: 'Hello, Saturn. We've got Papa.' (From Captain Prado's report.)*
>
> *Guevara was carried in a cape-sling by four soldiers to La Higuera, several kilometers from the site of the capture. There, Captain Prado turned his prisoners over to Colonel Selich, who was in charge of the post. An inventory was taken of the pack carried by Guevara: two diaries, a codebook, a book of notes containing coded messages, a book of poems copied by Ché, a watch, and three or four other books. (From the Bolivian Army report.)*

224

It was Colonel Selich that spoke with Ché. Both we (the wounded soldiers) and Guevara were in a hangar. But he was down at the other end of it, so we could hardly understand what they were saying, although we clearly heard the colonel, because he was shouting. He was saying something about Latin America. The colonel spent a long time with Guevara, maybe an hour or more. They were arguing over something the colonel wanted to get out of him, and Ché refused to tell him. Until finally Ché slapped the colonel with his right hand. At that, the colonel got up and left. Major Guzmán wanted to transport Guevara to a hospital in a helicopter but the colonel wouldn't allow it, so we departed by ourselves. (Account given by Giménez, enlisted soldier.)

The helicopter had no sooner taken off with the wounded and dead soldiers than the guerrilla's pain begin to grow much worse. He groaned something. I put my ear to his mouth and heard him say, 'I hurt. Please, I beg you to do something to ease my pain.' And I didn't know what to do, but he showed me what movements to make to make him easier. 'There, on my chest, please,' he said. He was in pain the whole night, groaning. (Account of the lieutenant in charge of the prisoner.)

Ché was taken with the other prisoners to a little schoolhouse in La Higuera, and he lay in one of the schoolrooms all that night. (Journalist's report.)

Here you have me now, you spaces I have abandoned—alone, without oblivion

On Sunday, October 9, at two o'clock in the afternoon, President Barrientos and General Ovando received the report of the capture. There was a General Staff meeting. Present were General Torres and General Vázquez, who presented the motion that Guevara be executed. No one objected; all remained silent. A little while later, General Ovando sent this order to Valle Grande: 'Say hello to Papa.' The order was received in La Higuera by Colonel Miguel Ayoroa. It was sent on to Lieutenant Pérez and, in turn, to his assistant Mario Terán and Sergeant Huanca. The executioners took up their rifles. In the

room where Ché was lying prisoner, the guerrilla named Willy
was also tied up. When Terán appeared, Willy insulted him,
and Terán shot him in the head. Huanca did the same with
Reynaga, who was held prisoner in the adjoining room. Mario
Terán was chosen by lot to kill Comandante Guevara. When
he came, nervous and agitated, out of the room in which he
had just executed Willy, he decided to exchange his weapon for
a more powerful one. He went to Lieutenant Pérez to requisition
an M-2 rifle, which fires rapid automatic bursts. Terán is a
small, short man. (Version given by Antonio Arguedas, former
secretary of state, to Prensa Latina news agency.)

Laid out, and held aloft by death for all to see
Behold me, you misfortunes and you glories, eternally borne on
Days, years, clouds, what will you do with me?

> *When I entered the room, Ché sat up and said, "You have come*
> *to kill me."*
> *This took me aback, and I lowered my head without an-*
> *swering.*
> *"What did the others say?" he asked me.*
> *I told him they'd said nothing.*
> *I didn't have the courage to fire. At that moment Ché looked*
> *very, very big to me, enormous. There was an intense gleam in*
> *his eyes. It was as though he were overpowering me, and I felt*
> *dizzy.*
> *"Be calm," he said. "Aim well."*

Tell us where you were hidden,
ay! you death which no one could ever see
Death mute, impossible, unbidden.

> *I took a step back, toward the door, closed my eyes, and*
> *fired off the first burst. Ché, his legs destroyed, fell, began writh-*
> *ing on the floor, and started to lose a great deal of blood. I*
> *recovered my courage and fired off the second burst, which hit*
> *him in the arm, one shoulder, and finally in the heart. (Account*
> *of Mario Terán as related to Arguedas.)*

226

The body of Ché Guevara was dragged, still warm, to a stretcher, and then carried outside to be picked up by a helicopter. The floor and walls of the schoolroom were spattered and stained with blood, but the soldiers refused to clean it. The cleaning was done by a German priest, who silently washed off the stains and in a handkerchief tied up the bullets that had passed through Ché's body.

When the helicopter arrived, the stretcher was tied to one of its struts. The cadaver, still wearing the guerrilla uniform, had been wrapped in a tarpaulin. Eddy González, a Cuban who had run a cabaret in Havana during the Batista regime, went over and slapped the Comandante's lifeless face.

When the helicopter reached its destination, the body was laid out on a board, with its head hanging backward and to the side, its eyes open. Almost naked, laid across a deep sink used for washing, it was illuminated by the photographers' flashes.

Its hands were chopped off with an axe, to prevent identification. But the body was mutilated in other parts, as well. The rifle became the property of Colonel Anaya, the watch went to General Ovando. One of the soldiers who had taken part in the operations stripped off the moccasins that one of Guevara's comrades had made for him in the jungle. But as they were almost unusable from wear and wetness, he threw them out. (From news reports.)

There will be flowers to remember you, and words, and skies,
rains like this rain, yet no change will come
You will still live on.
There sleeps, free of adversity, all the pride
of sadness.

NO, SILVIA, YOUR LETTERS DON'T BOTHER ME
but I have neither the time nor the inclination to meet Araujo. Tell him to start by reading Hegel, and he'll be able to see one "Marxist" Hegel and another Hegel who is "existentialist," and then he'll see why today's existentialism can carry on a fruitful and unifying dia-

logue with Marxism, or could, that is, if the two sides would stop threatening and insulting each other.

As for that word "metaphysical," just another typical accusation.

Araujo goes over me like a monkey picking nits, trying to find stigmata, or like those witch hunters trying to find the mark of the devil in the most secret folds of flesh. But as I've said before, I use that word "metaphysical" to refer to certain ultimate aspects of the human condition. One can see that a yearning for the absolute, the will to power, the impulse to rebellion, the pain and anguish of solitude, and death are ultimate aspects of every man and woman's life. They are not simply manifestations of bourgeois corruption and putrefaction but may (and do) attack the happy citizens of the Soviet Union as well.

Every person's life will face these emotions—these "problems." They are part of the totality of man. And that totality can only be apprehended by art. Which, by the way, is not just an idea held by certain lepers like myself: great Marxists say the same thing. All philosophers, when they have tried to touch the absolute, have had to employ some form of myth, of poetry. The existentialists, we already know about. But even the traditional, classical philosophers: think of Plato's use of myths, and remember Hegel using the myths of Don Juan or Faust to make the drama of ill-fated consciousness graspable.

And one last clarification: For many of the same reasons as these I've just given you, I use—to the eternal perplexity of typesetters, it seems—the word "eschatological," referring to the problems of death, not the word "scatological," which I leave to boards of censorship. *Eschatos* refers to the "other world" and *skatos* refers to excrement, no? Though for some critics it all comes down to the same thing: pure and execrable shit.

I'm tired, Silvia. It's two o'clock in the morning, and I'm sick. I can't explain why. If I ever manage to write the novel of this jumble, you'll be able to sense something of the world I live in—my *entire* world, not just the world you see in these philosophical discussions.

228

HE VERY SHYLY, VERY HESITANTLY ENTERS
the great studio at Channel 13, its rows of seats packed with people
waiting to see the show, but Pipo, with a microphone in his left
hand and his little arm waving about energetically, stretches a hand
out to him, shouts his name in delight and cries

LET'S HAVE A BIG, BIG ROUND OF APPLAUSE, LADIES AND GENTLEMEN!

at which everyone claps and shouts. He has him lie down on a couch
and then he kneels down beside him and begins a deep and somewhat heavy round of interrogation, a sort of psychoanalytical examination for mongoloid students, mentioning names of things,
events, words to which Sabato must respond with the first thing that
    comes into his mind:
a man going up a flight of stairs
an umbrella
a huge woman's purse
a train toiling heavily up a long mountain
a water faucet dripping milk
and each time his patient responds correctly, Pipo asks for ANOTHER
BIG ROUND OF APPLAUSE and doubles the prize, because now they're
on a quiz program of some sort. Sabato is sweating profusely, not
simply from the intense heat generated by the spotlights but also
because he is standing in his undershorts in front of hundreds of
people who refuse to take their eyes off him. He doesn't even get a
break when the show cuts to the commercials, because he's still on
exhibition, even while the people of Argentina are being told that
Aurora Brings the Future Home Today, that the people that really
know their business are at the Banco de Galicia, that they should
only drink wine whose making is overseen by experts, that it's stupid
to lose a boyfriend or a job because of BAD BREATH when Fresh-
Breez Mouthwash is available to not only swoosh away germs but
actually to kill them like THAT! (huge fist smashing ugly little mouth
germ), like THAT! (another germ smashed), like THAT! (and another), that they should all shop in Fravega because Fravega HAS IT
ALL—AND MORE, that Luxury Link is, quite simply, the Last Word,
that SuperFridge can hold everything (clip of an elephant emerging
from a refrigerator), that *that* (UGH!) was *her* (sweaty, upset, tense,

229

no time to watch TV or go to parties) till she started using Vero, that she couldn't go to the cocktail party because she'd forgotten to use her Odorono (close-up of sweat-stained armpit of blouse, then cut to faces of her friends turning disgustedly away) and that her constipation problems had been solved ONCE AND FOR ALL by Ross Pills (morning scenes of happy, smiling family) and by Waldorf, which offered her eighty yards of sweet-smelling softness, the advertising segment closing with two midgets dressed like children running around a house filled with appliances and other home products, the two midgets deafeningly screaming for a Drean!, at which Mommy enters smiling to soothe them and quench their thirst. Sabato feels ill at ease, because he is thinking that the spotlights are merciless with details, but just then the elegant and sophisticated actress Libertad Leblanc comes onstage, and Pipo once again calls for

A BIG, BIG ROUND OF APPLAUSE, LADIES AND GENTLEMEN!

after which he cries YOU'VE HEARD THE ANNOUNCEMENTS, LADIES AND GENTLEMEN, AND JUST AS WE'VE BEEN PROMISING, RIGHT HERE ON CHANNEL 13, ON *Circular Sabbath*, WE'RE BRINGING YOU, LIVE!, THE WEDDING OF ERNESTO SABATO AND THIS LOVELY STAR OF STAGE AND SCREEN, and his hand slowly steals toward Libertad who, following the saccharine but deafening orders of Pipo, the Master of Ceremonies, is about to kiss Sabato before the cameras. At last she does so, to A BIG ROUND OF APPLAUSE. Then once again there's a long list of commercial announcements, touting the definite advantages of dandruff shampoos, deodorants that last a full twenty-four hours, wines both dry and sweet, soaps of the stars, toothpastes, refrigerator-freezers, televisions, tougher and more absorbent toilet papers, cigarettes longer than any other cigarette ever known to man or woman before, in all the history of tobacco, washing machines, and automobiles. At the end of the commercials, Pipo brings out, to wild applause, Jorge Luis Borges, in a tuxedo, who is going to be the couple's best man. His white cane inspires general sympathy, which is augmented by a large seeing-eye dog and the comments of Pipo Mancera, underscoring the GREAT SACRIFICE it was for a man like Borges, in his condition, to be a guest on a TV show. *Poor old blind thing*, mutters a huge fat

230

woman picked up by the cameras, but Borges makes a trembling sign with his hand, as though to say "Don't give it a second thought." Libertad Leblanc, wearing a black dress with a neckline that plunges to her navel, is standing beside Sabato, who, still in his underwear, though now standing hand in hand with the star, looks sympathetically over at Borges, who is walking forward unsurely toward the center of the stage. Pipo then says MR. DIRECTOR, GET THOSE CAMERAS READY!, which is the cue for another long run of commercials, while Sabato thinks, "He and I both are public figures," and feels tears running down his cheeks.

HE OPENED THE BOOK AND FOUND HIS MARK,
his tiny but fearsome handwriting in the margin of the volume on occultism: "Break through the wall!" it tells him.

He would have to free the demon, even if it jumped out of the belly of that mummy straight at his face like some black, maddened, monstrous beast. But free it for what? He didn't know. To try to appease R.? It was some sort of terrible divinity to which mankind would be required to make sacrifice. It was insatiable, forever stalking, lurking in the shadows. He tried to put it out of his mind, but he knew it was there. A combination of poet, philosopher, and terrorist. Those barely glimpsed depths of knowledge, what did they mean? An aristocratic or reactionary anarchist who hated this civilization, a civilization that had invented aspirin "because it couldn't even bear a headache."

It gave him no rest. He couldn't open a book without coming across that crabbed, tiny, hateful handwriting. One day while he was yearning nostalgically for those years of mathematics, he had opened the Weyl book on relativity: in the margin of one of the major theorems, he found the comment IDIOTS! Nor was it interested in politics, in social revolution, which it considered subrealities, realities of a lower order, the sort of realities that keep newspapers in business. It put "The Real" between quotation marks, sometimes with a sarcastic exclamation point. The real was not umbrellas, the class struggle, laying bricks, not even the Andes Mountains. Those things were merely the forms taken by fantasy, the illusions practiced on people by delirious mediocrities. The only thing really real

231

was the relationship between man and his gods, between man and his demons. The really real was always symbolic, and the realism of poetry was the only sort that mattered, even though it was ambiguous—maybe *because* it was ambiguous: the relations between men and the gods were always equivocal at best. Prose only served for the writing of telephone books, an instruction manual for a new washing machine, or the annual report of some board of directors.

This world was crumbling, falling about our ears, and the dwarves in it were running about wildly, madly, frightened out of their wits, scrambling over the backs of rats and professors and leaving behind them a wake of plastic pails and buckets full of plastic garbage.

THERE SHE WAS
wearing her battered red raincoat, her head thrust forward, advancing over the rim of her coffee cup, pushing ahead into a world always just beyond her, just out of sight. Her myopia, her thick glasses, her modest raincoat moved him.

"You might wear a little makeup, you know." The words slipped out before he could stop them.

She lowered her head.

They sipped at their coffee in silence. Then he suggested they go out and walk for a while.

"But it's cold out."

He took her by the arm and led her outside without explanation.

Fall had set in, a fall of wind and drizzle. They crossed to the park from the steep hills of Belgrano, walked through the trees, and at last came to a wooden bench under an enormous rubber tree. The chess tables were deserted.

"You like parks," she observed.

"I do. When I was a boy I'd come over here and read. But let's walk, it's cold."

They walked through the big plane trees with their sere drooping leaves. They turned along Echeverría toward Cabildo. Sabato inspected everything as though he were about to buy it. To Silvia he seemed hermetic, somber. Finally she screwed up her courage to ask him where they were going.

232

"Nowhere." But the word didn't sound convincing.

"The novel as metaphysical poem," he suddenly muttered.

"What?"

"Nothing, nothing." But at a lower level his ruminations continued: the writer as the intersection of the planes of daily reality and fantasy, the border or gray line between the light and the darkness. And there, Schneider. There it was, the doors of the forbidden world.

"The Belgrano church," she said.

Yes, the Belgrano church. Once again Sabato looked at it with sacred mistrust, and he thought of its crypts.

"Ever been to this café?"

They went into the Epsilon to drink something and get warm. Then he took her by the arm again and led her outside. They crossed Juramento.

"Let's get through this hellhole fast," he said, his steps now hurried.

They passed Cabildo and went on up Juramento, until they were walking along the old streets paved with large paving stones, through the mystery of old Belgrano. At the corner of Vidal he stopped to look at the old mansion that sat there, gloomily, the remains of a villa that had once stood in lordly dignity on the lot. He studied it as though he were considering purchasing it, as Silvia had already noted once before. She told him, and he smiled.

"Something along those lines."

"I once read that you went out looking for houses for a novel. Is that true? Is that necessary?"

He laughed, but he left the question unanswered. Like some film director. Anyway, for which novel? It was like characters in search of an author, houses in search of characters to knock on their doors.

At the corner of Cramer the big old house had been turned into a Basque restaurant. Fads.

"Swear you'll never eat in a restaurant like that," he said to her with comic seriousness.

"But is it true that you're writing a novel?"

"A novel? Yes . . . no . . . I don't know how to explain . . . It's true that I seem to be obsessed by certain things, but it's all so hard . . . I suffer so much with the story, and also . . ."

After a few steps, he added:

233

"You know what happened with physics, at the beginning of the century? Everything began to be called into doubt. The fundamentals, I mean, the very most basic assumptions. It was like a building that creaks and groans and you have to go down to inspect the foundations. People began to be doing not physics but rather meditations on physics."

He leaned against the wall and stood for a moment contemplating the Basque restaurant.

"The same sort of thing has happened in the novel. The foundations have had to be looked into. Which is no coincidence, because it was born at the birth of this Western civilization of ours, and it's followed the same arc, the same trajectory, right down to this moment of collapse. Is there a crisis in the novel or is it rather a novel of crisis? Both. One delves into its essence, its mission, its worth. But it's all been done so far from the outside. There've been attempts to carry out the same examination from within, but one would have to go deeper. A novel in which the novelist him- or herself is included."

"But I'm sure I've read things like that. Isn't there a genre called metafiction?"

"Yes, but I'm not talking about that, I'm not talking about the *figure* of the writer inside the fiction. I'm talking about the possibility of the extreme case, in which it's the *author of the novel* that's inside the novel. Not as an observer, though, or a chronicler, or a witness."

"How, then?"

"As just another character, the same sort of character as all the rest, which however do come from the soul or spirit or *anima* of the author. The author would be a man maddened, somehow, and living with his own doubles, aspects of his own self. Though not 'acrobatically,' if you know what I mean. Heaven forfend. Just to see whether we couldn't penetrate that great mystery, rather."

He was deep in thought, even as they walked. No, no, *that* was the way. Into his own darkness, his own shadows.

It was almost as though he had it "on the tip of his tongue," and something, some enigmatic prohibition, some secret command, some sacred and repressive power were keeping him from seeing it with any clarity. He could feel it, though—as an imminent yet at the same time impossible revelation. But perhaps the secret was to be revealed to him as he went along, and perhaps he might at last be able to see it in the terrible light of a nocturnal sun, when the journey was over. Guided along by his own fantasies, toward the continent which they alone could carry him to. And so, his eyes blindfolded, he suddenly seemed to feel that he was being carried to the edge of an abyss, at the bottom of which lay the key that was tantalizing him.

They had turned down Cramer toward Mendoza and then, along Mendoza, they had slowly walked until they came to the railroad crossing. In the evening twilight the corner seemed to emanate an ominous melancholy: the vacant lots, the trees, the streetlight set shivering by the southwest wind, the railway embankment. A great sense of emptiness, of helplessness lay over the place. Sabato took it all in, fascinated. He sat down on the wall bordering the sidewalk and seemed to be taking the sad inventory of the place. And when, swiftly, dizzyingly, noisily, the tram passed by, the melancholy was shattered like a funeral procession scattered by gunshots.

It was drizzling rain, and growing colder by the minute.

"A nice place for a young man to commit suicide in," Sabato muttered suddenly, as though thinking out loud.

Silvia looked at him startled.

"Don't be silly," he said with a wry, sad laugh. "A young man in a novel, one of those novels that go out looking for the absolute and only come up with bullshit."

She murmured something.

"What?"

She said he always seemed to come back to the idea of suicide. She was thinking about Castel, about Martín.

Yes, it was true.

"But in the end, they *don't* commit suicide," he added.

"Why not?"

"I'm not sure. The novelist doesn't always know the reasons for his characters' actions. I always intended to carry Martín to suicide. And look what happened."

"Might it not be that, deep down, you don't approve of it?"

He seemed to accept that, though a bit dubiously.

"And that character . . ." Silvia began, then seemed to think better of it.

"What's that?"

"No, nothing."

"What is it? Tell me."

"That boy, I mean. That young man. This place. Is this something you plan to write?"

He didn't answer at once. He picked up a handful of little stones and arranged them into the shape of the letter R.

"Honestly, I don't know. By now I don't know anything about anything. All right, maybe I will write about a kid like that, somebody that comes here one day intending to kill himself. But then, of course . . ." He didn't finish the sentence. He stood up, said "Let's go," and walked with her to the Belgrano R station.

"I have to stay," he told her.

"Will I see you again?"

"I don't know, Silvia. I'm not well. I'm not well at all. Forgive me."

A WARNING

HE WAS ON THE POINT OF STARTING, he'd already rolled a piece of paper into the typewriter, but then his gaze began wandering about the room. Purposelessly. Then it returned to the typewriter. Finally he took a breath and wrote: "We must never forget Fernando's advice." Just at that moment the mail came. He leafed through the envelopes, then decided to open a large one, from the United States. It contained, he knew, Lilia Strout's article on "Evil in *On Heroes and Tombs*." Its epigraph, taken from the Bible (Eccl. 3:22), was "What is too wonderful for you, do not go further into that thing, do not dwell upon it; and that which is beyond your strength, do not investigate that thing." He stood for a long time, pondering. Then he ripped the paper from the machine.

INTERVIEW

"ARE YOU HAPPY WITH WHAT YOU'VE WRITTEN, SENOR SABATO?"

"I'd hardly stoop that low, I should think."

"Who *is* Ernesto Sabato?"

"My books have been my attempt to answer that question. I don't want to make you go out and read them, but if you really want an answer to that question, I'm afraid you'll have to."

"Could you give us a preview of what you're working on at the present?"

"A novel."

"Does it have a title?"

"That, I generally don't know until the end, when I've finished writing the book. For the moment, I'm not sure. It might be *The Angel of Darkness*. But it might turn out to be *Abaddon the Exterminator*."

"Gee, they're both a little spooky, aren't they?"

"Yes, they are."

"I'd love for you to answer a few questions for me: what do you think of the so-called Boom in Latin American literature? do you think a writer ought to be socially committed? what advice would you give a writer just setting out? at what time of day do you write? do you prefer sunny days, or cloudy days? do you identify with your characters? do you write your own experiences, or do you make them up? what do you think of Borges? should the artist have complete freedom? are writers' conventions useful? how would you describe your style? what do you think of the *nouvelle vague*?"

"Listen, my friend, let's stop this nonsense and once and for all tell the truth here. But no conditions: the whole truth. I mean, let's talk about cathedrals and whorehouses, ideals and concentration camps. I, at least, have no patience for joking around
because I am going to die.
The man who is immortal can afford
to go on and on about nothing.
Not me—my days are numbered (though what man's days, my interviewer friend, are *not* numbered, I ask you—tell me, cross your heart and hope to die)
and I want to add it all up, see
what the bottom line of all this is
(mandrakes or scriveners)
and whether it's true that the gods are greater things
than the worms

which soon will be gorging on my flesh.
I don't know, I do not know, I do not know anything
(why should I try to fool anybody)
I'm neither so arrogant nor so stupid
as to proclaim the superiority of worms.
(I'll leave that to the dime-a-dozen atheists.)
I confess that the argument impresses me,
since the coffin,
the hearse,
and those other grotesque implements of death
are visible testimony of the precariousness of our existence.
But who knows, who knows, my interviewer friend,
it well may be that the gods simply can't be bothered,
that condescending even to speak to man is beneath their dignity,
that they would never stoop to mean demagoguery,
to making themselves grossly understandable,
but rather that sinister spectacles await us,
after the last speech has been given
and our solitary body,
forever left to its own devices
(though, please note, abandoned truly, not with those imperfect,
     longing, and utterly futile abandonments that life affords us),
awaits the hordes, the thronging attack
of the worm.
Let's talk, then, without fear,
but also without pretensions,
simply,
and with some sense of humor
to downplay the logical pathos of the matter a bit.
Let's talk about all sorts of things.
I mean:
about those problematical gods
about the patent worms
about the changing faces of men.
I don't know a great deal about these curious problems
but what I know, I know for sure
because it comes from my own experiences

238

not from stories read in books,
so I can talk about love, or fear
like a saint talking about his ecstasies
or like a vaudeville magician (at a dinner party, among his closest
    friends)
might talk about his tricks.
You mustn't expect anything else,
don't criticize me for it afterward, don't be perverse, for heaven's
    sake.
Or mean-spirited.
I warn you, be a little more modest—
because you, too, are doomed (tralala, tralala, tralala)
to be food for those worms we were just talking about.
So, except for madmen and the invisible gods
(who might be nonexistent anyway),
all the rest of you would do well to pay attention, and to give me if
not your respect at least your ear for a moment."

"Many readers will ask, Señor Sabato, how it's possible for you
to have been trained in physics and mathematics."

"It's the simplest thing in the world to explain. I believe I told
you that I fled from the Stalinist movement in 1935, in Brussels,
with no money, no documents. Guillermo Etchebehere came to my
relief—he was a Trotskyite, and for a while I was allowed to sleep
in the attic of the École Normale Supérieure on the rue d'Ulm. I
remember it as though it were yesterday. A big bed, but back then
there was no heat; I would crawl in through a window at ten o'clock
at night and get into bed, the caretaker's double bed, wonderful man,
but it was a fierce winter and there was no heat—we'd put layer after
layer of L'Humanité on top of ourselves, so of course every time one
of us turned over, you'd hear the rustling of the newspapers (I can
practically hear it now). I was in chaos, many was the time I'd be
walking along the banks of the Seine thinking about killing myself,
but I felt sorry for the old porter, Lehrmann his name was, an Al-
satian fellow, he'd given me a few francs to eat with, to buy a cup
of café au lait with, he was a real trump, I'll tell you, so I kept on,
as long as I could, until one day I stole a book on mathematics from
Gibert's, Borel's calculus I think it was, and when I sat down in a

café to study it—it was freezing outside, I was drinking a hot cup of
café au lait—I began to think about those people who say
that this great bazaar we live in
is made up of a single substance
which is transmuted into trees, criminals, and mountains,
in an attempt to copy a petrified museum
of eternal ideas.
They claim
(old travelers, students of the pyramids, men who've glimpsed things
    in dreams, the occasional mystagogue)
that that museum is an astonishing collection of immovable, static
    objects:
immortal trees, ossified tigers,
plus triangles and parallelopipeds, of course.
And one perfect Man, also,
formed of crystals of eternity,
which a mass of universal particles—
once salt, water, batrachians,
fire, and cloud,
the excrement of bulls and of horses,
viscera rotting on battlefields—
clumsily try to imitate
(a child's drawing).
So (these old travelers go on, though now with the slightest touch
    of irony in their eyes),
out of that disgusting mess
of filth, earth, and the cold remains of dinner,
made pure again, distilled by sun and water,
zealously cared for and guarded
against the contemptuous, sarcastic powers
of the great forces of the earth
(lightning, hurricane, a frenzied ocean, leprosy)
there is formed a clumsy simulacrum of the Man of crystalline per-
    fection.
But though he grows, and even prospers (things going pretty well,
    huh?)
suddenly he begins to totter

begins to clutch at his throat and thrash about and struggle,
and, finally, dies,
like some absurd caricature,
and then returns to clay and cow dung.
Unless he is allowed the scant dignity of fire."

"Is there anything else you'd like to add to this interview, Señor Sabato? Some special preference in theater or music you'd like to share with our readers? Anything about the novelist's vocation, or his place in his society?"

"No, sir, thank you. Nothing."

THEN FINALLY THEY RAN INTO EACH OTHER.
They walked along the steep cliffs of Belgrano, then, not speaking. As always when he was with Marcelo, S. felt confused, uncomfortable; he didn't quite know what to say to him. It was as though he were trying to defend himself before a judge at once kind and of absolute uprightness. Someone had once defined a confessor as that paradoxical judge that absolved the man the confessor found guilty of sins. S. felt naked before Marcelo, he mercilessly confessed his sins to him, and although he took his absolution for granted, he always ended up unhappy. Maybe because instead of forgiveness his spirit needed punishment.

They sat down at a table in a café.

"What is a writer's first duty?" S. asked him suddenly, as though instead of asking him a question he were beginning his defense.

The young man looked at him with his deep eyes.

"I'm talking about a writer of fiction. His duty is no more and no less than telling the truth. But the Truth with a capital *T*, Marcelo. Not one of those small truths we read in the newspapers every day. Especially the most hidden truths."

He paused for Marcelo's reply. But Marcelo, realizing that S. was waiting for him, blushed and lowered his eyes; he began to stir the dregs of his coffee with his spoon.

"But you," said S., almost irritated, "you've spent your life reading good literature. Right?"

The young man murmured something.

241

"How's that? How's that? I can't hear you," S. asked with growing irritation. At least he heard something that sounded like a yes.

Then why wouldn't he talk?

Marcelo raised his eyes shyly, and in a soft voice he replied that he wasn't accusing S. of anything, that he didn't share Araujo's views, that he felt that S. had every right in the world to write what he wrote.

"But you are a revolutionary, too, aren't you?"

Marcelo looked at him an instant, then lowered his eyes again, embarrassed by the grand-sounding name. Sabato realized this, and corrected himself: he supported the revolution. Well, yes, he supposed . . . he didn't know . . . in a way, you know . . .

His few words came out filled with adverbs that attenuated his verbs, made them modest and self-denying, and with qualifiers for every noun, so that it was almost as though he hadn't said anything. If he hadn't spoken that way, his shyness, his desire not to wound S. would have kept him from opening his mouth at all.

"But you've read not only the war poems of Hernández. You've read his poems on death, too. And what's worse, you admire Rilke. I think I've even seen you with some books by Trakl. Wasn't that German book something by Trakl—that book I saw you carrying in the Dandy?"

Marcelo made an almost imperceptible gesture of assent. It seemed to him almost pornographic to talk about such things in public. He always put a brown paper cover on his books.

Suddenly, Sabato realized that he was performing almost an act of violation on Marcelo. He saw, with sorrow and something almost like a sense of guilt, that Marcelo had taken out his asthma inhaler.

"I'm sorry, Marcelo. Forgive me . . . I didn't mean to say such things. Honestly . . ."

But he had. The worst part of it was that in fact he *had* wanted to say exactly what he'd said. He sat there confused and angry, not with the boy but with himself.

"Your friend," he said after a while, not realizing he was starting on another unfortunate tack.

Marcelo raised his eyes.

"You're very close, aren't you?"

"Yes."

"He works in a factory?" S. thought he'd heard somebody say the young man had worked in the Fiat factory.

"He lives with you, in your room, doesn't he?"

Marcelo looked at him intensely.

"Yes," he replied, "but nobody knows that."

"Oh, yes, of course. It's just that, you know, he reminds me of a friend Bruno and I had, during the strikes in 1932. Carlos."

Marcelo used his inhaler. His hand was trembling.

Sabato felt guilty about this absurd scene, so with some effort he changed the subject and began talking about a Chaplin movie he'd seen at the San Martín. Marcelo grew calmer, like a man who, about to be stripped naked in the plaza by some madman, finds the madman suddenly walking away. But the relief was only temporary.

"Man is a dual creature," Sabato said. "Tragically dual. And the worst part of it, the most stupid thing about it, is that ever since Socrates, man has tried to outlaw the dark side. The philosophers of the Enlightenment kicked the unconscious out the door. But it sneaked back in on them through the window. Its powers are invincible. And whenever man has tried to destroy them, they've shrunk back, crouched down and at last broken out again, rebelled with even greater strength and perversity. Look at the France of pure reason. It's given us more possessed and demonic men than any other country in the world—from de Sade to Rimbaud and Genet."

Marcelo sat unspeaking, looking at him.

"Of course I couldn't say this the other day. I don't know . . . It seemed to me that your friend . . . I mean . . . How shall I put this . . . Sometimes it hurts me, or saddens me perhaps, to say certain things in front of somebody that . . ."

Marcelo had lowered his eyes.

"So as I was saying. People talk about the mission of the novel. As though one could talk about the mission of dreams! Look at Voltaire. One of the greatest men of modern times. Hah! All you have to do is read *Candide* to see what's underneath that veneer of enlightened thought."

Sabato laughed, but it was not sane laughter.

"And that other one is even more grotesque yet. The director of the *Encyclopédie*. What do you think? You've read *Le Neveu*, haven't you?"

243

Marcelo shook his head.

"You ought to. Did you know that Marx praised it? For other reasons, I suppose, of course. But anyway . . . That's why I said the powers sneaked in through the back door. It's no accident that the growth of the novel coincides with the growth of modern times. Where were the Furies supposed to take refuge? People talk about the New Man, always with capital letters. But we'll never create that new man if we don't reintegrate him. He's been disintegrated, so to speak, 'dissociated' some have called it, by this rationalistic, mechanical civilization of plastic and computers. In the great primitive civilizations, the dark powers were worshipped."

It was growing dark, and Marcelo was relieved by the lack of light.

"Our civilization is sick and dying. There is not only exploitation, and poverty: there is spiritual poverty as well, Marcelo. And I'm certain that you agree with me. We aren't talking about giving everybody in the world a refrigerator. We are talking about the possibility of actually creating a new sort of person. And meanwhile, the writer's duty is to write the truth, not to contribute to the decay and degradation with lies."

Marcelo had no comment, and S. began feeling worse and worse. Theoretically, he felt these things strongly, but his moralistic and even bourgeois side was perhaps tormenting him: poor blind creatures!, that sort of thing. Well, then, what did he want? Did he want Marcelo to applaud him for having discovered horrors? He knew, on the other hand, that in spite of his courtesy and his shyness, Marcelo firmly believed in certain things, and that no one would ever be able to get anything out of him that he didn't believe in. Or was it that essential honesty, that integrity, which drew S. to the young man, made him try to win some sort of approval from him?

He felt terrible. He excused himself and left.

He walked along Echeverría, and suddenly he found himself sitting on a bench before the Church of the Immaculate Conception. Its cupola stood out somberly against the gray sky. There was a drizzle of rain, and the night was turning cold. What was he doing there, like some silly fool? The Blind, he thought, looking up at the great church, imagining its crypt, its secret tunnels. It appeared that his dark obsessions had led him to this symbol of his anguish and torment. He was not well, a vague disquiet gnawed at him, and he didn't know what to do. Suddenly he realized how badly he'd acted with his friend, whom he'd left so brusquely and stupidly, whom he might even have hurt. He got up from the bench and returned to the café. They'd turned on the lights now. Fortunately, Marcelo was still there. He sat with his back to S., writing something on a piece of paper. If he had thought, S. later reflected, he'd never have come up on Marcelo so silently. When Marcelo saw S., he blushed and clumsily covered the little scrap of paper with his hand. "A poem," thought Sabato, embarrassed by the way he'd burst upon the young man. He pretended he'd not noticed; he pretended to pick up the conversation again.

"Listen, I came back because I'd intended to say other things to you. I mean . . . things different from what I . . . I want to ask you a favor."

The young man, leaning forward slightly, now himself once again, courteously awaited the request.

Sabato was irritated.

"You see? I haven't even begun to talk and you're already sitting there very deferentially, ready to listen to whatever it is I might have to say. That's exactly the favor I was going to ask of you. For you to stop being that way. At least with me. I've known you since the day you were born. I want you to argue with me, to tell me what your reservations are. Gosh . . . I don't know . . . You're one of the few people . . . And then . . ."

Marcelo's expression had drifted, although only very slightly, toward a kind of worried look; he was very serious and attentive.

"But it's that I . . ." he said.

Sabato took him by the arm, but with the same delicacy one would use with an injured man.

"Marcelo, I need . . ."

But he did not go on, and it appeared the conversation had petered out once and for all. The young man watched Sabato's head sink onto the table. Since he believed it was his duty to try to help him, he said, "But I tell you I agree with you . . . Or at least . . . I mean . . . in general, of course . . ."

Sabato had raised his eyes and was watching Marcelo with a mixture of attention and annoyance.

245

"You see?" he said. "Always the same thing."

Marcelo lowered his eyes. "It's hopeless," Sabato thought. And yet he felt the necessity to talk to the boy.

"I know I'm exaggerating, of course. I always exaggerate. It's just the way I am. Down deep what I am is an extremist, and I know that. I've spent my entire life going from one extreme to the other, being wrong with a vengeance. I was swept off my feet by art, and then I went into mathematics. And when I got all the way to the end of that particular swing of the pendulum, I gave mathematics up, almost resentfully. The same story with Marxism, and with surrealism . . . Of course maybe 'give up' is too . . . It's just a manner of speaking, you know. If one has loved something deeply and intensely, there are always marks of that passion left on one. In the words one uses, in one's tics, in one's dreams . . . Oh, especially in one's dreams . . . The faces you thought you'd forgotten forever reappear . . . Oh yes, I exaggerate things, Marcelo. I told you once that poets are invariably on the side of the demons, even though they don't always know it themselves, and I noticed that you didn't agree with me . . . That exaggeration is Blake's, but never mind—I repeat it all the time, there must be some reason for that. I also told you that that's why we're fascinated by Dante's Inferno while we're bored by his Paradiso. And that sin and damnation inspired Milton, while Paradise took his creative impulse away . . . Yes, of course—Tolstoy's demons, and Dostoyevski's, and Stendhal's, and Thomas Mann's, and Musil's, and Proust's. All of that is true, at least for that sort of person. And that is why they are rebels but rarely revolutionaries, in the Marxist sense of the word. That horrific condition—because it *is* a horrific condition, I tell you—makes them unfit for an established society, even that consummate society dreamed of by the Marxists. They might be useful as rebels, in the Romantic Age. But afterward . . . Mayakovski, can you imagine? Esenin . . . But that isn't what I wanted to talk to you about. I think I wanted to tell you that you shouldn't be so quiet, that you shouldn't just *accept* these exaggerations of mine, these stupidities of mine, my brusqueness, my rantings, this obsession of mine to choose examples to justify my wild ideas . . . I know that sometimes suddenly, when I'm talking to you, you think about Miguel Hernández, who may have been obsessed by death and many of whose poems may be what might be

246

called metaphysical, but who was most certainly not possessed by demons the way somebody like, say, Genet was. And you have every right in the world to think, 'Stop exaggerating, Ernesto, things aren't always that way, it's possible for a great poet not to be on the side of the demons . . . There may even be some poets who are Dionysian, euphoric, who are in harmony with the cosmos . . . And some painters, too.' "

His voice trailed off. He was feeling unhappy again; he sensed he was somehow lying. And with terrible distaste, he got up and left.

ONCE AGAIN HIS STEPS LED HIM TOWARD THE PLAZA,
and sitting on a bench he contemplated the circular mass of the church against the cloudy, drizzly sky. He imagined Fernando hovering about that entrance to the forbidden world, just at daybreak, and at last entering the subterranean universe.

The crypts. The Blind.

Von Arnim came to his mind: we are composed of many spirits, and they stalk us in our dreams, they utter dark threats, they give us warnings difficult to understand, they frighten and terrify us. How can they be so foreign to us that they frighten us? Don't they emerge from our own hearts? But what was this "us"? And what of that fascination which in spite of everything makes us evoke them, call them up, conjure up their presences, even though we know that they may well bring utter terror and terrible punishment?

No, he couldn't quite remember what it was that von Arnim had said. Something about the fact that if we were being spied upon by beings from a higher world, it would be by higher beings that only the poetic imagination could make visible. Clairvoyance.

But what if those invisible monsters, once invoked, were to launch themselves against us, and ourselves powerless to conquer or tame them? Or if our conjuration were somehow slightly off the mark, and we were not able to open the portals of Hell; or if it were *on* the mark, and we then ran the risk of madness, or of death?

And what had happened to von Arnim and his moral scruples? And Tolstoy? Always the same story. But what was it he had said, what was it? Was it sacred, that creator's faith in something still uncreated, in something that the creator was to bring to birth after

247

he had plunged into the abyss and given his soul up to chaos? Yes, it had to be. And it should never be impugned. The man had been punished enough simply by having to leap into such horror.

The wind blew gusts of frozen mist.

That was when he saw her walking like a sleepwalker across the plaza toward one of those old doorways near the Epsilon. How could he not recognize her? She was tall, with hair as black as night, and her steps were *her* steps. He ran toward her, spellbound, took her in his arms, and said to her (screamed at her) *Alejandra*. But all she did was stare at him with her gray-green eyes, her lips squeezed tightly shut. Out of disdain? Out of contempt?

Sabato let his arms drop to his side, and she walked away, without turning around. She opened the door of that house he knew so well and closed it behind her.

AROUND THEN, MEMÉ VARELA CALLED HIM.
A séance, she said, Friday night beginning at ten, with Daneri. She asked S. to bring someone else with the power, to add strength. He suggested Alonso.

"Alonso?" She didn't know him, but wonderful. He also suggested Ilse Müller. Super, she'd heard of her, she knew who she was, super. Suddenly, it seemed grotesque to Sabato, this bringing so many seers together, so many people with one distinguishing trait: as though everybody had to have a wooden leg, or a glass eye, or be left-handed. Oh, he'd mentioned Alonso, but now that he thought about it, he thought he was in Brazil. All right, that was okay, she'd expect him with Ilse Müller.

He took Beto, too, as though bringing along the head of the World Weights and Measures Laboratory in Paris. He didn't want to be swept along by mistaken sensations, by fallible experience.

Soon the famous Daneri arrived in his blue suit, his glasses with the remarkably thick black frames that stood out incongruously against his hairless, milky-white head like an egg set pointed side up on the man's shoulders. He was a little monstrous—lunar, ectoplasmic, like a creature from some sunless planet who had been dressed up in our own costumes and ways of behavior to be presented here on Earth. A creature that had lived always in the dark-

248

ness, or under fluorescent light. His flesh was no doubt soft and spongy, like warm lard. His skeleton must have been cartilaginous, as in some lower species of animals. Had he come from some trans-Uranian planet where the sun's rays shone like a memory of sunlight? Or had some cellar been uncovered after centuries of burial, to reveal this white creature with drool about his lips as he smiled?

Margot Grimaux came in as well, wearing those sunglasses that she never took off; her eyebrows were like two gables over her eyes, such as one saw in people who had suffered all manner of deaths, illness, operations on the womb, nervous breakdowns, fibromas. She was anxious to communicate with someone from the other world, someone now tragically far away. A child, a lover?

First there had to take place a technical conversation between Ilse and Daneri, the sort of conversation people in those international conventions of specialists (philologists or botanists, otorhinolaryngologists) had, using that hermetic jargon of theirs. People who'd never met personally but who kept up with each other via the journals. Common friends? Mr. Luck, of course.

Then began the jousting. Each person told of certain experiences, visitations (a word peculiar to the specialty), dreams, instances of clairvoyance, memorable séances.

Memé:

When she was a girl, she'd gone to an English-language school. In History, she'd said something or other about what had happened on the second flight of stairs of the prison Marie Antoinette had been held in. When the class was over, the teacher called her over and asked her where she'd learned that particular detail, which was only chronicled in a particular encyclopedia that Memé had never seen. Everyone hung in fascination on this anecdote, and at last it was concluded that the thing could only be explained by Memé's being the reincarnation of Marie Antoinette.

Ilse Müller:

During the summer she would always invite a certain group of friends to her house in Mar del Plata, where they would have séances under the direction of an extraordinary woman named Marieta. Surely they had heard of her? No, or maybe, maybe Memé had . . . Did she have this sort of hair, and stand so tall? No, she was so tall, with this sort of skin and that kind of hair . . . But anyway, her name was Marieta Fidalgo, a truly *extraordinary* creature . . .

By now it was very late; they had spent several hours trying unsuccessfully to establish contact. The efforts had been exhausting, and they were all dead tired. Sometime around three they all lay down or sprawled wherever they were, in armchairs or on sofas, to sleep for a while, when suddenly they heard a terrible banging and the table was flung violently into a corner.

Daneri nodded with pedantic placidity, smiling like some albino toad: he looked like some benevolent member of the Academy of Letters told, at a meeting of retired schoolmasters, about the brilliance of schoolboys in spelling, or the use of prepositions.

"There you have it, there you have it," he was muttering with lunar bonhomie.

Had anyone looked at him up close, he would no doubt have been seen to have a tiny thread of milky spittle dripping from between his lips.

A case of visitation offered by Memé: A piece of paper falls on the floor during a séance and her son-in-law Conito, who had attended the session with the classic attitude of skepticism adopted by scoffers and jokers everywhere, picks up the paper with a little sneer. But when he looks at the paper, he is struck dumb. What's wrong, what's happened? It was his dead father's handwriting; it was a letter to Conito.

People mentioned cases of communications written in Greek, Arabic, and even in the Gypsy language, transmitted by mediums who didn't know the languages.

A rest of about a half-hour.

Then the efforts began again. One and another rap was heard, ears were pricked up, there were messages from several people, but always the wrong ones.

"It's for you," Memé said to Margot Grimaux, who was still silent, sunk in sadness, with her circumflex eyebrows.

She listened attentively, she tried to decipher the message, but she couldn't make out anything really clear. A man swimming in the ocean? Memé anxiously asked if that might not be Bernasconi, but Margot shook her head disconsolately. Still, Memé kept trying to make out the message, with no success.

250

Then a series of arbitrary rappings occurred, some frankly non-sensical, like some sort of practical joke with pseudowords like *pli* and *pla*.

"They're making fun of us," Daneri explained. "It often happens."

"We might as well call it a night," admitted Memé, slightly miffed.

Then the conversation took a more careless and informal turn; people told stories, related memorable cases, remembered certain shocking or angry attitudes adopted from time to time by spirits. Did anyone recall something Mr. Luck had said once to Dr. Alfredo Palacios? No, yes, maybe, more or less . . . He had told Carlitos Colautti's fortune once, and it seemed Carlitos would be married by the age of forty-five. Great, just great, when you remembered that Carlitos at the time was a little over twenty and was always on the verge of marriage to somebody or other. Et cetera.

When they were outside on the street, Beto declared he was astounded at S.'s interest, at his concentration during all this.

"Such utter nonsense," he muttered in stupefaction, shaking his head and looking hard at Sabato.

S. did not reply.

"You aren't going to tell me you believe in that rubbish."

Sabato felt he had to say something, but nothing came to mind.

At last he asked Beto whether he'd seen *Rosemary's Baby*.

"Yes. So what?"

"I'll tell you what. That world in there," Sabato indicated Memé's apartment, "is full of charlatans, of poor old ladies ready to believe anything, of snobs, of fakes and smoke and mirrors. Of con artists. But that doesn't prove that the dark forces don't exist. There is a dangerous world, a world of terror, there, infinitely more terrifying and dangerous than you can imagine."

"And what does Polanski have to do with all that, if you please?"

"He intended to have himself some fun. And you see how it turned out."

Beto stood wordlessly, but Sabato had seen the expression of annoyance and skepticism on his face, even in the dark.

"Try to understand, Beto. It's like some sinister carnival: dressed as clowns, there are monsters, too."

FACTS TO KEEP IN MIND

ISAAC THE BLIND IS THE FATHER OF THE MODERN CABALA. He lived somewhere in the southwest part of France in the thirteenth century. Isaac "the Blind"!

Symbols, letters, and numbers. They come out of the old magic, the gnostics, and Apocalypse.

The number 3 in Dante. There are 33 cantos. There are 9 heavens, divided into 3 categories of 3. Was Dante inspired by the *Night Journey* of the Cabalist Mohiddin Ibn Arabi? Did Dante have any relationship to Isaac the Blind?

A chain of initiates, from farthest antiquity down to the disintegration of the atom. Newton belonged to that chain, and what he sets down in his writings no more than scratches the surface of what he actually knew. He wrote: "This manner of impregnating the mercury was held in secret by those who knew, and it most probably constitutes the doorway to something more noble [than the fabrication of gold], something which cannot be communicated without the world's being exposed to immense danger."

Thence derives the ambiguous language of the alchemists. Symbols for the initiate.

ANOTHER FACT WHICH SHOULD BE KEPT IN MIND

THE SUBTERRANEAN DEMONS FORM THE FIFTH CLASS OF DEMONS. Their abode is caverns and grottoes, and they may be either allies or enemies of those who dig wells and those who seek treasure buried in the depths of the earth. They lay constant traps for the ruin of man through cracks in the ground and abysses of all kinds, eruptions of the earth, and avalanches and collapses of mountainsides.

The Lucifuges, those who flee the light, are the sixth and last class. They may take body only at night. Among them, Leonardo is the great master of Sabbath orgies and of black magic; and Ashtaroth, who knows the past and the future, is one of the Seven Princes of Hell that appeared before Dr. Faust.

(JEAN WIER, *De praestigiis*, 1568)

252

CERTAIN EVENTS WHICH TOOK PLACE IN PARIS CA. 1938

I BELIEVE I ONCE MENTIONED TO YOU that the publication of *On Heroes and Tombs* openly unleashed the powers. But even before that, many years before, they had begun to make themselves felt, though in the most furtive and sinister way. Which, of course, made it all the more frightening. During a war a man can defend himself to an extent because the enemy is there before him, wearing a different uniform. But how can we defend ourselves when the enemy is one of us, wearing clothing like our own? Or when we don't even know that there's a war going on and that a dangerous enemy is mining our lands? If I had been aware of that silent, secret mobilization in 1938, I might perhaps have been able to defend myself. The signs went right by me, though, because in peacetime who pays any mind to that tourist taking photographs of a bridge? Ernesto Bonasso had just put me in touch with Domínguez, telling me that he was the painter who had put Victor Brauner's eye out—a horrifying and significant event, yet one that suggested nothing of the future to me. The second augury, perhaps the more chilling of the two, was the sudden emergence of R. out of the shadows. But of course that was an "augury" only in view of succeeding events. I think that if we knew our future, we would forever be seeing small events all around us, portending our days to come, and even foreshadowing them; as we don't know what the future is to bring, they seem random, coincidences of no real significance. Think of the fearful meaning, for someone who knew the apocalyptic ending of the thing, of seeing a corporal with a Chaplinesque moustache and wild eyes go into a brewery in Munich sometime around 1923.

Now I also see that it was not by chance that during that period I should have begun my abandonment of science: science is the world of the light!

I was working in the Curie Laboratory, and I was like one of those priests who is beginning not to believe anymore but who goes on celebrating the mass mechanically, only sometimes troubled by its, and his own, inauthenticity.

"You seem so far away," Goldstein would say, with that searching, fearful expression that a good, theologically orthodox friend of

253

the priest's might have after watching him during the celebration of the mass.

"I'm not well," I would explain. "Not well at all."

Which was, to a certain extent, true. And so I went on, distant and distracted, until one day I handled the actinium carelessly, and carried the small but dangerous stigma of it on my finger for several years.

I began drinking; I found a sort of sad voluptuousness in the alcoholic spinning of my head.

One very depressing winter day I was walking along the rue Saint-Jacques towards my *pension* when I turned into a bistro to have a glass of mulled wine. I looked around for a dark corner, partly because I had begun to shy away from people and partly because the light has always been bad for me. (I never realized this, though I've been this way my entire life.) I wanted to give myself over to that solitary vice of ruminating on fragments of ideas and feelings as the alcohol gradually took effect. The room had begun spinning pretty well already when I first saw him: he was looking at me fixedly, with a penetrating and (or so it seemed to me) ironic look, and that infuriated me. I looked away, hoping that would dissuade him from continuing to stare at me. But either because I couldn't help it or because I could feel his piercing gaze still on me, I had to meet his eyes again. He seemed vaguely familiar to me: he was my age (we are astral twins, he would say to me later, more than once, with that laugh of his that froze one's blood) and everything about him reminded me of some great bird of prey, a terrible night-flying falcon perhaps (and indeed I never saw him except alone and in the shadows). His hands were lean, thin, bony, grasping, predatory, pitiless. His eyes looked grayish-green to me, contrasting against his swarthy skin. His nose was thin but powerful and aquiline. In spite of his being seated, I calculated that he was tall and slightly stooped. His clothes were frayed and worn, but through the threadbareness of them one saw that he wore them aristocratically.

He went on observing me, *studying* me. But what made me more and more furious was not only that he was looking at me with that expression of irony on his face, but that the irony had actually increased.

254

I'm impulsive, as you know, and so after a few seconds of this I got up out of my seat to go over and demand that the man tell me what this outrageous behavior of his was all about. As his only reply he said to me, not even standing up:

"So you don't recognize me, eh?"

He had one of those voices that characterize the smoker: it was husky, masculine, and a bit rough, as though the man were hoarse. I looked at him in astonishment. A feeling of uncertainty, yet at the same time of aversion, began to take form inside me, something like what happens just as we wake up and at the foot of our bed our blurred vision makes out the shape that had tormented our dreams.

Since the suspense had become uncomfortable, he spoke the single word "Rojas." I thought of the surname, and so I began mentally running through the list of the Rojases I'd known. But as though he were able to read my mind, he broke in with annoyance:

"No, you fool. The town."

The town? "I left Rojas when I was twelve years old," I said curtly, trying to let him know that it was an arrogant presumption on his part to think I might recognize him or anyone else after all those years.

"I know," he answered. "You've no reason to tell *me*. I know all about your life. I've been following your career very closely."

My irritation grew; the man was a meddling boor. It gave me great pleasure to sneer:

"Well I, as you see, don't remember you at all."

He grinned a small, sarcastic grin.

"That doesn't matter in the slightest. Besides, it's only logical that you'd try to forget me."

"Try to forget you!"

I had finally sat down because, as you can see, there was no use waiting for such a man to ask you to have a chair. I'd not only sat down, in fact; I'd ordered another glass of warm wine, even though my speech was blurred and my head was really not functioning well at all.

"And why should I want to try to forget you, pray tell?"

I was growing belligerent now, and I could tell that this conversation could easily end in violence.

He smiled with that sneering smile of his and raised his eyebrows; his forehead furrowed into a series of very marked parallel ridges.

"You never liked me," he said, simply. "Or rather I suppose I should say that you always detested me. Don't you remember the sparrow?"

Now the figure out of my nightmare was there in perfect definition before my eyes. How could I ever have forgotten those eyes, that forehead, that sarcastic grin?

"Sparrow? What sparrow are you talking about?" I lied.

"The experiment."

"What experiment?"

"To see how it flew without eyes."

"It was all your idea," I shouted.

Several people turned our way.

"Don't get so upset," he scolded. "Oh yes, it was all my idea, but you were the one that put its eyes out with the scissors."

Stumbling, but with all the decision I was capable of, I threw myself on him and grabbed him by the throat. With quiet strength he pried my fingers from his neck and ordered me to calm down.

"Don't be a fool," he said. "All you'll accomplish that way is getting us thrown out of here by the police."

I sat down, crushed. A terrible sadness came over me, and I have no idea why, but at that moment I thought of M., waiting for me in the little room on the rue du Sommerard, and of my son in his crib.

I felt the tears begin to run down my cheeks. His expression grew even more sarcastic.

"That's it, cry, it'll do you good. Get it off your chest," he crooned, with that perverse perfection in the use of the cliché he'd been practicing since he was a boy.

I see when I read over what I've written that I'm hardly giving the most fair-minded picture of this encounter. Oh yes, I must confess that my relations with him were always those of one adversary to another, and from the very beginning I felt nothing but animosity for him. So what I've just written, the picture I've drawn of his manners, his voice, all that, is more a caricature than a true portrait. And yet, even when I try to change the words, I can't seem to see any

256

other way to describe him. I should at least say, I suppose, that there was a certain dignity about him, even though it was a diabolic sort of dignity, and a mastery of the situation, of the moment, which made me feel disconsolate and insignificant. There was something about him that reminded me of Artaud.

Before his silent, searching look, I paid for our wine and was about to leave when he spoke another name, and I was paralyzed: *Soledad*. I had to sit down. I closed my eyes so I wouldn't have to see his horrible, hated, inquisitorial face, and I tried to regain my composure.

I was in the third year of boarding school at La Plata, and one of my schoolmates was Nicolás Ortiz de Rosas. His father had been governor of the province, and since then they'd stayed there in La Plata, living modestly in one of those houses, peculiar I think to that region of Argentina, with two interior courtyards that all the rooms open on to—homes built around the time that Dardo Rocha founded the city. In the parlor, there exploded like a bomb on a quiet Sunday afternoon that oil portrait of Juan Manuel de Rosas, with the bright red sash.

The first time I saw it, I almost fainted: the effect of that school-room myth foisted on schoolboys by the Unitarians. The Bloody Tyrant looked down upon me (no, the correct verb is "watched" me) from his position in eternity with that icy gray stare of his, his pencil-thin lips squeezed together tight.

Nicolás and I were studying some theorem in geometry when I suddenly felt uneasy, as though at my back there had materialized one of those creatures that people say come down to Earth on flying saucers and have the power to communicate without speaking. I turned around, and I saw her at the door: her eyes were gray, and on her face was that same chilling expression her ancestor wore. All these years later, I still recall that apparition at my back, and I wonder whether she was unconsciously mimicking Rosas or whether the same features had been repeated in her, like a hand at cards with the same kings and jacks redealt after long years of play.

Nicolás had nothing in common with her, aside from the color of their eyes. He was spirited, gay, funny; he loved to imitate a monkey swinging from a tree, shrieking and peeling a banana. But when she was there, he would grow muted and quiet, and he would act like some underling intimidated by the presence of his superior. In a voice that I would now call quietly imperious, she asked Nicolás about something (it's strange that I can't remember what it was she asked him), and Nicolás, like some nameless yeoman before an absolute monarch, and in a voice which was not the voice I knew, told her that he didn't know. At that, she turned and left, as silently as she had come, never even deigning to speak to me.

We were a while getting back to that theorem. He was upset, distraught I might almost say, as though he were afraid of something. And I had been left with what I might call confusion, a feeling that I examined more closely when I grew up and looked back on that irruption into my life: it seemed to me that Soledad had appeared in that parlor for no other reason than *to have me know that she existed—to inform me that she was there.* But naturally, at the time it happened I was incapable of giving words to the scene that had just taken place, or of describing the characters that had played in it, as I'm doing now. It's as if the moment had been photographed and put into an album and only now were I taking the old snapshot out and looking at it, analyzing it for the first time.

I said that there was something about her that seemed to repeat what had lived in Juan Manuel de Rosas, but in truth I never learned (as though there were some ominous secret about her that was never to be revealed) how it was that she was related to Nicolás or to the Carranzas. Nor even whether there *was* any kinship at all. I rather tend to think that she was the illegitimate daughter of some obscure woman and an Ortiz de Rosas man I never knew, as frequently occurred in our part of the country when I was a boy.

As I was leaving, I got up the courage to ask whether she was Nicolás' sister.

"No," he answered, avoiding my eyes.

I didn't dare ask any more, but it did cross my mind that she was just our age, about fifteen. Now I would venture that she could as well have been a thousand, and have lived sometime in remotest history.

That night I dreamed about her. I was slowly and laboriously making my way down an underground passageway, which was growing more and more narrow and suffocating as I went along. The

258

floor of it was of wet clay, and there was hardly any light at all, and then suddenly I saw her, standing there, waiting for me in silence: she was tall, and her arms and legs were long, and her wide loins were out of all proportion to the thinness of her body. In the near-total darkness she glowed with some sort of strange phosphorescence. But what made her truly terrifying were the empty sockets of her eyes.

In the following days I couldn't concentrate on my studies; all I did was wait, with terrible agitation of spirit, for the moment when I could go to Nicolás' house again. But I'd hardly walked through the door when I realized that she wasn't there: there was that calm in the atmosphere that comes after a summer rain has washed the electricity out of the air.

I didn't need to ask, but I did anyway.

She'd gone back to Buenos Aires.

The fact that Nicolás had confirmed my feeling made me feel strong, it proved to me that some invisible but powerful thread joined me to her.

I asked Nicolás whether she lived with her parents in Buenos Aires. He answered with some hesitancy, choosing his words carefully; he told me that for the moment she was living in the Carranzas' house. The word "parents" was skirted, as though Nicolás were taking the long way around, at night, so he wouldn't have to pass by a spot it was better to avoid.

During those months I became obsessed with the idea of going one day to that house in Buenos Aires. Winter came and went, summer came, and school was over. I was by now desperate to meet her again, when one day I went to see Nicolás and he told me he was just leaving for Buenos Aires, to visit the Carranzas. It was Sunday, he was going to spend the day with the kids there. I realized that this meeting couldn't have been a coincidence; without any conscious will of my own, feeling that my heart was about to burst in my chest, I asked Nicolás if I could go along.

"Sure," he said, with his usual careless sort of generosity.

He moved through a different sort of dimension from that which I and Soledad inhabited. How could he have imagined my secret thoughts? He'd often spoken to me about Florencio and Juan Bautista Carranza, and he'd always said I'd like them, especially Florencio—and indeed he was right. But he was totally in the dark about my obsession.

I don't know whether you're familiar with the house at 1854 Acros. I seem to recall that I mentioned it to you once, that I told you that someday I'd like to make the characters in one of my novels live there. I had no idea, of course, since I *never* had any idea, what the meaning of that novel might be, much less whether I'd ever actually get it written. The house is empty at the moment; it's practically falling down, but even in those days it was in pretty bad shape, as though the owners were poor, or had neglected it terribly. From the street, you could hardly see the house for the tangle of trees and plants in the front yard. This front yard—front garden, it might have been, once—ran right down the two sides of the house, and then around the back of it, so the house, which at the turn of the century had to have been almost a palace, was totally surrounded by garden. During summer siestas, the silence of the house would be almost total, and you would have the sense of being in some abandoned mansion. Nicolás opened the huge rusty gate in the front wall and we walked around to the rear of the house until we came to the yard, or ruined garden, in back, where there was a little house which I guessed must at some time have been for the servants.

The kids lived back there, in the midst of total chaos. Now I laugh at myself worrying about whether I could go or not—in that house, with those kids, any bum in the world could walk in and take up residence in one of the rooms and spend the rest of his life there without anybody being in the least surprised.

That absurd place was where I met Florencio Carranza Paz, who was about my age, fifteen or so, and his brother Juan Bautista, who was a little younger. They resembled each other a great deal, and they prefigured Marcelo: their features were very delicate, their skin very white, almost transparent, and their hair was dark brown. One of the characteristic features of the family was their eyes—they were large and dark, but very deep-set under a brow that came down low and prominent, almost exaggerated. Their heads were narrow and their jaws a bit prognathous.

But although they looked like each other physically, there was something that one immediately noticed: Florencio's eyes were dis-

260

tracted, as though he were always thinking about something far from the things that surrounded him—a calm, beautiful landscape for instance. Something *somewhere else*, not there, not there where he was. Had it not been for the remarkable intelligence that manifested itself in everything about the boy, one would have thought he was what used to be called *"not all there"*—which as you see is an expression peculiarly apt for certain people.

As the years went on, I would become very close to Florencio, so close that I considered him one of my closest friends; for me, he was almost a judge as well, whose most terrible rebukes consisted of his silence, which he would break a few moments later, slapping at me affectionately as though he now wanted to take away the punishing edge of that slight coolness, that slight stillness that I always interpreted as disapproval.

I remember him always with that guitar that he never really played, but strummed at, as though he had not the will or the arrogance to actually bring music out of it. The way he played was more like the distant memory of a guitar, and what was hinted at in that strumming was the fragmentary echo of some gentle ballad. Years later, someone told me that they'd heard him when he thought he was alone, in the *pension* at La Plata, and that he played beautifully. But his timidity, or his delicacy, kept him from showing his talent. He never wanted to show himself superior to others in any way. When he started graduate school with me, he never took examinations, so naturally he never finished his doctorate, in spite of his gift for mathematics. He had no interest in titles or honors or position. He wound up going off as an astronomer's assistant to some modest observatory in the province of San Juan, where he's still no doubt drinking his *mate* and strumming his guitar. He got lost somewhere along the way, as though to him getting there were not the important part of the journey, but rather enjoying the little pleasures along the road.

None of this could be further from his brother Juan Bautista, who was practical, down-to-earth, realistic. And the curious thing about it is that Marcelo turned out nothing like his father, Juan Bautista, but rather like Florencio, his uncle.

I don't know why I've gone on like this talking about this young man, instead of explaining about Soledad. Maybe because in the dark

261

and forbidding shadows of my existence (and Soledad is almost the key to those shadows) Florencio has been like the far-off light of a refuge in which positive, kindly creatures still live.

On that hot afternoon in 1927 I hardly took part in the conversation; I was disturbed by the enigmatic nearness of María de la Soledad. Where was she, I wondered. Why hadn't she appeared? I didn't have the courage to ask the kids, but at last I got up the nerve to ask an indirect question. Who lived in the big house? Where were the grown-ups?

"They're in the country," Florencio replied. "And the rest, too, our big brothers and everybody. Amancio and Eulogio."

"So nobody's in the house," I said.

I thought I detected just one tic of uneasiness in them, but it could have been my imagination.

"Well, actually, Soledad lives in one of the rooms," Florencio said.

These words only increased my anxieties. Florencio strummed his guitar a little, and the others sat quiet. Later, Juan Bautista went to the bakery to get some croissants and Florencio brought the things for *mate* outside into the garden. There was hardly any light, now, when Nicholás climbed up into a eucalyptus tree and hung by one arm from a limb of it and began to shriek and howl like a monkey, and then to pretend he was peeling and eating a banana—his most celebrated talent. And then it was that I felt something at my back, and at the same instant a tingling along the nape of my neck, and Nicholás dropped from the tree limb and all the rest of the boys fell silent.

I turned around slowly, still feeling that prickling of the skin that always accompanies such sensations. And raising my head, as though I already knew the exact place that the sensation was coming from, I saw in the shadowy gloom of the evening, at a window in the second floor, the unmoving figure of Soledad. The dimness of the light and the distance made it very difficult for me to make out exactly where she had fixed her paralyzing gaze, but I felt absolutely certain that it rested on me.

Then she disappeared, as silently as she had come, and little by little the conversation picked up again. But I hardly heard what any of the boys were saying.

262

The mosquitoes started to bother us, so we went in. Later, Florencio whipped up eggs and fried huge quantities of potatoes and made a Spanish omelette, which we cut into wedges with a knife somebody found and picked up with our fingers to eat. Then we had some homemade candy they'd brought from the country in huge glass jars. Meanwhile, I was picturing Soledad eating up in her room, or in the kitchen of the great house, alone.

I don't have the strength at the moment to tell you what happened to me that day (though perhaps I will someday). I'll only say that Soledad seemed to me a confirmation of that ancient onomastic doctrine which states that there is always some occult relation between a person and the person's name, for her name expressed what she was: *solitude*—she seemed to hold or protect some sacred secret, like those secrets that members of certain hermetic sects swear to keep forever. She was silent and withdrawn—*restrained*, for there seemed to be a violence within her, kept under pressure as though in a steam boiler. But it would be a steam boiler fed with frozen fire. She never spoke about normal, day-to-day things. Instead, in the fewest of words (and sometimes in her silences) she would suggest facts, events, *knowledge* which did not correspond to those things one ordinarily calls "the truth"; she would seem to speak, rather, of the sort of things that happen in nightmares. She was a figure from the dark side, a being from the shadows. And even her sensuality reflected that. It might seem silly to talk about sensuality in a girl with severe, hard lips and a paralyzing gaze, and yet there you are— even if it was a sensuality that reminded one of vipers. Are serpents not a symbol of sex in virtually all the ancient cults of wisdom?

She knew "things" which astounded one, and made one think of "intermediaries." This word has occurred to me just now, as I type this, and it comes as a sort of revelation. Who were they? Where would she see them? For whom was she the intermediary?

Yes, the sinister figure that sat before me in the bar on rue Saint-Jacques was murkily linked with what had happened with María de la Soledad when I was sixteen. And I still do not really know whether those episodes were real or whether they happened in a dream.

Allow me for a moment not to talk about that. Let me go back to that dirty café in Paris, at the moment when R. spoke Soledad's

263

name to me. I've already said that I had to sit down to recover my composure. When I had pulled myself together a bit, I got up and left. The cold air outside began to clear my mind, and by the time I reached my room on rue de Sommerard at least I was walking straight.

I didn't think that encounter would ever be repeated. I didn't know that it would not only be repeated, but that the return of R. would mark a turning point in my life.

I didn't say a word to M. about the appearance of R., and now I think that was only natural. What on the other hand seems strange to me is that in all the years that followed I *never* talked to her about it—in fact, I talked to her neither about that particular encounter nor about the events of my youth nor any of the more recent events, either. The reason for this is perhaps that I thought she would suffer more than I did from the disturbing influence that creature had on me. Suffice it to say that *it was he* who forced me to abandon science, a decision which took everyone by surprise and which for the rest of my life I've had to give countless, repeated (and futile) explanations of. I have said, especially, that in *Hombres y engranajes* one will find the most complete spiritual and philosophical explanation of my decision. But I have also said, thousands of times it seems, that man is not a creature to be easily explained and that, in any case, the secrets of a man are to be found not in his rational thoughts but rather in his dreams and hallucinations. It was that same intruder who forced me to write fiction, and under his maleficent influence I began to write, during that dark time of 1938, in Paris, "La Fuente Muda." Then, somehow, he became the protagonist of what I called "The Memoirs of a Stranger," which soon aborted and which I have never published; then later, of a play, likewise abortive. But because he was transformed (I called him Patricio Duggan in those pieces)—both because the circumstances were different from those of real life and because Patricio's character was not exactly like R.'s—he continued to haunt me, as it were, to press me, until he began to appear to me again after so many years, and with redoubled resentment, and his presence has become virtually unbearable in recent years. Thus he gradually became the Patricio of this novel, a character who, as time has passed, has come to seem more and more like some mirage in the desert, one of those yearned-for

264

visions, hazily glimpsed in the distance, that grow farther and farther away as one approaches them. (Although in this case, it was more like an oasis in reverse.) And the more I shunned his presence (out of fear or whatever else it might have been), the more M. felt it, to the point that he even appeared several times to her in her dreams. On those occasions I always felt tempted to talk to her about him, about his life, his irruptions into my life, but I never did. Because as the years passed the idea grew stronger and stronger inside me that he was some sort of nightmare it was better to forget about, or at least never to consciously remember. Still, about the time *On Heroes and Tombs* was first published in Spanish, he crossed my path again, like some old creditor you keep paying little dribs and drabs to, and who keeps coming back, again and again, to collect his shameful, secret debt, threatening to expose you to all the people who think you honorable and upright. And when this latest appearance coincided with the sudden arrival on the scene of Schneider and his machinations, I thought that once and for all I should unburden my conscience to M., and speak to her about the problem. But I didn't. Since I had to free myself from the weight of it all in one way or another, though, I began to confide (in ambiguous terms, it's true) to Beba, who, I got the impression, would listen to me as though I were some schoolboy making up stories.

But let me go back to that incident on the rue Saint-Jacques. A little while later a second meeting occurred. I had left the laboratory one evening, and after I'd walked for a while I went into another bistro—I never went back to the one that had provided me with that first troubling intrusion into my life—to give myself over to the solitary consolations of wine and the ever more confused ruminations on my fate. It must have been quite late when I decided to leave the refuge, and as I was walking along the rue des Carmes toward my room, I felt someone take my arm in silence. Even before I saw him, I knew who it was. I reacted violently:

"I have no desire to see you!" I shouted. "I should think that was obvious!"

"Oh, all right," he replied. "All I wanted was to talk to you a little bit more. So many years . . . Besides, I keep telling you that we have common interests."

He said the words "common interests" with that ironic twist he always gave clichés. His tone of bonhomie irritated me even more, since I knew he was incapable of such feelings of goodwill for anyone.

"Look," I said, "I don't know what your idea of 'common interests' is, but I have not the least intention of finding out. I want nothing to do with you. Not now, not ever. In fact, the idea that you and I might have 'common interests' makes me laugh."

He shrugged his shoulders, smiling.

"All right, we'll leave it at that, for the moment," he said. "But I'd like for us to have a drink together."

I was already pretty tipsy, and I couldn't wait to get home and go to bed. I told him so.

"The home fires, eh?" he murmured.

It was a cheap strategy, but it worked, as it always did. So I found myself having a drink with the man in another bar, this one as sordid as the first. The smoke, the drinks, my exhaustion kept me from thinking very straight, while his mind was like hardened steel. His words cut me mercilessly, they opened all the old wounds and let the pus that had accumulated over those last years of science in the laboratory run out. I found myself, out of simple self-esteem, defending positions I no longer believed in, while he battered me with the very ideas which I had, somehow, begun to hold. But this, it seems to me, is what I *now* see; I'm not sure how much I saw of all this that night. Talking about "ideas," "debating," "analysis" seems totally wrong. It wasn't ideas we debated, in the strict sense of the word; there was nothing systematic and coherent about it. There was no systematic, organized illumination—it was more like the explosions of gasoline tanks in a city dump, at night, and I would be trying to ward off being burned and then suddenly be blinded by the explosions, while at the same time I would be floundering about in mud and trash and offal. I seem to remember that at one point he became a huge, overwhelming Inquisitor of some sort, and the dialogue went something like this:

"Ever since you were a child you've been afraid of caves."

It wasn't so much a question as a statement that I was to confirm.

"Yes," I nodded, unable to take my eyes off him.

"Soft, slimy things disgusted you."

266

"Yes."

"Worms and maggots and slugs."

"Yes."

"Trash, and excrement."

"Yes."

"Animals with cold skin that hide in holes in the ground."

"Yes."

"Animals like lizards and rats and weasels and ferrets."

"Yes."

"And bats."

"Yes."

"Probably because they are winged rats, and animals that live in the dark."

"Yes."

"And you would run toward the light, toward the clear and bright and transparent, toward what was crystalline and cold."

"Yes."

"Toward mathematics."

"Yes! Yes!"

Suddenly he threw his arms open, raised his face, and looking up exclaimed, like an enigmatic invocation:

"Caves, women, mothers!"

We were no longer in the café. I don't know how or when we'd left, but we were in a lonely, silent place somewhere, on the side of some little hill. It must have been almost dawn by then, and in that dark, solitary place his voice took on awesome, terrifying resonance.

He turned to me, and he put out his right arm and pointed his finger at me menacingly:

"You must have the courage to return. You are a coward and a hypocrite."

And taking me by the arm (for by now I felt like a child), he dragged me over to a place where there was a wet, dark cave. We went farther and farther inside, until I felt the earth under my feet growing soft and clayey. Then he forced me to bend over and put my hands into that marshy muck.

"That's it," he said.

And then, "This is only the beginning," he added.

I had to tell someone about all this, and I went to Bonasso's

267

place rather than to the laboratory. He woke up grumpy. What did I mean, waking him up at that hour of the morning. It was his standard little joke. I sat down on the edge of his bed and for a while said nothing. Bonasso yawned and rubbed his hand across his face, gauging the growth of his two-day beard.

"There are years when you don't feel like doing *anything* when you get out of bed." He stood up heavily, yawned again, and finally took his first steps. He slipped on a pair of slippers and slapped down the hall to the bathroom. When he came back he looked at me for the first time, inquisitively.

"Something's happened to you, my man."

Then he washed his face a bit, and as he was drying himself off he eyed me curiously.

I told him the story of my night. Bonasso looked at me amazed as the tale went on; he gradually stopped drying himself; his motionless hand still grasped the towel.

"What? You don't believe me?" I asked sharply.

Pensively, he hung the towel in its place, and then he turned his head and looked at me sidewise. I was growing angrier by the second.

"What is it?!" I cried.

"My friend," he wrinkled his brow and said, "you were with me and Alejandro Sux last night. You aren't going to tell me you don't remember."

That was a blow.

"What . . ."

"I'm telling you. The idiot wanted to talk to you about something to do with the Protection Society."

"The Protection Society?"

"Yes, of course, man. One of those societies he's always inventing. The Atomic Physicists against Something or Other, I don't remember."

Words escaped me. Bonasso was still looking at me, a worried look on his face.

I left, lying that I had to get to the laboratory, I'd be late. But I went to Sux's place. The concierge told me I'd find him at the Dupont Latin. And there he was, talking to some Frenchman I didn't know.

"What a coincidence," he smiled as he spotted me, "just last night I was telling Sabato about this. He works in the Curie Laboratory, you know."

I was stupefied.

Around that time Cecilia Mossin arrived in Paris with a letter of introduction from Sadosky. She wanted to work on cosmic rays, but I dissuaded her: in my opinion, I told her, she ought to work in the laboratory with me. "A slave," I cunningly thought, in my state of mental confusion at the time. "A nice girl." I introduced her to Irène Joliot-Curie, she took the job, and she immediately began to come to work in her very proper little white smock. She'd see me come in unshaven, half-asleep, at ten or eleven o'clock in the morning. She stood by in horror at my distracted meetings with Madame Joliot.

It was around that time that Molinelli came around one day with somebody that looked the way Trotsky must have looked during his student days: just the same, in fact, except that this fellow was tiny, and very very thin from the privations of his life. His aquiline nose was sharp, but he wore the same rimless glasses the famous Bolshevik leader had worn, and had the same broad forehead, the same tangled hair. His gaze, of great keenness and intelligence, came from little, burning eyes. He took in everything around him with that intellectual avidity that can only belong to a Jew, the avidity that could lead an illiterate Jew from some ghetto in Cracow to listen feverishly, for hours, to a lecture on the theory of relativity though he didn't understand a word of it. The man might have been dying of hunger, as the frayed and tattered clothes he wore, handed down from someone larger than he was, seemed to indicate, and still be obsessed only by the fourth dimension, the squaring of the circle, or the existence of God.

I don't know whether I had told you that Molinelli, an enormously fat man, looked in turn like Charles Laughton, with that double chin of his and the half-open mouth out of which at any moment one expected to see a thread of spittle drop. The contrast with Trotsky was so grotesque that had I not been in the state of soul that held me during that time, I'd have had a hard time not laughing, even though I knew how tender Molinelli's feelings were.

Molinelli said, mysteriously, that he'd like to talk to me alone.

269

The picture formed by the fat man and the skeletal, extremely nervous creature beside him was not the best thing that could have happened to make Cecilia and Goldstein change their opinion about my future in the world of science. They stared at me the way people stare at a person about to faint in the middle of the street.

We went off into a corner, where we no doubt looked to Cecilia and Goldstein like a farce being played out against a stage set of electrical meters and gauges. In a low, conspiratorial voice, Molinelli informed me that his friend Citronenbaum here (with a *C*, he had me know) had some important things to ask me about alchemy.

I looked at Citronenbaum. His little eyes glittered with fanaticism.

My feelings were curiously mixed: on the one hand I wanted to laugh, I thought the idea of linking him, because of his tiny size, to Citroën automobiles was very funny; on the other hand I somehow had a sense of fear or danger.

"Alchemy?" I repeated, in a voice as neutral as I could make it.

"What do you think of Thibaud?" Molinelli asked me.

Thibaud? I really didn't know, I'd read a little book of his once, a long time ago, in which he'd talked about his discoveries.

And what about Heilbronner?

Heilbronner was a physical chemist—yes, of course.

"He's an expert witness at trials," young Citronenbaum said, never once taking his eyes off me, as though he wanted to catch me in some slip.

At trials?

Yes, an expert in alchemy.

An expert in alchemy? I didn't know what attitude to take about all this, but I decided the best thing was to stay as natural and expressionless as possible. Molinelli got me out of my fix: There were people always going around inventing things, perpetual motion machines, that sort of thing. But that wasn't the point: Citronenbaum here (he waved a hand at him, indicating again who he was talking about) had managed, by way of Heilbronner, to get in touch with someone of great importance. Had I read Fulcanelli's books? No, I wasn't familiar with them.

"You have to read them," he told me.

Well anyway, how could I help them? Molinelli shook his head, as though more or less to say "that isn't important" or "you've missed the point." The man had disappeared, hadn't been seen since the fission of the uranium atom had been announced.

Who'd disappeared? Fulcanelli?

No, he was talking about the alchemist that Citronenbaum had met through Heilbronner, a very mysterious man . . .

Then why had he mentioned Fulcanelli?

Because in their opinion he might be the same person, the alchemist and Fulcanelli might be the same person, they meant.

"You know," Molinelli said, glancing around fearfully at Cecilia and Goldstein, who were standing there doing nothing, watching us in fascination, "you know there's some great mystery about Fulcanelli?"

At that moment something happened, utterly unexpectedly, that still embarrasses me terribly when I think about it, something absolutely alien to the sleepless anguish I was suffering during those days: I began to laugh almost hysterically.

Molinelli, with his half-open mouth and his great hanging dewlap, was taken utterly aback.

"What's wrong with you?" he asked, his voice trembling.

I then committed the stupidest error I could ever have committed: instead of keeping my mouth shut, I told him—Molinelli and Fulcanelli. I wiped my eyes with my handkerchief, and when I was ready to listen again to what my visitors were saying, I realized the enormity of what I had done: Molinelli was still standing there with his mouth half-open, in hurt, stunned silence, and his friend had achieved the maximum possible electrical charge in his glowing eyes. They looked at each other, and without saying a word they left.

At first I couldn't do anything. All I could do was turn and look toward Cecilia and Goldstein, who were still standing there motionless, following the scene. Then I ran toward the door. I called out to Molinelli. But they didn't turn around. Then, seeing the two men, one huge and flabby, the other tiny in his too-large, ragged suit, walking on down the hall, I stopped.

Pensively, I went back into the laboratory and sat down in silence.

For days I was very depressed and it was hard for me to sleep, or if I did, the dreams would start. One of them was not so bad, at

271

least apparently, but I woke up in dread and anguish. I was walking along through one of the underground areas of the laboratory; I went into Lecoin's room and saw him leaning over some X-ray plates, with his back to me. But when I spoke to him and he turned around, he had Citronenbaum's face.

Why did I wake up in such distress? I don't know. Perhaps my conscience was hurting me over the interview with Molinelli. I woke up from this dream with my mind set on finding Molinelli and apologizing. By the time the sky grew lighter, however, and I got out of bed, I was convinced that the nightmare was not the result of some simple sense of guilt, but rather of something deeper. But what?

I went straight to that shabby room of his filled with cabalistic books and papers of all kinds. It was early, and still foggy out, and through the fog I could see the cupola of the Pantheon, which made me feel more melancholy than worried. The things that had happened with R. now seemed far away; the terror had been replaced by that melancholy that grew heavier and heavier as I lived through that year of 1938 in Paris.

I went up to his room and knocked again and again, figuring he must be asleep. When I heard his voice at last and I told him who I was, there was a silence that lasted much too long. I didn't know what to do, what to say. On the other hand, I didn't want to go away without apologizing.

After a while I put my face near a crack in the door and said loudly that I hoped he'd forgive me, that I hadn't been well, hadn't been well at all, that I'd been hysterical when I'd laughed like that, et cetera. I've told you that he was a wonderful person (he died about two years ago), incapable of carrying a grudge. So finally he opened the door, and while he washed his face I sat down to wait for him on a three-legged couch—a pile of occult books replaced the lost leg. I tried to explain, to apologize, but with excellent good sense he asked me not to.

"I feel bad for Citronenbaum," he said, although he didn't tell me why, didn't tell me what my laughter had done to that fanatical little man.

As he dried himself off, he repeated: "Only for him."

I was ashamed of myself, and I believe he could see that, since he had the kindness to change the subject as he went about making coffee. Nonetheless I asked him to talk to me about what they had wanted to discuss with me the day they'd come to the laboratory. He raised a hand as though to say that it didn't matter anymore, and tried to go on about something or other that had happened the day before with Bonasso.

"Please," I urged him.

Then, although disconnectedly, he returned to the subject of Fulcanelli. He pulled out one of his books and handed it to me: I had to read it.

"You know, no one has ever seen him, ever. This book is dated 1920, you see? And in almost twenty years there's not a single person who can tell you who this person is."

What about the publisher?

He shook his head. Did I recall the case of B. Traven? The manuscript would arrive by mail. With Fulcanelli at least they knew that the manuscript had come by way of a certain Canseliet.

So it ought to be relatively easy to find out something about the author.

No, because this Canseliet had absolutely and completely refused to talk. Did I understand now why that conversation with Citronenbaum was so very very important?

No, I still couldn't quite see it.

"Good lord, man," he said. He began again, very patiently. Professor Heilbronner was an expert often called to testify at trials, and he had had contact with more than one alchemist, real or pretended. One day he sent Citronenbaum to interview a man who worked in the testing laboratory of the Société du Gaz. This man warned Citronenbaum that not only Heilbronner but Joliot and her associates as well, to mention only the French investigators involved, were standing on the edge of a precipice. The man talked to Citronenbaum about the experiments they were doing with deuterium, and he told him that certain men had known about these things centuries ago—but, he said, there was a reason they had kept their silence, had put everything into hermetic archives when their experiments reached a certain point, and then related what they knew in a language apparently nonsensical though in truth ciphered. He told Citronenbaum that such things as electricity and accelerators weren't even needed, that all one needed in order to unleash the nuclear powers were certain geometrical arrangements of extremely pure elements. And why had all this been so utterly silenced? Because unlike modern physicists, heirs of those enlightened and libertine salons of the eighteenth century, the concern of the ancient alchemists was fundamentally religious. Not all of them, of course: the immense majority of them had been fakes and charlatans, men who had the ear of the king's uncle or took a tale to Duke Such-and-such, and who in fact often wound up tortured or at the stake. But this man was talking about the genuine alchemists, the true initiates, men who belonged to the chain of knowledge that came down from Paracelsus and the Comte de Saint-Germain, all the way down to Newton. Did Citronenbaum know the ambiguous but meaningful words that Newton had spoken before the Royal Academy? The entire story of alchemy, at least that part of the story that had come down to those of us who live in this materialistic civilization of today, seemed to be concerned with the transmutation of copper into gold and other such folderol, but those were mere *applications* of a principle unimaginably more powerful. The essence was, in fact, the transformation of the alchemist, the investigator himself, an ancient secret reserved for one or two privileged men in each century. The Great Work.

We sat for a while in silence, as we drank our coffee.

"And this is the man who has just recently disappeared?" I asked.

"That's right, just a few days after the newspapers of the world began reporting the fission of uranium."

But why disappear? I didn't understand.

He shrugged. Citronenbaum's hypothesis was that the man in the Société du Gaz was none other than Fulcanelli. Another friend of his, one Berger, thought so, too.

I sat meditating over this, but I still couldn't quite understand why these two men had come to see *me*.

"That's a long story," he replied. "And besides, it has a lot to do with Citronenbaum. But unfortunately, now it's too late. I don't think he'll want to see you again."

That stung me: I'd already apologized profusely. What more could I do? Yes, of course, of course. But Citronenbaum was another sort of person. And looking me in the eye, Molinelli added gravely:

"A genius."

274

I asked him whether he'd be seeing him soon. Of course he would be. But he had me understand that at least for the moment there was nothing more I could do.

I wandered around for several days, figuratively speaking at least, trying to put my thoughts in order, but I could find no solutions.

I stopped by the Dome. Marcelle Ferry was there with Tristan Tzara and Domínguez, inventing *"cadavres exquis."*

"What is a can of sardines a hundred yards long?"

Mongol camouflage.

"What is the tragic minute?"

The love of a forgotten flower.

"What is the breakfast minotaur?"

Nothingness.

From a little table off to one side, Alejandro Sux was protesting: "The war coming, and you people over there acting like fools."

Domínguez looked at him with his tender, sleepy ox-eyes.

Sux asked me about the uranium issue. It was urgent—we had to organize a committee. He already had the acronym for it: DEFENSA. It was a weakness of his, organizing committees and societies—on paper, of course. The last cause had been organizing the League Against the Use of Aluminum Cookware in the Kitchen. Of course, as he always organized the committees in Spanish, while living in Paris, they hardly got off the ground, and this committee had been no exception.

"The important thing is a good acronym, something people can remember easily. Defensa de Eminentes Fisicos, Electricistas, Naturalistas, Sociedad Anonima"—The Eminent Physicists, Electricians, Naturalists Defense Society, Incorporated.

I found the idea of an entity as absurd as that committee organizing itself into a corporation (madness allied with commerce) very funny.

Which irritated Sux.

And why electricians? That amused me, too: the man-in-the-street's idea of what a physics laboratory is like.

It was for the letters! The acronym! Didn't I know it had to be something catchy, make a good first impression?

Ah, well, then, all right.

They'd stopped their games at the other table. Domínguez, as

275

though performing a ritual either very sad or very boring, with that sad-eyed ox's face of his with the hanging dewlap, disheartened, began to insult people that looked French. Every Saturday and Sunday (he explained) the Dome filled up with Frenchmen and Frenchwomen, disgusting bourgeois types. He finally stood up unsteadily and stumbled over to an old gentleman with a white goatee and wearing the medal of the Legion of Honor. Domínguez was determined to insult the man who, accompanied by his wife, was tranquilly drinking a Ricard. Domínguez bent himself double, making a bow that reminded one of the kinds of bows clowns make in those circuses with trained elephants, and greeted the couple in his abominable French. Madame, Monsieur, he said, and then he picked up one of the lady's gloves and began to bite at it and chew it as though he proposed to eat it. The old man was paralyzed with shock; he sat there transfixed. But then suddenly he stood up in a manner much more indignant than his size would have led one to expect him capable of. Domínguez stopped chewing. He looked at the man with that exaggerated tenderness his blank bovine eyes gave his expression, his acromegalic head tilted delicately to one side.

Sux, who was watching every move in this pantomime, had quickly paid his bill, and now grabbed my arm and pulled me out of the place, reminding me what happened the time that Peruvian boxer had had to step in and save us.

We'd no more than gotten outside when the noise started.

Sux was indignant.

"Idiots!" he cried, as we sat down at a table in La Coupole. "The war's upon us, and those madmen acting like that!"

He took some papers out of an inside pocket and wrote some numbers down.

"Each signer will pay a dollar a year."

I took advantage of Wilfredo Lam's arrival to get away. I had nothing in particular to do, nowhere to go; Sunday always made me especially sad. I wandered up one street and down another, but then suddenly I found myself in the rue de la Grande Chaumière. Unconsciously, my steps had taken me to Molinelli. I went up and found him making coffee, as usual. He seemed to have overheard my conversation with Sux.

"It means the end," he said.

"The end? What is it that means the end?"

"The fission of uranium. The Second Millennium. And you have had the privilege to be witness to such a great event."

In his pockets he had little bits of paper all folded up every which way, wrinkled and crumpled and of all degrees of wear: letters, sketches, old bills. (My brother Vicente used to do this, too.) He rummaged in his pocket and found the piece of paper he was looking for at last; he showed it to me. It had a diagram on it: there was Pisces, he pointed, there was the Sun. As the Sun had entered Pisces, Christ had appeared and the Jews begun their diaspora. It had lasted two thousand years. Now, as we approached the end of that period, they were returning to their homeland. This prefigured some fundamental event, because the Jewish people had a mysterious and profound, supernatural destiny. I thought of Citronenbaum, though I said nothing.

With the chewed stub of a pencil he showed me: this is the sign of Aquarius. We were now entering the sign of Aquarius, the final years of the First Millennium.

And then, raising his eyes and pointing at me with the stub of pencil, he added:

"Great catastrophes."

What sort of catastrophes, I asked. Well, first of all, a huge war, a trial for the Jews. But they would never be exterminated altogether, because they still had a great mission to carry out. With his little pencil, on the back of one of his pieces of paper, he wrote in block letters, with a box around them:

FINAL MISSION

and then he turned and looked at me with a very serious, very calm expression on his face.

The catastrophes would have to do with atomic power. The Great Lamas had foreseen that such cataclysms would be the prelude to the Final Battle for control of the world. But he wanted me to understand him: this had nothing to do with politics. It was the most naive kind of mistake to think that this was just politics. Nothing

277

could be further from the truth. The political powers (France, Germany, England) were the form in which the STRUGGLE (he wrote this word, too, in block letters on the piece of paper) would manifest itself to men. But behind the appearances there was something much more grave: Hitler was the Antichrist.

Humanity was now in the Fifth Cycle.

The Fifth Cycle?

Yes, the moment at which science and rationality would reach their highest power. A terrible and sinister magnificence. But the foundations were invisibly being laid for a new, spiritual conception of the universe. Pointing the stub of the pencil at me again, he added:

"The end of materialistic civilization."

I was growing more perturbed by the moment, because this conversation seemed in some way to be related to my encounter with R. and that mysterious scene I had had with him.

Did I know what the Fifth Cycle of Eastern prophecy referred to?

No, I didn't know.

It referred to the Fifth Angel of the Apocalypse, in Revelation.

Uranus first, then Pluto, were the messengers of the New Age. They would act like volcanoes in eruption, and would signal the boundary between two eras, the great universal crossroads.

"Pluto," he affirmed, tapping his papers with the pencil stub, "will rule over that renewal by destruction."

After a silence in which he seemed to be looking into the very depths of my eyes, he added these surprising words:

"I know that you know something. Maybe not at all clearly, *yet* . . . But there is something in your eyes."

I said nothing, but lowering my head I stirred the dregs of my coffee with the spoon. I heard him go on:

"Pluto rules the inner world of man. He will reveal the deepest secrets of the soul and the abysses of the sea, the mysterious subterranean worlds which are under his jurisdiction."

I raised my glance. For a moment he didn't say anything. Then, stabbing the pencil stub at me again, he said:

"We are at the moment going through the third and last house

278

of Pisces, under the sway of Scorpio, where Uranus is in the ascendant. SEX, DESTRUCTION, AND DEATH!"

He wrote these last words in capital letters, too, on another dirty little slip of paper, and he looked at me again as though I had something to do with all this.

We were sitting almost in darkness by now. I told him I had to go, I was very tired.

"All right," he said, putting a hand on my shoulder. "All right."

I went home to sleep, but I couldn't. Molinelli's words kept going around and around in my head—and I don't know why, but so did Citronenbaum's face. I told you before that it looked like what Trotsky's face must have looked like during his days as a student, but now I realized that that was not really a very good description of it at all. I'd perhaps been struck by the physical resemblance and the fire of fanaticism in the eyes, which glittered electrically behind the lenses of his rimless glasses. But that wasn't quite it. Not quite *all* of it, anyway. But what did I mean to tell myself with that "all"? His threadbare suit handed down to him from some bigger man, his bony shoulders, his sunken chest, his long, thin, nervously restless fingers. But there was something else, and although I could sense it, I couldn't put words to what it was that troubled me about that tiny little man possessed by a supreme truth. Maybe it was precisely that, that "supreme truth," that revelation which went beyond mere politics, that lent him an air almost of awesomeness.

I finally got up and went to the laboratory. I asked Cecilia whether she'd done the measurements I'd asked her to do. Yes, of course. Her eyes scrutinized me; they were filled with reproach, like a mother's when she hands clean, starched clothes to her son who is living a life of dissipation.

"What is it!" I shouted at her.

She was startled, and went off to her electrometer.

I found the container of actinium and took it out of its lead tube.

But my mind was not on it, I fumbled. I returned the actinium to the tube and decided to go out for a cup of coffee.

Outside, the cold air helped restore my mind.

I felt the old obsessions that had terrified me as a child, coming

279

back to haunt me. And now they were even more terrifying, precisely because they had seized a grown man surrounded by other grown people who only believed in mathematical formulas and atomic particles, in rational explanations.

I recalled Frazer, the soul that travels during dreams, and doubles. We Westerners were so base, so stupid, so coarse. Were men like Hoffmann and Poe and de Maupassant really just simple storytellers, liars even? Weren't nightmares *true* in some deeper sense? And the characters in fiction (I'm talking about the authentic ones, the ones that spring up like dreams themselves, not the made-up ones)—did they not visit remote regions, like the soul during nightmares? Somnambulism. Where was I going when I was a boy and would get up and walk at night? What continents had I traveled to on those journeys? My body would go into the parlor, or into my parents' bedroom. But what about my soul? The body goes one place, or stays in its bed, but the soul is a wanderer.

Ever since then, I have tried to unravel the secret design in the weave, and although sometimes I think I can almost make it out, I am still waiting, for my long years of experience have proven to me that underneath one design there is always another more subtle, or less visible. In these last few years, however, I have tried to tie up the loose ends of some threads which seem to lead through the labyrinth. In fact, those episodes occurred just at the time I began to abandon science, which is the universe of light. Afterward, sometime around 1947, I noticed that in Sartre everything derived from the sense of sight, and that he too had taken refuge in pure thought, while his guilt feelings forced him into good acts. Guilt = blindness? Finally, the *nouveau roman*, the school of the eye, objectivism. Science again—that is, the pure vision of the object posited by the engineer Robbe-Grillet. There was some reason that Nathalie Sarraute laughed at the "pretended abysses of consciousness." She laughed. . . . Just a manner of speaking. Because down deep, they were all frightened—every one of them fled from the universe of the shadows. Because the powers of night do not forgive those who try to unearth their secrets. Which was why they hated me, in fact: for the same reason collaborators hate the men and women who risk their lives combatting the enemy that has occupied their homeland.

This is confused, I know, you don't have to tell me. Many people will think it bears a certain resemblance to the fantasies of a madman, or a paranoid. Let people think what they will: all I care about is the truth. And I have tried, although in a fragmentary way, like the flashes of lightning that allow one glimpses, in tenths of a second, of the verges of bottomless abysses, to express that truth in my books.

All this, I think now. Because back in that winter of 1938 none of it was clear to me. My laboratory period coincided with the half of the road of our lives on which so often, according to some occultists, the meaning of life is inverted. It had been thus with eminent people, Newton and Swedenborg, Pascal and Paracelsus. Why shouldn't it happen with more humble folk too? Unknowingly, I was turning from the illuminated part of life to the darker side.

It was at that moment and in the midst of a profound spiritual crisis that I came in contact with Domínguez, through Bonasso. I have never before now told anyone what really happened back then, the danger I ran. It was a danger that Domínguez wouldn't or couldn't avoid, and it ended in suicide. (On the night of December 31, 1957, he slashed his wrists in his studio, his blood soaking the cloth he had draped over his easel.) I know what powers were involved. And involved long before Victor Brauner's eye was put out, because that was only one of their manifestations.

One finds what one is consciously or unconsciously seeking. I am speaking of encounters that are fated, not of stupidities. If you bump into someone on the street, that encounter hardly ever has any decisive consequences on your life. But it does when that encounter is not casual, when it has been provoked by the invisible forces which operate upon us. It was neither coincidence that I should run into Domínguez nor was it by chance that the encounter occurred just as I was on the point of abandoning science. Our meeting was of enormous importance, although at the time it didn't seem so. Time ranks events, sets them into their proper degree or weight, and things which at first seem trivial are later revealed in all their transcendental importance. And thus the past is not fixed and crystallized, as some people believe, but rather an order which changes as our lives advance, only achieving its final shape, its true significance at the instant we die, when once and for all the order of things is petrified. If at that moment we could turn our gaze back upon the configuration of our life (and it is entirely possible that the dying man does look back), we would see at last the true landscape on which our destiny worked itself out. Tiniest details that we had given no importance to in life would then show themselves to have been grave warnings or melancholy good-byes forever. Even the things we had believed to be simple jokes or mere puzzles, perplexing coincidences, would become, from that perspective on the edge of death, sinister foreshadowings.

That was more or less what happened around that time with Surrealism.

I was on my way to D.'s atelier to work (and please give that word its most grotesque meaning) on that bad joke I baptized with the name Lithochronism, and which Breton later would take over for the last number of *Minotaure*. All that and the other absurd word games we invented (and which made us roll on the floor with laughter), and that letter to Deladier on the Pope, and the practical jokes in the Métro, seemed mere diversions, games, "having fun," like so many things that other people were doing and which made a lot of relatively unconscious people think Surrealism was the cat's pajamas, to use an anachronism. The truth was that even at those moments when we actors in the "farce" thought we were just clowning around (which is precisely what happened with D. and me), we were unwittingly in mortal danger: like a child in the middle of a battlefield playing with shells he thinks are duds—suddenly they blow up in his face, spewing death and destruction. The grandiloquent theoretical declarations of the movement claimed that Surrealism proposed to open the portals of the secret world, the doors to the forbidden; yet those promises seemed belied by the capering and nonsense. Then, unexpectedly, the demons appeared. Who better than D. to illustrate that grim paradox?

I don't know whether you know the story of Brauner, a Rumanian Jew very much preoccupied with the phenomena of premonition and clairvoyance. He arrived in Paris in 1927, and I think it was through Brancusi, who was also Rumanian, that he met Giacometti and Tanguy. They then introduced him to Breton. Now, pay attention to what I'm about to tell you. For ten years, that is to say from 1927 to 1937, he painted images of the unconscious—obsessive, repetitive images, all having to do with eyes, and some extremely

282

unpleasant—shocking, I suppose—and unsettling. There were paintings in which the eye would be replaced by a vagina or turned into a bull's horn, or in which the characters were partially or totally without eyes. But the most frightening thing is that one of his self-portraits, painted in 1931, exactly prefigured the tragedy in which Domínguez was to be the protagonist, in 1938. Brauner for some time had been painting a series of self-portraits in which one of his eyes was gouged out, the socket empty and gaping. But the 1931 painting was even more incredible: his right eye is blinded by an arrow from which hangs the letter D. There is still one more, and even more fantastic, fact: that same year, 1931, Brauner photographed the façade of the house that one day would be the scene of the horror: Domínguez's atelier, at number 83, boulevard Montparnasse. He thought he was taking a picture of a clairvoyant who was sitting in front of that building, but in reality he was photographing the house in which one day his own sacrifice would be consummated. Brauner went back to Rumania. But he returned to Paris in 1938 "in order to" receive his mutilation. Some years later he would write: "This mutilation is as alive today as on its first day. Through time, it remains the essential fact of my existence."

I transcribe his own words: "There were quite a few of us that night, but it had not been at anyone's particular instigation that we should get together, there was no occasion, no real reason or intention behind it. Boredom in fact was the dominant emotion that hot August night. I myself was drowsy, yet filled with anxiousness—since for more than forty-eight hours, beginning on that long evening walk with U., I had had an inexplicable, powerful fear, and it had grown as the hours passed. The friends all began to go, and Domínguez, quite excited and overwrought, began an argument with E., but since it was all in Spanish the rest of us didn't understand much of it. But suddenly they both grew pale and trembled in fury, and then rushed at each other with a violence that I don't recall ever having seen before in my entire life. With a sudden feeling of death, I leapt to hold E. back. Then S. and U. grabbed D., while the others left because things were getting ugly. Domínguez managed to free himself, but I barely had time to look at him, because I was thrown to the ground by a terrible blow to my head. My friends picked me up and tried to carry me away. Feeling my senses grow more and more dull, and at the same time that my sight was somehow muddied, I asked them to let me go home and lie down. But I was carried out by my friends. On their faces, I could see there was terrible pain and grief, but I understood nothing of what had happened until the split second when, as we passed in front of a mirror, I saw that my face was bloody and that my left eye looked like an ugly open wound. At that moment I thought of my self-portrait, and in that confusion of my mind, its resemblance to the gaping wound woke me to the reality of the situation."

I return to the idea of the soul which journeys during sleep and which, because it is freed from the body (which in turn chains man to his prison of space and time), can see things in the future. Nightmares are the visions of our hell. And what we ordinary people achieve in sleep, mystics and poets achieve through ecstasy and the imagination: *"Je dis qu'il faut être voyant, se faire VOYANT."* And in one of those ecstatic visions, through that terrifying privilege given the artist, Victor Brauner saw his own horrific future. And painted it. The visions are not always so clear; almost invariably they come in the enigmatic and ambiguous shape of dreams. This is partly because of the dark nature of those regions of horror, which the soul perhaps glimpses as though through a fog, for the soul has achieved only an imperfect disincarnation, it has not been able to entirely free itself of the weight of the flesh and of its bonds to the bloody, furious present; and it is partly because man is apparently incapable of bearing the cruelties of hell, and our life-instinct, the instinct of our body, which in spite of everything sustains with all its might that soul peering into the abysses, protects us with masks and symbols of the monsters and torments of that hell.

I went back to the laboratory very late. Goldstein had already left, and Cecilia, who had no doubt been waiting for me, was all ready to leave for the night—she had taken off her ever-present smock. The expression on her face was supplicating, with the pain-filled eyes of the *Yiddische momma.*

"It's all right, Cecilia," I said to her. "It's nothing. My head hurts, that's all."

She left the measurements for me and left. At the door, she asked me if I'd like to go to an organ concert with her that night at some church or other. No, I didn't think so, thanks. I watched her walk away—her small, neat figure, her little steps. "I mistreat her," I thought. From the very beginning she had seen Madame Curie's mediocrity, and she had almost cried. I swore to myself that the next day I'd show her that the woman had once been a genius.

Again I took out the lead tube that contained the actinium and set it on my workbench. My eyes stung from lack of sleep, and the light bothered me more than usual. I turned off the light and sat in the silence of the deserted laboratory illuminated now only by the pale light that came in from the next office.

I stood up, walked over to the window, and looked out onto rue Pierre Curie. A light rain had begun to fall. Once again the old melancholy oppression of the spirit began to weigh on me. I returned to my stool and fixed my eyes on the lead tube which enclosed the dreadful actinium. Slowly, imperceptibly, I grew drowsy and began to nod: the face of Citronenbaum, with its indecipherable but demonic expression, made me start.

My eyes came to rest once again on the lead tube which seemed in some way linked to my dread and anguish. It looked so harmless, so neutral. And yet inside it there were furious cataclysms occurring in miniature—tiny, invisible microcosms of the Apocalypse that Molinelli had spoken to me about, and which enigmatic prophets had directly or indirectly been prophesying for century upon century. It occurred to me that if I could somehow shrink myself, became a Lilliputian inhabitant of those atoms locked in their impregnable prison of lead, so that one of those infinitesimal universes became my own solar system, I would be a witness, seized by a sacred terror, of unbelievably enormous catastrophes, of hellish bolts of terror and of death. Now, after thirty years, when history has seen more than one of those dreadful prophecies come true, I remember those days in Paris. On August 6, 1944, the Americans prefigured the final horror, in Hiroshima. August 6. The Day of Light, the Day of the Transfiguration of Christ on Mount Tabor!

Poor Molinelli: the gross messenger of truths higher than his own life, his own appearance, almost laughable intermediary between men and the gods of darkness. "Uranus and Pluto are the messengers of the New Age: they will be like volcanoes in eruption, and will mark the boundary between the two Eras," he said as his eyes bored into me. And he spoke those words in 1938, when we had no idea that the atoms of uranium and plutonium would be the sparks that ignited the catastrophe.

Enough. I would prefer not to remember a time so filled with dread and anguish. Friday, when we see each other, I'd rather talk about what's happening to me now.

A MAGAZINE ARTICLE
DURING THOSE DAYS, A YOUNG MAN NAMED DEL BUSTO visited S. to do an interview for a glossy weekly magazine.

Why had S. left La Plata?

How should *he* know? His whole life had been a series of absurd and disconnected actions, a secret pattern, he meant.

Had leaving La Plata been leaving the scientific universe behind forever?

That was possible, he supposed. But be that as it might, he had come to Buenos Aires. Enrique Wernicke had said he could put him in contact with somebody who might be able to rent him a hut in the Sierra de Córdoba. That was how he'd met don Federico Valle, the cave man. And how it came about that he went to live in that lonely place above the Chorrillos River, in a wooden hut without electricity or water or glass panes in the windows.

While S. conversed with del Busto it all seemed to fall into order, light began to emerge from the chaos: the black sun. And they inevitably started talking about caves and other underground phenomena, and about the Blind.

"Porters," said del Busto.

Porters? What about porters? Sabato asked the question with a shiver that may have shown itself in his voice as well, because del Busto looked at him cautiously. And then he told S. what S. already knew, what sooner or later somebody had had to come to tell him. Tell *him*. Still, S. listened with grave attention:

"From the ground floor up, apartments. Those clean apartments of the modern world, made of cement and plastic, of clear glass and shining aluminum, and all air-conditioned. Impeccable."

"Abstract," offered Sabato, almost impatiently, to cut the story short.

286

"That's it, abstract. And down below, the rats. At night, among the shining boilers. The porter. A mysterious class of person, the man who holds the key to the gates between the two worlds."

Sabato stared at him in silence.

"Of course," he nodded after a moment.

It was growing dusky, and one could hear the birds twittering as they settled down into their nests.

"You had to come here."

"Yes, of course."

"Sooner or later."

"Yes. The Blind have always fascinated me," commented del Busto. The expression on the young man's face could hardly be made out.

"I'd like to dedicate this piece on porters and rats to you, that is," he added.

"Dedicate it to me?"

"Yes, if you wouldn't mind that. Because of the Blind. Since the moment I wrote it, I have been disturbed by it. It has made me listen to certain voices, a certain kind of whispering."

"Whispering?"

"In my own soul, I mean."

"Do you write?"

"No, this is really the first thing I've ever done. Walker commissioned me to do it because I was talking to him about it, he wanted to see it. I'm actually a photographer."

"A photographer?" Recorder of light, S. thought. And he, too, had made a decision to abandon the realm of light.

Young del Busto told S. other things, the results of his research: the Mint's struggle with rats, which kept eating the bills. After years of study, years of painstaking projects and failed battles, they finally built a formidable vault of reinforced concrete. And it failed too. Did the rats come in through the plumbing? Did they reproduce inside the vault?

They talked about the possibility of doing a complete study of subways, cellars and basements, sewers, drains. It would be a terribly complex and presumably terrifying study.

As del Busto was leaving, he almost brought up the subject of porters with S. again, but then he decided it wasn't the proper moment.

And perhaps not necessary, either.

HE WAS WALKING ALONG CORRIENTES

when he saw Astor Piazzolla coming down the street toward him. He spoke to him, and then he realized he'd made a mistake: it was some sort of caricature of the man. The person stopped, surprised, while S. walked away embarrassed and turned down the first street he came to, as though running away. He was on Suipacha. He stood for a moment pretending to look in a shop window, and when he had calmed down a bit he looked about for a café where he could get something to drink. He was next door to Tio Carlos, as it turned out. Kuhn was not at the cash register, so he found himself a table, and then he looked up to find Piazzolla smiling at him.

"What's wrong, did my beard scare you?" Astor joked.

"No, it's not that."

"What on earth is wrong with you? What's happened?"

S. hesitated to tell him what just happened, but then he finally did. He was much more distraught than Astor thought the case merited.

"It's just a coincidence, man," he said.

S. looked at him angrily.

"In a city of nine million or more people?"

Astor changed the subject; he wanted to talk to S. about his plans to write a "Requiem for Buenos Aires."

"What?" S. asked absentmindedly.

"A mass. A mass for Buenos Aires."

S. was very ill, his nerves, you know. He'd see about it. Then immediately he got up and made some weak excuse and left. He continued on to El Ciervo.

Bruno found him strange, and he asked how S. was feeling.

"All right, all right," S. replied distractedly.

He drank a beer and after a while said to Bruno:

"You may think I was exaggerating about Dr. Schneider."

"In what sense?"

"Well, in general . . . his powers . . ."

288

Bruno started fiddling with the toothpicks.

"I lost sight of him years ago," S. went on, "but he's here. I'm sure of it. He's here somewhere in Buenos Aires."

(*"Lost sight of him,"* he thought with a shudder.)

Bruno raised his sky blue eyes and waited.

"I told you how he reappeared in 1962, didn't I?"

"Uh-huh."

"Did I tell you about my following him in the subway?"

"No."

"After seeing him that once in 1962, remember, I saw him on three or four other occasions. Sometimes alone, sometimes with Hedwig. Of course I saw *her* pretty often, until she disappeared. It was in Zur Post, I think, that we ran into you too?"

Bruno nodded.

"Yes, they just disappeared. But you know, I always had the feeling they were around somewhere, somewhere in the city. And in fact I did see him, I saw him on the corner of Ayacucho and Las Heras. But the second he saw me (or at least that was my impression) he ran into a café." S. grew thoughtful. "It was him, I'm sure of it," he murmured, almost to himself.

"As for Hedwig . . ."

"You never saw her again?"

"No, but she's in Buenos Aires, I know it. A tool. And she suffered because of that mission. That man's power? Or some sort of dependence or servitude that she was forced to assume? That's it, that's it: servitude. That's the word. And to make it worse, in this case the servant is superior to the master. I'm not saying that because of her social class, of course . . . In spite of her physical and moral decay . . . You would see him and suddenly . . ." His words trailed off, as though he had begun talking to himself again, and Bruno realized that he had had that same impression—Hedwig had seemed not only physically tired and worn-looking, so that her old splendors could hardly be seen through the briars and brambles, the abandonment and depredation (like the antique beauties of a manorial garden seen through the rusty gates and rubble of a fallen wall), but actually *spiritually* degenerated, by time and the terrible vicissitudes the flesh is subject to, by disillusion and disappointment and bitterness, and above all by her servitude to that despicable person; and so, it was true, one only saw her old spirit in fleeting, incredibly sad instants, and through her moral ruins. S. had ordered another beer.

"I don't know what's wrong with me. I'm dehydrated."

He looked vacantly at the beer, lost in thought.

"I told you that around the time *On Heroes and Tombs* first came out in Spanish our paths crossed and I started trying to follow his movements. And then one day, after weeks of futile efforts, I made a discovery."

Looking at his friend, he added:

"A terrifying discovery."

After a few moments he went on:

"It was one day when we had agreed to meet. When we supposedly left each other, I followed him. He went into the Munich, on Constitución. I waited in the plaza for him to come out. He was inside for a couple of hours; by the time he came out, it was getting dark. He went into the subway, and I got in the next car so I could follow his movements. When he got to the Obelisk, he changed trains for Palermo, and I got in the next car again. I kept having the feeling that there was something in his manner . . . something about him seemed to make me think that he was waiting for something to happen there in the subway. For a second I imagined, with fear, that his powers somehow allowed him to know that I was near him, and I was nervous that he might catch me by surprise. But if he did, I'd attribute it to coincidence. And if he didn't believe me (still by virtue of those powers he possessed), what would I have lost? At least he would see that I was on my guard, that I had no intention of being easy prey for him. I'd probably even rise a few notches in his estimation. Those were the kinds of thoughts I was thinking when I saw, coming toward me—walking back through the train, I mean— the blind man that sells pencils and combs and whatnot on the trains. He had aged since the last time I'd seen him, but he was still as gross and disgusting and spiteful as in the days when Vidal Olmos pointed him out to me. I shuddered and my head began spinning when I remembered Fernando in that same subway, in the same persecution (but who persecuting whom?), and I had a sudden presentiment of what was about to happen: the blind man didn't walk by Schneider as though Schneider were just another passenger on the subway—his sense of smell, his sense of hearing, maybe some secret sign passed between them that only they recognized, *something* made him stop and sell Schneider something out of that dirty box of his. As Schneider was paying the man, it gave me another shudder to remember how dirty the man's shirt collars invariably were. The blind man went on his way. And when the train came to a stop, Schneider got off, with me behind him. But I lost him in the crowd."

S. fell silent. He seemed to be lost in thought, and he sat for so long that it seemed he'd forgotten about Bruno's presence. Bruno didn't know what to do, but at last he asked S. if he didn't think it would be better to walk, or at least to try to find a café that wasn't so noisy. What, what? S. seemed not to have heard or understood what Bruno said.

"I was saying, it's too noisy here."

"Oh, yes. It is. The noise is terrible. I find the noise of Buenos Aires harder to stand every day."

He stood up, saying he had to make a telephone call. Bruno watched him look all about him as he made his way to the telephone. When he came back, S. began again:

"I told you that things began to get complicated directly after I published *On Heroes and Tombs*. I *did* tell you that, didn't I?"

Yes, he had told Bruno that.

"But when those poor people came to me, that séance in the basement, remember?, a door seems to have opened . . . Although of course forces such as those aren't easily defeated. And I think I told you that they'd warned me: the tide of battle would run in my favor so long as I was prepared to defeat those forces once and for all, forever. I swore myself to that, and then I fainted. I told those people how optimistic I began feeling the next day. Now I see that it was premature of me to believe in such people, and probably indicative of the naiveté that one can come to when one is as desperate as I was: I was like an aborigine armed with a stick against atomic warfare. But be that as it may, I did feel the desire to fight, and I did begin to feel a certain hopefulness. M. now tells me—she didn't have the heart to, before—that she had a dream at the time: she saw a sort of miniature garden below her, and in it there were frenzied yet impotent little dwarves, tiny people moving about; it

291

looked like some sort of Lilliputian prison yard, and they were gesturing and apparently shouting, though you couldn't hear them, it was like a silent movie: they were looking up, very nervous, very excited, maybe angry, and it seemed they were calling for help. 'They're the characters in your novel,' she said to me; 'if you don't set them free, they're going to drive me mad.'

"I looked at her without a word.

" 'For the love of God,' she implored me.

"Her expression shocked me: it was an expression of sheer terror, and of desolation.

" 'If you don't write, those people will drive me mad. They'll be back. I know they will.' So I shut myself up in my room, sat down at my desk, and sometimes I would take out the pages—hundreds of pages, confused, absurd, disorganized pages. I would set them before me with actual physical effort, and then I would sit there staring at them, for hours sometimes, as though I were totally lifeless and spiritless. When M. stuck her head in for some reason (on some *pretext*, I should say), I would shuffle the papers around or pretend I was making some correction with my ballpoint. Then, even as she left the room, I would feel her eyes still on me. I would go out in the garden, dejected, but I never really fooled her.

"This would happen especially before I met those people. Afterward, as I told you, I felt some hope begin to kindle. (And what a significant verb that is!) I would blow on the spark, protecting the tiny flame from the wind, trying to make the fire grow.

"The séance in the basement made a great impression on me, particularly when the blond girl played the piece by Schumann. But the day afterward I thought a great deal about the disproportion between these nice people, lovely people, you understand, and the magnitude of the powers involved. And I began to downplay what had happened in the basement: many piano students play that piece at a certain stage in their lessons. Was it not possible that she knew the piece and had played it at the urging of my own telepathic anxiety?

"There was no call to exaggerate, it didn't mean anything out of the ordinary. Not that I thought they were frauds—they were real enough, they were authentic, they were nice people.

"I realized, too, that they were not altogether powerless. I saw

292

great improvement in my spirit, I felt like a man who had been gravely ill and who has begun to feel like eating something again, to take a few steps.

"It's that it is a constant struggle, a battle virtually to the death, with no quarter given, and it has its good days and its bad days. One must be constantly at war—you can't drop your guard even for a second, you can't put too much faith in taking some hill or forcing the enemy's retreat, because it could be a trap. I have been waging this battle for years and years, fighting all sorts of strange skirmishes—like that skirmish I fought with the statue.

"The kids in the neighborhood were almost afraid of it (which I only saw *afterward*, of course). It stood in the garden back there, almost hidden by limbs and branches, under the palm tree at the rear of the yard. From the time I realized that the kids in the neighborhood, and especially don Díaz, would eye it a little apprehensively, I began to see that it did have something sinister about it. One day I mentioned it to Mario. 'But Papa,' he said to me, the way you'd talk to some irresponsible child, 'don't you know that no actor will work on a stage where there's a plaster statue?'

" 'Why not?'

" 'Don't ask *me*. But everybody knows it.'

"That night I couldn't sleep, until suddenly it came to me—how could I not have realized it before? The next morning I told M.

" 'Has it never occurred to you that that statue's showing up one morning on the sidewalk in front of the house is awfully hard to explain? Why would anyone leave a huge statue, made out of plaster, a life-sized woman, on my sidewalk? Where did it come from? It's the work of a sculptor, not some manufacturer of garden statuary for the masses—the work of a sculptor of today. Who in Santos Lugares would own such a thing—a working-class neighborhood full of people who at best decorate their houses with dime-store figurines? And besides, why leave it there on our sidewalk? And at night? What do you think?'

"She thought for a moment, because she always resisted my harebrained ideas.

" 'Just think back,' I said. 'For years I'd been wanting to put a statue out in the yard, a copy of one of those Greek or Roman statues like in the parks. Remember how I looked everywhere to try to find

293

one like the one in Lezama Park, or in the yard of that house in the novel—Liniers and Yrigoyen's house. A lot of our friends knew about that. Several people promised me they'd try to find one for me. Even Prebisch, when he was superintendent.'

" 'Uh-huh,' she said.

" 'And another thing,' I said, 'what did we think when we first saw that statue on the sidewalk?'

" 'We thought it was a joke. A friendly practical joke one of those people was playing on us. We thought somebody had left the statue on the sidewalk during the night to give us a surprise when we got up the next morning,' she remembered.

" 'That's exactly right,' I said. 'But you left out one little detail.'

" 'What's that?'

" 'We never learned who that friend was. Why remain anonymous? Was there something dishonorable about it? If someone had left it to give me pleasure, what was the reason for this silence? In fact months passed, and it all started to become more and more ominous, things went from bad to worse, and the statue standing out there began to look more and more sinister. Don Díaz asked me several times why I had that thing standing out there in the garden.'

" 'Uh-huh,' she said.

" 'So let's think about this another way, the *opposite* way. Let's suppose that someone wanted to cause me harm with some object, some object that had to be gotten into my house. It would be someone who knew that I wanted a statue like that. It would be very easy to have left the statue on my sidewalk that night; the person bringing the evil charm would surely know that I get up early every morning and go out in the garden, would deduce that I would immediately see the statue there on the sidewalk and bring it right in, etc. Might not that be true?'

"She stared at me in silence. I demanded an answer.

" 'Yes, of course it might,' she finally admitted.

"I spent the rest of that night very distraught, and that face with its abstract gaze, like the gaze of a blind woman, or a member of the Blind with the figure of a woman, seemed to be standing directly before me, with a malignant expression on its face, so close I could reach out and touch it.

"The sun was barely up when I ran out into the garden. There

294

it was, staring at me out of the foliage with that ominous sightless gaze.

"I first thought that I'd carry it away myself, but it was too heavy. I anxiously stood out on the sidewalk and waited for don Díaz to arrive, as he did every morning, and I asked him to help me. We dragged the thing out into the street, then he went home to get a rope and he tied it around the statue so that he could pull it onto his back and drag it over his shoulder. He told me to leave it to him, he'd carry it off somewhere.

"Where? I never tried to find out. And strangely enough, Díaz never told me, either."

Sabato turned his eyes on Bruno, as though asking him what he thought about all this.

"Very strange, very strange indeed," Bruno commented after looking into Sabato's eyes for a few seconds.

"Isn't it?"

He was deep in thought. Castel and the revenge of the Sect. When he realized what was afoot, Fernando had been terrified; he had decided to put an ocean between himself and "it." But on that complicated voyage, all he managed to do was once again come face to face with his fate. The curious thing about it is that he could sometimes actually foresee that, yet still he ran. S. too would have liked to flee his destiny, but that perverse force made him sink deeper every day into that very thing he would have liked to flee. Yes, many times he had thought of leaving it all, setting himself up in some little garage in some anonymous neighborhood somewhere, maybe growing a beard.

And the more cornered and persecuted he felt, the more he treasured that misguided possibility. That is the word: *treasured*. Now he realized that in these pages it would all come to its consummation. And although he didn't know exactly what that culmination was to be, he did have the certain sense of the revenge.

Yet how interesting life was! There were so many things he wanted to write about!

And in a way he could, too, so long as he wrote only about ideas. The Forces had no fear of ideas, the Gods didn't even bother about them. It was dreams, the dark imagination, that was what they feared.

"And now this Dr. Schnitzler," he suddenly said.

"What? Isn't his name Schneider?"

"No, I'm talking about somebody else. A professor, a very queer bird—*too* queer. He's sent me letters."

"Letters?"

"Uh-huh. Letters."

"Threats?"

"No, no, nothing like that. He's a professor. He started by writing me letters about some of his ideas on sex." S. rummaged in one of his pockets.

"Here, here's the latest one."

On the piano, dear doctor, the lower (darker) notes are found at the left. The higher, or clearer, brighter tones, at the right. The right hand plays the rational part, the "comprehensible" part, the melody. Observe how the right hand begins to gain importance among the Romantic composers, eh?

Once, primitively, writing went from top to bottom, as with the Chinese, or from right to left, as with the Semitic peoples. Then the words GNOTHI SEAUTON, *on the temple of the Sun, went from left to right. Notice, Dr. Sabato: the first way of writing came down to earth, while the second, the Semitic people's, ran toward the unconscious or the past; now, the last way of writing, our own, turns toward the awakening of consciousness.*

Heracles, at the crossroads, took the road to the right. Just men, in Plato's opinion, in death take the road to the right and upward, while the unjust take the road to the left and downward. Think, my dear doctor, think: you still have time. This is urged on you by one who, please be assured, has only your best interests . . . et cetera.

"But I don't see why this should alarm you."

"My experience of such things has been painful. There's something in these letters, a certain insistence on seeing me, something connected with the world of science, meaning the world of light, that, well . . . I *smell* it, you know? It's just something I feel. His letters have gotten increasingly insistent, there's something underneath all this amiable formality, or formal amiability. And I've de-

296

cided to take the bull by the horns once and for all. In fact," he looked at his watch, "I'm supposed to be at his house around six. I've got to go. I'll see you soon."

DR. SCHNITZLER

WHEN HE RANG THE BELL, he first felt an eye scrutinizing him through the peephole for a time he thought altogether too long. Then the door opened a crack and he saw a head looking at him that appeared to have been obtained by crossing a bird and a rat.

In a shrill, nervous little voice, Dr. Schnitzler expressed his likewise birdlike pleasure at S.'s arrival. He was thin, worn away by the years he had spent among books. His small ratlike eyes glittered behind the thick lenses of round, steel-framed glasses like those the hippies had recently made popular again, but which he had no doubt bought half a century ago in Germany and cared for with the same tenderness that he cared for the books in his library: they were aligned like a small German army, clean and disinfected, and all numbered.

Yes, that was it: he moved with the quick, nervous jumpiness of a bird when it lights on the ground, with the same flicks of the body and startled hops—like the staccato in some grotesque score by Haydn. He turned to the exact page he wanted to show S., and then returned the book with the utmost carefulness to its proper place. S. thought: if this man were forced by some respectable authority (some law passed by the German government, say) to lend one of these books, he would suffer exactly the same way an overprotective mother would suffer if her son were sent to war in Vietnam.

S. looked around circumspectly and took inventory of the study while Schnitzler was showing him some quotation or other. Then the door opened a crack and through the minimum possible opening there appeared a tray carrying two demitasses of coffee, passed in by the aged hands of an invisible woman. The tray was taken without a word by Dr. Schnitzler.

Where had S. seen that bird's face with the eyes of a rat?

He looked familiar, huh? Smiling in a most Mephistophelean

way, Schnitzler gestured to a signed photo of Hesse on one of the shelves.

Of course, of course: that same ascetic face of a criminal restrained just this side of murder by philosophy, literature, and probably a certain invincible, though secret, professorial respectability.

How had he not seen it before? No doubt because the look-alike smiled constantly: the vivacious brother of the somber murderer.

"We corresponded."

What a pity, what a pity he couldn't find *Heterodoxy*. But he'd made a copy of what he needed on the photocopier in the library. While Sabato explained that he had agreed to republish it, he asked him, preventively, how it was possible that he'd become so interested in him. With a series of little jerks and hops, Schnitzler opened a very clean file cabinet and pulled out a disinfected manila folder:

"You see, you see. Your position has always interested me, doctor."

Germany, S. marveled. If a German discovers that one has a doctorate, even if it was given in some previous incarnation, there is nothing in the world (except the government, of course) that can make him stop calling you by that title. With a hint of irony, S. tried to remind Schnitzler that the title belonged to his protohistory, his batrachian period, but Schnitzler shook his index finger at S. in quick little negative shakes, like a metronome marking an *allegro vivace*. For Schnitzler, that was like trying to make him believe in the nonexistence of a hand because it was inside a glove. It was useless, S. knew, from long experience.

Yes, as he was saying, S.'s evolution had always interested him.

"Very curious, doctor, very curious!"

And he studied S. with the sharp smile of a little bird that belonged to some Masonic organization, S. told himself. His expression said "You can't fool me," while Sabato wondered, in growing alarm, what kind of fooling he might mean.

But Schnitzler had found it even more curious when he read *On Heroes and Tombs*. S. waited for Schnitzler to go on: Why? Because of what?

They sat for a second in the most absolute silence, a second which S. found disturbing. Suddenly he had the sense that he knew what the man was thinking, but he was careful not to say so. On the contrary, he waited for the man to speak as though it were out of total ingenuousness that he wondered what it was that Schnitzler could have found so "very curious."

His words came with dry precision. And although they were the expected words, they made S. shiver:

"The Blind, doctor."

As he spoke the words, he looked directly into S.'s eyes.

Why in the world had he agreed to meet the man? And in his own apartment, on top of all. He concluded that it was because he was afraid of him, that there had been something that subtly emanated from his letters. What had that insistence on seeing him been aimed at? It had somehow been better to confront the possible menace face to face, take a sounding of the invisible (and dangerous) reef below, try to map it. It was an inquiry that made S.'s head spin, while the other man kept his eyes fixed on S.'s own. He had a sudden flash of illumination about that woman with the tray. Why hadn't she shown herself?

"But you are married, are you not, Dr. Schnitzler?"

For a long time after that first interview, S. asked himself what he had meant by that "but."

The professor grew serious, and seemed to be calculating the enemy's position. Then, controlling his reactions, he replied with an affirmative-sounding murmur.

That "but" had put him on guard, as there had been no phrase from either of them to justify it. It had undoubtedly showed him (thought Sabato) that my mind is working on two planes at once: the superficial plane of our conversation and another plane, more profound and secret. And as a finely tuned horse halts in a hayfield when he senses the presence of something strange, out of the ordinary, yet invisible, in the grass, so Schnitzler started, to the point of not being able to maintain that fixed smile which had hidden his intentions.

"Yes, I am married," he said, as though apologizing.

And immediately the smile returned, as he fumbled around in his library for that book by the Oxford professor.

Ah, there it was: the problem of the right hand, and so on and so forth.

Sabato nodded mechanically, but his brain went on thinking

299

quickly: the apartment was tiny, no one but the husband and the wife could live there, certain things he'd said indicated that he had a deep hatred for women or, in the best of cases, that he held them in satanic contempt. What S. could not manage to clarify to himself was why Schnitzler's praise made him feel uncomfortable, since most of the books the man had pulled out confirmed certain of the ideas on abstract civilization that S. had expounded in *Hombres y engranajes*, although Schnitzler went to extremes that S. couldn't share. At any rate, his instinct warned him that he was in the presence of an enemy, not an ally.

"You said it, doctor," he repeated merrily, "don't forget that!"

Now standing, with his index finger pointing at his own head like some histrionic teacher of languages pointing out the various parts of the body as he recited the corresponding word: "The head, eh?"

A rationalistic, masculine civilization
the right hand
abstract order, norms, standards, rules
law (a significant word, my dear Dr. Sabato!)
objectivity
et cetera, et cetera, et cetera

In his enthusiasm, he seemed to have forgotten about the coffee. Enthusiasm? Forgetfulness? He drank a little cold coffee and with a German volume in his hand he began enumerating all the things that this masculine civilization had repressed: the life-affirming, the unconscious, the illogical, the paralogical, the perilogical, the subjective.

He took another little sip of coffee, and above the rim of the cup his tiny, apparently gleeful rat's eyes glittered as they watched Sabato.

Sabato thought at double time. What made him, S., so alarmed? Wasn't this man repeating the same things that he himself had written in two books? It seemed nothing more than a philosophical joke, yet his panic grew.

Hesse's smiling double, all the more sinister for his sharp little smile, now took S. by the lapel and asked him a question, like a teacher asking a student a problem on a quiz: Which is the right side of a thing? The side that counts, no? The other side is the side that should be hidden.

With obvious delight he ticked off calamities: the left, or sinister side, is connected to ill-fortune, to perversity, to unlucky fate, to wrong and injustice. All feminine. One took oaths with the right hand, and made the sign of the horns with the left.

"Horns?" asked Sabato, to gain some time.

"Of course, of course. And as for Christianity, it is a solar, masculine religion which sees the left as demoniacal."

S. concluded that this little man either wanted to save him or was an agent of the Sect trying to find a way to keep him from going on with his inquiries. Unexpectedly, even to himself, he found himself asking whether the woman who had brought the coffee was his wife. And the words had hardly left his mouth when he realized that he was frightened by the step he had just taken. But it was too late now. He thought he saw an almost imperceptible stiffening in the man's expression, but in less than a second he had recovered his stereotyped smile:

"Yes, yes, indeed she is," he replied, as though some vaguely comic secret had been revealed, his voice almost tittering. "But she's awfully timid."

He's lying, thought Sabato.

"Poor women!" the professor cried, disclaiming any personal consideration.

He laughed, but it was obvious that he felt real repugnance.

"And the punishments inflicted on the left by languages! From Sanskrit right on down, good heavens! *Rectus, regula, corrigere, recht, right, orthodoxy.* He-he-he!"

The door opened a crack again, and another tray appeared, with more coffee.

S.'s head was spinning. He drank the coffee as quickly as he could, said he was running terribly late, and fled. Schnitzler saw him off in the elevator. His little Voltairean rat's eyes showed uncontainable glee.

Why? Why, Sabato asked himself when he was out in the street again.

He went up to Beba's apartment.

301

"Give me a whisky," he said as he walked in the door.

Beba gave him her inquisitorial look.

"What's wrong with you?"

"Nothing. I just feel like whisky. I'm tired, Beba, beat."

"I thought you were Quique."

"Why?"

"He's supposed to come by."

Sabato got up to leave.

"Don't be absurd. Come back in the other room and lie down on the couch, there you go, lie down for a while if you're so tired. Nobody'll bother you. He's coming with Professor Gandulfo. And in fact I may need your advice."

"Gandulfo?"

"Some man that Quique's discovered."

"That's too much. I'll just finish my drink and go."

"I tell you you can lie down back here and rest. You don't have to talk to Quique. But I'd like very much to hear your opinion."

Sabato gave in.

"Listen, Beba, I'd like to know whether you've ever heard of a man named Schnitzler."

"Aside from reading some of his short stories, no. I've never been introduced."

"I'm not joking, Beba. I'm not talking about that Schnitzler. I'm talking about a German man living at this very moment in Buenos Aires."

No, Beba hadn't the least idea who he might be. And what about Schneider, had she ever heard of him? Oh, heavens, it had been years since she'd heard that international troublemaker mentioned.

Sabato looked at her with tired sarcasm: "international troublemaker"? Why, what was it? Nothing, nothing. And what about Nene Costa?

"What about him?"

What was he doing these days, where was he, what was he up to?

"How should I know? In his house at Maschwitz, since he's dared to come back."

Since he's dared to come back?

Of course, silly, since that fat Villanueva woman's husband said

302

he wouldn't kill him after all. Unless, of course, he's ruined another marriage in the meantime, and has run off to Caracas or London or somewhere.

"So he's in his house in Maschwitz, huh?" Sabato muttered to himself thoughtfully.

"What's that?"

"Nothing."

Quique came in then, bringing a little man about four and a half feet high with a well-fed baby's face, all round and rosy, with gold-rimmed glasses. Very charming. A sort of long-haired little angel, but a nice sort of person. Your humble servant.

DOCTOR ALBERTO J. GANDULFO'S STORY

"GO AHEAD, PROFESSOR, PLEASE," Quique urged him. *"Nous sommes tout oreilles."*

S. walked away, to the far end of the living room, ill-humoredly.

"Once, in the remotest past, humanity lived in the celestial realm. It was one great family that surrounded the Divine Father. They had no bodies, they were a community of angels. These angels were led by a spiritual hierarch named Satan, a hierarch of great power. Power such as may be held by a general in time of war. Ambition, the love of power, though, is what brings all beings down, no matter what sort of beings they may be. And angels do not lack ambition merely for being spiritual. And so ambition began to cloud the mind of Satan, who at last came to consider himself omnipotent, like the Divine Father, when in truth he lacked the power of creation. And believing this of himself, Satan began to work, very cunningly, to incite that organization which he commanded to rebellion, promising his followers high rank and power."

"Like an ambitious soldier in any little Third World country, right, Professor?"

"That is exactly what he was like. I should say, of course, that not all the angels were followers of Satan. But those who were, were the most ambitious—that is, spiritually speaking, they were the least pure."

"But excuse me, Professor. I don't see how the Divine Father could not know about this plot. I mean, being omniscient and all."

303

"Of course he knew about it. He not only knew about it, he followed it very closely. Yet far from trying to prevent it, he let the idea take root and begin to ferment. Freedom of thought and action, instituted by the Divine Father himself, is as sacred as the Creator. God does not want to control our minds, to make them run in one predetermined direction, and channel our will to power, because that would mean depriving us of the freedom to develop our consciences, which is that which allows us to progress on the spiritual plane. The Divine Father knew, then, the rebels' plan, yet he continued his own work by dividing the infinite into heaven and earth."

"*Tiens!* What object did he have in mind by that, Professor?"

"You'll see. The heaven was divided into regions into which the several different families of souls were set, according to their spiritual state. Earth was destined for the egoists. In carrying out this idea, the Creator used his hierarchs, among these Satan, or Jehovah."

"Jehovah!"

"Yes. That is the name by which Satan later became famous in the Scriptures. These hierarchs were *gods*, in the plural: *elohim* in Hebrew, which has been erroneously translated into Spanish *Dios*, into English *God*, into French *Dieu*, and so on, in the singular."

"Just one point, Professor," said Beba.

"Yes, of course."

"You say that Satan and Jehovah are the same being."

"There is no doubt of it. I should tell you that I must reveal a fundamental secret. The Old Testament is not the holy word, as claimed by virtually all religious doctrine, including Catholicism. Only part of it is truth, that part which refers to the stages of the Creation. The rest is the work of Satan, who subjected the Semite patriarchs to his will and made them spokesmen for his thoughts, apologists for the acts he performed under the guise of Supreme Creator."

"*Un deguisé!* Diabolic! Uf!"

"Precisely the word. Such cunning, such audacity on the part of that powerful and invisible entity—to pretend to be the True God, and to make God, in turn, look like a Satanic being."

His voice was a little shrill and didactic, a schoolmaster—though one who rather than explaining long division was explaining the mechanics of a terrifying conspiracy. His tone was quiet and impartial. He didn't seem to be declaring that the Devil ruled the world, but merely to be setting forth the Pythagorean theorem in some sunny, clean schoolroom, just before the bell for recess.

"This trick became feasible for Satan at the instant he was sent out of the celestial region to become God of Earth. He governs the Earth through our passions, our egoism, and our ignorance. Now you'll see what happened with the cattle."

"With what, Doctor?" Beba inquired.

"With the cattle. Abel was the angel in charge of cattle, as Cain was put in charge of agriculture. Jehovah, which is to say Satan, inspired Cain to murder his brother. Why, you may ask."

"Indeed."

"Very simple. When the guardian of the cattle was eliminated, the cattle became easy prey for man, easily butchered for his consumption. By that one act vegetable nutrition, which had been instituted by the Divine Father, was abolished, and in its place was set nutrition by the fruits of butchery."

"Fascinating. So Cain becomes the protobutcher. Without him there would be no butcher shops," Quique concluded.

"Of course there wouldn't be. The purpose of this change was to neutralize the Divine Plan, because vegetarianism preserves health and encourages the spiritualization of man. Eating animals, or rather *cadavers*, brings on diseases of all kinds, cuts life short, dulls one's conscience and one's mind, stupefies the senses, incites passions, and feeds the ego. Not to mention being immoral, since every act against another being's life constitutes an immoral act, and a crime. We are brought to this pass by carnivorousness, and by it humanity is kept in the most total and complete darkness, prevented from seeing the truth and from reaching spiritual perfection."

"Interesting theory, Professor."

"It is not a theory, it is proven fact. Another thing: Noah and the Flood. Look how everything confirms what I have just said. Since Satan was incapable of creating humans or animals, he set aside Noah, his descendants, and their progeny, plus a certain number of all the *animal* species, for reproduction after the Flood. How ingenious men must be to attribute such a monstrous, criminal and

305

despicable act to the Divine Father! Satan, of course, had not the slightest interest in saving the *plants*. But the Earth, which had been saturated with seed since the Creation, made the vegetable kingdom reappear, in virtue of its spiritual essence."

"Turning the tables on old Satan."

"Of course. Which goes to show, by the way, how error-prone he is. But going back to what I was saying—both the sinking of Atlantis and the destruction of Sodom and Gomorrah, like the murder of Abel and the ills that have spread across all the face of the Earth since then, are the work of Satan. The Celestial Father, who is the essence of kindness, was never, nor could ever be, so bloodthirsty and cruel as to be able to destroy with such ferocity and hatred what he had created with such love. Learned and unlearned men alike, all of those who attribute these horrible acts to God, are in reality tricked by Satan, and their eyes are clouded."

There was something about him that reminded one of some grotesque marionette, some puppet controlled from above by Somebody. (But who? and where?) Or a ventriloquist's dummy, appearing to say what the Other, apparently unmoving and impassive, is actually speaking. There was something studied, unnatural, unreal about him. And yet one felt that his message was real, though ambiguous; terrible and terrifying, though amusing, almost comic.

"Very interesting, Professor. But how do we know it was really Satan and not the Divine Father who was the perpetrator of all this evil? Couldn't all this mayhem be explained just as well by a Bloodthirsty Father?" Beba wondered.

"No, because the Divine Father is perfect, and perfection assumes the good. But there is another proof, and quite an impressive one. The Assyrian story of the Deluge. It coincides point for point with the Jewish story, but it states that it is the spirit of evil that rules the world, not the spirit of good."

"So the Jews have been lying ever since the Flood. Biased journalism ever since back then! Wow! *Too* much!" exclaimed Quique.

"Precisely, sir. After the Flood, Noah and his family served to multiply the species. The interrelatedness by blood of all humanity was the inevitable result, and with that inbreeding you may well imagine whether the subraces that resulted could compare to those

306

marvelous Atlanteans that existed before the Deluge. From among these subraces, Satan chose one and excited its passions, its egoism so that he could manipulate the people of that subrace at his whim."

"The Jews."

"That's right. And he chose one of the representatives of that race as his earthly spokesman. Jehovah said to Abraham: *I will make of thy people a great people*, and that dazzled Abraham so much that Jehovah won his will entirely."

"Don't take this the wrong way, Professor, but I'd like to know whether you're an anti-Semite."

"Not in the least, sir. On the contrary, I feel that we should honor that race which was tricked and deceived by the Devil and by whose deception the link between Israel and Satan was established—a link that has been preserved down through the ages through the pact of circumcision, through the liturgy, and through other Luciferian mandates such as the festival of Passover to celebrate the events in Egypt."

"The events in Egypt?"

"Yes, of course, events obviously satanic. Just as we've seen that the Devil committed monstrosities such as the Deluge, the sinking of Atlantis, the destruction of entire cities by fire, not to speak of the inspiration of incest and the other repugnant acts of the Sodomites which led to that destruction. But all that is nothing beside the plagues he sent down upon Egypt: frogs and lice, hail and locusts, flies and vermin upon the cattle. How do those events strike you? As 'paternal'? And now look at what happened with Christ. Christ was one of the spiritual hierarchs who aided the Holy Father. The means that Satan used to turn the Hebrew people into his slaves (in return for riches and protection) made the Holy Father decide to send Christ down to Earth, incarnated in the body of Jesus (from which the name Jesus Christ) in order to emancipate that people from the terrible rule of the Devil, although the benefits of the mission would also be extended to all the rest of humanity as well. By the working of the Messiah to waken the conscience of mankind. Otherwise we would have remained in the most profound darkness and ignorance, since having confused Satan with the Divinity we would never have known of the satanic rule over us. Seeing this stratagem, and realizing what was about to occur, Satan at first tried to bribe the Son of God by offering him the kingdoms of the earth and its glory, just as he had previously bought off the Jewish people with deceitful promises. But when Christ rejected the offers with disgust and repugnance, Satan determined to scuttle the mission by even more iniquitous means. The preachings of Christ opened deep rifts in the Hebrew people, and that healthy reaction was the most serious threat to Satan's dominion. It was then that the God of the Earth divided the opinion of men and had Christ accused of heresy, choosing Judas to be the one to betray him. Filthy lucre was the means by which the conscience of this disciple was corrupted, just as vile lucre has been the greatest corruptor of all times, and just as the Church itself has diminished the greatness of its own mission by subjecting religious offices and rites to the blandishments of gold. But let me return to the mission of Christ. That mission was actually aimed at the special awakening of the Jewish people, since it was they who were most enslaved to the satanic influence, though all unwittingly. As they still are, of course. That is why Christ took the body of a Jew, so that He could work His influence as the Spirit of the Race and provoke in that people the reaction against Satan that he so ardently desired."

"But excuse me, Professor. How could the Celestial Father not foresee that the mission was going to fail? Did he not know the Jewish people would persist in their error?"

"Yes, yes, of course He did. But it was only a *partial* failure, because the Truth did take fire in a good part of that Chosen People, and in all of humanity. As for the rest of them, the Hebrew people who still believe in Jehovah, they follow their same path down to this very day, under Satan's terrible powers of suggestion."

He was not shouting, yet it inexplicably seemed to S. that the man was virtually shrieking. It was a shrill and penetrating voice, like one of those drills that burglars use on bank vaults in the dead of night.

"Don't you think, Professor, that for a chosen people protected by the God of the Earth, the Jews have not had altogether the best of it? Concentration camps and so forth, I mean . . ."

"There you have it! It is precisely because that people has not faithfully kept its religion, its promises—to Satan that is to say, that

308

Satan has decided to punish it with inquisitions, slaughters and beheadings, concentration camps, and the like. You have heard more than once that Hitler was the Antichrist, sent by the Devil. How much unconscious truth there is in those statements!"

"You've convinced us, Professor. What other proofs are there that the Jews are the slaves of Satan?" Beba asked.

"There are many, many of them. Remember that passage where Saul repeats the words of Christ, words after which he became converted into the Apostle Paul, to the effect that the evangel should be preached among the Jews and the Gentiles: 'Open their eyes, and turn them from darkness to light, and from the power of Satan unto God.' [Acts 26:18] And also those words of Christ in the Gospel of St John: 'Ye are of your father the devil, and the lusts of your father ye will do.' [John 8:44] It would be impossible to be clearer. And Satan had already said to Christ: 'All these things will I give thee, if thou wilt fall down and worship me.' [Matt. 4:9] Which is what without knowing it the Jews do. Worship Satan, for their entire liturgy is aimed at praying for material wealth and the remission of their everyday sins. The Holy Father is not the giver of material goods. And this is what the faithful of any religion should keep in mind, including Catholics: When we pray for wealth or evils, it is Satan who hears our petitions, and it is Satan who grants the wishes of those who are turned to evil, and thus they act as instruments of his perverse designs. The principal instruments by which Satan exercises his powers are: first, medical science . . ."

"Medical science?"

"Yes, medical science. Second, the clergy. Third, Catholicism. Fourth, Judaism."

"But explain to us, Professor, please—that part about medical science."

"I would be delighted. The harm done by Satan by means of doctors is perhaps the greatest harm of all. Neither wars, nor plagues, nor crimes, nor the earthquakes sent by Jehovah surpass the monstrous killing and butchery carried out by medicine in its recommendations for the eating of meat. By that means alone the individual conscience is made brutish, and illness and bad health multiplied."

"But excuse me, Professor—why should Satan want to keep us sick, if we're his allies? Wouldn't we be of more use to him healthy?

309

An army of lame, scurvy-ridden dwarfs is not the best army in the world."

"Ah, but you'll see, sir—in no way is it in Satan's interest that we be healthy, because physical health is likewise spiritual health. And because we are in condition to see the truth if we are healthy. When we eat the cadavers of our lower brothers and sisters, we are not simply committing a kind of anthropophagy, since they are in fact our brothers and sisters, but also rendering ourselves stupid and brutish, more prone to sin, as is proven by sexual corruption, which is infinitely greater among meat eaters. But going back to the crime that we commit with animals, I have had very interesting experiences. Animals are like children; they learn by way of human language and from constructive discipline. The experimental tests which I have carried out over a period of years have produced splendid results, and I have proven that all animals, without exception, are elevated, raised up—they come to identify with man—the instant they are placed under this discipline. And for that education no more than the human language needs to be used, for they respond to human language in a way that can only be called wonderful. Dogs, birds, cats, doves, chickens identify with the person who teaches them."

"Any language in particular, Professor?" Quique inquired.

"No, any language at all. Any language at all. So long as it is spoken carefully, slowly, and patiently."

"I mean, because Russian, or say German, ought to be harder than Spanish. Especially for a chicken, *disons*."

"Not at all, sir. It's wonderful, I tell you, absolutely wonderful the way a dog or a chicken responds."

"So, there don't seem to be problems with the declensions of Russian or German? I only go on like this, Professor, not because I want to cast doubt on your truly remarkable research, but rather because I myself had a good bit of trouble learning the accusative and dative when my mother was making me take German. And Russian, from what I'm told, *n'en parlons pas*."

"No problem whatsoever, sir. It is a question of patience, of applying oneself with affection and perseverance. People who use whistles and shouts and guttural noises of one kind or another, because they think animals won't understand them if they simply

310

speak naturally and correctly, commit a grave mistake. Not to mention the fact that we have an obligation to raise our lower brothers and sisters up, to educate them in our highest instrument, language. Would you educate your children with whistles and grunts?"

"No."

"There you are. The same goes for our lower kin. The animal kingdom is a deep secret, veiled to us by our Creator. And we sense that that kingdom is so sacred that to sacrifice the creatures which are part of it is a crime, an act of terrible immorality and monstrousness, a crime both against natural law and its evolutionary end, which is living together in peace on earth. What would we think of a monster that ate children too young to have learned to speak? I would add that while meat dulls the mind and conscience, as I have explained, vegetables sharpen and sensitize it."

"Any vegetable in particular, Professor? I ask because I myself am very fond of lettuce."

"Lettuce? Excellent! But there are no exceptions—any kind of vegetable at all: lettuce, of course, but also spinach, radishes, carrots. It's all excellent for sharpening our minds and consciences. Observe the herbivores, such as the horse or the cow: they are gentle and peaceable by nature."

"Bulls, too, Professor? I mean, I was thinking about bullfights."

"Bulls, too, yes, of course. It's only by such savage customs as bullfighting that an animal as noble and peaceful as the bull could bring itself to perform such atrocities as attacking men. We should be ashamed that the human race is capable of such extremes of cruelty and barbarity! The bulls aren't the villains, believe me, it's the men and women who go to bullfights and encourage such crimes. I repeat, all herbivorous animals are gentle. Compare a horse with a tiger or a vulture. Meat perverts the senses and makes the creatures that consume it aggressive."

"So wars and murders are the consequence of eating meat."

"You should not for a moment doubt it, madam. And it not only makes us insensitive to the next person's suffering, it leads us ever deeper into the world of the flesh, the merely physical world. And that is the aim of the satanic plan: to keep us from knowing the Truth, and thereby to avoid our emancipation from Satan's rule."

"So medicine . . ."

311

"I could talk for days on end about the horrifying crimes committed by that so-called 'science' of medicine, a science based on the consumption of meat, and on the idea of microbes and intravenous tubes. In one passage in the Old Testament we are told that Jehovah, which is to say Satan, created the plagues of flies and lice and locusts to punish Egypt. Jesus Christ, the Lord of Lords, cured illnesses by touching the body of the sick man and casting the filthy spirit out of it—which is to say casting out the Devil, who is what's actually responsible for disease. All those monstrosities that doctors call bacteria are nothing but creations, manifestations of Satan. And only those who live outside the Divine Law are attacked by microbes. So medical science does not cure, it simply lends itself to the satanic sleight-of-hand by which disease and illness are created and spread."

"So if somebody gets bitten by a rabid dog, there's no reason to run to the Pasteur Institute for a rabies shot; what the person ought to do is go find somebody to exorcise the demons?"

"Exactly."

"And what if the person can't find anybody that can do it? Or what if there's no time?"

"It will be a pity—but it's the only thing to be done. Let's look now at the second instrument I mentioned: the clergy. This is the strongest prop on which the power and might of Satan rests, because of the influence the clergy holds over a great part of mankind."

"Of course, like a person that trusts the police, and runs to the police for help, only to find that the police are in the pay of the underworld. Chesterton. *Drôle de police!*"

"You have hit the nail squarely on the head, sir. One proof is all that's needed: the clergy do everything for money. From performing a baptism to giving extreme unction. And money is the Devil's standard instrument. Oh my, eight-thirty! I'll just give an outline. The Catholics. The conduct of most Catholics shows the absolute negation of their doctrines. Priests and laymen alike diminish and cheapen their religion with their passions and their selfishness. Both priests and laymen are greedy for material wealth, and they will stop at nothing to gain it. As for the Jews, I have already said the most basic things to be said. The Semites are tied to Satan, whom they

312

call Jehovah, by the rite of circumcision. As in every diabolic pact, there must be blood spilled. But I must be short, unfortunately, since I could say even more important things. The struggle now being waged is a satanic struggle against the Divinity, a cruel, merciless, pitiless struggle which aims for the satanization of the world. And the world will be turned into a springboard for a battle for universal power. Atheism is the first step toward that satanization. Unfortunately, the victory of satanism would be equivalent to our eternal perdition, for we would be condemned to live in this hell for reincarnation after reincarnation."

"*Que Dieu nous préserve!*"

"Good-bye, madam. Good evening, sir. Some other time, we might pursue this subject which affects us all so gravely."

Doctor Gandulfo left the apartment with little hopping steps.

"Reincarnations!" Quique exclaimed, raising his hands to heaven. "Great future. According to the way we behave ourselves, imagine, a roster exactly backward from the army's: you start as a major-general and in one of those reincarnations you work like a dog to be a colonel. And the bureaucracy there must be! Some guy dies, he thinks he hears somebody tell him to go into the Cossacks next time around, so he stands in line for one or two hundred years waiting to come around again, and when he gets to the counter they look at the books, rummage through papers, go through the drawers, and it turns out the guy's made a little mistake, he must've heard wrong, he was supposed to be a cockleshell this time. Well, my chickies, I'm off, too, I think. This professor's got me worried. For the time being, I'm eating my daily allowance of lettuce, anyway. It's holy, I wouldn't stop eating it for the world. And you better leave off that whisky, or you'll wind up a cockleshell."

Bowing toward Sabato, he said, "Maestro," and left.

"Clown!"

"He's a wonderful person, a friend of Mabel's."

"I'm not talking about that poor sod."

He got up and browsed absentmindedly through some books in the library.

"Poor bastard. It's like the author of *Marital Bliss* trying to explain de Sade's sexual ideas to frigid housewives. And you people acting so clever. Laughing. The devil can rest easy. These shenanigans he plays with the truth seem to work. He uses poor bastards like that to make people laugh."

"You mean to tell me that you think this Dr. Gandulfo is proclaiming some theological truth."

"Of course he is, you idiot! You people laugh at that nonsense about the lettuce, but he is essentially in the right. Don't you remember what Fernando used to say?"

"Fernando Cánepa?"

Sabato looked at her disgustedly. "I'm talking about Fernando Vidal Olmos."

Beba raised her hands and rolled her eyes toward the ceiling in amused amazement. "That's all we needed, for you to start quoting your own characters!"

"I don't see why I shouldn't. God was overthrown before the beginning of time by the Prince of Darkness, or by the being who was later to become the Prince of Darkness. I'm capitalizing the title, by the way."

"No need to tell me, I know you by now. But that's not exactly what Professor Gandulfo was preaching."

"Leave that poor man out of it for now, if you don't mind. There are several possibilities, you understand. Once God was overthrown, Satan may have circulated the version that the one overthrown was actually the Devil. And thereby caused God a great loss in prestige, since that would have made God responsible for this miserable world. The theodicies which are later invented by desperate theologians are feats of acrobatics engaged in to demonstrate the impossible: that a good God is capable of permitting the existence of concentration camps in which people like Edith Stein die, and of allowing children to be mutilated in Vietnam, innocent people turned into horrible grotesques by the bombing of Hiroshima. All of which is sinister and perverse nonsense. What is true, what is indisputable, is that Evil rules the Earth. Of course not everyone can be deceived, there are always men and women who suspect the truth. And so, for two thousand years they have faced torture and death for daring to speak that truth. They have been dispersed, sent into banishment and exile, annihilated, tortured, persecuted, and burned by the Inquisition. Since the Devil isn't going to play by the Marquis of

314

Queensberry rules. And the very existence of that Inquisition should be enough to prove who rules the world. Entire peoples banished or destroyed. Remember the Albigensians. From China to Spain, the religions of the state (another organization of the Devil) wiped the planet clean any time there was an attempt at revelation of the terrible secret. And one might even say that they almost achieved their goal."

"Of course *almost*. The exception being Professor Alberto J. Gandulfo, for example."

"Keep laughing. Little deviltries of Satan's. Making a ridiculous person speak the truth is one way to condemn that truth to ridicule and therefore to impotency. Men like Gandulfo are not only *allowed* to live: they are actually *inspired* to talk. But I insist—there are other sources of confusion that are even more diabolic. Some sects which could not be wiped out, or maybe it was that Satan didn't wipe them out *ex profeso*, but at any rate they became in turn another source of lies. Think of Mohammedans. According to the gnostics, the sensible world was created by a demon named Jehovah. For a long time God allowed that demon to do his work as he wished, freely, but at last God sent his Son to temporarily inhabit the body of a Jew. That was the way God planned to free the world from the false teachings of Moses, the prophet of Jehovah—which is to say of the Devil. And by the way, remember what Papini said about Michelangelo's Moses? Was Michelangelo in on the secret? But let's not go into that now: if we accept the fact that Jehovah is the Devil, but that with the coming of Christ the Devil has been overthrown, buried in Hell (as the Mohammedans and other gnostics believe), then the only thing gained is an increase of mystification. We now have a double mystification. We still have the same world of miseries and horrors, because Hiroshima and the concentration camps have come after Christ, don't you see? In other words: each time the lie is weakened, this class of wretches consolidates it again, and the Devil tranquilly rules for another thousand years or so, while the true God lies in Hell. That's why Satan allowed the Mohammedans to grow and develop and raise such a wide and powerful empire. You'd have to be crazy to think that one fanatic on horseback could conquer the Western world and rule it for centuries."

"So?" Beba's eyes were ironic.

315

"Fernando's conclusion is inevitable. The Prince of Darkness still reigns. And that reign is achieved via the Sect of the Blind."

The conclusion seemed so self-evident to him that he would have laughed out loud had he not been possessed by terror.

"And do you agree?"

Sabato stared at her in silence.

When he got home, he found the

THIRD MESSAGE FROM JORGE LEDESMA

GIVE ME A LITTLE WHILE YET; DON'T FORGET I DON'T KNOW THE JOB TOO WELL, I'm in the process of discovering myself in a strange medium and in total solitude. I have little time to write, but I do think a lot. Now I'm selling sausage for Tres Cruces wholesale meats. I think about Gogol, stewed to the gills, sitting on some table with his legs hanging off it, saying How sad is Russia, while he laughs till he cries with Pushkin, and then starts crying for real. Argentina, on the other hand, is incomparable. When my sausage gives me a few minutes off, I run off and write.

To the point: a very large, strange animal has emerged from me. I'll have to shorten its neck a little and make it a bit less unbeliev-able. Its legs are as heavy as the ones on Hobbes's Leviathan, and comfortless, like the work of Schopenhauer. I will explain the book to you:

1. The record set clear about God. God cannot exist. If He does exist, it's nothing to us one way or the other.

2. What we are doing on earth.

3. The metallurgical and strategic arguments for death. The re-ligious argument not only puts the cart before the horse, it puts man in the place of the horse. Now all we need is for the horse to climb into the wagon. It must most energetically be prevented from doing that.

4, 5, and 6. The whys and wherefores. Why we are liquid. Why there are two sexes. Why the only thing that belongs to us is what we no longer possess: the past. I will explain Angst, dissatisfaction, this damned incompetence. Schopenhauer saw it at thirty. Incredi-ble. Intellect vs. will. That is the great struggle of mankind, the plane

316

taking off from its aircraft carrier, the man in search of being. It will leave this ramshackle world full of madmen behind, it will pulverize morality, it will break and destroy everything. The knowledge of the Truth is the greatest event of the century, not some stupid trips to the moon like the schoolboys think. I don't know why I was one of the select few. I could have been a bum, gone to the dogs and taken to drink, written love stories, maybe even have won mention and moolah. Still, I am going to sing. Ever since I was a tyke I've been a standout in the field of jigsaw puzzling. Inclination for work somehow didn't come altogether naturally. But anytime I had to put something together, unravel some mess, there, there was the subtext, the infrascript, the figure in the carpeting. The Truth was in the world already, ready and waiting, most amiably standing by to be at our service, but in pieces all around us. Every philosopher said his little piece of it. It had to be put together, not added to. Remake the old Dumpty, not make a fancier omelette, or whip up a soufflé. Which is why all the old standby sages failed: the sager the sages spoke, the darklier and more scrambled it all looked. I had the rotten luck to put Truth back together again, because I know virtually nuttin' about nuttin'. And since I've got no professors to insult or make look bad, I'm totally irresponsible.

ALL THAT NIGHT SABATO MULLED
and in the morning, when the sky began to grow light, he had managed to overcome the myriad fears which had been holding him back: he would find Schneider, wherever he might be. For the moment there was one lead—Nene Costa's house in the country.

He looked at the calendar; Sunday was still two days away. He walked outside. The sky was clear, the air dry. He cut a little piece of paper, held it up, and let it go: the wind was from the north. All indications were that come Sunday the weather would be warmer, with little chance of clouds—and even less of rain. A sunny day in February: everybody would be in swimming.

The decision calmed him, and he began to feel his strength return, the strength he'd squandered in all this hesitating and looking back he'd been indulging in.

317

in that way he had, with his head tilted down and to one side, and the skin-deep sort of smile which constituted his veneer of diplomatic friendliness; under this first layer there was a second which tight control of his facial muscles kept barely perceptible but which nevertheless might be noted by an observer who knew him very well—it was a level at which ironic enjoyment of all this took place, where he asked himself questions along the lines of "Has he picked up the scent?" or "How can he be so naive?" For Nene Costa was thinking, surely, of the depths of ingenuousness implied by the fact that S. had made a trip all the way to Maschwitz, to this conventional weekend of sun and swimming, to ask questions about Schneider. The questions asked, of course, reflected suppositions on the part of Sabato, and therefore might or might not actually be germane, the suspicions leading to them perhaps on target, and perhaps not. So that arrangement of the muscles in the second layer—a layer that unquestionably existed (because under the mundane smile there had to be feelings of irony, or even resentment, or hatred)—was not necessarily produced by the fact that Costa knew whether or not Schneider was in Buenos Aires. Costa's knowledge—that was a hypothesis for the moment, no more than that, a mere hypothesis, which S. was trying to confirm by snooping around this country house, talking the way he was talking to this person whom he detested, and even noting his negatives:

"Schneider?"

Costa wrinkled his forehead in that interrogative way that was his alone, a manner he used not only for asking questions or listening to something that intrigued him but also for making statements such as "I don't really think Lenin was a revolutionary." It was this sort of statement that created about him that halo of mysterious sagacity he had: he would say such things with no support or foundation whatever, as though what he said was so obvious that it did not merit discussion, though when he added that almost interrogative wrinkle of the brow to the words he spoke, he seemed not to be taking an authoritarian or Solomonic tone at all, but rather offering his words as proposals for some future discussion (which of course, S. wryly said to himself, would never later come about).

No, Schneider was still in Brazil, no doubt, it had been years since Costa had seen him. And as for Hedwig, he had not the slightest idea. But she must still be with him, surely she was, which meant somewhere in Brazil as well.

HE BROODED ON FERNANDO'S WORDS

and remembered his warnings. No, there was nothing going on there that ought to worry S. *Apparently* not, that is! The same naiveté that Fernando himself had shown, no less! The equivocal role played by Domínguez, who *apparently* knew nothing of his doom of Blindness and of fire. Brauner, who had returned to Paris in 1938 *apparently* because of his painting, though in truth to meet his bloody fate: returning to the perfect place at the precise moment for the glass hurled by Domínguez to gouge out that eye which he had dreamed and painted for years as hanging, bloody, from a flap of skin. Men moved like sleepwalkers toward places they were darkly drawn to. Now, for example, what part in that gang of fools did destiny play, and what part chance? He tried to see, under their false faces and sophisticated poses, the terrible meaning, like some expert in espionage might try to find the real words under the rambling jokes and anecdotes of some woman's giddy letter. *Could they imagine Aunt Teresa*, Quique was exclaiming, theatrically flinging his arms wide like the blades of a fan, *if, after spending her life on her knees praying in the cathedral, she should die and go upstairs there and find that the Big Guy in charge of the Big Deal is not Christ at all, but rather, disons, some blue man with lots of arms coming out all over his body?* That was the thing: terrifying messages brought by clowns. Every word, every gesture had to be studied; not a single corner of the world, or of one's life, could be left unexamined, not a single step taken by Schneider or his friends left unwatched. Remember de Maupassant mad, Rimbaud dying in delirium, wrote Fernando. And so many other anonymous men and women, as well, ending their days horribly: caged in the four walls of an insane asylum, tortured by the police, drowned in wells, swallowed by quicksand, eaten by ravenous ants in Africa, devoured by sharks, castrated and sold as slaves to sultans in the East. Naturally Vidal Olmos had forgotten to mention subtler forms of punishment—whose subtlety made them all the more frightening.

the little gathering turned radical—and though they cooled it from time to time with dips in the pool and trips to the bottle of 100 Pipers, certain of the invited guests entered into a heated discussion of the State of the Masses in the Third World, not failing by the way to scold Nene (who apparently was doing the bartending) for being so preoccupied with mere literary concerns.

"You're still mucking about in Nabokov when it's time to grab a rifle and head for the front," Coco summed up as he energetically rubbed oil onto his chest.

And then, perhaps because of some small sign that his Secret Police antennae picked up—in spite of my care not to so much as blink—Coco turned to me and asked:

"And you, Quique, might one inquire what the fuck *you* think? You aren't a Peronist, you aren't a Bolshie, so could you please explain to us what it is the fuck that you exactly *are*?"

A reasonable question, under the circumstances, I thought, and to which I, in a tiny, humble, barely audible voice, replied, in a tone of hurt and grief:

"It's true, Coco, I'm not a Peronist or a Bolshie. I'm very poor, you see."

These were words that I would later (for nothing is secret) be severely judged for.

Then the personal lives of several ladies and gentlemen present, several ladies and gentlemen absent though linked to those present, and several ladies and gentlemen merely absent were brought out for examination:

"As long as it lasted it was great. Then it got a little wearing. I began to see the light in analysis."

"You talk, but you still haven't got past the homo stage."

"With grass everything's rosy, we talk more, we cry if we feel like it."

"We share *everything*. We met in this friend's apartment where we were watching *The Hour of the Ovens*, and we began this great no-strings relationship."

"We had therapy as a couple. We split up okay; we're good friends now."

"Listen, buster, you're projecting."

320

"But you're a masochist, which is very frustrating."

"Yeah, but at least I've got some *insight*, you know?, so I can see the conflict. And besides, Panchita turns me on, she's so-o-o-o foxy, so what do you want from me, because I mean there's empathy, you know? When we're together there's so much rapport you wouldn't believe it."

"So I split. I admit it's a cop-out, okay, you can say I'm immature, but I just couldn't take it anymore. If he's gay I think he ought to come out of the closet once and for all, what the fuck difference does it make? The 'undecided' are the worst, don't you think?, they don't see you as a woman, they want to be 'friends,' right, and you can never get rid of them."

At which point Coco apparently couldn't stand any more, because all of a sudden he screamed *What it is, is, that you people have got to realize for once that in this miserable fucking life you're not the only ones who have got conflicts. Conflicts are not so special, all they are is the subproducts of the general alienation of consumer society.*

There he goes with the Revolution again, I thought. And sure enough, the talk got *very* political, and important verdicts were soon being handed down:

"No sir, what I want is to be accepted as a woman, not as a consumer object. What do you think, asshole, that I'm Isabel Sarli because I've got a nice pair of tits?"

"It's an urban problem—the city cries out for change, a basic change, a change in its very structure," said Arturito, who's an architect, and who, one must say in his favor, had until that moment not opened his mouth.

"Well, but it's different if it's aimed at the *lumpen*."

"And what do you have against the masses, if you don't mind my asking?"

"It's that you can't de-class yourself. There's a context and you have to live in it."

"But the fact that one insists on remaining in the upper class doesn't mean that one has license to overlook or ignore or *deny* the errors in the system. Nor can one become mechanistic."

"Yes, but there's one quantum you ought to take into account!"

"If you step outside the lines that your environment imposes on you, you're punished."

At which point poor Cristina, who had very prudently stayed on the sidelines during all this, no doubt so as not to appear too stupid, said something about the interpretation of some book or other. Poor dear! Everyone looked at her like somebody riding a buggy in the Age of the Locomotive. Reading, you idiot?! Reading! The reading of *Guernica*, for example, from the point of view of the bourgeoisie.

So Cristina shut her mouth, and I watched her slip away little by little until she was over by Nene Costa, who was lying under a tree reading *Playboy*.

LOOK AT THIS FACE, NENE SAID TO HER.

"So. Some woman. She looks awful, all wasted. Must smoke a lot."

He read her name: E. Kronhausen.

"And this face down here," Nene pointed. "P. Kronhausen."

Cristina asked if they were sisters.

"No, they live together. They're married."

"Two sisters married?"

"You goose. The one up there is a man. Eberhard."

"Okay. So?"

"So nothing. They're on a panel on new sexual styles."

"Wow. They look like they've had their mugshots taken by the cops after a night at the swingers' ball."

"Read, read."

Curriculum vitae: when he was a boy he was attracted to Tarzan. He married, had two children, and then discovered that he was homosexual. He asked for a divorce and founded the Metropolitan Community Church, for gays only. He was once described by a reporter as the Martin Luther King of the gay movement, to which he replied, 'I don't know if I'd go that far. Just call me the Martin Luther Queen.' He is constantly on the go, from taking part in picket lines and marches to giving sermons and appearing in high schools and colleges. He has set up a hot line for gays in crisis.

"And now for the two that you thought were sisters. The Kronhausens. They were married while they were doing their doctorates at Columbia. They are the authors of *Pornography and the Law* as well as the famous two-volume *Erotic Art*, a collection of fifteen

322

hundred plates representing the holdings of their renowned International Museum of Erotic Art in San Francisco, a nonprofit institution. Then there's Betty Dodson, known for her work in the feminist movement and her efforts to 'liberate society' through her explicitly erotic art. Her 'celebration of the art of heterosexual and homosexual lovemaking, which depicts behavior ranging from orgies to masturbation,' has been exhibited in one-woman shows in New York City galleries. She was a judge in the Wet Dream Film Festival in 1971 in Amsterdam, and she's the director of a sex clinic. Al Goldstein, with the face of a practical joker with lots of money, founder of *Screw* and *Gay*, a weekly homosexual tabloid, once imprisoned in Havana as a suspected CIA agent, actor in the first hardcore epic film, which *Screw* produced, teaches New Sexuality at New York University. Let's hear what these people have to say:

"*Goldstein*: If my wife cheated, I'd kill her. She's part of my property. I mean, I am a sexist. And since I pay the bills, I feel I *own* her, the way I own my car, and I don't lend my car out to people.

"*Perry*: Al, are you really sure that you're the editor of *Screw*? Maybe you should drop your wife and try having a loving relationship with some of your other property, like your sofa.

"(This guy's not so bad after all, he's got a sense of humor.)

"*E. Kronhausen*: I don't see, Al, how you can sit there and say such things. I feel embarrassed for you. How can you kid yourself that you're part of the sexual revolution with attitudes like that?

"*Goldstein*: Everything has its price. Let's not bullshit ourselves that marriage, one-night stands, orgies or anything else don't have their price. I just want my wives to know the terms of the sale before they sign the contract."

Nene flipped several pages.

"Ah, on group sex parties:

"*P. Kronhausen*: It's fun. You go there just to have a good time. If we could get just one message across to the young, it would be that sex should be for recreation, not procreation.

"*E. Kronhausen*: Actually, swinging can be amusing as well as erotic. We've often laughed our fool heads off at a sex party. When you've got twenty people on a bed, something funny is bound to happen—like someone's falling off. Or making a human pyramid and having the whole thing collapse.

323

"*P. Kronhausen*: I'll never forget the party we went to last spring, where the men turned on the TV to watch a basketball game. They were actually carrying portable sets from room to room while there was sex going on. Ebe and I couldn't believe it. When it came to sports or sex, they chose sports.

"*Playboy*: What's the usual ratio of males to females at a group-sex party?

"*Pomeroy*: Usually, people come in pairs, but an ideal swinging party has about twice as many males as females, because females can keep going longer. They usually wear the males out.

"*Playboy*: What kinds of erotica are used to get a group-sex party going?

"*Pomeroy*: Porn movies are very common at swinging parties. The films are much like swinging: terribly genital, very specific, non-emotional. They also help people develop their fantasies, give them ideas of what to do sexually.

"*E. Kronhausen*: Well, I'm not in the habit of going to sex parties with a tally sheet, but my guess would be that sex films have played a role in no more than ten percent of all the parties I've attended. And, more often than not, they have a decided turn-off rather than turn-on effect under these circumstances. After all, if you have live stimuli all around you, who needs people fucking on the screen?

"*Dodson*: At one party, the women brought vibrators and we initiated sensual massage and masturbation. We also showed the men the best position for fucking while using the vibrator. Like, you can have penetration and use the vibrator on your clitoris and the man can feel the vibrations inside you. One of the exciting developments was that as the women became more aggressive and said what they wanted, there were more female orgasms.

"*Goldstein*: I've got to give Betty credit for teaching me the wonders of the vibrator. Vibrators always used to be a no-no, something you had to buy under the counter in a sex-book store. Now the poshest drugstores on Fifth Avenue are selling them for $2.95. You've probably noticed they never sell square vibrators; they're all cock-shaped, which probably accounts for a lot of wives' smiling even when their husbands aren't around. The marketing of dildos is another great step forward for middle America. In fact, the ultimate dildo would be for insecure people like me, who need an emotional accompaniment to their raw sexuality. It would have a voice box inside, saying 'I love you, darling.'

"*Davis*: Personally, I find such devices a little inhuman. I guess I'm just really hung up on flesh, as opposed to plastic and metal. But with or without vibrators, the mythology is that Lesbians can't live without being fucked—and that's absolutely ridiculous. Women don't necessarily need intromission. The seat of women's sexuality is clitoral. If more women realized that, they might develop a lot more power and autonomy in their relationships.

"*Perry*: From the experiences of homosexuals who come to me for counseling, it would seem that vibrators and dildos are often used in group-sex situations. Some individuals especially like vibrators for anal intercourse. If they're sixty-nineing, for instance, they might use vibrators on each other simultaneously. Their attitude is that if it helps heighten the sex act, then that's cool.

"*Lovelace*: It really depends on how good the vibrator is. I have a vibrator that's not one of those long thin ones you put inside your vagina but the kind that you attach different things to the end of— more of a clitoral vibrator. It's really fantastic.

"*Pomeroy*: The primary negative aspect of group sex, as I see it, is the danger of emotional involvement—the problem of meeting somebody you tune into and then get emotionally involved with. When I talk about this with my patients, I always emphasize this very strongly—that they're sort of playing with dynamite. This is also a part of their life that they really have to cover up from their children, and even from their straight friends."

"Donkeys are better than dogs," murmured Nene, pensively examining Linda Lovelace's face. "And now observe the minister: the Reverend Troy Perry."

He gazed at him, his head tilted to the left.

"I'll bet he was a terrific football player, but one of those guys that are brutal and introspective at the same time. A cross between a boxer and a down-and-out philosopher. Look how carefully dressed he is, how perfectly his hair is combed.

"Linda Lovelace, twenty-two (but she looks forty!)." Under the photo she was saying that if she didn't have at least one orgasm a day she got "very nervous, very uptight." She was famous for her appearance in the hard-core film *Deep Throat*: "the very mention of her name at cocktail parties invariably precipitates either a spate of sword-swallowing jokes or a chorus of opprobrium." The magazine *Screw* had called her "America's favorite mouth."

"Mouth?" asked Cristina. "But it's awful." Nene smiled at her in ironic pity. They went on reading: " 'Drawing upon her extensive personal experience she recently became a monthly columnist for *Oui* magazine, dispensing advice on sexual matters from analingus to zoophilia.' "

MEANWHILE, QUIQUE WAS FOLLOWING A NEW TURN IN THE CONVERSATION.

People had swung from the psychosocial aspect of modern life to the aestheticosocial aspect, and Nene Costa immediately pricked up his ears. Imagining a discussion of that sort without him, in fact, was like imagining a boxing match without Howard Cosell. Judgments were handed down on:

John Cage and *la musique d'ameublement*
official culture
the need to shit in good taste
antipainting
antiopera
antipoems
antinovels (but how passé—the anti-antinovel, better)
musical collage
Schoenberg

"But what is *idea* for Schoenberg?" Nene asked. One had to distinguish between the idea of music and its phenomenological aspect.

"One must unmask the extreme embodiment of idealistic bourgeois thought."

"Our warmest felicitations. 'Idealistic bourgeois thought.' More or less like saying 'an orange painted orange.' "

"Action music."

"Precisely. Mixed with applause, shouting, sneezing and burps from the performers."

"But in that case, what about Penderecki?"

That "in that case" devastated me, showing me in the most bru-

326

tal way what sort of intellectual wreck I'd become since I'd joined the Fourth Estate with *Radiolandia*.

In that case?

I, in a state one might call *agitato con vertigo*, noted the presence of the following statements in the discussion that ensued:

"Happily dissociate Balzac from Dostoyevski."

"How can one go on writing like Balzac?"

"Or even like Camus."

"Those great lumbering tortoises!"

"And what do you have to say about Osberg?"

"Osberg?"

"Yes, of course, Borges, that article on Nabokov, dummy. Weren't you talking about that? He said he'd fascinated him, until he'd seen that it was a façade without a house behind it."

"Good one, good one! That Nabokov, too!"

"The man who made the world in his own image."

"Die Walt als Wille und Vorstellung," emphatically intoned Nene Costa.

And then Coco yelled ENOUGH LITERATURE! WHAT *IS* ALL THIS BULLSHIT, and while he poured himself another Pipers he said What needs to be done is you need to grab a rifle. To which Pampita replied Oh stop all this sectarianism, it's all very fashionable but it's totally mistaken, the Revolution has to be fought at every level, and how can anybody talk seriously about a revolution if at the same time he's still writing like Camus?

Literature had to be demythified, they had to do with literature what had already been done with the plastic arts, unmask all those guys that believed in characters and telling stories and all that.

When suddenly Pampita asked me whether I'd seen Luisito's last show. The question caught me by surprise, but I pulled myself together and said I'd gotten there too late—by the time I got there they were redecorating the gallery.

"Redecorating the gallery?"

"Yeah, there were cans of paint all over the place, and piles of sand and stuff."

"But you idiot, that was the show!" she cried.

I mentioned Domenicone, so the damage would not be quite so total. But that only made things worse: the man was utterly out of

327

it. Show-off of the century. By the time he started working with all those neon gadgets, nobody was doing the tacky things anymore.

HE HATED HIMSELF FOR BEING IN THIS HOUSE,
for having, in any way whatsoever, anything in common with these people. But could anyone in all honesty boast of being better than anybody else? Someone had once said that in every living creature lay the seeds of all humanity: all the gods and demons that any civilization had ever imagined, feared, and worshipped were found in every one of us, and if even one small child were left alive after a catastrophe that destroyed the entire planet, that child would re-create the whole panoply of luminous and perverse divinities, the same race of deities all over again.

S. walked to the station in the silence of the night and then stretched out on the grass, near a stand of grand, solemn eucalyptus trees, and he looked up into the blue-black sky. The novas from his stint in the observatory returned to his mind, those inexplicable celestial explosions. He had his own idea about them, the idea of an astrophysicist driven mad by heresies:

There are millions of planets in millions of galaxies, and many of them repeated our amoebas and megatheria, our own Neanderthal men, and then our Galileos. One day they discovered radium, the next they managed to split the uranium atom and couldn't control the fission, or weren't able to contain the atomic race, weren't able to prevent the atomic cataclysm, and their planet had exploded in cosmic inferno: the Nova, the new star. Throughout the ages, those explosions had signalled the ends of successive civilizations of plastics and computers. And in the peaceful, star-filled sky that very night a message about one of those colossal cataclysms was coming to him, a cataclysm produced out there at a time when on the Earth dinosaurs were still grazing on the Mesozoic plains.

He recalled the pathetic figure of Molinelli, that risible inter-mediary between man and the deities that ruled over the Apoca-lypse. Those words he had spoken in 1938, as he pointed his gnawed pencil at S.'s chest: Uranus and Pluto were the messengers of the New Age; standing like volcanoes in eruption, they would signal the boundary line between two eras.

328

Yet that starry sky seemed to stand so remote from any hint of imminent catastrophe. It emanated serenity, harmonious and inaudible music. *Topos uranos*, the beautiful refuge. Behind and above men being born and dying, many times at the stake or by torture, behind and above the empires arrogantly raised and inevitably fallen, that sky seemed the least imperfect image of that other universe, the universe incorruptible and eternal, the greatest perfection, which one could only pretend to scale with the transparent but rigid theorems of mathematics.

He had attempted that ascent. He had attempted it each time he had felt pain, because the tower was impassive and invulnerable; each time the garbage heap was unbearable, because that tower was limpid and clean; each time the ephemerality of time tormented him, because in that realm reigned eternity.

To lock oneself in that tower . . .

But the distant murmur of men had always wound up reaching his ears, it slipped in through the chinks and rose into the very heart of the tower. Because the world was not just outside; it was in the deepest and most secret corner of his heart, as well, in his viscera, in his excrement. And sooner or later that incorruptible universe wound up looking to him like some sad simulacrum, because the world that counts for us is this one, here—the only world that wounds us and pains us and makes us feel our terrible loneliness and hunger, but also the only world that gives us the fullness of existence, this blood, this fire, this love, these hopes for death. The only world that offers us a garden at twilight, the touch of a hand we love, a glance cast on putrefaction, but *our own* putrefaction: warm and close, carnal.

Yes, perhaps that universe invulnerable to the destructive powers of time did exist, but it was an icy museum of frozen and petrified forms, perfect but stiff, forms ruled and perhaps conceived by pure spirit. But pure spirit is alien to humankind. The essence of this unhappy race is the soul, that region torn between corruptible flesh and pure spirit, that *halfway* region in which the gravest acts of existence occur: love and hate, myth and fiction, hope and dream. Ambiguous and filled with anguish, the soul, dominated by the passions of the mortal body yet aspiring to the eternity of spirit, wavering perpetually between rot and immortality, between the diabolic

329

and the divine, suffers. (And how can it not suffer!) There are moments of horror and ecstasy when it creates poetry out of that anguish and ambiguity, poetry which bursts forth from that confused region and as a result of that very confusion. A God does not write novels.

THE NEXT MORNING HE WANTS TO WRITE
but his typewriter suddenly has a series of problems: the margins don't work, it skips, the ribbon spool won't rewind automatically, he has to rewind by hand, and finally something in the carriage breaks.

In desperation, he decides to go downtown to get his mind off all this; he'll walk through the south side of town.

On Alsina, between Defensa and Bolívar, he decides to buy a notebook, to write in in longhand. Something new, a symbol of the new beginning, something that will let him write in a café, in spite of his handwriting, in spite of the weariness that producing legible script makes him feel. He might be able to break this evil spell that way.

A tired, unpleasant clerk waits on him and is almost obviously irritated by the fact that S. is looking for exactly a certain kind of notebook. S. tells the salesclerk to go to hell and leaves the store, in increasingly bad humor. He decides to go to the University Bookstore on the corner of Bolívar and Alsina. His spirits pick up at the thought that he'll be able to find exactly what he's looking for in the huge stationery section there. But then he sees, through the window bars of an old house, a huge rat glaring out at him fixedly from the darkness of the basement, its little red eyes malign-looking; it brings back the memory of that conversation with young Busto and their talk about the bats in Francisco Ramos Mejía's little parapeted fort in Tapiales: winged rats, filthy, disgusting, ancient creatures. He tries to put these memories aside, and strides on purposefully toward the bookstore. Purposefully? Well, to a certain point. It should be phrased, to be perfectly precise, that he walks with a *degree* of purpose.

With the timidity that salesclerks always make him feel, S. goes over to a tall, thin young man with long hair. Although he sees that

330

the young man recognizes him, he tries to remain neutral and un-
affected, to overcome the shyness that this sort of recognition always
produces in him. Things are getting complicated, he thinks; it embarrasses him to have to explain what he's looking for (he knows so
clearly what it is, but there are so many details—just about this size,
black outside and red inside, etc.), but overcoming his resistance he
finally tells the young man what he wants—though he keeps back
the details, out of lack of courage:

"A notebook," he says, clumsily.

The clerk shows him some things, but they are far from what S.
is looking for: he wants a notebook neither too big (which would
be unpleasant; it would intimidate him with its huge, unmanageable
pages, like great white sheets in the wind) nor, of course, too small
(in which he couldn't write with any looseness, in which he would
feel straitjacketed). Of course he doesn't declare all this to the salesclerk; he only says that he "had been looking for something else."

The clerk then begins to show him other binders and folders
and the like, but unfortunately each one is ever more remote from
the ideal model he carries in his mind. "My damned habit of getting
into something without first locating absolutely what it is I want,"
he thinks. He's so often felt himself obliged to carry away the most
unpleasant or useless inventions. Bitterly he ponders that closet in
which the object, whatever it is, winds up, a closet filled with un-
wearable shirts, too-short or too-long socks, ballpoints whose tips
are too fine or outlandishly broad, letter openers with brightly
colored seashell handles that say SOUVENIR OF NECOCHEA, a pair of
castanets that he can't bring himself to remember how he was cowed
into buying, a gigantic bronze Quixote that he paid a small fortune
for, and even a chrome vase he felt obliged to buy when he went
accidentally into a little shop he thought might sell keyrings. These
were the things he had kept. But he was even more bitter about the
things he actually wore, in virtue of that damned European spirit of
frugality he had inherited from his mother, or that she'd forced on
him like the soup he'd had to swallow—a habit which (like the soup,
too, he thought) leaves some mark on the body, even if you've swallowed it grudgingly: a pair of sporty pants he hated, a polo shirt, an
awful handkerchief. He wore these things for no other reason than
to keep from throwing them away, or putting them in that museum

331

of monstrous objects. Especially that handkerchief, a dirty pink color with little red flowers on it that was so ugly that he had to use it with extreme caution, when no one was looking. Often he found himself in the humiliating position of not being able to blow his nose for long periods at a time, even if he desperately needed to, just because somebody was around that might see him use that handkerchief. The clerk showed him some binders which were even further from that notebook he had dreamed of in his latest day-dreams.

"No," he said vaguely. "I mean yes, of course, but I don't know . . ."

The clerk looked at him inquisitively. Gathering all his strength, yet still not looking him in the eyes, S. added:

"I don't know . . . yes, that one's not bad . . . . but maybe a little smaller . . . something along the lines of a large notebook . . ."

"Ah, so you aren't looking for a binder, you're looking for a notebook," the clerk said, a little sternly.

"That's right," Sabato replied, with discouragement and misgiving. "A notebook . . ."

And just as the clerk turned, he added with embarrassing ambiguity:

"But a ring notebook, like a binder."

The young man, without turning his body (which was already headed toward the notebook counter), turned his head and stared at Sabato with obviously increasing sternness. S. hurriedly nodded—yes, yes, what he wanted was "more like" a binder.

He followed the salesclerk to the counter, through whose display glass he saw, with disheartening clarity, that nothing on display there bore even the faintest resemblance to what he wanted. But the die was cast.

The clerk took out and showed S., one by one, several items which were ludicrously unsuitable; S. didn't know whether it was because by now the young man had forgotten what he had just told him about the notebook's being "more like" a binder, or out of the clerk's simple stupidity, or out of some secret irritation with S. for his uncertainty. S. was shaking his head in negation, though modest negation. And out of some sort of perversity of bad luck, the young man kept pulling out not larger and larger notebooks, but smaller and smaller ones. S. of course could have stopped that descent by

332

one firm word, but did he dare? The young man wound up offering S. an infinitesimal little notebook, which would only have been good for writing either very expensive telegrams in, or for satisfying the whim of a little girl, like that little woman walking down the street by her mother's side very seriously pushing a miniature baby carriage with a plastic baby inside. A tiny little notebook for keeping microscopic lists for microcosmic housekeeping in.

He admitted that the notebook was very pretty, and even, hypocritically, pretended to test the rings, the flexibility of its cover, the paper.

"Leather?" he asked, thinking that requesting such a precise piece of information would indicate that he was not altogether uninterested in buying the miniature pad.

"No, sir. Plastic," replied the young man curtly.

"Ah," S. commented, checking how the rings worked again.

As he carried out this apocryphal inspection, he realized that his body was covered with sweat. How can I tell him, at this stage of things, that this *toy* is exactly the opposite of what I'm looking for? How do I dare, what words can I use? For a second he was on the verge of buying it, to put it in that museum of sterile objects of his when he got home, but he felt that if he did that, he'd be beneath contempt. He decided, therefore, to overcome his weakness once and for all.

"Very nice, really very nice," he said almost inaudibly, "but what I need is a large spiral notebook. Really, what I want is *almost* a ring binder."

The salesman looked at him with stern severity.

"Then," he said coldly, "what you are looking for is a notebook."

Suspecting beforehand that this was going to be worse than with the binders, which at least were interesting, he dubiously nodded. The clerk, with a decisiveness that Sabato thought a little exaggerated, went over to that counter where the monsters of the species lay. With premeditation, it was clear, he looked for the largest of them, a gigantic, repulsive thing, one of those artifacts used no doubt in government ministries for enormous bureaucratic papers, and with a question more like an order, said:

"Something along this line, I suppose."

333

They looked at each other for a second, but that second seemed to Sabato an eternity. An almost classical, textbook case of the difference between astronomical time and existential time. It was a grotesque "instant": a tough, unbending salesclerk holding a behemoth ledger in the air before the face of an intimidated and embarrassed petitioner.

"Yes," murmured Sabato, with a barely perceptible voice, and terribly dispirited.

Brusquely and noisily the salesclerk wrapped the swollen object, then wrote up and handed the ticket to S.: it was a sum of money as outlandishly huge as the package that lay between them. With this amount of money, S. calculated bitterly on his trip to the cash register, I could buy three or four notebooks like the one I was looking for.

He left the store possessed by dark and tenebrous thoughts: it was now indisputable that everything was against him.

When he got to Santos Lugares, he unwrapped the monstrous ledger and, trying not to look at it, put it in the closet with the other acquired frustrations; he laid it between a pair of yellow-striped underwear and the bright chrome vase. Then he sat down at his desk and there he stayed for several hours, in silence, until he was called to dinner. Then he watched one of those series on TV that picked up his spirits: as the gunshots rang out and the bad guys kicked half-dead people sprawled on the ground in the face, he promised himself to do something decisive the following day.

That night, a fiery Alejandra walked toward him, her eyes wild and hallucinatory, her arms open, ready to embrace him and make him die with her, in flames. As before, he woke up screaming.

Long before daybreak he got out of bed and splashed water on his face and tried to put aside his obsessions. But he found it impossible to write as he had made up his mind to do the day before. He was still convinced that Nene had not told him the truth in the house in the country, and that that lie was one reason the more to be alarmed and stay on guard. The way he'd pooh-poohed the presence of Schneider in Buenos Aires was altogether too "natural." So the prudent thing to do was watch that café. For the time being, he called Bruno and told him to meet him at La Tenaza instead of at the Rousillon.

WHEN BRUNO GOT TO THE CAFÉ

he found S. sitting as though in a daze, or under a spell, as though his mind were on something far away, as though he were absorbed by thoughts or visions that separated him from the reality around him—for he hardly seemed to see Bruno, and didn't even say hello. He had his eye fixed on a perverse, sleepy, catlike woman a few tables away. She was reading, or seemed to be reading, a large book. And as he studied her, he pondered the abyss that often lies between the person's age recorded in the civil registry and that other age that results from disasters and passions. Because while the blood courses through cells and years, while it follows those channels that doctors naively examine, and even measure with instruments and try to palliate with pills and bandages, while we celebrate (but why?, why?) the anniversaries marked by calendars, the soul, at the behest of implacable powers, experiences decades and even millennia. Because that body that country doctors innocently take in hand, trying to cure its rashes and kill its plagues of fungus or mites, is a country below which, in dark caverns, there live dragons which have inherited the soul of other dead and dying bodies—of men or fishes, of birds or reptiles. So a man's age might be measured in hundreds or thousands of years. And also because, as Sabato said, even discounting the soul's aging through the process of transmigration, the soul ages while the body rests, for in the night it visits infernal caverns. Which was the reason one so often observed even in children those looks and emotions and passions which can only be explained by some dark legacy inherited from the bat or the rat, or by nocturnal descents into the Inferno, descents that calcine and craze the soul while the sleeping body remains young, able to deceive those doctors that consult their manometers instead of looking closely at the subtle signs in a man's movements or the glitter of his eyes. Because it is possible to detect that calcination, that degeneration, in a certain trembling as the person walks, a certain awkwardness, certain peculiar lines in the forehead—but also, or above all, in a man's gaze, since the world the man is seeing is not the world of the innocent child but the world of a monster that has witnessed horror. Men of science, then, ought to pay closer attention to the face, analyze with extreme care and even suspicion the tiniest, subtlest marks that appear. And especially try to surprise some instantaneous, fleeting glitter in the eyes: because of all the chinks through which one can catch glimpses of what occurs down there below, the eyes are the most important, the supreme recourse—though impossible to observe, of course, in the case of the Blind, who in that way preserve their shadowy secrets. From where he was sitting, it was impossible to study those signs in her face. But there were the other signs—he could follow the movements of her long legs as she resettled herself, her hand as she raised the cigarette to her lips, so slow as to be almost imperceptible—and those signs told him that the woman was infinitely older than the twenty-odd years her body had lived. She embodied the experience of some prehistoric serpent-feline, an animal that perfidiously gave the impression of indolence, but which had the slithering sexuality of the treacherous and mortal viper, ready to strike. Because as time passed and his scrutiny of her deepened, he felt that she was coiled, lying in wait, or stalking perhaps, with that ability felines have of perceiving, even in darkness, the most insignificant movements of their prey, of sensing the hushed sounds that would be unnoticed by other animals, of catching the slightest sign of their adversary. Her hands were long, like her arms and legs. Her hair was very black, and straight; it fell to her shoulders and swayed with muffled, morbid softness at every movement she made. She smoked as though in slow motion, with deep drags on her cigarette. There was something in her face that made one feel distaste, somehow, and then he realized that it was the wide spacing of her eyes: they were large and almond-shaped, but almost defectively separated, which gave her a kind of inhuman beauty. Yes, it was obvious that she was watching Bruno and him, too, under her half-closed, somnolent-looking lids, giving the two men slow hidden looks out of the corner of her eye, as though she were not looking at them at all, but just raising her eyes from her book to think, or to abandon herself to those deep but vague currents to which one gives oneself up when one reads a book that makes one contemplate one's own existence. She stretched her legs voluptuously, threw a wandering glance over the other people in the café, appearing to pause for a moment on S., and then submerged herself once again in her impenetrable felino-reptilian universe.

Bruno sensed that a lump of some mysterious substance had fallen into the deep waters of his friend, and that from below, as it dissolved, it was giving off miasmal gases that were rising to the surface and clouding his friend's consciousness. Obscure sensations, but in him, in S., they always prefigured some decisive event. And they produced an uneasiness, a nervousness in him, too, like that nervousness felt by animals at the approach of an eclipse. Because it was hard to believe that she could watch them like that, with her eyelids almost closed, with those long lashes of hers that must have even further veiled the wan light of the café. Silently, equivocally, she sent her radiations over S., who felt the presence more with his skin than with his head, through myriads of infinitesimal receptors on his nerve endings, like those radar systems on a country's borders that detect the coming enemy. The woman emitted signals that he picked up with complex networks of detectors and felt viscerally, and which not only put him on edge, but (as Bruno knew all too well) alerted him as well, and filled him with anguish and anxiety. There he sat, as though huddled in some deep den, until suddenly he stood up and said only, by way of good-bye, "We'll talk some other day about what I mentioned to you on the phone."

As HE LEFT,
S. passed beside the woman, and she closed the book and put it to one side. Did she do that so he could read its title? It was a large, hardcover book with a dust jacket of bright colors, a reproduction of a painting that looked like one of Leonor Fini's: on a mirrorlike lake there was a naked woman with a mane of silvery hair against a red sunset, surrounded by carnivorous lunar birds and ichthians and wild-looking eyes. The title startled him: *Eyes and Your Sex Life.* Outside, he began to think. Ever since he had seen Dr. Schneider go into that café, and then Costa, he had been visited, haunted, by a sense of danger. And now, after telling Bruno to meet him there, another significant event had taken place.

He pondered: Schneider, seeing him come out of the Radio Nacional building, had quickly ducked into that café, but not quick enough for S. not to recognize him. Still, knowing Schneider, it was conceivable that everything had been cunningly planned: he had followed S., and then waited for him at the corner so he could run into the bar with premeditated haste, though in reality giving S. just

337

enough time to recognize him. The fact that Nene Costa had gone in afterward made the episode even more troubling, because that meant they knew S. would be going to Radio Nacional. How?

Then—he continued reasoning—Schneider has foreseen that S. would go snooping around Costa's house in the country, and would sit around La Tenaza again, as well. So he had sent that woman as bait and was now waiting for the next step, which S. had just taken.

Of course this was a chain of suppositions that might correspond to reality, but that might just as well be nothing but a train of coincidences. It was possible that Schneider hadn't followed him at all, that he'd been on that street corner for any number of reasons and that he had really and truly wanted to avoid meeting Sabato.

Still, that night S. couldn't sleep. And a curious thing—there returned to his mind the crime that Calsen Paz's gang had committed. But the details kept changing. Under the direction or supervision of a Schneider no longer gross and disgusting but now sinister and severe, Calsen turned into Costa, the poor waif of a girl turned into the woman in La Tenaza, and she in turn was Costa's sister and lover, while Patricio, ambiguously, witnessed the moment when Costa plunged the awl into first the bound boy's eyes and then his heart, twisting the metal instrument with cold, mechanical perversion.

THE NEXT DAY, AT THE SAME HOUR,
he went back to La Tenaza. He had decided that if she wanted to meet him, he wanted to meet her, too. But he intended to be sure, so he half-hid himself in the doorway of an apartment house across the street. When he saw her coming, he had the sudden impression that she'd studied dancing, but besides whatever it was that dance might have given her, he noticed something that couldn't be taught but that all blacks had: she moved slowly, with that rhythm that marked the walk of blacks, though nothing in her face or skin would make one think she was black. She was rather tall, and wore very dark glasses and a violet miniskirt with a black blouse.

She went into the bar, stayed for about an hour, and then came out again. She was hesitant in her movements, looked in various

338

directions, and then at last went off down Ayacucho toward Recoleta.

S. followed her at a distance until he saw her turn into La Biela. At that, his suspicions were confirmed. La Biela was one of his most frequent hangouts: she was looking for him. He waited for her to come out again; he followed her. Back to La Tenaza.

S. hesitated for a moment, but the turbulent decision then came from his soul—where it was hard to tell whether it was fascination, or lust, or irresponsibility (given the danger) that led him to want to meet the woman face to face. He went in and walked over to her, saying, "I'm here." She heard the words without surprise, with a slight, indecipherable smile.

And thus began the descent into a phosphorescent swamp with that slinking black panther of a woman who moved with the haughty, elastic sensuality of the cat but as though her mind were controlled by a serpent. Her voice was deep, and grave, and it seemed to catch as it passed through her throat, as though she were walking through the dark and were afraid of waking up the person ready to rip her heart out. It was a somber, warm voice, like thick chocolate. A singular fact: if Schneider were behind her, S. never found out. But he sensed that with this instrument Schneider was setting in motion some complex and slow corruption.

There are, S. thought at one point, many kinds of torture. Perhaps, he thought—though long afterward—one of its manifestations would be the sacrifice of Agustina.

OH, MY BROTHERS AND SISTERS!
30th, Jujuy—Two sisters, 13 and 9 years old, were found frozen to death yesterday. The victims are Calixta and Narcisa Llampa, who with their older brother had left P.S. #36, in the high plateau country, on their way home. Freezing and exhausted, they stopped by the side of the road and sat down, while their brother went for help. But by the time the boy found a muleteer and returned with him to aid his sisters, the two girls had frozen to death. Perhaps seeking some last warmth, they had thrown their arms around each other; death came to them as they lay there together.

Nacho cut out the story and looked around for his shoebox, on the top of which, in black marker, he had written:

SMILE, GOD LOVES YOU
(IN CASE OF FIRE, PLEASE
SAVE THIS BOX)

He added the new clipping to the stack.

Los Angeles.—John Grant, 38 years old, of this city, was deeply in debt, so to get himself out he insured his wife and two young children for $25,000. He then arranged a plane trip for the three of them, at the same time putting a time bomb in one of their suitcases. He was arrested when he attempted to collect the insurance. A stewardess who remained on the ground, exchanging her shift with another stewardess, was in on the plan.

WE ARE PROUD TO OFFER YOU the services of our able and experienced listeners, who will listen to anything you wish to say, without interrupting you, for a very modest fee. When our listeners listen, their faces express interest, pity, sympathy, understanding, hate, hope, desperation, fury, or joy, as the case may require. Lawyers and politicians, presidents of clubs and civic organizations, and preachers will find comfort in rehearsing their speeches or sermons before our experts, as will lonely people who have no one to talk to. Anyone can tell our listeners about their domestic or sexual problems, their ideas for business or inventions, with no fear that their secrets will be revealed. Thousands of testimonials, which we will be happy to send you upon request, support these claims. Give free rein to your emotions with our listeners, and you'll very quickly see the benefits.—The Southern Listening Bureau, Little Rock, Arkansas.

Stockholm (France Presse).—Gregori Podyapolsky, 47 years of age, an eminent geophysicist belonging to the Soviet Com-

340

mittee on Human Rights, was called to a military hospital in Moscow for psychiatric examination. It is presumed that after the examination he will be committed to a psychiatric institution for special treatment, as is usual in such cases.

Rome (AFP).—Bishop Helder Cámara has told journalists and members of the Church that the police department attached to the Brazilian army gives classes for torturers. On October 8, 1969, around 4 o'clock in the afternoon, a group of 100 soldiers, most of them sergeants from the three services, attended a class given by Lt. Haylton. In this session, Lt. Haylton showed the class members slides taken during torture sessions and explained the advantages of each method. After the theoretical explanation, his assistants (four sergeants, two corporals, and one private) carried out demonstrations on ten political prisoners.

Buenos Aires (Telam).—Early yesterday morning Daniel Fuentes, 20, tape-recorded the reasons for his decision. He then strapped the tape-recorder to his body, went out into his backyard, tied one end of a thick cable around a crosspiece on the grape arbor and the other around his neck. Finally, he climbed up onto the eaves of his house and shot himself in the right temple, "in case one of the other methods fails," he explained on the tape. As his dead weight fell, he was hanged by the cable. His father, who ran outside when he heard the gunshot, found him in that position. When the girl mentioned on the tape heard the news, she said, "God, was he crazy or something?"

Buenos Aires.—Mr. Alvan E. Williams, as he steps off the plane smiling. Williams plans wide distribution of his famous dry deodorants. "The future," he stated with conviction, "is in dry deodorants, and there's no reason this great market won't be able to see that. I'm sure that very soon the worries we have now will give way to a much more encouraging picture of things."

341

SPECIALIZED MANUFACTURERS PREDICT MADE-TO-ORDER PERFUMES, fragrances that will evoke memories of scenes dear or otherwise memorable to the person ordering them: the sensation of a pine woods the first time the client was with his current wife; the country just after rain; the auditorium where the client made the speech launching his company or celebrating the anniversary of his club, etc. There are plans for manufacturing imitations of the fragrances of vegetables, of wet leaves, of the trunk of a tree, of watermelon rind, of pickles or mushrooms, of lichens, smoke, pigskin, horse sweat, cigars, saltwater. Some flavors, such as that of burning charcoal, are destined to be added to electrically grilled steak so that it will perfectly imitate the flavor of beef barbecued on a campfire. —The American Perfumer.

Lansing, Texas.—Dudley Morgan, a black man accused of attacking Mrs. McKay, was pursued by enraged whites carrying guns, rifles, baseball bats, and other weapons, and was caught and tied to an iron stake; a huge pyre of firewood and other inflammable material was prepared. By the time he was about to be burned, a crowd numbering close to 5,000 people had formed. When red-hot pine knots were ready, Morgan's eyes were gouged out with them. Then the burning brands were held to his throat and parts of his chest, while Morgan, screaming, begged for the crowd to shoot him so he could die quickly. The crowd shouted to make his death as slow as possible, and some of the firewood was pulled away so the black man would not be burned all at once, which made him kick and try to pull his body back, howling from the increasing pain. The smell of burning flesh grew stronger and stronger, but in spite of this the crowd pushed and shoved so as not to miss a second of the spectacle. Mrs. McKay, who had just arrived at the scene in a car with four friends, could not get close, however, due to the pushing crowd. Before dying, Morgan stammered, "Tell my wife good-bye," and his head dropped lifeless to his chest. When the fire had done its job, many people in the crowd

342

approached to gather souvenirs: pieces of the man's skull and bones were carried away. His captors, carried on the shoulders of the crowd, were photographed as the crowd cheered.

London (UPI).—During the summer, the tourists who came to the Frisian Isles off the north coast of Denmark had to dig a path along the beach to reach the water, as the beaches are covered with oil. Lord Byron's hymn to the purity and blueness of the North Sea refers to a landscape which no longer exists. For these hundred years, the industrial wastes carried by the noisome Dutch canals have been, according to Engineer Luck, "the price we pay for progress." Sir Gilmore Jenkins stated that a half-million tons of petroleum covers the surface of this sea. Acids, ammonia, insecticides, detergents, cyanides and cyanates, phenols, sewage, and carbon-bearing wastes flow into the sea here daily, as do titanium and mercury wastes. As a consequence, on the coasts of Britain alone 250,000 marine birds die each year. Within a short time all marine life will be decimated or even eradicated by industry.

"Only a born diplomat could meet a *fait accompli* head on. On May 25, at Government House, the invitation for the president's reception called for black tie, but the ambassador to whom we are referring, not totally familiar with the customs of our country, attended in morning coat. When he arrived on the scene and realized that everyone else was in black tie, he showed not the least sign of distress (thanks to his inborn self-possession), but simply took his assigned place in the line."
> —Sunday supplement to *La Nación*, Buenos Aires.

Buenos Aires (La Razón).—Miguel Kiefer, a 59-year-old Rumanian, was the owner of a small farm in Pampa del Infierno, in the state of Chaco, where he worked alongside his wife Margarita, 46, and his sons Juan and Jorge. Jorge was married to Teodora Diebole, 21 years of age. Teodora was

343

about to be a mother, and since the child would be a burden, the mother-in-law resolved that Margarita should abort the pregnancy, to which end the mother-in-law inflicted terrible suffering on the daughter-in-law, while the son did not dare to come between them. When the attempt to produce a miscarriage proved fruitless, the mother-in-law, after consulting with the family, decided to kill the girl by having her bitten by a poisonous snake native to the area, the *yarará*, which was put into a basket of clothes. When Señora Kiefer ordered her daughter-in-law to get a shirt out of the basket, the girl was bitten by the snake. Since the venom appeared to be working very slowly, and fearing that it had not been enough to be fatal to the healthy young woman, the family got into a car and forced Teodora, with a rope tied around her body, to run along after it. Crazed with thirst and the effects of the poison, her husband later told the court, the girl begged for mercy. But the sentence of death had been given. To bring it about more speedily, the mother-in-law strangled her with a kerchief around her neck.

Paris (AP).—Thor Heyerdahl made the voyage of the *Kon-Tiki* in 1947, and the voyage of the *Ra* in 1969. On this last expedition he noted, he says, one great difference from the first. "In 1947 we had a completely open sea, on which we saw no sign of the hand of man for the entire 101 days of the journey, across 4,300 miles of water. But in 1969 there was not a single day when we did not sail through every kind of waste imaginable—plastic jars, glass bottles, cans, and oil slicks. These were not traditional objects thrown overboard from ships, for example, which sooner or later become usable by organic life. They were synthetic substances, which are not part of the cycles of nature. We have no guide for where we want to go, but we keep making things," he concluded somberly.

New York (AP).—Private Arnold W. McGill, accused of genocide, stated that he did not understand why such a fuss is being made over a Vietnamese village, when that procedure

344

was followed regularly, as the generals who have been running the Pentagon know perfectly well. "All I did was follow Captain Medina's orders," he said. And he added, "Anyway, the village had been a pain in the ass all along."

Bronwich (UP).—Bill Corbet stated before the magistrate that he had not spoken a word to his wife in more than seven years, although they live under the same roof. In the local court, Mrs. Corbet confirmed this fact: "It's been years since we've spoken. When one of us comes in a room, the other leaves. But we run into each other very seldom, really, sometimes on the stairs, you know, or at the door to the loo." She added that up until a short time ago she would prepare her husband's meals, set them out on the table, and leave him written messages: "the soup has salt in it, the stew's very hot, that sort of thing." But recently, she said, she's stopped that sort of communication as well.

Tokyo (AP).—"On the morning of the Hiroshima bombing," recounted Mr. Yasuo Yamamoto, "I was on my bicycle when I heard the sound of planes. But I didn't pay it any attention, because during those days we were used to it. Two minutes later I saw a huge column of fire rise out of a horrendous explosion, like the sound of a thousand crashes of thunder all at once. My bicycle was thrown into the air, and I fell behind a wall. When I looked out, I saw terrible confusion all around, and I heard the sound of the mad crying and shouting of children and women and the screaming of people that sounded terribly hurt, or dying. I ran toward my house, on the way seeing many people clutching great wounds, other people covered with blood, most of them burned. They all showed the most frightful terror I had ever seen in my life, and the worst suffering conceivable. Beyond the station you could see a sea of fire and flames, and all the houses destroyed. It distressed me greatly to think of my only son Masumi and my wife. When I came at last, through mounds of rubble and burning buildings, to what had been my home, there were no walls, and the floor was tilted as though there had been an earthquake, with piles of broken glass and fragments of doors and ceilings everywhere. My wife, who had been injured, was calling for our son, who had gone out on some little errand. We looked for him everywhere, in the direction he'd taken, until over that way we heard groaning and we saw a naked creature, with almost no skin, and its hair all burned off, lying on the ground in great pain, moaning, and almost without the strength even to writhe as it lay there. In horror we asked who it was, and in a strange voice, we could barely hear him, he whispered that he was Masumi Yamamoto. We lay him on a board, what was left of a door, very very carefully, you know, because he was one great exposed wound, and we carried him off to find help. About ten blocks away, we came upon a line of people injured and burned who were waiting to be seen by the doctors and nurses, who were also injured. Thinking our son couldn't stand it any longer, we begged a military doctor to at least give us something for the boy's pain. He gave us some oil to pour on him and to cover him with, and we did. The boy asked us if he was going to die. We immediately told him that he wasn't, that he'd soon be well again. We were about to carry him back to our home, but he asked us please not to move him from where he was. Around nightfall he became easier, but he was asking for water constantly. And although we didn't know whether that might not make him worse, we gave it to him. Sometimes he would grow delirious and we could not understand what he was saying. His words made no sense. After a while his mind seemed to clear, and he asked us if it was true that there was a heaven. My wife was very disturbed and could not answer, but I said yes, there was a heaven, a very pretty place where there were never any wars. He listened to those words very attentively, and they seemed to calm him. 'Then I think it's better if I die,' he whispered. He could hardly breathe now, his chest would rise and fall like a bellows, while my wife cried in silence so that he would not hear her. Then our son began to be delirious again, and he

346

stopped asking for water. A few minutes later, fortunately, he stopped breathing."

Letter from Mr. Cornelius Lippmann, of Eureka, Colorado, to the Secretary-General of the United Nations, published in the *New York Times*:

Dear Sir:
I am writing to inform you that I have decided to resign my membership in the human race. Therefore, in future you may disregard my interests in the treaties or debates in which your Organization engages.
Most sincerely yours,
Cornelius W. Lippmann

FROM THESE CLIPPINGS
Nacho chose three to add to his gallery on the wall.
A huge advertisement two columns wide by twelve inches long, bearing the title

Another advertisement had caught his eye, in *La Nación*, appearing among the most important stories of the day:

When he'd stuck this ad up on the wall, he called the number given on it, and when a young woman's voice answered, "Astral Studio, may we help you?" he replied, "Woof! Woof! Woof!"

To end his day's work, above the photograph of the tuxedo'd Anouilh emerging from the church he tacked the back cover of an old *Reader's Digest*. The cover consisted of a large picture of the distinguished diplomat and metaphysical poet Paul Claudel, fat but with grave dignity, looking out of the photo with his penetrating, admonitory eyes and saying to the reader READ THE *READER'S DIGEST!* The admonition was accompanied by sensible words below.

Then he decided he'd go to the zoo.

THAT AFTERNOON S. TOOK A LONG WALK,
waiting for the hour when he was to meet Nora. He walked aimlessly to the Plaza Italia, then took Sarmiento to the Monumento a los Españoles, along the wall bordering the zoo. That word "aimlessly" had simply popped into his mind, which went to show, in Bruno's opinion, that even writers get swept up into using clichés, which are as superficial as they are false. Because we always walk with some aim, sometimes determined by our own visible will, but other times, perhaps the most decisive times in our lives, determined more by a will unknown even to ourselves, though nevertheless powerful and unmanageable—a will which makes us march off to places where we are to meet people or things that somehow are, or have been, or promise to be, essential to our fates, a will that helps along or stands in the way of our apparent desires, helps along or stands in the way of our anxieties, and sometimes (which is the most astonishing thing of all) turns out in the long run to have been more right about it all than our own conscious will. Under his feet S. felt the soft leaves of the plane trees, which the wind had blown off. It was a depressing holiday afternoon, especially in that neighborhood, when the children that play in the zoo have been taken home by their parents or their nannies, and the sailors, run inside by the cold and the drizzle, take refuge in the bars along Santa Fe with their regular girls or the modest little whores that share their warm croissants with chocolate.

There was no one about along all that solitary sidewalk, except for one skinny young man gripping the bars of the fence with both hands, his arms wide. He was standing motionless looking into the grounds of the zoo, apparently indifferent to the drizzling rain, for all he wore was a pair of faded blue jeans and a T-shirt as worn and faded as the jeans. All in all, an awkward, perhaps even grotesque figure.

Until, on coming a little closer, S. realized that it was Nacho, and he stopped, as though he were doing something vaguely wrong or had surprised someone in an act of absolute intimacy. He turned, then, and began to walk away, taking the long way around, trying not to make any movement or sound that might startle the boy, or wake him from his revery, make him stop looking hypnotically into that silent park, with its lost animals like inoffensive ghosts. Then, when S. was far enough away, he paused behind a plane tree and looked back, fascinated by the presence of the boy and by the way he stood motionless, contemplative, his eyes fixed, outside the wall of the zoo.

MEANWHILE, NACHO

was, as he so often liked to be, seven years old, and far from the land of dirtiness and desperation, sitting on the ground in the shade of the little newspaper stand, picking out the words in a comic book, hearing the quiet breathing of Milord lying there half asleep at full length beside him. Milord was Nacho's faithful dog, whose coat was that café-au-lait color with the white spots of a mongrel. Milord, Nacho knew, was dreaming quiet dreams; he knew he was safe, protected from the Forces of Evil by the much more powerful Forces of Good, the Heroes that sat beside him, especially Carlucho, doubly a giant because of the toy-sized stool he squatted on, sipping his *mate* with slow thoughtfulness, meditating during his philosophy hour. Carlucho's silent meditation, according to Bruno, was never troubled by the boy's or Milord's presence; on the contrary, it was aided and even encouraged by them, since his spirit was so wide and so deep that his Thoughts were not for himself alone but for Humanity in general, and, for those two helpless creatures in particular. So while the boy read his comic book and Milord snoozed and dreamed of wonderful bones to gnaw on and of long walks on holidays along Maciel Island, Carlucho brooded on new ideas about The Mission of Money, The Role of Friendship, and The Sadness of War.

Just then, pricked by some memory or some thought inspired

349

by the comic book, Nacho, keeping the magazine open on the page he had been reading, looked up at his friend and said "Carlucho," and the gray-headed giant with the broad athletic shoulders, without abandoning the ideas that at the moment filled his head, mechanically said, "Uh?"

"But are you listening or not?"

"I'm listening to you, Nacho, I'm listening."

"What animal would you like to be?"

They had talked about lions and tigers other times before. The general idea was more or less this: tigers were more like cats, lions were more like dogs. How funny—they both liked dogs better. But this question was more complicated, and anyway—Nacho, who knew Carlucho like a book, was not going to ask anything so silly. No sir.

"What animal?"

"Uh-huh, what animal would you like to be?"

He didn't expect a quick answer, he knew that Carlucho was fair-minded and that he wasn't going to blurt out just any answer that popped into his head. It was not, for example, a question of just saying "elephant" and letting it go at that. He would never lie or give a false answer or say anything that might offend any animal, or bird, or beast, or *anything*. So, it was a big question. It was not for nothing that Nacho had thought about it many, many times; it was a question long pondered.

Carlucho sipped at his *mate*, and as he always did when he was concentrating deeply, he fixed his blue eyes on the greenish-blue roof of the house across the way there, on Chiclana, meanwhile murmuring to himself, "If I had to be an animal . . ."

"Uh-huh?" Nacho prodded him impatiently.

"Hold on, just hold on . . . What do you think, Nacho, that things are as easy as that? If things was that easy, why . . . Just let me think a bit . . ."

Nacho knew all too well that when the veins in Carlucho's neck swelled it was because he was thinking as hard as he could. So the swelling this time made Nacho happy, because he had been hatching this question for a long time, and he'd been pretty sure it would put Carlucho on the spot. It wouldn't do that to lots of people, of course. If you asked most people, they'd say elephant or lion or tiger, and that would be that. But not Carlucho. Carlucho was different, he had to weigh things, the pro and the con, he had to say just exactly what he thought was right, or true, or necessary, "because right is right."

"I'm going to tell you the truth, child. I never thought about this before, never in my whole life. You ask the goldarnedest questions."

He softly pushed Milord away with his foot (Milord had the bad habit of creeping closer and closer to the fire until he was right under the can of boiling water) and then he resumed his concentration. His eyes returned to the greenish-blue roof across the park.

The longer Carlucho took, and the more his veins swelled, the more Nacho enjoyed this. "Well?" Nacho insisted.

Carlucho got mad. Nacho always got scared when Carlucho got mad because, as Carlucho himself admitted when he'd grown calm again, he was capable of just about anything when he lost his temper.

"What are you bothering me about!" he shouted, his eyes growing bright with anger. "I told you to wait a minute! Or didn't I tell you that? Uh?"

Nacho shrank away and waited for the storm to pass. Carlucho got up and began straightening the magazines, the bars of chocolate, the packs of cigarettes, setting everything into absolutely perfect ranks. It was like a clean, well-disciplined army—the least irregularity upset him; there was hardly anything that bothered Carlucho so much as seeing something "out of line." Little by little he calmed down, and finally he sat back down on his tiny stool.

"You surely do expect a person to bust his rear end thinking for you. Look how many animals there are: tigers, lions, elephants, eagles, condors, goats, all kinds of animals . . . not to mention the bugs, the ants and the mites, and rats and things like that . . . It isn't easy, Nacho. And according to you a person ought to be able to pick up and solve it all *snap*, just like that, in two shakes." He meditatively sipped at his *mate*, and Nacho realized that the thinking was coming to its end—there was a sort of inward smile that was beginning to flicker on his face.

"If I had to be an animal . . ." he now muttered, almost grinning, just to drag out the pleasure.

He stood up, set his little jug of *mate* on the metal box that served him as a stove, and then, with great calm, he turned toward the boy and said:

351

"I'll tell you the truth, child—I'd want to be a hippopotamus."

Nacho almost jumped. He was not exactly surprised, he was almost angry, because for a second he thought Carlucho was pulling his leg.

"Are you crazy?" he cried.

Carlucho looked at him sternly and his face took on that cold calmness that preceded his worst explosions of wrath.

"What's wrong with a hippopotamus?" he asked icily. "Speak up."

Nacho turned humble again; he didn't say a word.

"Speak up, I said. I want you to tell me what's so bad about a hippopotamus."

Milord had pulled his long body together and was watching the two warily, his ears alert; he was almost frightened. Nacho looked at Carlucho cautiously. When Carlucho took that attitude, it was dangerous as could be, and the slightest wrong word could set off a terrible explosion.

"I didn't say there was anything wrong with a hippopotamus," he got up the courage to stammer, never taking his eyes off his friend's face.

Carlucho listened, looking at the boy inquisitively.

"You jumped like a fish."

"Me?"

"Yes sir, you. You're not going to tell me you didn't jump like a fish."

"I didn't jump. I just thought you'd probably like to be some other animal. That's all."

The icy calm of Carlucho did not go away; there was a spring wound tight inside there.

"I said I wanted you to tell me what was so bad about being a hippopotamus."

Nacho gauged the danger. If he totally denied any misgivings, any repugnance, anything bad at all about the hippopotamus, Carlucho would suspect he was lying. He sensed that it was better to tell at least part of the bad stuff.

"I don't know, Carlucho," he began hesitantly, "they're pretty ugly . . ."

"All right. What else? You're not going to tell me now that be-cause they're wild animals they're not first-class animals."

"I think they're pretty dumb, too."

Carlucho glowered at him.

"Dumb? Who told you they were dumb?"

"And . . . I don't know . . . it seems to me . . ."

"*It seems to me! It seems to me!* So since it seems to you hippo-potamuses are dumb, that means that hippopotamuses are dumb!?"

Nacho put out his hand to him, like a person before a hand grenade he's not sure is going to go off or not. He tried to calm him down.

"Well, I don't know, really. Maybe not. Maybe . . . Aw, I don't know, Carlucho. . . ."

"Maybe! Maybe not! When you learn to weigh things and be fair in your thinking and think before you talk—then, *maybe*, we'll talk about dumb!"

He got up to sell a pack of cigarettes, arranged the ranks of his implacable armada once again, and then sat back down. Nacho knew that it was better to let him calm down slowly, and then never again say anything else about hippopotamuses. How many times had he had to let declarations of Carlucho's—on money or armored trucks, on women's fashions or too much grease in the frying pan—remain wrapped in the most profound mystery.

Nacho let many days pass before he went back to the subject of animals. Carlucho was like a powerful river running through a plain—slow and apparently calm, with waters that seemed hardly to flow at all, but that had incredibly dangerous whirlpools that a per-son risked falling into and drowning and never coming up out of again. Not to speak of the furious strength the river had when a storm came and made a flash flood. Carlucho hated for a considered judgment to be taken lightly. Of course, sometimes he made jokes. But when a man talked in earnest, it infuriated him that people couldn't see he was talking in earnest. A great deal of bitterness was caused him by that discussion about hippopotamuses, and he was hurt and resentful for days afterward; he wouldn't talk, or he would answer in monosyllables.

Until the day came finally when it had all blown over and they could talk like old friends again about all kinds of things. Nacho brought the subject up again, but this time in the most general way. Zoos, that sort of thing.

"If I was the gover'ment," Carlucho pronounced, "I'd do away with zoos. What do you think of that?"

"How come, Carlucho? I like to go to the zoo. I like to see all the animals. Don't you?"

"No sir. I don't like it a bit. Not a bit. I'll tell you the truth, child—if I was the gover'ment I wouldn't only do away with zoos, I'd take every one of those people that go off to Africa to catch wild animals and throw 'em in jail."

Nacho looked at him in puzzlement.

"That opens your eyes, does it?"

He stood up, sold a pack of cigarettes, and sat back down again.

"Yes sir," he declared with solemn certitude, "I'd take every one of those scoundrels and throw them in the jail. They'd see whether *they* liked being behind bars, like the lions and the tigers."

He turned to Nacho.

"Would you like to be in a cage?"

Nacho looked at him in surprise. "Me? Why, no."

Carlucho shot to his feet, and with his face radiant he jabbed a finger at Nacho, like the district attorney who's got the witness where he wants him, and exclaimed:

"Ah-HA! You see? You see what I mean? I got you there, didn't I, Nacho, I surely got you there!"

He sat down again, calmer now. He sipped at his *mate* and seemed pensive, looking across at the bluish-green roof.

"That's the way the world works, Nacho. The world is an old bitch."

Then, suddenly furious, he turned.

"Tell me the truth, Nacho—if you wouldn't like to be in a cage, how can you expect a lion or a tiger to like it? Uh? Poor animals, and they're used to the jungle, too, where they can run around free, and do whatever they feel like, wherever they feel like it. Uh? What do you say to that?"

Nacho remained silent.

"I'm talking to you, Nacho!" the man insisted.

"Uh-huh, Carlucho, that's right."

Carlucho began to grow calmer, but he sat for a long time on his tiny stool without saying anything. Several customers came along.

"Cigarettes! Cigarettes! I'll tell you, I'd put the people that make cigarettes in jail, too. Everything's business. At thirty—when my daddy was thirty, I mean—when my daddy was thirty, Dr. Helguera told him, 'I'll tell you, don Salerno, you either stop smoking or you'll be dead in six months!' "

"And what did he do?"

"My daddy? What do you think he did? My daddy was hard as iron. He quit smoking, bam!, just like that, right there and then. That was a *man* for you, not like these namby-pambies you see today, that'll tell you they'll stop, then they don't, then they will, then they won't, cigarettes are bad for you, but just two or three a day, telling you that it makes you an addict, that it doesn't . . . Pansies."

"Pansies?"

"That's something you'll know about when you get bigger."

"So he quit smoking."

"My daddy, may he rest in peace, he did it like *that*. And to the day he died he never smoked another stogie."

"A stogie?"

"Why of course, Nacho. Do you think my daddy was going to smoke these little things with filters on them, like these sissies do? There was never a cigarette in my house, nor a soft drink, either."

Nacho was dying to get back to the subject of hippopotamuses.

"But tell me something, Carlucho. If there aren't any zoos, where are people supposed to go to see the animals?"

"To see the animals? Nowhere."

"What do you mean, nowhere? You mean you can't see wild animals anymore?"

"No, child. Nobody's going to die because they didn't get to see a lion in a cage. A lion's got to be in the jungle. With his own daddy and mother, if he's a cub. Or with his own lady lion if he's big, and his own children. And I'd take those people that go out and hunt animals and I'd put them where the lion used to be, in the zoos. I'd like to see those people sit in their cages all day long and eat peanuts. I would dearly love to see that."

Nacho looked at him.

"You like to talk to me, don't you, child?"

"Uh-huh."

"Well, the animals like to talk to each other too, don't you imagine? Or do you think that just because they growl and roar and whatnot they're not talking? Do you know what happens when a bear's in a cage all day, going around and around and around in that cage, day and night, always by himself, always thinking, and nobody to talk to?" He was once again staring off into the distance, his eyes on that bluish-green roof. "It's hard to believe that nobody ever thinks about that."

His words trailed off, and then after a while he went on:

"I like to do experiments. You know what I did one day?" A smile announced that the experiment had been as successful as he could ever have wished.

"You know what I did? I went to the zoo, around vesper time."

"Vesper time?"

"You know, Nacho, toward evening, when everything gets dusky. After the zoo was closed for the day, I went. You know the gate on Sarmiento over there?"

"Uh-huh."

"Well, like I say, it was in the evening, and the children had all gone off home to drink their milk, and the gate was already closed. There was nobody there. You ought to see what the zoo is like when there's nobody there. You try it someday."

"Try what?"

"Try going to the zoo when nobody's there, to see what it's like."

"What *is* it like, Carlucho?"

Carlucho bowed his head and started making lines in the dirt around the newsstand with a broomstraw. "It's the saddest thing in the world, is what it's like," he whispered.

"Because there aren't any children, because there aren't any children to give the animals candy and popcorn and things, all that?"

Carlucho looked up irritated.

"When will you learn, child? Can't you see what I'm saying? When the children are there, they take the animals' mind off their troubles, sure, they do that, of course they do. A piece of candy here, a funny face there, some popcorn, some peanuts, and the time goes. Of course the animals like that. All the animals like children, there's no doubt about it. I'm not going to deny you that. But don't you see what I'm saying? *It gets their mind off things!*"

Nacho didn't understand. Carlucho looked at him like a teacher with a slow student.

"Let's say (just saying, you know) that your daddy dies, just for an example, and a friend of yours comes over to your house and talks about baseball and football and soccer, and the strike at the post office, little things like that. It takes your mind off things. I'm not saying it's not an awful nice thing to do, and that friends ought to do that for you, if they love you. Of course they ought to, it's the natural thing to do, it's lovely."

Nacho was still looking at him.

"You don't understand me, do you? I can see it in your face." He concentrated. The vein in his neck began to swell. "What I'm saying is, what if that friend of yours didn't come? Your daddy doesn't have to die. Do you see what I'm getting at?" He observed the boy's face, to see whether the idea had gotten home yet.

"I suppose that's not a very good example. But don't you see, Nacho? I'm not opposed to children going to the zoo and seeing the animals and giving peanuts to the elephants and monkeys and things. What I'm trying to tell you is that there don't have to be any zoos. That's why I did my experiment."

"What experiment?"

"Looking at the animals, in the evening, when it begins to be night all around, when they're all by themselves, and I mean by themselves, all alone, without any children or candy or peanuts or anything at all—I mean *all alone.*"

He began tracing lines in the dirt again, and after a long silence he raised his head and it seemed to Nacho that his eyes were veiled.

"What did you see, Carlucho?" he asked, though he didn't know whether he should or not.

"What did I see?" He got up, straightened some boxes, and then replied:

"What do you think I saw? Nothing. Animals. All by themselves. That's what I saw."

He sat down, adding almost to himself:

"There was one great huge animal, some kind of . . . well, I don't know what it was. You'd have to see it. It was all droopy and bent

357

over, its back was humped over, looking at the ground, just looking at the ground. The night getting darker and darker, and the poor thing all alone. Such a big huge thing, and as lonesome as it could be. It didn't even move to shoo off a fly that was flying around it. It was thinking. Do you think that just because animals don't talk out loud they don't think? They're just like human beings: they take care of their babies, they kiss them and pet them, they cry when their mate gets killed. So who knows what that big old animal was thinking. And I'll tell you—the bigger they are, the worse I feel for them. I don't know, the little tiny creatures, bugs and things, sometimes I don't like them, I'll have to admit that. They're a bother, you know, troublesome creatures, like fleas and things. But those big animals . . . A lion, say for example. A hippopotamus. Don't you see how sad it must be to know you're never going to be in the jungle again, never ever in your whole life? The big rivers and the lakes?"

He stopped.

"And you know what happened then?"

"What?"

"I talked to him."

"To who?"

"To who do you think, goose! To that animal, a buffalo or a bison, I don't know."

"You talked to him?"

"Why not? But he didn't move. Of course, he might not've heard me. I mean I couldn't start yelling at him from way over at the bars there, could I? I'd have gotten myself thrown in the insane asylum."

"But what did you say to him?"

"I don't know . . . Things . . . pretty silly things, I imagine . . . 'Hey,' I said, 'hey, animal, hey.' That was all."

"But he didn't say anything?"

"No, of course not. But I thought at least he might look at me. But he didn't."

"Maybe he didn't hear you."

"Oh I know, I know. I had to just barely whisper."

They sat in silence. Then they talked about other things, but finally Carlucho went back to the subject.

"You know something?"

"What?"

358

"I could be a doctor, but I would never be a veterinarian."

"Why not?"

"Because of what I was telling you. They can talk to each other, I know that they can talk to each other as good as you or I. If you're a doctor and a man tells you 'This is where it hurts, doctor, and over here, too,' then you're okay. You know whereabouts to start, you see? But how're you going to know where to start looking for what ails a hippopotamus? Or a lion? Imagine, the king of the jungle lying there without the strength to get up and find himself something to eat, and looking at you with those sad eyes of his, like he was begging you to do something for him, actually counting on you, you know, trusting in you to make him feel better . . . Rotting inside from the cancer for all you know, and you not even knowing where to start looking."

Slowly, the fall evening was turning to night, the darkness growing deepest first in the most sheltered places, inside the animal houses, and then rising, little by little, everywhere, while Nacho went on looking in through the bars of the gate, making out the dim shape of an elephant, he thought, and perhaps, over there, that same bison that Carlucho had watched during his experiment, that same bison to which he had spoken those quiet, unanswered words.

BECAUSE WHAT AMOUNT OF TENDERNESS,
what wise or kindly words, Bruno thought S. was probably thinking, what gentle touch could reach the hidden, solitary heart of that creature so far from his own country, from the jungle he'd been taken from; what words could touch that creature so brutally separated from his own kind, his own sky, the cool lakes? It was not strange, then, that Nacho should realize that sad truth at last and drop his arms and stick his hands in the back pockets of his jeans and walk pensively off down Libertador, his back bowed, kicking absentmindedly at a stone. Where was he going? What solitude awaited him, still? And then once again S. felt in the pit of his stomach that disgust for literature which was coming to him now stronger every day, and he thought once again of what Nietzsche had said: one might manage to write something real, and true, when one's repugnance for literary men and their words became unbear-

359

able—but it would be real repugnance, a repugnance that would make you vomit if you had to go to one more of those "artistic" cocktail parties where people talk of death while jockeying for position in some provincial literary prize. And then, a million miles from those (those?) vain, mean-spirited, perverse, filthy, hypocritical creatures, be able to breathe clean, pure, fresh air, feel able to talk unashamedly with an illiterate like Carlucho, do something with one's hands: dig a ditch, build a little bridge. Something small, humble, yet clean and precise. Something useful.

But since the heart of man is unfathomable (Bruno told himself), with that thought in its head the body of S. walked off toward Cramer, where he was supposed to meet Nora.

SOME TIME PASSED
without any further word from Dr. Schnitzler. And S. thought, relieved, that there wasn't going to be any further word, either. But then one day he answered the telephone and heard the foreign gentleman's ratlike squeals. What was wrong, Dr. Sabato? Was he sick? He had to take care of himself. Hadn't he promised to come by when he had more time to stay? A most fascinating book, from Oxford, had just arrived. Etc.

S. let a few weeks go by, not knowing how he should feel about this, or how to react, wavering between fear of seeing Schnitzler and fear not to, either case provoking lord knew what reactions from the man. Then he received a letter with a somewhat chilly and probably ironic interrogatory about his health, those attacks of gout and the shooting pains of neuralgia in his face. Cases of hysterical paralysis (was he not aware of this?) most often occurred on the left side, the side most subject to unconscious influences. S. put his hand to the left side of his face. For quite a while now he had been haunted by a strange idea: someone was creeping up on him with a sharp-pointed knife; the person grabbed his head with one hand, at the base of the skull the way barbers do, and with the other hand he jabbed the point of the knife in Sabato's left eye. Well, not in the eye exactly, but rather between the eyeball and the bone of the socket. Once the unknown person had done this, which he did with great care, he would slice the knife all around the socket until the

360

eye fell out. The eyeball usually fell at S.'s feet, but then it would bounce like a rubber ball across the room.

This whole scene was extraordinarily vivid to Sabato, and of course terribly unpleasant. Each time he felt the experience coming on he would begin to suffer the most terrible anxiety. The curious thing about it was that it didn't help in the least to think about other things or try to shun the event: it happened inexorably.

An example. One night he was sitting with Señora Falú, talking about Eduardo's trip to Japan, when he sensed that it was about to happen to him again. Señora Falú saw him suddenly go pale, and she was instantly concerned.

"Is something wrong?" she asked, looking at him worriedly. As one could well understand, S. was not about to explain what was happening to him. He simply said he was all right, perfectly all right. That was at the exact moment the unknown person was plunging the point of the knife into his eye and beginning to make that circular sawing motion with it that S. was now so horribly familiar with.

Señora Falú went on talking about whatever it was—Sabato, of course, was in no condition to follow the conversation. The woman obviously sensed something, though S. tried to remain as calm and composed as possible, in spite of the horrifying sawing of the knife blade around his eye socket. Of course the experience was not always so disturbing. It seldom came over him when he was with other people. Sometimes he would be in bed, or sitting in the darkness of a movie theater, where the thing was not so conspicuous. It was very seldom that the operation was performed on him in such uncomfortable circumstances as those with Señora Falú, since she was not the only person who had been there—several other people had been present as well, and some had watched him from a distance.

THEY HAD PICKED UP HIS TRAIL AGAIN.
He thought his part in it had been secret; it seemed impossible to him that anyone could even suspect him. Why were they nosing around, then, asking questions? What did that half-whispered conversation over in that corner there mean? Who were they, those people whispering, and why were they talking like that to each other?

361

He thought he recognized Ricardo Martín whispering with Chalo and Elsa, who kept furtively looking over toward him from time to time. But there was so little light it was hard to tell. Then somebody else came in; he'd have sworn it was Murchison if he hadn't been sure Murchison was at the university in Vancouver. The man bent over to Anzoátegui, said some word in his ear, and it became obvious that everybody was in on some grave secret that somehow concerned him. Then other people came in: it was like a wake, but a wake for a corpse still alive, and very suspicious. Among the newcomers he thought he saw Cio with Alicia, Malou with Graciela Berethervide, Siria, Kika alongside Renée. The room grew more and more crowded, the air more and more suffocating, the whispering louder and louder—not because people were raising their voices but simply because there were more and more people whispering. Iris Scaccheri, Orlando and Luis, Emile came in. Tita. And alone in a corner, S., as though awaiting the verdict for some crime he'd committed. The word had gotten around, that was clear enough. Who was that woman that was shoving her way in now? Matilde Kirilovsky, but the Matilde of years ago, the Matilde of university days, when she was just a girl. People pushed, shoved, elbowed each other, squeezed tighter and tighter together by the people still coming in— it was getting frankly disagreeable, particularly for him, needless to say. The Sonis, Ben Molar, Dr. Savransky, Chiquita, the Molins, Lily with José, and other people who by now were more guesses on his part than clear images.

Then he lost consciousness, he fell into a deep, deep well. He woke up screaming.

It took him a long time to shake off the remnants of that nightmare; little by little faces began growing blurry, fading away, dimmed by the powers of wakefulness. But his anxiety grew not less but even worse, since he realized that the news of his crime was spreading wider every day through his nocturnal landscape, and that the police and their interrogations were becoming increasingly oppressive.

He got up groggily, washed his face and head with cold water, and went out into the garden. The sun was just coming up. The trees, unlike men, received the sun's first rays with peaceful nobility, the nobility of beings that did not have to undergo (or so S. assumed) that sinister experience each night.

He sat for a long time beside a flowerbed. Finally he went into his study and sank into a chair, looking at the rows of books. He thought of the number of books that now he'd never read again before he died. Then making an effort, he stood up and took out Weininger's *Diary*, which he had seen from the chair. He opened it at random and read the words of Strindberg, in the preface: "That strange and mysterious man! Born guilty, like I. Because I came into the world with a guilty conscience, afraid of everything, of man, of life. I believe I committed some crime before I was born."

He closed the book and sank once again into his chair. After a while he went back to bed.

When he woke up, it was almost dark outside. He had barely enough time to make it to his appointment with the woman in La Tenaza. When he found her, he had an alarming impression: in the darkness, among the trees along Calle Cramer, he thought he saw the fugitive shadow of Agustina.

The next day, in La Biela,
Paco brought a folded piece of paper over to him: "Gothic steeples and the Eiffel Tower (*ad majorem hominis gloriam*) rise, strain upward, symbolically seeking the heavens. They flee from the feminine earth, the essence of the horizontal. The bed, the symbol of sex, is also horizontal."

He didn't need to look, but he couldn't help it: there the man was, in a corner of the café, watching him with those gleeful rat's eyes of his. He made a gesture to Sabato and winked, as though saying How's that! The least sign from S. would bring him rushing over, in spite of McLaughlin. But S. made no sign, though he looked at him in hypocritical friendliness. He sat there thinking about the message and the man's insistence. It was obvious he was following him, since he had never seen him in La Biela before. But was he doing the following himself, or did he have agents at his service?

"Mac what?" he asked.

The man wrote it for him on a napkin.

It was pronounced maclaflin, wasn't it?

There were supposedly places in Ireland where it was pronounced maclaklin.

Of course: as though the arbitrariness of English pronunciation weren't bad enough, Irish madness had to be factored in.

He wanted to write a thesis: Sex, evil, blindness.

S. looked at him in surprise. "It's a complicated subject, I don't know much about it myself. That is to say, everything I know is in the Report."

"I understand. But there is one other thing. I believe I read in a biography on you that your Albanian ancestors fought the Turks in the fifteenth century. Do you know the legend of the city of the Blind?"

S. was very much taken aback. What was that?

"I'm not really terribly sure about this, I still have some looking into it to do, but somewhere in that area there's supposed to have been an underground city of the Blind, with kings and vassals and everything—all Blind."

S. was petrified; he knew nothing about it. There was a silence, and for a while there seemed to be some sort of cabalistic triangle: Mac, looking at S. out of his sky blue eyes, S. himself, and Dr. Schnitzler, who had not taken his eyes off him, like a cat watching a bird. If a director had been staging this as a play and could avoid the conventions of naturalism (S. thought later), he'd have removed all the other people with their wineglasses and cups of coffee, all the chairs, tables, waiters, and the remains of sandwiches; it was all false, a disguise, in a way, or a camouflage, of the real reality—which went to prove what a lie that sort of realism was. Three characters at the vertices of a triangle, observing each other, watching each other warily.

It was too much. He told McLaughlin that he was unfortunately beginning to get an attack of neuralgia, he could barely talk; they'd get together another day. When the young man left, S. observed that Schnitzler was feverishly writing. After a few minutes, he sent S. the results: "I'm beginning to think, my dear Dr. Sabato, that you don't wish to see me, that in fact you don't like me very much. What a pity! You have no idea how sorry that makes me. We have so much in common! I have so many things to tell you; you are so very close to the truth. I've already lost all hope (I must say very frankly, word of honor) of your coming to my home again for a cup of coffee. So

364

allow me to take advantage of this happy coincidence to send you some observations that I think you will find interesting:

"1. The increase in the world's population.

"2. The uprising of the lower classes.

"3. The rebellion of women.

"4. The rebellion of the young.

"5. The rebellion of the colored races.

"All these things, my dear doctor, and I mean *all* of them, are *manifestations of the vital asserting itself over the rational.* This could in all justice be called *the awakening of the Left.* I hardly need to explain to you, my dear sir, that I am not speaking of the Left in any trivial sense more fitting to those poor devils who have no idea of the real problem. I am speaking of the Left in a much more profound sense, linking it to the repressed and instinctive powers of the race. You have said so yourself, in a way. How close you and I are! And one of your characters expressed the idea brilliantly in the 'Report on the Blind.' That is why I have followed you with such interest in these last few years, and have wanted to help you, go to you, give you my spiritual support. But I am, as I say, beginning to think that you do not wish that. I tell you in all frankness: it hurts me deeply."

S. could not go on reading; the reference to Fernando left him stunned. It was true, all those ideas could perfectly well have been pronounced by Vidal Olmos. And he, Sabato, what did that make him, then? He motioned for Paco to bring him another coffee, meanwhile scrupulously avoiding looking in the direction of that other man. It was only when his second coffee came that he could start reading again. "From the time of the Renaissance, technology and reason have swept the world along before them. The age-old struggle between the cortex and the inner brain ended (but only *apparently* ended, doctor! only *apparently!*) with the victory of the cortex, and the vital element in man was replaced by the mechanical: the clock, mathematics, plastic. But the subjugated inner brain will not surrender, it lies there, filled with fury and resentment, and at last attacks the triumphant society with psychosomatic illnesses, neuroses, the rebellion of the masses, the uprising of all the repressed and suppressed people of the world—*they are its soldiers!*—be they women or children, black or yellow. The entire Left. Even in clothes: bright, shocking colors (the feminine), irrational art, the arts of primitive peoples come into fashion, hippies dress almost like women, the 'lower world' becomes feminized. One must not be deceived by the woman's cigarette, her pants, her work in the workplace, or universal suffrage: that is an act of cunning, to make us believe that they are becoming like ourselves. A bit like what happens in the East, which in a profound sense also belongs to this Left: in order to resist this masculine Western civilization, it first dexterifies itself, if I may coin a word, takes a turn to the right, with Western technology—from transistors to Marxism, from plastic to the calculus, and even including atomic weapons. You will see: the yellow peoples of the world will someday rise against us. They have already begun to invade us, with Zen Buddhism, yoga, karate. And it is the intellectuals—the brain, the very nucleus of this Western civilization—that have been the first to succumb, like so many scatterbrained ducklings following the first moving creature they lay their newborn eyes on. Careful, my dear Dr. Sabato, careful!"

S. finished reading but he did not lift his eyes from the paper. He knew the man was watching him. Quickly he tried to think: who was this Dr. Schnitzler? Was he on the side of Western civilization? But this civilization was a product of the Light. So he couldn't be an agent of darkness. Or was he telling S. all this as a smokescreen, in order to catch him unawares? Was he trying to keep S. from snooping about anymore in that shadowy world by exciting a kind of egoism in S., a pride in things Western, in the masculine sex?

S. stood up, waved at the man from a distance, and left. After a long circuitous walk to throw anyone who might be following him off the track, he went into La Cueva, on the corner of Quintana and Ayacucho. On a paper napkin, he jotted down words in automatic writing. It had always worked for him. The first word he wrote was SCHNITZLER, and then almost immediately, underneath, the word SCHNEIDER. How could he not have seen it before? The two names began and ended the same, and had the same number of syllables. Of course, it was true, they might be apocryphal names. But if they were, then it was significant that they'd been chosen with those identical characteristics. Was there some relation, then, between the two men? They both, as though that weren't enough, came from somewhere between Bavaria and Austria, they were both grotesque creatures, and they both had contempt for women. But while Schneider was obviously an agent of darkness, Schnitzler defended rational science.

He thought a long time about that "but." Couldn't they simply be dividing up the work?

He went out to walk until it was time to meet Agustina.

And when they met, he felt the abyss that had opened between them.

SHE WAS TRANSFORMED INTO A FLAMING FURY,
    and he could feel the universe crack
shaken by her anger and her insults
and it was not just his flesh that was rent by her claws, but his
    consciousness
and there he stood as though cast out of his own spirit
the towers split and collapsing
in the cataclysm
and calcined by the flames.

MEANWHILE, NACHO
was minutely studying the features of Señor Pérez Nassif: the lechery and the mean-spiritedness, the hypocrisy and the low ambition, the sly cunning and the typical Buenos Aires wheeling and dealing, all with the most correct sort of conspicuously executive haircut. He cut out the picture and tacked it up with the others in his collection. Standing back a bit, he contemplated the effect with an expert eye. Then he looked over at the wall in front of him: the lions gleamed in purity and beauty.

He lay down on the bed, after putting on a Beatles record, and began thinking, looking up at the ceiling.

They were born already dirtying their diapers, spitting up milk (*I give him all I can, you hear*), they got fat (*look how cute*, wiping up his drool with the bib), grew up, reached the one magical, real moment of their lives (*unconscious, dreaming madmen*), and then switches, uplifting moral advice, and little schoolteachers turned

367

them into a herd of hypocrites (*you mustn't tell lies, children, or bite your nails, and don't ever write bad words on the wall, or miss your classes*), a herd of realists, social climbers, and niggards (*a penny saved is a penny earned, and if you take care of the pennies the dollars will take care of themselves*). Never ceasing to eat, to defecate, and to dirty everything they touch. Then a job, marriage, children. And once again the little monster spitting up milk as the gaga ex-milk-regurgitating monster looks on in idiotic delight, and the comedy begins again. Struggle, an argument over seats in the bus and a chair in the boardroom, envy, slander, a satisfaction to feelings of inferiority when people see a parade of their all-powerful nation's tanks down the main street (the dwarf feels himself a giant). Etc.

He got out of bed and left the apartment and began to walk. *Julia, Julia, oceanchild, calls me.* When he came to Mendoza and Conde he sat down on the curb and looked at the trees against the dusky light of the sky: the noble, beautiful, quiet trees. *Julia, seashell eyes, windy smile, calls me.* That fucking woman, that fucking Japanese bitch had to ruin everything. The trains were beginning their nightly transport of cattle; night was beginning in the great anthill with the exit of all the little ants that came scurrying out of their offices, their little numbers still on their backs, after their hard day of rushing around carrying Papers and Files, saying Good morning, sir, Excuse me, Mr. Badneighbor, 'Afternoon, Mr. Droolgood, Mr. Pretty wants to see you, curtsying to the ants immediately above them, kneeling down and shining their shoes, smiling at the stupid things they said, crawling on their bellies, then running wildly for the subway, being pushed and shoved along, stepping on each others' feet, arguing sullenly over seats, traveling like sardines in a can, smelling each others' smells, sensing that life was a tiny office and an interminable trip on a subway, with Marriage somewhere in the middle and gifts of irons and mantel clocks, and then the Baby, two (*this is a picture of my older one, he's all boy, yes sir, quite a live wire, you won't believe me when I tell you what he said the other day*), and Debts, the Promotion put off a while, Bar Bets in the Café, Soccer Games and Horse Races Saturday and Sunday, with Ravioli by the Little Lady, I've never eaten Ravioli like the Little Lady makes. And then Monday again, with the train to the city and the subway to the office.

368

And now they were going home on the same train, like cattle. The night was beginning, with its phantasmagoria of sleep and dreams and sex—first *La Razón*, then robberies and other crimes on TV, then a quiz show, and then sleep, where all things were possible. The omnipotent dreams in which the little ant is transformed into the Hero of World War II, the Boss at the Office, the Man Who Singlehandedly Wins the Battle, courageously crying *Just because you're the boss doesn't mean you can step all over me!*, the Unconquerable Don Juan standing amid the girls from the secretarial pool, the Sharpshooter, the Owner of a Swell New Sportscar, Carlos Gardel, Socrates, Aristotle Onassis.

The trains were going past.

It was night now. He stood up and began to walk back to his house. *Julia, sleeping sand, silent cloud.*

He found his sister lying on the bed looking up at the ceiling.

SILENTLY, IN ANGUISH

he stared out the window. How many horrors like the horror of the two of them were there at this moment in the world, how many unknown solitudes in this execrable city? Behind him he could feel that other rancor, the rancor that she held. He turned around: her hard face, the tightly squeezed jaw, her wide scornful lips showed that her resentment had reached its limit: a little more and that cauldron of hatred would explode. Almost without thinking, compelled by his unbearable suffering, Nacho screamed at her—what had *he* done to her, he screamed. *He*, he said, stressing the word in fury and pointing at his own chest with his rigid hand. And why should she have this hatred for him, this anger, why *her*?

He saw, in desperation, that she was getting up to leave.

He grabbed her arm. "Where are you going!"

It was a cry, not a question.

She ducked her head, and Nacho saw that she was biting her lips till she brought blood. Then she walked over to the wall and laid her two fists against it, not so much to lean on it as to push against it, beat it.

"There are no absolutes in life," she said after a long silence.

"And if there are no absolutes, that means that everything is permitted."

She seemed not to be talking to her brother but to herself, in a low but angry voice. Then she added:

"No, that's not it. It's not that everything is permitted. It's that we are *forced* to do everything, to destroy everything, to dirty everything." Her brother looked at her stunned. But she was concentrated on her own thought, and she continued to stand with her clenched fists against the wall. Then she began to scream, or really to howl, as she beat the wall with all her strength.

When she was calmer, she went over to the bed, sat down on the side of it, and lit a cigarette.

"It's cost me a lot to learn that," she said.

Nacho walked toward her, and when he was standing directly above her, he exclaimed, "But I will never accept it!"

"So much the worse for you, then, you fool! That's what makes me most furious of all!"

And then screaming "Imbecile!," she leapt at him, her fists beating against his chest, trying at the same time to kick him, to do anything to beat him down. And at last she did; he collapsed.

Then she sat down on the edge of the bed again and began to cry. It was not gentle crying, though, but dry, savage, angry sobbing.

When she was quieter she sat looking up at the ceiling. Her face looked as though it had been ravaged by the barbarians: fire, sacking, rape. She tried to find a cigarette, and when she had found one she lit it, her hand shaking.

"I see you've put up a picture of Señor Pérez Nassif right there between Sabato and Camus. I thought the idea was to put up photos of those disgusting people who talk about the absolute. The idea was, if I'm not mistaken about the vow I seem to remember you taking, to exhibit the faces of the great con artists of our time. Not just of any old maggot."

For a time which seemed to Nacho eternal, all that could be heard was the ticking of the alarm clock. Then, the bells of some church.

"Pérez Nassif," murmured Agustina, pensively, "I'll have to think about that one."

370

WHEN HE GOT TO HIS HOUSE

Lolita growled at him, as she had started doing recently, but this time she almost bit him, so he had to pick up a stick and brandish it at her, though what he really wanted to do was crack her skull for her if she kept this up.

Dogs have an instinct for things, he thought, and they're seldom wrong. When had he ever seen a dog behave like that with a member of the family? He'd tried to establish when it was that she growled at him, what thoughts or occurrences it coincided with, but he couldn't come to any conclusion.

When he reached his desk, he found the

LAST COMMUNICATION FROM JORGE LEDESMA

YOU GOT MAD AT ME, BUT I DON'T CARE. Whether you like it or not, our friendship rises above all the pushing and shoving of this great rapid transit bus the two of us are riding in, it has a dimension you've never suspected, I suspect. I don't care about all your disagreements with me—you're my heir. I've named you in my will and there's nothing you can do about it.

Your latest work(s), your ruminations over nothingness, the void, fear and loathing and the sickness unto death (anguish and anxiety, I mean—I didn't mean to joke), and the powers of hope and hopefulness have shown (have shown at least *me*) that you've come to a dead end. And you can only get out by backing out. Abaddon or Apollion, the Beautiful Angel or Satan. Enough middlemen. *God the Exterminator*. Do we want to be engines or cabooses?

The world is still a sorry wreck, a mess, a dark chaotic wrack and ruin, and nobody can set it right. And since I've got all the time in the world, I think I'll sleep.

My book progresses, slowly. What I need is some good weather, a goad, some nice air to breathe, and a little money. Plus, I must confess, I am a coward. I'll have to see if one of these days I can't pluck up the spirit to climb naked up that lamppost on Corrientes again. We'll see.

371

HE WENT OUT WALKING, AIMLESSLY,
until he found himself in front of the Boston. How had he gotten
there? He used to come here often, years ago, when he would stop
by to have long talks with the kids at the university. But now?

He ordered gin and as on so many other occasions when he was
deeply troubled, he concentrated his attention on the stains on the
old walls. As he studied them, he began to make out a cavern in
which he thought he could glimpse three people familiar, somehow,
to him. Their poses, the cellar or catacomb-like space in which the
ceremony was taking place, it all seemed to configure some grave
ritual that he almost believed he had experienced in some previous
life.

His eyes grew tired from his stubborn insistence at picking out
the details, especially of the mystagogue who led the rite. He closed
his eyes, rested a little, though his anxiety continued to grow, and
then, with the conviction that there was some crucial link to his life
to be found in that scene, he turned his scrutiny on the stains again.
At last the details began to come together, to form a familiar, perverse face, the face of someone whom he had tried, fruitlessly, for
years and years, to keep out of his life—the face of R.!

The moment he found the key to that secret code, the rest was
instantly revealed to him. Closing his eyes again, but this time
squeezing them shut as though refusing to admit the memory into
his mind, he was once more swept by the lustful horror of that night
in 1927.

But that was not the most uncanny part of it, and he might
perhaps have attributed it later to the normal human tendency to
find in the stains on the wall whatever it was that one was obsessed
by. What was almost impossible to believe was the entrance of R.
into the café at that very moment, as though he had been spying on
S., waiting for the instant S. finally deciphered the hierogram. S. had
not seen him since 1938.

He sat down nearby, also ordered gin, drank it, paid for it, and
left, all without making the slightest effort to speak to S.

S. was dumbstruck. He had followed him, that was clear. But in
that case, why hadn't he come over to pester and harass him the
way he'd done back in the days of the Curie Laboratory? S. reflected
that the man no doubt possessed countless techniques for harass-

ment, and that his silent but significant presence was one of the means he employed for his warnings. But in this case, what was the warning?

S. meditated in more and more dizzying slow motion over the horror in that cavern, until he saw or thought he saw that he had to return to the underground vaults and passageways of Calle Arcos.

When he saw the ancient house again, surrounded by modern office towers, he had the sensation of gazing upon a mummy in a store filled with chrome-plated artifacts.

A long sign hung up along the fence announced the court-ordered auction. Looking at those grimy, leprous ruins, and knowing R. as he knew him, it occurred to S. that R. would never have stepped into his path again just to invite him to cast one last look on a family album that some indifferent stranger was about to consign to the flames: S. sensed that something much more profound was at stake. And much more terrifying.

He looked at the gate. It was chained and locked with a padlock, though everything was as old and rusty as the antique gate itself. S. was almost certain that it had not been opened once during all these years of lawsuits and wills. Why not? Most likely because don Amancio had never wanted to see it again, even from the street.

One used to drive up to a lovely wrought-iron gate and through it down the driveway to the porte-cochere, but the beautiful iron gates had been stolen now, no doubt by those combination thief–antiques dealers that filled Buenos Aires these days. And now in place of the gates there stood two ugly sheets of corrugated tin hung by crazy hinges. They were weather-streaked, rusty, dented, and across one of them someone had spray-painted VIVA PERON. The tin sheets were precariously wired shut with a couple of loopings of thick wire threaded through two gouged-out holes.

He found a hardware store on Juramento, where he bought a pair of wire-cutters and a flashlight, and then he began walking, to wait for nightfall.

He walked down Juramento to Cuba, and then into the square at Belgrano, where he sat for a long time on a bench, entranced by the church, which penetrated into deeper and deeper realms of his spirit as the evening drew on. He began to not see, not hear; the sound of the rush of people that thronged Belgrano at that hour went unheard, and S. felt himself more and more alone. The dusk was somehow ominous, an hour reigned over by occult and evil deities, crisscrossed by bats waking to their nocturnal lives—those denizens of the shadows whose song is the shriek of winged rats, those messengers of the gods of the shades, those gelatinous heralds of horror and of nightmare, those minions of rat and weasel kings in their theocracy of caverns.

Voluptuously, he abandoned himself to his visions; it was as though he were witness to the theophany of the most exalted monarch of darkness, the king surrounded by his court of basilisks, cockroaches, ferrets, and toads, of lizards and frogs and weasels.

But then he woke to the ordinary noises of every day, the neon lights and the thunder of cars. It was dark enough now, he thought, that in the tree-lined quietness of Arcos no one would notice what he was doing. Still, he took even more precautions. He waited for a pedestrian to get farther down the street, he kept his eyes on the front of the great apartment houses, and then just as he was about to cut the wire, he thought he saw someone scurry out of one of those buildings, as though the person had been hiding until then— it was a heavyset figure, and S. knew it all too well.

He was paralyzed with fear.

If that fleeting shadow had indeed been Dr. Schneider, what link was there between him and R.? More than once S. had thought that R. was trying to force him to enter the universe of shadows and explore it, as he had once before with Vidal Olmos, but that Schneider was trying to keep him back or, if he couldn't prevent him, to see that it turned out to be the punishment long prepared for.

After a few moments, S. grew more calm; he reflected that he was altogether too worked up, there was no reason for the silhouette to be Dr. Schneider—and anyway, if Schneider had in fact been watching him from the dark doorway (as he had no doubt watched on so many other occasions), he would not have had the slightest interest in showing himself to S.

S. cut the wire and went in, being careful to close the tin gate again behind him.

On that summery night, with its clouds scudding across the sky, flickering moonlight lit the funereal setting. His pulse racing ever faster and his heart pounding ever louder in his chest, S. walked

374

through the garden. It was being devoured by a horribly spreading cancer: up the palm trees and the magnolias, through the jasmines and the cactuses, vines and creepers unknown to S. had made strange alliances, while tall grass and weeds lived like beggars among the rubble of a temple whose cult they had never known.

He contemplated the ruins of that mansion, its friezes fallen, its shutters rotted and hanging off their hinges, the panes of its windows shattered.

He approached the servants' house at the rear. He had not the strength, at least for the moment, to turn his eyes up toward that window in the big house. He sat down on the ground with his back against a tree, to look half pensively, half horrified at the ruin it had all fallen into, and to gather his strength and his wits, for he knew that when he was done looking at this yellowing album he would have to confront the horror face to face. And perhaps because he was so certain of that meeting, he took his time in his recollections of Florencio and Juan Bautista, the two of them prefigurations of Marcelo: that same matte skin, black hair, and big dark moist eyes; ready, when their beards began to grow, to attend the burial of the Count of Orgaz. Florencio—preoccupied, somehow, his mind far away (on some other thing, some other continent, some other planet), "a little absent" as the country people of that time, with instinctive accuracy, would say. There was a contrast, though, in spite of the virtual identity of their physical features, between Florencio's distracted expression and the realistic, sensible expression on the face of his younger brother. And then S. reflected once again that Marcelo had inherited the character, the air not of his father Juan Bautista but rather of his uncle Florencio, as though someone in the family had to inherit the job of keeping up a useless but quaint tradition.

He rested his eyes on the eucalyptus tree that Nicolás had climbed up that afternoon in 1927 and swung on as he did his famous imitation of an ape. And S. remembered how Nicolás had suddenly stopped shrieking and squealing, how they had all fallen silent, how he himself had felt the touch on the back of his neck. Turning with fearful slowness, raising his head, knowing the exact place the call had come from, he had seen at the window, up there, to the right, the frozen image of Soledad.

375

It was hard to see in the tenuous light the place from which she had cast down her paralyzing stare. But he knew where it was.

Then she had disappeared, and little by little each one had taken up whatever it was they'd been doing before, though not, now, with the carefree euphoria of a minute earlier.

He had never told anyone (unless you counted Bruno) about the events connected with Soledad. Although naturally he had not even told Bruno of the monstrous ritual that he had participated in. And now, sitting in that garden, after almost half a century, he sensed that the circle was closing. He recalled that night, Florencio absent-mindedly strumming his guitar, Juan Bautista interminably frying potatoes for the Spanish omelet, Nicolás singing some idiotic song over and over, until somebody yelled "Enough!" and they managed to go to sleep. Not him, though, of course.

He had told Bruno how he had met her in Nicolás' house, in that parlor presided over by the great oil painting of Rosas. They had been studying some theorem in geometry when he felt the presence behind him of one of those beings who have no need to talk in order to communicate. He had turned around, and for the first time seen those same grayish-green eyes, the same stern, tense mouth, the same authoritative expression that made the ancestor's face so memorable: she the bastard heir of the man, as she surely was. Nicolás had gone mute, as though he were in the presence of an absolute monarch. In a quietly imperious voice, the girl had asked him about something, and Nicolás had replied in a voice that S. had never heard before. After that, she withdrew as silently and secretly as she had come. It took them awhile to get back to their theorem, and S. even then had a confused and disturbed impression which only as an adult could he put into words: She had appeared to let him know that she existed, that she was *there*. Two ways of saying it, and many times he had wavered between them, until he had decided at last to use them both, even knowing that they didn't mean at all the same thing, and might even, terrifyingly, be self-contradictory. But that characterization he could only make, as he had said, some forty years later, when he told Bruno the story for the first time, as though back in that faraway time he had somehow taken a snapshot of the moment and only now, so long afterward, were able to interpret it.

376

That night, the night of the theorem, he dreamed that he was walking down a subterranean passageway, and at the end of it Soledad stood, naked, waiting for him, phosphorescent in the darkness.

From that night onward he could hardly keep his mind on anything except that dream. Then summer came, and at last he could go to the house on Arcos where he knew she was waiting for him.

And there he was, now, trembling in the darkness, waiting for his friends' breathing to take on the rhythms of sleep. Then he got out of bed with great care, tiptoed out with his shoes in his hand, and put them on outside, in the garden.

He cautiously walked to the back door of the great house, the glass door of the conservatory.

Just as he had imagined it, the door was unlocked. When the clouds allowed, rays of moonlight filtered in through the panes of glass and illuminated the interior of the conservatory, everything in it weirdly colored by the carmine and azure lozenges scattered in the glass walls. When his eyes had adjusted to the semidarkness, he saw her, standing at the foot of the stairway that led to the floor above. The glimmering, uncertain light was the truest setting for her. He had once told Bruno that Soledad could well have been the confirmation of that ancient doctrine of onomasia, because her name was the perfect reflection of her essence: hermetic and solitary, she seemed to hold the secret to one of those powerful, bloody sects, a secret whose revelation is punished with torture and death. Her inward violence seemed held in under pressure, as though in a boiler almost bursting with steam. But this boiler was fired by an icy flame. As he had tried to explain to Bruno, it was she herself that was the oxymoron, not the precarious and contingent language that might be used to describe her. Even more than the few essential words she spoke (or her cries of sexual pleasure), her silences suggested knowledge that did not correspond to "the things of every day" but rather to that other sort of truth, the truth that governs nightmare. She was a creature of the night, an inhabitant of caves, and she had the same paralyzing stare, the same cold sensuality, as snakes.

"Let's go," was all she had said.

And going in one of the doors down the short hall, they came into a sort of butler's pantry, a room off the great kitchen. Carrying an old kerosene lantern in her right hand—which proved to S. that

377

all of this had been perfectly foreordained—she went straight to a corner of the room and pointed out to him the trapdoor to a cellar.

They descended down brick steps, little by little beginning to feel the underground wetness of the passage. They made their way through all sorts of rags and refuse to a place where Soledad pointed out another door to him, which he raised. They began a second descent, but this time down a stairway of flat, heavy bricks from colonial times, half destroyed by more than two hundred years of moisture. Mysterious little trickles of water dripped and ran down the walls, making this second cellar even more frightening and eerie.

The dim light of the lantern did not permit him to see what there was there, but from that muted echo of the footsteps that one only hears in deep, empty caverns, he was inclined to assume that there was nothing in the chamber but the stairway. They walked across the space until they came to a narrow passageway dug out of the earth, without even the support of walls of brick. This tunnel barely allowed one person to pass, and Soledad walked along in front of him, with the lantern; through her almost transparent robe he could see her body swaying in morbid majesty.

He had read more than once in magazines and newspapers about secret tunnels under Buenos Aires, built during the colonial era and discovered from time to time during the construction of subways and skyscrapers. And he had never read an acceptable explanation for them. He especially recalled the tunnel almost a half mile long between the Church of Our Lady of Succor and the Recoleta, the catacombs of the Manzana de las Luces, and the tunnels and passageways that connected those tunnels with the old mansions of the eighteenth century, those crypts and tunnels the components of a vast labyrinth whose purpose no one had ever been able to puzzle out.

They had been walking now for more than half an hour, although it was hard for him to gauge the time exactly: the almost claustrophobic passageway, the lurid darkness, the ghostly girl, the night journey in all its details kept time from ticking at the same rhythm as life in the day, in the light. In one sense that silent, almost hallucinatory march would later seem to have taken all eternity, as he followed the twists and turns and forks in the passage. He was amazed at the sureness with which Soledad walked the route to the

378

place they sought. And then he thought, with horror, that if one didn't know the exact plan of that labyrinth, one would never see the streets of Buenos Aires again, one would be lost in that tunnel forever with the weasels and ferrets and rats that he suddenly heard (more than saw) scurry off ahead of them, into their own, even more nauseating and impenetrable labyrinths.

Then he realized they had arrived at their destination, for he could see ahead a vague luminosity. The tunnel gradually opened, and at the end of it they found themselves in a cavern more or less the size of a bedroom, though very rudely constructed, with walls of heavy colonial bricks and a staircase he could hardly make out over to one end of it. On one of the walls there was a torch, like the kind used in the times of the viceroys, and it was that which gave off the flickering, wan light.

In the center of this cavelike room there was a straw mattress that looked as though it might have come straight from some dank, nightmarish jail cell, though it gave the impression of being in use even today, and some rough wooden benches sat against the walls. Everything was sinister, and somehow suggested the image of a dungeon more than anything else.

Soledad had just put out her lantern when S. heard the footsteps of someone coming down the stairs. He soon saw the hard face and nyctalopic eyes of R.! S. had not seen him again since he had left Rojas to study in La Plata, and he had always remembered the torment of that blinded sparrow; he now found him standing there before him, when he'd imagined (and hoped) that he would never cross his path again.

What link could there be between R. and Soledad? Why was he there, as though waiting for S.? Suddenly he had the sensation that Soledad and he had something in common, some shared habit of the night, at once horrible and fascinating.

"You didn't think you'd ever see me again, eh?" R. said in that hoarse, sarcastic voice S. despised.

The three of them stood in that cavelike dungeon like figures in some nightmarish triangle. He looked at Soledad and found her more hermetic than ever, hieratic, with a majesty out of all keeping with her years. If not for her breast, which rose and fell with some deep emotion, he might have thought she was a statue: a statue which

379

secretly quivered with life. Under her tunic, S. caught glimpses of the snake-woman body she possessed.

He heard R.'s voice again, speaking to him, and saw R. make a gesture with his head toward the ceiling:

"We are under the crypt of the church at Belgrano. Do you know the church? That round one? The Church of the Immaculate Conception," he added, his voice ironic.

Then, in a voice that seemed changed to S., a voice almost of fear (which was difficult to believe in him), he said:

"I will tell you that this is also one of the navels of the universe of the Blind."

After a silence, he added:

"And this will be the center of your life, from this moment on. Everything you do or fail to do will lead you to this spot. And when you do not return of your own will, we will see to it that you remember your obligation."

Then he fell silent, and with slow, ritual movements Soledad took off her tunic. As she raised her robe, her arms crossed before her, her body emerged: her full loins, her narrow waist, her navel, and then, at last, her breasts, which trembled as she moved.

Once naked, she knelt down on the mattress facing S. and slowly leaned backward, opening her legs and extending them out toward him.

S. felt that at that moment he was indeed at the center of the Universe.

R. took the torch down from the wall. It gave off a suffocating smell of burning oil, and a great deal of smoke. He walked around the circumference of the room, came to S.'s side, and imperiously said:

"Now look at what you must see."

Bringing the torch down to Soledad's body, he illuminated her loins, which up to that moment had been in shadow. In dread and fascination, S. saw that in the place of her sex Soledad had a huge grayish-green eye, looking out at him in somber expectancy, in harsh anxiousness.

"And now," said R., "you must do what you are fated to do."

A strange force began at that instant to rule S. Without taking his own eyes off that enormous vertical eye, and unblinkingly watched by it in turn, he slowly removed his clothes. Then R. made him kneel before Soledad, between her open legs. He knelt there for several seconds, looking with utter terror and sadistic fear at the grave sexual eye.

Then she raised herself up, with savage splendor; her great mouth opened like a devouring beast's, her legs and arms wound around him and squeezed him like powerful claws of flesh, and little by little, like an inexorable vice, she forced him in contact with that great eye whose fragile elasticity he could feel below him, splitting, rending, bursting. And as he felt the frigid liquid spew out, he began his descent into another cavern, still more mysterious than this cavern that witnessed this bloody rite, the monstrous blinding of that eye.

Now, after forty-five years, he had come again to the house on Arcos. "When you don't come of your own volition, we will see to it that you are recalled to your obligation." So R. had told him on that night in 1927, and reminded him in 1938, in Paris, just when S. had believed he could find shelter in the luminous universe of science. And now he had just repeated the same words, in silence, at the time when . . . When what?

He didn't know, and might never manage to unravel it all. But one thing he did know—R. had sought him out in the Boston in order to make clear the reminder, the terrible warning. And so he found himself amid the ruins of the old garden.

Until that moment he had not had the strength to look over toward the glass door of the conservatory. Everything, apparently, was repeated: the summer's night, the heat, the moon running through the stormy clouds. But between that other time and now there lay misfortune and tempests, ostracism and disappointment, the sea, battles, love, and the sands of the desert. What sort of return, then, was this return?

Who knew whether it was because of the state he was in, or the enigma that had always surrounded Soledad, or something actually real, but the moonlight had an ominous and twisted cast to it. He began to feel that he was not in the garden of an old and well-known Belgrano house but on the surface of some abandoned planet, its inhabitants flown to other regions of the cosmos, fleeing some terrible curse. Fleeing a planet on which there were no more, nor would there ever be again, journeys of the sun from east to west, a planet given over forever to the unmoving and livid light of the moon. But it was a moon which in virtue of that permanence it held in the sky had taken on a supernatural power, become endowed with both infinite melancholy and violent, sadistic, yet funereal sexuality.

He realized that it was time now.

He stood up and walked to the glass door, its panes cracked and shattered, its frame twisted and rotted by time and neglect. He wrestled with the rusted door, and at last it opened; he went in, and began his walk toward the underground chambers, with his flashlight tracing again the path he had so long ago taken.

He knew that at the center of that labyrinth something was waiting for him. But he didn't know what it was.

THE WAY UP

was infinitely more difficult than the way down, because the path was slippery and he was suddenly terrified at losing his balance and falling into the wet, gooey abyss he sensed beneath him. He could barely keep his footing; he allowed himself to be carried along by instinct toward that dim glow that filtered down through some crack above him. Little by little he was ascending, cautiously but hopefully—a hopefulness that grew as the glow became gradually brighter. Still, he thought (and the thought disturbed him terribly), the light did not seem to be the light that came from the sun he knew; it was more like the light from a midnight sun that cast its wan rays on the glacial landscape of the pole. And though this idea had no rational foundation, it began to take root in his mind, and became so overpowering that it turned into what one might call a disheartened hope: the same sort of emotion that takes shape deep inside a man who returns to his native country after wandering for many years through realms of horror and who suspects, with increasing anguish, that the homeland to which he returns has been devastated in his absence by some grave calamity, by invisible and cruel demons.

He was extremely overwrought through the difficult ascent, though his tortured emotions might also have stemmed from that suspicion that clutched at his heart. He would pause but never sit down, not only because the path was wet and clayey but also be-

382

cause of the fear distilled in him by the gigantic rats that he could hear skittering between his legs and which from time to time he glimpsed in the dimness: they were nauseating creatures, with malign, red-glowing eyes, shrilly shrieking and ravenous. When he sensed he was reaching the end of the path, he grew more and more certain of the catastrophe that he was about to discover, for it was not the characteristic sounds of Buenos Aires that came more and more audibly to his ears, but rather an ever-deepening silence. At last his eyes dimly made out what appeared to be the entrance to the cellar of a house. It was. Through a hole in a wall built of bricks half-crumbling from wetness and time, he entered that basement room, where at first he could only make out heaps and mounds of unidentifiable things, covered with the clayey soil that the rains had deposited there over the years and piled with rubble and rotting timbers, and where pale weeds stretched upward longingly toward the light filtering in from above.

He stepped gingerly through those spongy hillocks of debris, trying to find the way out; it would surely take him to the first floor of this building, whatever the building was. The roof was of masonry and cement, which had perhaps kept it from falling in, but there was a huge crack in it through which the scant light filtered, dimly lighting the cellar room. The light made him think, in fact, that perhaps there was no building above at all, but rather that this was some sort of vacant lot with the remains of some primitive building. The crack was not in the masonry, either, as he had first thought, but in an ancient wooden door, now splintered and rubbery from rot. He presumed the door must lead to a stairway of some sort, though he could not yet see it for the mounds of trash and rubble. He tried to scale one of the mounds, but it sank beneath his weight (for it was not solid but spongy and wet) and out of it scattered hundreds of huge rats, some of which in their hysteria rushed straight at him and madly ran up his legs, his torso, his neck, until they were about to reach his face. In unspeakable horror and desperation, waving his hands and trying to brush them off him, he tried to step back, tried to get the creatures off him, tried to keep his body from the attack. But he could not keep some of them from reaching his face; they were squeaking madly, shrieking, and then he felt the nauseating brush of their skin against his cheek, and for one second his eyes met the glittering, red, perverse eyes of that incarnation of rabid putrefaction. He lost control, and from his throat there came a shriek of horror, and then it was muted by a convulsion of vomiting, as though he were screaming as he drowned in the middle of a swamp filled with green, slimy water—because he did not vomit food (he couldn't remember how long it had been since he'd eaten), but a viscous liquid that hung in slimy threads from his lips like some nauseating green drool.

He stepped back, instinctively, and found himself where he had started again, at the irregular hole in the wall through which he had entered the cellar, or what once had been the cellar. The rats were scurrying madly in all directions, and for a few seconds he could rest; he dragged his shirtsleeve across his mouth, to wipe off the rest of the vomit. He stood paralyzed with fear and nausea. He could hear, in every corner of that room, dozens and perhaps hundreds of rats, and he felt that they were watching him with their burning eyes. He was seized once more with a terrible heaviness; his heart failed him when he thought of having to cross that horrible swamp of living trash. But even more unthinkable was staying there, where sooner or later he would be defeated by sleep and would collapse into that quicksand, at the mercy of the ravenous rats. That thought gave him the strength to launch his final ascent. That thought, and the conviction that the barrier of spongy filth and rats was the last trial that kept him from the light. Like a madman, he set his jaw and leapt toward the door; madly, blindly, he scaled the heaps of garbage, trampling shrieking rats and flailing his arms to keep them off him, keep them from running up his body as they'd done before, and at last he came, breathless, to the door of rotting spongy wood. He kicked at it, and it gave way sickeningly.

A GREAT SILENCE LAY OVER THE CITY.
Sabato walked along beside the people, through the crowds, but no one noticed him, no one seemed even to see him, as though he were the only living creature in a city of ghosts. He grew desperate, and he began to scream. But all the figures continued on their way, in silence, indifferent, showing not the slightest sign of having seen or heard him.

384

He got on the train for Santos Lugares, where he lived.

When the train came to his station, he got off and walked down Bonifacini. No one looked at him or said hello. He went into his house, and there was only one small sign of recognition of his presence: the hair of Lolita's coat stood on end and she barked softly. "Hush," Gladys said, irritated, "you're crazy, what are you barking at? There's nobody there. Hush." He went into his study. Sabato was seated at his desk, as though he were meditating on some misfortune, his exhausted head resting on his two hands.

He walked over to him, stood before him, and he could see that Sabato's eyes were withdrawn, infinitely sad, looking vacantly into space.

"Here I am," he said.

But Sabato sat unmoving, his head between his hands. Almost grotesquely, he corrected himself:

"Here you are."

But this did not produce any sign, either, that the man had heard or seen him. Not the slightest sound came from his lips, not the slightest movement came from his hands or his body.

The two of them were alone, cut off from the world. And to make matters even worse, cut off from each other.

Suddenly he saw that from the eyes of the seated Sabato there had begun to fall two large teardrops. Almost in disbelief, he then realized that he, too, could feel, running down his cheeks, the telltale chill of tears.

THEY RUSHED UP OUT OF THE SUBWAY BY THE HUNDREDS, bumped into each other, stepped off crowded buses, and disappeared into the inferno of Retiro, where they got back on other trains. A new year, a new beginning, thought Marcelo with pious sarcasm, as he watched those desperate and despairing people rush off to grab a piece of the New Year's hope that everyone in Buenos Aires seemed to think came served up with the cider and *pan dulce*, with the sirens and fireworks and shouting.

From his bench he looked up at the clock on the tower: nine o'clock. And of course, there she came, unspeaking but punctual. "A little present," she said, showing him the green bow on the package, then smiling: César Vallejo, bound by hand. By a German book-binder in La Lucila. Not many of them left. Her almost silver hair glowed in the evening light. "Ulrike." He could hardly say it, as his slender fingers touched her hand to accept the little package. They sat down, like two shipwrecked souls on a tiny island in the midst of a stormy ocean, with the anonymous, alien tempest beating about them.

Then they walked toward the docks. There was a ship decked with streams of bunting there, with all its lights turned on, waiting to blow its siren at midnight.

Did he believe in that stuff about a new beginning? she asked him in her choppy way. "You know I stuttered till I was ten," she always explained, with that characteristic honesty of hers for confessing her own defects.

Conversation between them was as tortured as the ascent of Aconcagua by two invalids. They shunned the personal, trying to talk about books, texts they shared in classes, which was a way of not talking. But sometimes they sat down together to translate things from German: Rilke, Trakl. That was not easy, either, though: how could one correct Marcelo's errors without wounding him, without its somehow turning into a boast? "But it's natural, your father's German," he would manage to stammer out, wanting to apologize for her. Or she would say, "Those *lieder*. They're better with the music, you know. The words become almost automatic, they're easier that way." But he would sing too softly, abashedly, somehow, self-consciously, hitting false notes both in the music and in the German, making it worse than it had to be, worse than he was capable of: *Gewahr mein Bruder, ein Bitt.* "No, Marcelo, wait, excuse me," she would interrupt him sweetly, to correct him. But of course Schumann moved them, the songs of that virile friendship, the grenadier about to die who begs his comrade to carry him back to the Homeland, to bury him there, so that he can be near when the Emperor calls him again: that song of combat, of melancholy, and of patriotic loyalty in distant lands. In the soft evening light of the plaza. And he would feel the temptation to tell her that she looked beautiful with her long pale hair lying on the soft black blouse she wore. But how could he say anything so long, so intimate? So they walked without speaking, until they came closer to the ship: the

386

lights and the bunting spoke of people there, too, who wanted to be happy, who were waiting for the sirens and the magic of midnight, the hour that would divide their lives in two, so that they could leave behind their troubles, their heartaches and suffering and poverty and the disappointments of the year gone by, and begin anew. Then the two young people turned back and sat down again on the same bench. At last she said it was ten, and she had to be back in La Lucila before eleven.

Oh yes, sure, of course.

Was he going to his parents' house?

Marcelo looked at her. His parents' house? Well actually . . . Scarecrow was all by himself, and he thought . . .

They stood up; she was a little taller than he. Then Ulrike brushed his cheek with her hand and said "Happy New Year," with that soft irony they used when they disguised real emotions behind clichés, as though to hide behind slogans and gaudy colors. And then, for the first time—and also for the last—she brought her lips to Marcelo's, and they felt that something very profound was begun with that light touch. He watched her go off toward the station, with her black blouse and yellow pants, thinking it was almost incredible that she had no sense of, not the least conceit about, her own beauty: the beauty of a hidden, secret garden, a place that never appeared on glossy tour folders, that has never received (and will never receive) that sickly-sweet, hypocritical treatment of the promoters.

He walked down the Avenida del Libertador toward his parents' house, and when he reached it he stood and looked up at it from the fence at the walk. Yes, there were lights on the seventh floor. They were getting everything ready, they were probably hoping he'd come by, even if only for a minute. He wondered if it weren't mean of him not to go up, and selfish of him to sadden his mother, even if her mind was now gone. He stood and wavered a long time, thinking of the way she mixed up words, of the way her hair was always messed up, tangled, of the way she couldn't get anything straight. Bécquer? What was wrong with Bécquer? What was all the fuss about—when she was no more than *this* high she could recite Bécquer by heart. Beckett, Mama, Beckett! he would correct her, with his hard, intellectual bent for exactness. But it was like trying to beat a sack of cotton into shape: Bécquer, Bécquer! What on earth is so new and wonderful about Bécquer!? she'd insist, her eyes on her crossword puzzle.

He stood and looked up at those seventh-floor windows for a long time, and then at last he crossed the avenue. But he continued on, down to Heras, to catch the number 60 bus. Several went by full, but he finally caught a handhold on one. He got off on Independencia, went into a grocery store, and bought a bottle of cold cider and a loaf of *pan dulce*. He had the *real* gift in his pocket already. It was going to be a wonderful surprise for Scarecrow. "I need words, Marcelo, that's the trouble. If I only had a dictionary." All right, there he'd have it, even if it was just a little one—like his needs, thought Marcelo. Those fantastic needs of his: copy down ten words a day in a notebook, and memorize them *here* (he would tap himself on the forehead). The Comandante always told them it wasn't just guns and bullets.

He walked downhill down Independencia, but as he crossed Balcarce, just as he was going into his rooming house, several men jumped him. It all seemed so unreal to him that he didn't even run, though it would have been futile anyway: he was completely surrounded. First he felt a terrible blow to his groin and then a blow to his head, and then a rag was stuffed in his mouth and he was thrown into the trunk of a car waiting with its engine running. Everything happened within seconds. In the trunk, his mind dulled with the pain, he could hear the car race down streets, turn, go down long avenues, then turn again, until little by little there was silence. The car stopped.

He was pulled from the trunk, thrown on the ground, and kicked in the kidneys and the scrotum, and though he writhed in pain his cries were muffled by the filthy rag that had been stuffed in his mouth. He heard one of the men say to another:

"Hey, Gordo, gimme a cigarette."

After they had lighted their cigarettes they half-dragged him along a corridor and down some stairs, and there he began to hear screaming: the howling, actually, of someone being flayed alive.

"Listen good, 'cause you're next," one of them said to him.

They continued along a hallway lit by a sickly light bulb. There was a nauseating stench, as though of toilets, of dirty urinals. They opened a cell door and threw him in. He sprawled across the floor.

388

He could not see for the darkness, but there was a smell of excrement.

"You better get ready to start remembering, because you're going to have a lot of it to do."

Little by little his eyes grew accustomed to the semidarkness. The air was fetid; he almost retched. Then suddenly he heard moans, and he noticed another body sprawled on the concrete floor. After a while he heard the man murmur a few words, something like Pedreira or Pereira or Ferreira. Hugo, he added later. It was important, he said. And with an effort, Marcelo at last made out, after several tries, what the man wanted to tell him: if Marcelo ever got out of this place, he was saying, he wanted him to tell them he hadn't talked. "I beg you, my brother," he finally moaned.

TWO MEN CAME IN WITH A FLASHLIGHT,
went first to the man who'd said his name was Pereira or Pedreira, and bent down to examine him. "Son of a fucking bitch," one spat, "and he knew something, I know he did." He kicked the lifeless body and then they came over to Marcelo.

"Let's go," they said.

As they shoved him into the corridor, he heard those howls again.

They kicked and shoved him into a room with a kind of operating table in the middle of it. They stripped him and went through his pockets: aw, a little black book, how nice, and a book of poetry, the faggot: 'To Marcelo, this December 31, 1972—Always, always, Ulrike.' Ulrike, eh? And everybody thought he was gay . . . And a little dictionary in his coat pocket—look, Turco, listen to this—'To Scarecrow, I hope this comes in handy. Best wishes, Marcelo.' To Scarecrow, no less! I told you the asshole didn't even know his ABCs!"

Another man, the one they had called Gordo, said enough bullshit, they had to get to work.

They dragged Marcelo up onto the marble table, spread-eagled him, and tied his wrists and ankles down. Then they threw a bucket of cold water on him and brought the prongs of an electric cattle prod close to his eyes, so close he tried futilely to pull his head away. They asked him if he knew what this was.

"It's an Argentine invention," laughed Turco. "And people say all we Argentines know how to do is steal other people's ideas! Biggest national industry, and you better not deny it!"

Gordo, who seemed to be in charge, came over to Marcelo and said:

"You are going to tell us everything, my friend, absolutely everything. And the sooner you start talking, the better. We're in no hurry, see? We can work on you for a day or a week, and you won't croak on us. We know how to do that. So I'd say that before we get started on you, you'd do well to tell us some things. And I warn you—we've got another friend of Scarecrow's next door there. You heard all that screaming? And he talked about all kinds of things, too—but we want to know what *you* know. So start talking: how you met him, what he's told you, his contacts, whether you know Rubio, or Cachito. Scarecrow's disappeared, you know. Where's he hiding? You live with him, you're his best friend. We already know that. So there's no point in you denying any of it. What we want to know is other stuff. Who he's working with, who the people are that he sees, who the people were that went to his room on Independencia, that kind of stuff. And who's Ulrike?"

Nobody ever went to that room. Ulrike was just a friend. He never asked Scarecrow anything.

So they'd just decided to live with each other for no reason? Where had he met him? Was Marcelo by chance not aware that Scarecrow had been in the guerrillas with Ché?

No, he didn't know any of that.

So one day he just happened to run into Scarecrow on the street and they decided to become roommates.

Marcelo did not reply.

Nobody had introduced them? He just liked the asshole's face? Who was the connection? Why had Scarecrow come to Buenos Aires in the first place? How had he wound up here? Where had Marcelo first seen him?

In the café on Rivadavia and Azcuénaga.

Okay, very good, excellent. But thousands of people go there. How did they get together? Did he know who Rubio was?

Marcelo didn't answer.

All right, do it.

First they put the cattle prod to his gums, and he felt as if he were being stuck with thousands of burning needles. His body arched violently, and he screamed. When they stopped, a terrible shame swept him. How could he have screamed? He'd never hold out. It was with horror that he thought it—he would never be able to hold out.

"Listen, that was just a little demonstration. A free sample, you know? It's barely the beginning. You saw the guy on the floor in the cell? So come on, let's not waste time here. There are lots of things we already know, don't worry. And you shouldn't let your body get messed up forever just to keep a few stupid secrets. In the long run they'll come out, but by then you'll be pretty fucked up. So come on. You can start by just telling us how you met Scarecrow."

"In the café on the corner of Azcuénaga and Rivadavia."

"Yeah, so you said. I'll buy that. But how was it? Did he come up to you all of a sudden, just sort of say Hey, I'd like to come live with you?"

"He asked me for a light."

"And you gave him one."

"Of course."

Gordo turned and asked if anybody'd found any cigarettes or matches in his pockets. No. Just a little tiny dictionary, a book of poetry, one of those asthma inhaler things, an address book, and seven hundred and some pesos.

Gordo turned back to Marcelo and said sweetly:

"See? It's no use lying to us. You didn't have any cigarettes or matches. I'm telling you for your own good, my friend, don't fuck around with me."

He'd run out.

Huh?

He'd run out of matches.

Cigarettes and matches at the same time?

They laughed.

So let's see: what brand did he smoke?

Jockey Club, he said at random.

Oh? Jockey Club? How much did a pack cost?

He couldn't answer, he didn't know. They stuffed a dirty rag in his mouth.

"Give it to him. Turn it up."

They turned up the voltage and held the prod under his arms, to his groin, the bottom of his feet. His body was violently shaken.

"Okay, stop. . . . All right, my friend. I see you're the hard-headed type. Stupid. You're going to ruin your life for nothing. When the government changes, we'll still be right here. And you will be, too. *If* you survive. So let it out, kid."

They removed the rag from his mouth.

"We know that one day Rubio was there, that you met Rubio through a law student named Adalberto. Adalberto Palacios. So see, we know you've been lying. And you can also see, my friend, that other people have been more cooperative."

Marcelo was stunned and terrified. But it couldn't have been Rubio. That left Palacios.

"That's not true," he said.

Gordo smiled at him good-naturedly.

"Listen, I'm going to tell you something—we know you're not a guerrilla, that you couldn't kill a fly. We know a whole lot more about you around here than you could ever imagine. We're not torturing you because of that, I want you to understand that—we're torturing you because you know things, and you're going to tell us. We're putting a lot of faith in you right now, for that very reason. Because you like poetry, I mean, because you're, I don't know, delicate. Right? Don't take that the wrong way. I mean, do you think I gig you a little because I like it? I've got a family, too, you know. What do you think we are, monsters? You think we never had a mother too?"

His face was almost kindly.

"Well anyway, now that we've broken the ice a little, now that you see we're not as bad as people say, let's talk about this. You said he came up to you to ask you for a light, and you said you gave him a light, is that right?"

"Yes."

"And we've proved that you were lying."

"Yes."

"So now you see there's no use lying. We always wind up finding

392

out when people lie to us. So let's go back to the café on Rivadavia and Azcuénaga. We know you met him there, that much is true. How did you become friends? Did he just walk up to you and start talking about the guerrillas? Because you know very well that nobody in the guerrillas talks to anybody about it unless they trust the person with their life. Why should he have trusted you, I mean, a perfect stranger? Because he *has* talked to you about the guerrillas, hasn't he?"

No, never. He didn't know who Scarecrow really was. He just knew he was a Tucumano, that he'd worked at a sugar mill, that the mill closed down, that he didn't have a job, that he went to work at Fiat and then lost that job, too.

But he'd never explained why he'd lost those jobs?

No.

Or why he'd gone to Bolivia?

No.

So Marcelo didn't know that Scarecrow was in a guerrilla group here?

No.

And there had never come to their room a guy about twenty-seven years old, tall, with glasses and curly black hair, a guy that limped a little?

That was a perfect description of Lungo. Marcelo was shocked. Now he was sure of it—it was Palacios that had talked.

No. He'd never seen such a man.

Gordo looked at him for a long time, without a word. Then he turned around and said, "Give it to him, all the way."

They stuffed the dirty rag in his mouth again and he heard Turco say, "This one's going to sing the national anthem. Watch."

They started with his gums, then went under his arms, the bottom of his feet, his testicles. It was like his flesh being ripped off with red-hot pincers. Then everything went white and his heart was pounding against the walls of his chest like somebody banging his fists against a door, trying to escape from a room filled with raging, slathering dogs. Then the discharges stopped.

"Take the rag out."

Where were the weapons? Who were the ringleaders? Where did Lungo live? Where was their hideout? Had they had any connection with the attack at Calera? Who were the people that went to the café on the corner of Paseo de Colón and San Juan?

He could hardly speak, his tongue felt like dry, fluffy cotton. He moaned something; Gordo brought his ear down. What?

"Water," Marcelo murmured.

Yes, they'd give him water, of course they would. But first he had to answer.

He thought of Scarecrow, that sad childhood in the impoverished hut, his sufferings in Bolivia, the stoic silence of Ché Guevara. At that moment, Scarecrow's life depended on one word that Marcelo might speak. Marcelo had never done anything brave, never done anything that mattered, even—never done anything to relieve a single child's sadness or hunger. What had he ever been good for?

Gordo held up a bottle of cold Coca-Cola.

Was he going to talk?

Marcelo made no sign.

The man opened the bottle and poured the bubbling liquid over Marcelo's body.

"The rag," he said angrily. "And give him the maximum."

The horror began again, until everything went black and he lost consciousness. When he came to himself once more, as though he were rising up to the surface through a sea of red-hot coals, he heard words he couldn't quite make out, something about a doctor, a needle. He felt a sting somewhere. Then he heard somebody say, "Leave him be for a while."

They began to talk among themselves, something about Sunday, a beach at Quilmes. They were laughing, complaining about missing a New Year's Eve party. He heard names: Turco, Petrillo or Potrillo, Gordo, Chief. The screams and howls began again in some nearby room. Why don't they just cut it out of him? somebody said. Then one of them came over to him and said, "Hear that? That's your friend Palacios. We ain't puttin' a rag in his mouth so you c'n hear it real good for yourself—we'll bring 'im in here and show 'im to you later." The man laughed.

His head was full of cotton burning with a blue alcohol flame, he was so thirsty he couldn't bear it, and he heard them say, "Shit, this beer's hot." The screams continued. Scarecrow, no more than skin and bones, the rickety hut, the Comandante, the New Man.

"Okay, boys, back to work," somebody said, Gordo no doubt. "The doctor says to let him off for a while."

They took off the ropes that tied him down and threw him on the floor.

"Bring in that little whore and Buzzo what's his name."

They dragged the two people in by their hair.

Marcelo had been propped up against one wall, and they forced him to watch: the girl was nineteen or twenty, the boy a little older. They looked like working-class kids, good kids.

They stripped the young man they'd called Buzzo and tied him down to the same table on which they had tortured Marcelo, while the others held the girl. Gordo told Buzzo it would be a good idea for him to talk before they used the cattle prod on him or had to use his girlfriend.

"We already know that the two of you are in the Montos. Cachito already told us everything—the attack on the Tigre detachment, the assault on the hospital in San Fernando, the death of Corporal Medina. Now *you*, my friend, are going to give us some details we still need. Tell us about the connection with the Córdoba group."

What connection?

He didn't know anything about it? "May as well get started on this one," Gordo ordered.

Marcelo began to see from the outside what he himself had been put through; the same horrors were repeated, the same monstrous contortions.

"Stop."

They brought the girl over to him.

"What's your name?"

"Esther."

Esther, men have done you wrong, somebody sang.

"Shut up," Gordo said. "Now, then, Buzzo, where'd you meet her?"

"In the factory."

"And what's she to you?"

"My girlfriend."

"Nothing to do with politics, right?"

"No, nothing. She's just my girlfriend."

"And you never talk about politics, right?"

"Everybody talks about politics these days."

"Oh, I see. So she knew that you're with the Montos, I presume."

"I'm not with the Montos."

They all laughed out loud.

"Okay, all right. We aren't going to argue. Strip her."

Buzzo screamed out, "Don't! Stop it!" His cry was almost savage. Gordo looked at him. With icy courtesy, he asked:

"Are you going to stop us?"

Buzzo looked at him and said, "That's true, I can't do anything now. But if I ever get out of here alive, I swear I'll find every one of you, and I'll kill you."

They all stood for a moment without moving. Their faces showed great delight at this. Then Gordo turned to them and asked them what they were waiting for. They ripped her clothes off her. Marcelo could not take his horrified eyes off the scene; there was a kind of nightmarish fascination about it. The girl was modest, poor, but she had the humble beauty of Indian features that some of the women of Santiago del Estero have. Yes, now he remembered the few words she had spoken; she had the Santiago accent. The men ripped her clothes off with shouts and sick laughter, one of them above all, a huge, dirty man who yelled "Me first!"

As the one they called Turco, maddened, almost drooling, threw himself onto her, and as the others egged him on with shouts and laughter, some of them pawing her, others beginning to masturbate, Buzzo shouting *Esther! Esther!*, Marcelo lost consciousness. From then on he had no sense of time or of place. He suddenly woke up on the filthy floor of a cell again (the same cell as before?), with the same smell of piss and excrement, then he was carried off to be tortured on the table, or was kicked in the belly, or had his scrotum squeezed and twisted. Everything was mixed up, jumbled, confused—the names they asked him about, the shouts, the insults, the spittle in his face. At one point he woke up to find he was being dragged by the hair down a barely lit hallway and thrown again into the sticky, stinking cell.

He thought he was alone. But in a while, in the dimness, through eyes so swollen and inflamed that they felt like they were bulging out of their sockets, and through which everything looked like some

396

murky phantasmagoria, he thought he saw another man, sitting on the floor.

The man murmured something. He didn't know, they were accusing him of being a member of FAR. FAR? He'd said yes to everything, he was so afraid. What did Marcelo think? He was pleading, apologizing.

"Yes," mused Marcelo.

Yes what? the other man pleaded.

Everything was all right, he shouldn't worry.

The other man fell silent. They could hear more screaming, and then came the intervals of silence (the rag in the mouth, thought Marcelo). He heard the other man dragging himself over to him.

"What's your name?" he asked.

"Marcelo."

"Did they torture you much?"

"Pretty much."

"Did you tell them everything?"

"Of course."

The other man fell silent again. Then he said he needed to pee but he couldn't.

Marcelo dozed off. It was a sleep like sleep on a burning desert bristling with tongues of fire. Then he's kicked outside. They've come back. How much time has passed? One day? Two? He doesn't know. He just wants to die and get it over with. They drag him by the hair into a brightly lit room, another torture chamber. They show him a shapeless mass, a body covered with bruises, wounds, blood, and filth.

"You don't recognize him, huh?"

It's Gordo again, with his icy voice.

Now Marcelo thinks he does recognize him, maybe, when he moves a little, tries to make a sign, maybe a sign of friendship. When he realizes who it is, he faints again. He wakes up in that same room, they've given him something, a shot of something in the arm.

They bring in a pregnant woman, a doctor examines her. "You can go ahead," he says, "she's okay for it."

"You're going to lose that baby, you little whore," he says.

They use the cattle prod on her breasts, on her vagina, on her anus, under her arms. They rape her. Then they ram a wooden rod up her, while beside him someone is screaming, howling.

"It's her husband," Gordo tells Marcelo.

He feels like he's about to vomit, but he can't. They want him to tell them whether he knows this pregnant woman, whether he knew Buzzo, Esther, when he had seen Cachito. It all gets mixed up in his mind, he doesn't understand anything anymore. They continue torturing the woman, they tell her they're going to make her have the baby there on the torture table, they're going to pull the baby out of her.

Gordo tells Marcelo he's going to make him wish he'd never been born if he doesn't tell them what Scarecrow was doing in the last few weeks. Was there a tall boy, with lots of freckles? Did they call him Red? Did he know this other guy? Had he seen him with Scarecrow in the café on Independencia? They have untied the woman and now have begun to use the prod on Marcelo. When he faints, he wakes up again on the cement floor of his cell. Everything seems darker. In a while the men with the flashlight come in. They look for the other man. "Son of a bitch," one of them disgustedly says, turning the flashlight on the man. "Look at that. Where'd he get that razor blade? There was a lot left to get out of this motherfucker, too. Son of a bitch." They drag him out, and Marcelo is alone.

He feels like urinating, but he can't—the pain almost makes him faint. He has a strange dream, almost like a dream out of his childhood—like utterly pure images in a pigsty. Half awake, he finds himself murmuring a prayer, he's kneeling beside his little bed, asking for sweet things from Jesus, his mother is there beside him, "Now it's time to go to sleep," she says. Baby Jesus, that was it. And suddenly, in a hoarse whisper, he is murmuring *God, my God, why hast thou forsaken me!* But then he feels ashamed of himself, he thinks about that pregnant woman. That walk with Ulrike in the Plaza Retiro seems a century ago, a million miles away, on another planet. God has had an attack of lunacy, and the whole universe is breaking into pieces, there is howling and blood everywhere, oaths and imprecations and the mutilated corpses of men and women and children. He thinks about Toribio again, he repeats the prayer from his childhood, as though in that hell it could have some power. Where was God? What was he trying to prove with all this torture, with the

398

rape of a woman as lowly and humble as Esther? What did he mean, what was he trying to say? Maybe he was trying to tell them something, tell everybody something, but they just couldn't understand. At that moment boyfriends were taking girlfriends by the hand, there were kisses, a good outlook for happiness, there were signs of it everywhere, there was laughter, the ships were blowing or had already blown their sirens. "A new year, a new beginning." Or had several days already passed? What day was it? It was always night where he was. Oh, yes, the other man had said he'd told them everything, but that it was all lies, he'd accused innocent people, they'd made him sign something. He thought he'd cried, though down there you couldn't make out gestures, couldn't hear anybody crying. What? He'd killed himself with a razor blade? What about the women, he thought, the women: Marta Delfino, Norma Morello, Aurora Martins, Mirta Cortese, Rosa Vallejo, Ema de Benedetti, Elena da Silva, Elena Codan, Silvia Urdampilleta, Irma Betancourt, Gabriela Yofre. It was like a parade of ghosts through Hell. The Christian martyrs, he thought. Being devoured by flames was nothing in comparison with this. Then he began to rave again, he became delirious, and all the names ran together, and the times.

Then the men with the flashlight came back. They dragged him by the hair to the torture room.

"Okay," said Gordo, "the fun's over. You tell us what we want to know or you're not getting out of here alive."

They put him up on the table again. The room was filled with smoke, there were cries, laughter, insults. Everything had become a nightmare of hellish confusion. "We're going to keep working on you, faggot, till you spill everything you know." They twisted his testicles, stuck the cattle prod into his mouth, his anus, his urethra, they slammed their hands into his ears. Then he heard them bring in a woman and strip her, then they threw her on top of him. They used the cattle prod on the two of them at once, yelled horrible things at the woman, threw pails of water on them; then they untied them and threw them onto the floor, where they beat and kicked them. He fainted, and when he came to, there was the doctor, with the needle. "He can't take any more," the doctor said. But it was like a pack of wild dogs turned loose on him. They grabbed him and dunked his head into a bucket full of piss, and when he thought he was going to die they pulled his head out and started with the same questions again. But he didn't understand what they were saying anymore. Everything had disappeared, into a landscape convulsed by earthquakes and fire, earthquakes and fire over and over again, and one could hear the screams, the heartrending cries of people crushed by blocks of iron and cement, bleeding, mutilated, crushed and torn by glowing-hot bars of iron. Before he lost consciousness, he felt a wave of unspeakable joy: *I'm going to die*, he thought.

THE THREE WISE MEN ARE ON THEIR WAY NOW,
Nacho told himself, with glum sarcasm. From the darkness thrown over him by the trees on the Avenida del Libertador, he saw, at last, the pearl-colored Chevy Sport driven by Rubén Pérez Nassif. It pulled up and stopped in front of the building across the street. Pérez Nassif got out of it, with Agustina. It was approximately two o'clock in the morning of January 6. They went into the apartment building.

He stayed at his observation post until about four, and then he left, presumably to go home. He walked with his hands in the pockets of his faded jeans, his back bent and stooped, his head down.

MORE OR LESS AT THE SAME HOUR
the body of Marcelo Carranza, naked, unrecognizable, was lying on the floor of a dimly lit hallway. The man called Gordo asked if he was still alive. One of the men, Correntino, went over to it, but it made him sick to touch it; it was covered with spittle, blood, and vomit.

"Well?"

Correntino gave it a kick in the kidneys, but there was no moan.

"I'd say he was ready," he nodded.

"Okay, sack him up."

They brought in a canvas sack, put him in it, wrapped a rope around and around it, and went off for a drink. Then they came back and took the sack out to a car. They threw the awkward bundle into the trunk and drove off toward the Riachuelo. At a place alongside the river they came to a garbage dump, where they stopped the car. They took out the sack, but when they put it on the ground one

400

of the men thought he saw a movement. "Hey, I b'lieve this guy's still alive," he muttered. They put their ears to the sack and it did seem like they heard moans, some sort of murmur, coming from inside. They carried the sack over to the edge of the river, tied several large chunks of lead to it, and then, swinging it back and forth to give it impetus, they hefted the body into the water. They stood for a moment looking, and then Correntino said, "I'll tell you, we had our work cut out for us with that one, brother." They got into the car again and one of them said he'd like a cup of coffee and a mortadella sandwich.

"What time is it?"

"Not quite five."

"Well then, let's go back. They won't open for a while yet."

THE LITTLE HOUSE SEEMED MORE FORSAKEN THAN EVER
and the squeaking of the rusty iron gate louder than at other, less lonely, times. Milord greeted him with the noisy barking that was inevitable when he'd been shut up all by himself for a long time in that rundown shack. Nacho absentmindedly pushed him away with his foot and threw himself down on his bed. With his hands crossed behind his head, he stared at the ceiling. He felt like listening to the Beatles one last time. Making a great effort, he got up and put them on.

Julia, Julia, oceanchild, calls me.
Julia, seashell eyes, windy smile, calls me.
Julia, sleeping sand, silent cloud.

Sitting on the floor, his head drooping on his chest, he could tell that his eyes were swollen. With a sudden blow of his fist, he smashed the arm of the record player.

He got up, left the shack, and began walking along Conde toward the railroad tracks, followed clandestinely by Milord. When he came to the crossing at Mendoza, he stopped a moment, but then almost immediately he began climbing up the embankment, scrambling through the trash and papers and rusty cans that littered the side of the steep hill until he came to the tracks. He sat on the ties

401

between the rails. From up here his cloudy eyes could see the first timid signs of the dawn, which in silent modesty was beginning to shine on the scattered clouds, on the glass windows of the tall buildings that had been constructed among the remains of old houses, on distant roofs here and there: those windows that open, slowly and with a degree of renewed hope, in the house from which the coffin has just been removed. *Julia, Julia, oceanchild*, Nacho murmured as he waited for the train, thinking with glum hopefulness that it couldn't be too long now. Just then, though, he felt the dog's tongue lick his hand. He realized the dog had been following him at a distance. With fury apparently out of all proportion to the dog's offense, he cried, "Leave me alone, goddammit!" and hit him.

Milord, panting, looked at him with pained eyes. As Nacho contemplated the dog, the fragment of a hated book came to his mind: War may be absurd or wrong, but the platoon to which one belongs, the friends that are sleeping in the trench while one stands guard, that is absolute. D'Arcangelo, for example. A dog, perhaps.

"Stinking son of a bitch!" he cried, thinking of the author.

And an even more insane fury made him leap at the animal and kick him wildly. At last he collapsed onto the rails, crying.

When he could look to see what had happened to the dog, there he was, still sitting there, so old he was useless.

"Go home, stupid," he said with the remains of his anger, little flames of it still rising up here and there after the great fire. But since the dog didn't move, but just kept staring at him with those eyes (of pain? of reproach?), Nacho began to grow calmer little by little, until desolately, patiently, gently, he begged the dog to go home, to just leave him alone. His voice was soft and loving and although he didn't dare even to whisper it, he wanted to say, "Forgive me, my friend."

Milord's uneasiness was soothed at that, and at last he wagged his tail, though more with the remains of old happiness, those crumbs left on the floor after the party's over, than with real strength or cheerfulness.

Nacho climbed down the embankment again, and when he got to the bottom, he patted Milord and begged him again to go on home. Milord looked at him for a moment, not quite sure whether he could trust him, and then, almost grudgingly, he turned and began to go, limping, and every once in a while casting a look back.

Nacho climbed back up onto the tracks, through the litter of dirty paper and cans and rags, and sat down again between the two iron rails. Through his tears he looked once again, for the last time, at the trees on the vacant land around him, the mercury lamp down there, the length of Conde: fragments of a life without meaning, the last fragments he would ever see.

Then he lay down across the tracks and closed his eyes, and now, isolated in the darkness of that phantasmagoria, small sounds began to take on importance. Soon he heard a noise he thought might be a rat. He opened his eyes and saw that it was Milord again. The dog's grieving eyes seemed some new kind of blackmail, and Nacho once again was enraged; he struck the dog again and again, shouting insults at him, and threats. But then he began to grow calmer; he was tired, and he was defeated by the dog, and then he heard the train. Slowly, dejectedly, he began to climb down the embankment and walk toward home, followed closely by Milord.

He went in his room and began to pull out his clothes and throw them into a duffel bag. He took from the Treasure Chest of his childhood a magnifying glass, a badge that had belonged to Carlucho, two marbles, a little compass, and a magnet. He took *The Catcher in the Rye* and two or three other books down from the bookshelf, pulled the picture of the Beatles when they were still together down off the wall, and then the photo of the naked little Vietnamese girl running alone through a flaming village. He put it all into his duffel bag, along with the package of the things he was writing. He went out into the yard, tied everything to the motorbike, then tied the dog on top of the duffel bag, and started the motor. But just then he had an idea. He turned off the engine, got off, untied everything, and took out the notebook with his manuscripts. He set the package down on the ground and lit it, and he watched those searchers for the absolute who had begun to live (and suffer) in those pages go up in flames. Forever, he thought at that moment.

He began putting everything back on the scooter when Agustina arrived. Mutely, like a sleepwalker, she went into the bedroom.

Her brother sat there on the motorbike, paralyzed, not knowing what to do anymore. Pensively he got off and slowly went into the house. Agustina was lying on the bed, still dressed, staring at the ceiling, smoking a cigarette.

Nacho went over to her, looking at her morosely. And then, suddenly, screaming *Whore!*, repeating it in hysterical fury, he threw himself at her, took the body of his sister between his knees, and began to smash her face with his clenched fists. She did nothing to defend herself; she lay there inert, her body as slack and yielding as a rag doll, which only increased her brother's fury. He ripped her clothes into tatters, tearing them from her in sadistic rage. And when, weeping and still screaming, he had stripped her naked, he began to spit on her: first on her face and then, spreading her legs, on her sex. And at last, since she still lay without the slightest resistance to his attack, looking at him with open eyes filled with tears, his hands fell and he collapsed onto the limp body of his sister, sobbing. He lay there for a very long time. And then he got up and left. He started the engine and sped off down Monroe. He still didn't know where he was going.

ON JANUARY 6, 1973,
Natalicio Barragán woke up very late, his head filled with needles and shards of broken glass. He lay staring at the ceiling for a long time, but he wasn't really seeing it. He was trying to think about something, but he didn't know what it was exactly that he wanted to think. Like water pipes that grow slowly more and more corroded from the effects of time and the acids they are exposed to, his thoughts, like drips of dirty, clotted water, could barely pass down channels now closing, clogged, constricted. And he was about to get out of bed to fix himself some *mate* when suddenly, like a flash of lightning through a murky, lowering night sky, there came into his mind the memory of the vision.

He squeezed his head between his hands and sat there for long seconds, wavering and afraid.

Then he did get up, and as he fixed his *mate* the image of the fire-breathing beast grew more and more vivid, more terrible, until at last he could not bear the memory, and throwing the *mate* to the floor, he ran out into the street.

404

The morning was sunny, the sky perfectly clear. It was about eleven o'clock, and on this festive day—the gifts to children, the visits to friends and family, the celebration of Epiphany, the day of the Three Wise Men's visit to the Child—people were strolling down the street or sitting in doorways drinking *mate* and chatting with their neighbors, the children beside them playing with their toys. Loco Barragán studied their faces, and tried to hear what they were saying. But neither their expressions nor their words were strange in any way: it could have been any holiday in La Boca.

Standing on the corner of Brandsen and Pedro de Mendoza, leaning against the same wall that had propped him up at midnight last night, he looked up at the same sky, through the same masts. He could hardly believe he was looking at that clean, clear sky, without a cloud in sight, without anything out of the ordinary at all, in fact, while people were walking around like nothing had happened.

He decided to go down to Nicolás' shoe-repair shop. There he was, working, like always, holiday or not. Barragán chatted with him for a while. About what? Nothing, nothing, but it was as clear as could be both that he hadn't seen anything strange the night before and that nobody had mentioned anything to him about seeing anything strange.

Toward nightfall, after he'd sold all the papers Berlingieri gave him to sell, he went to the café. In the face of the absolute ignorance of the vision which everyone showed, his terror grew from hour to hour. Everybody in the bar was talking about the Boca team's chances against Racing. But he sat mute, with his little glass of raw-tasting rum between his folded hands. He was waiting for the day to end, for night to fall, with a fear that he carefully tried to conceal but that revealed itself (curiously) in a tingling, itching sensation all over his skin and a coldness of his hands and feet, in spite of the summeriness of the afternoon.

He wandered around, here and there, but at night he was back in the café, and he stayed until closing time: two o'clock in the morning. Then he took the same path he had the night before, down Almirante Brown, then down Brandsen to Dársena, all the while keeping his eyes carefully on the sidewalk. At the corner of Brandsen and Pedro de Mendoza he leaned against that wall, that same wall, and he closed his eyes tight. His heart was pounding, the tingling of his skin had grown unbearable, and his hands were covered with icy sweat.

At last he got up the nerve to open his eyes and look up. Yes, there it was, flames shooting from its nose, with eyes of blood. It writhed there in silent fury, which made it all the more terrifying: as though someone had come up to him and in absolute silence threatened him, and he were totally alone, and no one else could see the terrible danger.

He closed his eyes. Almost at the point of fainting, he collapsed against the wall. He stood there for a long time, until he could finally find the strength to go off to his room in the run-down rooming house, keeping his eyes firmly fixed on the ground.

The next day the same weird phenomenon occurred: everyone acted like nothing had happened, talked the same way they always did (about politics, the soccer game), made the same jokes in Chichín's bar. Barragán, mute, looked at them all in stupefaction, but he didn't have the nerve to tell them what once he would have said. And when he returned to his room, he was very careful not to look up at the sky.

Several days went by like that, and he began to feel sadder and sadder; he felt that he was alone, that he had no one to talk to, yet that he was committing some shameful act of cowardice or betrayal. Then one night, when he went into his dark room, there was a glow, a glow that he had seen before. In the center of the glow he saw the face of Christ, looking at him with a mixture of pity and sternness, as though Barragán were a child whom he loved but who was doing something he ought to know better than to do. Then the vision disappeared.

Natalicio Barragán knew very well what he was being reproached for. Fifteen years ago, almost twenty now, he had seen this same vision, and he had begun to preach in the street, at Chichín's bar. He had foretold a fire that would sweep over Buenos Aires, but everybody laughed and made fun of him. "Come on, Loco, tell us what that Christ of yours told you," they would call, and he, with his glass of harsh *aguardiente*, would tell them. There would be times of blood and fire, jewould say, shaking an admonitory finger at the scoffers and laughers mocking him, pushing and jeering him; the world, he would say, would

406

be purged by blood and fire. And then one frigid afternoon in June, 1955 death rained down on thousands of workers in the Plaza de Mayo, and Barragán's own wife was killed, blown to pieces by the bombs; when night fell, fires lit up the gray sky of Buenos Aires, and everyone remembered Loco Barragán, who from that black day forth was not the same half-crazy but gentle man he had been. He grew silent, his eyes seemed to hold some terrible secret, and he withdrew into himself, as though into some deep cave: something in the most profound depths of the man's spirit told him that the day that had been was almost nothing, and that much greater sadness, many more sorrows, were to be loosed on mankind, all mankind, one day not far away. Meantime, for all these years, he had not spoken of what he knew. Yet the new guys who came into the bar, kids who in years past might have inherited the tradition of laughing at Loco Barragán, now fell silent when he came in.

He did not preach anymore. He turned sullen and withdrawn.

But when the dragon appeared to him, he realized that the times were coming, and that he had a duty to fulfill.

So Christ knew what that expression of pity and stern sadness would mean to Barragán. Yes, Barragán was a sinner, he lived on the charity of other men, from the sale of the newspapers Berlingieri let him have. He was a bum, and to cap it all off, he kept the Vision secret.

That day, as night was falling, and after meditating for hours as he walked along the Dársena, Loco Barragán went to the café. He went in and ordered a drink and then he turned and faced Loiácono, Berlingieri, the little bowlegged Olivari, and poor lame Acuña. They were discussing the soccer game against Racing. He began to speak:

"Boys, last night I saw Christ."

A deathly silence fell in the bar. The young men playing pool froze, and everyone's eyes turned on Barragán. No one smiled. Barragán, standing stiff and tall, looked at each man in turn. His body was trembling. Then he went on:

"But before that, late the night before, after midnight it was, I was standing on the corner of Brandsen and Pedro de Mendoza, and I had another vision."

Everyone looked at him tensely. In a quivering voice, Barragán continued:

407

"Up in the sky, far out at sea, and it covered half the sky. Its tail curled all the way down to the earth."

He stopped, frightened, perhaps, or embarrassed to go on. But then he said, in almost a whisper:

"A red dragon. With seven heads. And fire and smoke coming out its nostrils."

There was a long silence. Then Natalicio Barragán continued:

"Because the time is near, and this Dragon foretells blood. Not one stone will be left upon another. Then the Dragon will be enchained."

A WINGÈD RAT.
UNABLE TO MAKE A MOVEMENT OR A SOUND (why call out? so people would come running in and see him and be so filled with disgust and revulsion that they clubbed him to death?), Sabato watched his feet turn slowly into the shriveled black claws of a bat. He felt no pain, not even the tingling that one might expect from the shriveling and drying out of the skin. But he did feel repugnance, and the repugnance grew stronger and stronger as the transformation continued: first his feet, then his legs, then, little by little, his torso. The revulsion grew even more terrible when the wings formed, perhaps because they were of flesh, and had no feathers. At last, his head. Until that moment he had followed the process with his sense of sight. Although he had not had the courage to touch those bat's legs with his hands, which were still those of a human, he could not bear not to stare in horrified fascination at the gigantic rat's claws, covered with the wrinkled and leathery skin of some ancient mummy, that were now his. Then had come, as we have said, an even more striking and horrifying thing—the sprouting of the enormous cartilaginous wings. But when the process reached his head, and he began to feel his face stretch and lengthen into a muzzle, the hairs on his nose grow long and black, and his nose begin to sniff at the air about him, the horror of it was indescribable. He lay for a time paralyzed in his bed, where the transformation had come upon him by surprise. He tried to stay calm, to invent some plan. The plan would have to include silence, because one cry, one scream would bring people who would kill him without mercy, beat him to

408

death with iron bars. There was, of course, the fragile hope that they would recognize in that nauseating creature the features of himself, especially as it was not logical that such a creature would have taken over his room, his bed, so inexplicably.

In the rat's head he now possessed, ideas were furiously boiling.

He sat up, at last, and once upright he tried to calm himself, to take things as they were. With care, as though inside a body that did not belong to him (which in some way it did not), he shifted on the bed until he was in the position a human would take to get out of it: on the edge of the bed, that is, with his feet hanging downward. But he realized that his feet no longer reached the floor. From the contraction of his bones, he thought, he must have shrunk, though not all that much, really, and that would explain, too, why his skin was so wrinkled. He figured his new height at about four feet. He got up, and he looked at himself in the mirror.

He stood unmoving for a long time. And then he lost his composure—he wept in silence at the horror.

There were people who kept rats in their houses—physiologists like Houssay, for instance, that experimented with the repulsive creatures. But he, Sabato, had always belonged to the class of people who are nauseated at the mere sight of a rat. It is easily imagined, then, what he felt as he stood before a four-foot-tall rat with cartilaginous wings and the wrinkled, black skin of those hideous creatures. And him *inside it*!

His eyes had grown weaker, and then he suddenly realized that the weakening of his vision was not some passing phenomenon, some product of his emotional state, but rather would actually in time grow worse, until he became totally blind. And he was proven correct: within a few seconds, though those seconds seemed centuries filled with nightmare and disaster, his sight faded to utter blackness. He stood paralyzed, though he felt his heart pounding in tumult and his skin shivering with cold. Then, little by little, he groped his way toward the bed and sat down on the edge of it.

He stayed there a while. And then, unable to contain himself, forgetting his plan, all his rational precautions, he heard himself give a terrible, chilling cry of anguish, a cry for help. It was not a human cry, though; it was the shrill, stomach-turning shriek of a gigantic wingèd rat. People rushed in, naturally. But no one showed the least surprise. They asked him what had happened, if he felt ill, if he wanted a cup of tea.

It was obvious that no one noticed the change in him.

He did not answer, did not speak a single word, thinking that they'd think he had gone mad. He simply decided to try to live somehow, keeping his secret, even in this horrendous state.

Because that's the way the will to live is: unconditional and insatiable.

GEORGINA AND DEATH,
two words Bruno had tried never to think together, as though by way of that primitive magic he were enabled to stop time. He grew more inclined to this magic as the years went by, even as they swept away, like the icy gusts of August wind that sweep away the dry, bruised leaves, the things he had wanted to preserve forever.

He wandered through the city without direction or aim, until he found himself walking along the Río Cuarto. Soon he picked out the pink Mirador against the gray autumnal sky: it was not just melancholy, it was as lugubrious and enigmatic as Alejandra and Fernando themselves. And the Olmos house reminded him of that strange Señor Valdemar, held on the verge of death by the hypnotist, with the body's viscera exposed, millions of maggots waiting, "the worm," until there came a whisper from the almost-corpse, from the threshold of the sinister portal, begging, desperately, for the love of God, for them to let it all end. And then, when the magus broke the spell, the corpse collapsed into death and instantaneous putrefaction, and the myriads of worms leapt upon it like an army of infinitesimal monsters ravenous with eager hunger.

The tall smokestacks and modern bridges of the Riachuelo stood in contrast to that mansion out of another time—a hard reality, and wavering phantoms. But if the smokestacks and bridges were the reality, then what was the meaning of that enormous leprous house in ruins? And even more than that, what was he himself, then, since his spirit shrank as it beheld the leprosy on the face of those pink and greenish walls? A son, a grandson, a great-great-grandson of hard sailors and soldiers, conquistadors, was he, too, a ghost like don Pancho Olmos, like that Bebe with his honking, out-of-tune

410

clarinet, like that Escolástica with the head of one of her ancestors? Because otherwise, why should he feel that he was beholding the end of that gloomy mansion and its ambiguous inhabitants? Why in that Buenos Aires autumn should he feel that for him, too, there was fast coming a time of desolate, empty streets and dry leaves? His whole life he now saw as a dizzying voyage into nothingness. Saint-Exupéry, sure. He had cheered Martín up, cheered up so many other helpless souls lost in chaos and darkness. But what about himself?

HIS FATHER, HIS FATHER

THE CURT MESSAGE HAD COME ONCE AGAIN, and who could say how many more times it might come yet: "Papa dying. Nicolás." He knew, though, that that last word in the cable was not simply "Nicolás"— in that ironclad system in which the younger owed unconditional obedience to the elder it represented the signature of *all* his brothers. So "Nicolás," hierarchically and economically, meant Nicolás-Sebastián-Juancho-Felipe-Bartolomé-Lelio. And was a tacit rebuke, too, saying "I've had to tell you, to find you, far away, and call you, you who've always been so removed from our house, our fate, and even though you knew that our father was never comforted, never consoled, but who even now is waiting for you to return, before it's too late." Although neither in the telegram nor in any conversation, by any word, would anyone even intimate those feelings, in keeping with the law which required the brothers to keep their deepest emotions hidden. So when they came in contact with other people, people accustomed to ways less harsh, the brothers seemed superficial in their affections; they were only open about emotions connected with matters of no great importance. And so while they could express grief in long discussions about hailstorms or the locusts destroying a friend's crop, they felt it was bad form, somehow, to "go on" about the death of their own child—cases in which the old man Bassán, his face the most rigid of them all, would always say "it is fate." No one ever heard this phrase spoken to refer to the loss of a crop, as though those grand and terrifying powers which acted under the generic name of "fate" were not to be invoked in vain, or for some trivial event.

411

TWENTY-FIVE YEARS LATER, EVERYTHING—THE THINGS,
THE MEN—

everything was the same, and everything was different. Because that
modest railway line was still using the same coaches, the same rails,
the same bridges and stations and outbuildings, the same colors
they'd always used. More worn, older of course—but not as old and
worn as the men that had lived and suffered for the same number
of years. Because, he thought, men wear down faster than things do,
and disappear faster, sooner. And so some humble rocking chair in
the attic recalls the death of the mother that sat in it. Though with
a stupid pathos, after all. Because it could be any little trifle, a ribbon, a book, a matchbox present at the flowering of a grand amour,
some scrap of cloth which once vibrated with magical intensity in
the light of that glow which passion sometimes confers on the simple objects which witness it, any *thing* which, with the clumsy stubbornness that inert *things* possess, survives—yet at the same time
still cannot escape the insignificance of its own nature, and is as
dull and leaden and mute as stage settings when the magic of the
play has gone and the lights are dimmed.

Yes, the coaches on the train were the same, but the men had
changed, or died. And most of all, I am different. Many catastrophes,
and terrible ones, had buried one city on top of another in his soul,
as the burning and the depredations and the earth itself had done
to the nine cities of Troy. And although those who lived on top of
the ancient ruins seemed to live like other men, beneath them they
sometimes heard muted whispering, or murmurs, or faint legends of
extinguished passions, or found scraps of bones, the remains of palaces once kingly, proud.

As Buenos Aires fell away behind him, the stations seemed to
grow more and more like the archetype of the train station of the
pampas, like the successive sketches of a painter trying to find the
ideal form of that obsession which lies far down within his deepest
self: a warehouse of bare brick walls, standing hieratically on the
other side of a dirt road; country men and women in long, loose
black coats and high pants, pensively picking their teeth with a dry
stalk of grass; a buggy, the horses tied up to a rail in front of a
country store, a corrugated-tin shed, a wagon, the stationmaster's
boy in shirtsleeves with his hand on the bell rope.

412

And the train had come to the Santa Ana station, and his child-hood burst forth with straining urgency, because that small corner of the Santa Brígida ranch was suddenly the whole world of the Olmos family, of Georgina, and he could see her, standing behind that fat albino steward of theirs that was always laughing, now saying *Pero qué cosa, ¿no?*, the accent of the pampas, the exclamation of delight so native to that land, and then slapping his pants with the palm of his hand and shaking his hairless head—a man who for Bruno had had no other attribute than that, and only standing still and unchanging in his memory because behind him Bruno had seen, for the first time in his life, Georgina, shy, skinny, redheaded Geor-gina. Yes, those pampas were linked to the most important people who'd ever come into his life. Yet now there was hardly anything left of Santa Brígida, and those fifteen thousand acres of land which was their patrimony in his childhood (even then much reduced from its original size) now did not even belong to the Olmos family, or the Pardos family either, but to people actually indifferent to the fate of those people to them anonymous and unknown. Those lands, on which little Brígida had been killed in an Indian attack long ago, just like in the Westerns from America, those pampas which once had been traveled on horseback for days on end by Captain Olmos, that land which he and his sons Celedonio and Panchito had left, never to return, to follow Lavalle, stood now as distant from his blood as the streets of Buenos Aires (which sometimes bore the names of people of his own line) stood from all those hurrying, indifferent men and women come from all parts of the world to make their fortune, people who in many cases considered their lives there no more than a transitory stay in a second-class hotel.

Now the train began its descent, chugging around the curve to-ward the west, leaving the peak of Santa Ana behind, and then all at once the steeple of the church came into view, and a little while later the grand towers of the mill—those elevators full of wheat at Bassán's mill, his own house, his childhood. And when the train at last pulled into Capitán Olmos—identical to what it had always been—Bruno almost felt that for all those long years he had been living under some sort of illusion, in some pointless creation of lights and setting and sound without weight or texture, and the events that he'd thought he had lived through faded away, the way

413

dreams lose life, lose force when a man wakes up, and turn into uncertain fragments of some play, every second more unreal. And that sensation induced him to think that if "the real" is what remains identical to itself, a hard, unchanging piece of eternity, then the only thing really real was his childhood. But just as when we awake the life of day is still contaminated with baseness, and we ourselves not what we were before those dreams, so the return to childhood was sullied, saddened by the sufferings through which he had lived. And if childhood was eternity, that sadness, that sullying of it by life kept him from seeing it as it seemed it ought to be seen, clean and crystalline; instead, he saw it dimmed and blurred as though through a clouded, dirty pane of glass. It was as though the windows through which we can at some fleeting instants of our lives peek at our own eternities were glass which suffered the changes of time, the passing of the years, growing dirtier, grimier from rainstorms and windstorms, from the crusts and cobwebs of time.

Like a man looking out of the darkness into some bright place, he recognized faces though he himself went unrecognized: Irineo Díaz, with that same (though now threadbare and faded) black hood on his buggy; Commissioner Bengoa, waiting, as he had always done, for the train to arrive; and finally, sitting like some idol, old Medina, who had already been an old man when Bruno was a child, and who apparently was still sitting in the same place he had been when Bruno had seen him last, thirty-five years ago: thoughtful, utterly undaunted, like all Indians, who after a certain point undergo no change—as though time did not run inside him but along beside him, and he could sit there and smoke the same cornsilk cigar forever and watch time run by him, the man as hieratic and indecipherable as though he were the idol of all the Americas, as though he were watching a river flow past carrying things that were merely mortal, things that merely perished.

"Don't you recognize me?"

The old man slowly, slowly raised his eyes. Bruno felt the man's eyes, sunken into the parchment-covered bones of his earthen face, examine him calmly but with minute care. Accustomed to look out at the universe with caution, carefully, almost in fact with no other labor to occupy him but observing that world and registering within himself its meticulous particulars (and with a kind of subtly ironic muteness about him), Medina belonged to that race of scouts, of guides, of men with quiet, probing eyes who knew every rock and blade of grass in the pampas for miles and miles around them, who could pick out the hoofprint of one horse from among the hoofprints of a thousand, and who could direct an army by means of the almost imperceptible scent of a weed. He looked at Bruno with that cunning mistrust he had, which only showed itself in certain tiny wrinkles at the corners of his eyes. And in the same way as erasing a pencil sketch leaves those features which because they were essential were the lines most impressed into the pad, the features of the long-ago Bruno began to be revealed to him. And then, rising up through the thirty-five years of absence, of rains and deaths, of winds and happenings, came a sober yet implacable pronouncement from the enigmatic depths of Medina's memory. He moved his lips almost imperceptibly and said, without the least emotion or nostalgia, if in fact that sort of feeling even existed in the heart of that impassive man:

"You are Bruno Bassán."

And then he was rigid again, sitting impassive before the simple events of the world, removed from the violent and almost frightening emotional turmoil of that creature who had gone from boy to man before him.

Bruno walked down the dusty streets, crossed the plaza with its acacia trees and its palms, and at last caught sight of the heavy shape of the mill, heard the measured, regular pounding of the machinery. A fearsome symbol: the indifferent march of things, while in the midst of them the man who with love and hopefulness created them lies dying.

THE DEATH OF MARCO BASSÁN

"HE'S SLEEPING," Juancho said.

In the near-darkness, Bruno heard for the first time the muffled groaning and the short, agitated breathing. As his eyes became used to the dimness of the room, he began to make out what remained: a bedful of bones in a sack of suffering flesh. Rot.

"Yes. You can hardly bear the smell when you first come in. But you get used to it."

415

Bruno looked at his brother. He had been his idol when Bruno was a kid: with his wide-brimmed hat, his broad shoulders, atop that long-tailed dapple gray mare. And when he finally left home, his father had said, "You will never again set foot in this house." Yet to show how precarious such words were before the forces of the species, the forces of blood, Juancho had not only returned, he it was who now cared for his father, day and night.

"Water, Juancho," the old man murmured, waking from his drugged dreams, which in relation to his dreams of old must have been like a dank and slimy swamp full of snakes and wild animals in comparison to a beautiful lake dotted with water birds.

Juancho raised his left arm a bit and gave him a spoonful of water, as though to a sick child.

"Bruno has come."

"Huh? What?" he stammered, his tongue clotted and raglike.

"Bruno. Bruno has come home."

"What? What?"

He peered up, out of his bed, with his whole face, like a blind man.

Juancho opened the shutters a crack. It was then that Bruno saw what survived of the man once so powerful, so filled with energy. From his sunken eyes, like dingy, crazed and cracked balls of greenish glass, milky and almost totally opaque, there seemed to come a little gleam, the tiniest flicker of a dying coal breathed on one last time.

"Bruno," he whispered at last.

Bruno went over to him, leaned over, and made a clumsy attempt at an embrace, always smelling the awful smell.

The old man's words came like those of a drunk.

"Ah, Bruno. I'm a ruin."

It was a struggle that lasted for many days, and fought with the same energy he had marshalled against all the other obstacles of his life. Dying was defeat, and he had never admitted defeat. Bruno told himself that the old man was made of the same stuff as those old Venetians who had raised their city in the face of water and pestilence and plague, who had fought against pirates and hunger. He still had the profile of the Jacobo Sorranzo painted by Tintoretto.

416

He asked himself if it weren't mean-spirited and cowardly of him to leave the room, try to distract himself sometimes, walk through the streets of the town, rather than to keep always before himself the pain of his father, to bear it, to take it upon himself as Juancho did. Then, like a coward, in fragments of thoughts, bits and pieces, snatches of words which were afraid of coming together into one whole thought, he told himself that there was nothing wrong with putting the horror out of his mind. But then almost immediately he would remind himself that even though his father would suffer neither more nor less because he, Bruno, took his mind off the suffering from time to time, put it just for a while out of his memory, it was, somehow, betrayal anyway. Then, ashamed, he would go back to the house and for a while longer pay his niggardly tribute, the tax he owed to the blood, while Juancho would stay in the room, sit in his chair and go on watching over their father—alert to the least sound, helping him, listening to his long, mad fits of delirium.

"Juancho!" he would suddenly cry. "The bed! They're setting the bed afire!" And half sitting up, he would point at the flames—there, at the foot of the bed.

His son would jump up and put out the fire with exaggerated gestures, the exaggeration mimes use when they have to be understood by gesture alone. The old man would be calm, then, for some time.

Then the bed would fall apart, it would have to be fixed. Get a hammer and some nails. Juancho would bring in boards, a hammer, would crawl under the bed and fix it. Later, cringing and shrinking from the headboard, the old man would be terrified; he would point in rage and horror at people, accuse them of being cowards, babble incomprehensibly. Juancho would get up, loudly and theatrically scold the imaginary intruders, and shove them out of the room.

"Juancho . . ." the old man would hiss suddenly, as though he wanted to tell his son a secret.

Juancho would go to the bed and put his ear down to the old man's lips, where the terrible smell of rot came from.

"Robbers," the old man would say. "Robbers have broken in. They're disguised as rats, and they're hiding in the closet. Gaviña—

417

he's the leader. Remember? He was mayor during the time of the conservatives. He was always a thief, a good-for-nothing. He thinks I won't recognize him disguised as a rat."

Old, forgotten faces paraded through the room, old forgotten friends. His memory had grown at once sharp and grotesquely distorted, twisted by his delirium and the morphine.

"Don Juan! Who'd ever've thought you'd turn out to have to work for another man! With the fortune you used to have!"

He would point to the man, shaking his head and smiling as though it were really hard to believe, with a look of ironic disappointment. His son followed the old man's gaze.

"Over there, currying his horse. See who it is? Don Juan Audiffred. Who'd ever've thought it."

"Ah," Juancho would say. "Life has a way of turning sour on you, all right."

Their father talked about it all so normally, and for such long stretches—first he would see monsters or ghosts and then immediately he would be acting sensibly again, he would talk with men dead twenty years as naturally as a minute later he told his son his throat was dry, he'd like a sip of water. When Bruno returned from his walk, his brother would shake his head and laugh at the crazy things that had come into their father's head, Juancho like a father himself, laughing in tenderness and condescension at the comical things that came out of his little son's mouth. But then the delirium would return, and Juancho would have to perform the magical pantomimes again, while Bruno slipped into the parlor, where the brothers all sat and talked about the harvest, the crops, the buying and selling of land, of animals. Bruno would listen to them and, wanting to enter that community of spirit, he would remind them that when he was a kid they would let him weigh the wheat in the balance scale. His brothers would look at him. He mentioned names: Favorito, Barletta, other kinds of wheat they'd planted. His brothers shook their heads scornfully: it was at least twenty years since they'd even heard those names. One of the brothers put out his cigarette and went into his father's room for a moment, to pay his due, and then came back in, somberly.

"What about don Sierra?"

They looked at him in incredulous irony.

418

"Huh?"

He reminded them.

The older brothers had a monopoly on certain memories, and they refused to share them even with the younger ones, much less with Bruno. But surely they remembered: he was a big, fat, potbellied man, with those big ears with long white hairs sprouting out of them.

It was not enough. They looked at each other in mute consultation, and Nicolás, fixing his eyes on Bruno sternly, like a professor at a dissertation defense, demanded that Bruno give the most memorable event or characteristic associated with don Sierra.

Yeah, they all nodded, we'll see.

Bruno thought furiously. They all looked at him slyly, with country cunning. Don Sierra's most unforgettable trait, that was all they wanted to know. The silence was absolute, while Bruno pawed feverishly through his memory.

The pocket watch?

No sir, that wasn't it.

Bruno could see him as clear as day, driving up in his sulky, getting down out of it with the buggy whip in his hand, with that wide belt of his cinched below his huge potbelly, dressed in a shirt and vest, sweaty, wheezing, with his hat fallen down around the nape of his neck, the rope-soled shoes he wore spattered with cow dung.

Did he give up?

He didn't know. If it wasn't his pocket watch, he didn't know.

"The pocket watch!" one of them sneered.

"So what is it then?" Bruno asked, under the impression that they'd set a false trap for him.

"What's what?"

"What's the famous unforgettable thing that's associated with don Sierra?"

The older brothers all looked at each other: another of the peculiar rules of the game, leave the victim gnawed by doubt. Bruno considered those big clumsy men with their broad shoulders and graying hair, waiting for their verdict, not realizing how mad it somehow all was. Then gravely, the oldest of them produced the missing fact: tricking that Englishman O'Donnell.

"Tricking that Englishman O'Donnell?"

Bruno exaggerated his puzzlement, so as not to seem totally defeated—as though even if that trickery had in fact taken place, it was hardly so essential to don Sierra as to be considered even in the mysterious code of the Bassáns as the single most significant fact associated with the man.

Nicolás looked at his brothers: Could anybody think of old man Sierra without thinking of the way he lied to that Englishman O'Donnell? No way, they agreed.

"You're all kidding. This is some kind of joke."

Bruno tried to discover some wink of conspiracy, some gleam in their eyes that would reveal the malicious humor of it all.

Nicolás turned to Marco, the youngest of them (forty-five years old) and ordered him curtly:

"Tell Juancho that if papa goes to sleep, we want him in here."

"Just a second," Bruno suddenly said, mistrustfully.

He went with Marco, fearing Marco would let Juancho in on the joke. When Juancho came into the parlor, he showed the exhaustion of days of sleeplessness and suffering.

"You didn't hear what we were talking about," Nicolás said to him, "so you tell this fool what it is that you always associate with old don Sierra."

"Telling lies to the Englishman O'Donnell."

Marco came back in. "He woke up, he wants some water."

Juancho left the room, and the reality which had lain in muffled silence below the tender memories, like the constant war during the sweet, short interval while the soldier opens the package and reads his letters from home, broke in sharply, harshly. No one said a word, and for a while they all smoked in silence. Moaning came from the other room. Nicolás looked out the window, pensively. What were they thinking?

Bruno went outside.

Everything, beginning with the very name of the town, was linked to the people who had weighed most upon his life: Ana María Olmos, her son Fernando, Georgina. And though he yearned to walk and walk and walk until he came to the old house that the whole town had started from, something held him back, he could only walk in circles in the part of the little town that lay near his home. As he walked along the dusty streets, the names awoke his memo-

420

ries: Salomon's dry goods store, Libonatti's shoe store, Dr. Figueroa's office, His Majesty Victor Emmanuel's Mutual Aid Society.

But Bruno's memories of his childhood had always come as bits and pieces unconnected and therefore unreal. Unreal because he had always conceived reality, life, as flowing and alive, a throbbing, palpitating thread, while those memories of his boyhood seemed to lack interconnections; they seemed static, separate, each one valid in its own way, in and of itself, each one on its own strange and solitary island, possessing that peculiar unreality of snapshots, of a world of people suddenly petrified, the boy holding the hand of his now-dead mother, the mother long ago become earth, plant, seed, and the boy almost never that great doctor, soldier, hero of the country the mother imagined, but rather some obscure clerk who, going through his papers one day, comes across that photograph and gazes on it through suddenly tear-filled eyes. That is why every time he had tried to reconstruct the earliest parts of his life everything had seemed so blurred and faded to him, why he had only been able to see, here and there, episodes or faces which were usually not even out-of-the-ordinary enough to justify their haunting durability. How else could he explain how he could remember so clearly something as trivial to his life as the arrival of that big motor for the mill? Well, maybe not "so clearly," maybe that overstated it a little. . . . Because when he tried to put that scene into words he did realize that it grew less definite, somehow, its outlines less marked, more hazy, and that everything grew pale and insubstantial, as though one could pass one's hand through it without touching it. No, he didn't know, he couldn't really give details; and when he tried, the scene shivered and faded away like dreams when we awake. And besides, it was impossible to force memories, unless one found the key, the magic word, because memories were like princesses that slept through an ancient sleep and would awake only when the secret word was whispered in their ear. Down there below slept moments of happiness and terror, and suddenly a song, a fragrance would break the spell and the ghost would stir from its graveyard of dreams. What melody, what uncertain fragment of melody was it that he had heard that evening he'd sat alone in the Jardin du Luxembourg? The song came from somewhere far away, from a world now lost, and suddenly he found himself in Capitán Olmos, on a summer night, sitting in the

421

circle of light cast by those great arc lamps they used to have. Who were they? All he could be sure of was the figure of Fernando cutting off the hind legs of a frog, and then the frog's grotesque attempts to get away from them using the two legs it had left, crawling horribly over the plot of dried-out clayey ground. But it was an imprecise ghost at best, without flesh or weight, a Fernando without concrete eyes or lips—an idea, almost, a horror, a shiver of repugnance. And that monster had arisen from some region of darkness to mutilate a frog, by the grace of a song. How strange it was that the sadist, the song, and the mutilated frog had all survived together, were to be forever linked, outside time, in a dark and somber region of his soul. No, he couldn't remember his childhood with any logic or order. His recollections floated up at random from some nebulous, neutral depth, and he could somehow never establish any temporal link between them. Because those fragments, which emerged like islands in an indifferent ocean—it was impossible for him to determine which followed or preceded which; the time that lay between them had no meaning, was no longer tied to births or deaths, or to lives at all, or to rainstorms or friendships, misfortunes, loves. And so, the arrival of that imprecise machine might have been before or after the horrible mutilation, for between the two events there lay a gray ocean without beginning or end, nor was there any claim of causality by which to draw up the things that had fallen into eternal oblivion.

Then Juancho collapsed under the weight of that unequal struggle; he suffered an attack of screaming and convulsions, and had to be given sedatives to make him sleep. The old man immediately sensed his absence, and from the well in whose depths he floundered he imagined that they'd taken Juancho off to Pergamino and killed him, in some act of dark revenge. They were hiding him. Why were they hiding him? Huh? Why? he moaned tearfully, although there were no tears in his eyes, because he no longer had any water in his body; but from the sound he made and the unmistakable shaking of his body one knew that it was weeping that came from that almost-corpse. Where was Juancho? Huh? Where was he? In Pergamino, he moaned again, before lapsing into the crisis that they all took for the end: he was breathing as though someone were trying to strangle him, he thrashed and wriggled furiously in the bed, from his mouth came fragments, chunks of words. Then he

422

threw off the covers and howled. And then suddenly his face grew rigid, and he had to be held down to keep him from throwing himself from the bed. From between his lips, as though they were bats flying from the chink in the ground that leads to a stygian, putrid, sulfuric cavern beneath the earth, there flew accusations, insults for the enemies who had killed his son. And then he fell, lifeless, as though collapsing inward upon himself.

All the brothers looked at each other. Nicolás went to the bed to check whether he was breathing. But once more he came through the crisis. He was no more than a bagful of bones, a mass of rotting flesh, but his spirit resisted—it took shelter in his heart, that last fortress that remained to it, while the rest of the body tumbled, discouraged, into death.

In a barely audible voice he was mumbling something. The effort was obviously exhausting. Nicolás put his ear to the old man's lips, and he deciphered the message: "It's so sad to die." That was what he thought he'd said. And then the struggle recommenced, and like a warrior gathering his last tattered, beaten followers together to stand and fight with them once more the futile (but lovely) battle, the old man rallied.

His followers! thought Bruno. He barely had even his heart left to count on, that weak and exhausted heart. Yet there he lay, and in every one of the fluttering beats of it he declared that he was still there, at their side, and that they would fight on yet.

The ruin of the man had one moment of lucidity, he recognized Bruno, and smiled at him sadly, and even seemed to be trying to speak to him. Bruno approached the bed, but he could understand nothing, though his father gestured at his body, the remains of his body.

He had stood a moment with him, and in his eyes, now calmer, he thought he glimpsed a smile of incredulity, a mixture of happiness and irony. He made another gesture, as though trying once more to talk. Bruno put his ear to his lips. "Juancho," he murmured. Juancho was trying to sleep. The old man thought for a moment, and then once again he mumbled something. What, what? Land? What land? This seemed to irritate him, he frowned, then he made a great effort to speak, random-seeming words that would never have been understood by a person who didn't know him, but which Bruno

423

managed to put together in their proper order, the way a man who knows an ancient language may pick out a text from fragments virtually illegible: from what he was leaving to Bruno, he wanted part of it to go to buy some land. His old obsession: the land that holds a man.

His errant son's promise seemed to make him smile. Then he asked again for Juancho, he wanted water, he wanted him to turn him. Bruno tried clumsily, but the old man gestured in irritation, no. Bruno had to wake him up; the two of them turned their father, and they gave him a spoonful of water. For the first time in his life Bruno felt that he was actually of some use, he felt himself much more Juancho's brother, and with a sort of tender humility he saw that he, Bruno, who had wandered through all the lands of the earth and through many of its doctrines, who had read many books on pain and death, was inferior, somehow, to this brother who had never done any of that.

The old man made another sign. Juancho bent over to him and then nodded. The father then seemed to drift off to sleep, peacefully. Bruno looked questioningly at his brother.

"The garden."

"What about the garden?"

He loved that garden, didn't Bruno know? It was the light of his life, and he cared for it like a baby. Juancho had to go out and spade it, loosen up the soil a bit, that was all.

Bruno watched his brother as he prepared to go out into the backyard. What? He wasn't going to go try and get some sleep? Where was he going?

"I just told you, I'm going out and spade up the garden."

Bruno was dumbfounded. Good heavens, the old man was never going to see it again, that garden and all the rest of it would be gone forever.

"He's asleep like that now," Juancho nodded toward the peacefully sleeping man, "because I promised him I'd do it."

Bruno said nothing, he only looked at him: he was wasted, aged by the terrible exhaustion of days and nights of vigil.

"But at least send somebody, one of the peons."

"No, he never let anybody else touch that garden."

When his brother left, he sat in the chair. He felt like dirt, worth-

424

less, racked with guilt for having felt nausea at the state his father was in; he heaped blame upon himself for having tried to forget that suffering, for having tried to take his mind off it by wandering through the town, for having thought about other things, for having read the newspaper during these days, a book. It was all frivolity, even thinking about things as profound as fate and death, because one thought about them in general, in the abstract, not about that suffering flesh that was actually lying there, and not for the sake of that suffering flesh.

When his brother came back in, he gave him the chair. And they remained in silence, listening to the moaning, the fragments of delirium. Standing behind him, Bruno contemplated Juancho's wide, exhausted, stooping shoulders, his white hair, his head drooping forward with weariness. For a moment he felt the temptation to reach out and lay his hand on his brother's shoulder, that shoulder that he had sat on when he was a boy, but then he realized that he would never be able to do it.

"Well, I'm going back out to the garden. Watch for me."

When he sat in the chair he felt a pride which must have been something like the pride a sentinel feels when he relieves his comrade at a dangerous post. But no sooner had that feeling taken shape than he was ashamed of himself, and a little embarrassed.

Night fell. From time to time the older brothers came in. Juancho was forced, at last, to resume the sleep he had interrupted. And so Bruno spent, for the first time in his life, an entire night with a dying man. And he sensed that he had just become a man, because only death can truly prepare one for life. The death of someone one loved allowed one to understand the life and death of other men, no matter how distant they were, and even of the lowest animals. He gave his father water, and even managed to give him his shot of morphine.

The old man was speaking Venetian, perhaps talking about things that had happened when he was a child, because he mentioned names that Bruno had never heard. There were words about a rudder or something of the sort, as well. And then suddenly an expression of terrible anguish would come over him. Other times, he would struggle with enemies and thrash about in his bed. Then Bruno heard him singing, and the expression on his face was of

425

happiness; when Bruno put his ear to the old man's mouth he could make out snatches of "Le Campane de San Giusto," that song of the unredeemed Triestianos his father had sung to him when he was a child.

At two o'clock in the morning, the last agony began.

Bruno was shocked by the courteous indifference, the mechanical gestures with which the priest touched him with the oil and prayed. Even so, Bruno felt the solemnity of the act of extreme unction: it was his father bidding farewell to life forever, that life he had lived with such courage, and such tenacity.

Two candles were lit before an engraving of San Marco, his father's patron saint. Juancho placed a medal of the Venetian saint about his father's neck. And the old man, from that moment on, was mysteriously still until he died.

HE WALKED ALONG ALMIRANTE BROWN

but when he came to the corner of Pinzón he saw that Chichín's old café had been transformed: formica had replaced the marble of the tables. He sat down timidly, fearfully, like some ghostly intruder in a place he did not belong in, after almost twenty years of absence. Many of the men who had argued over soccer matches must long since have died, and the kids that had pestered and wearied Loco Barragán would now be men, and have married, and had children of their own. Chichín, where was he? The waiter that came to take his order was new, he didn't know Chichín. He thought he was sick, an invalid, or maybe he had died. The owner? His name was Mourente, that Spaniard over at the cash register. The photograph of the Boca team had been taken down off the big mirror at the bar. Gardel's, too, and Leguisamo's.

A MAN FROM ANOTHER AGE

HIS EYES CAME TO REST ON AN OLD MAN NO MORE THAN SKIN AND BONES. His hair was white, his nose was sharp and aquiline, and he had little eyes set in the sides of a narrow face, so that he looked a little like a bird, a bird in anguish over something it's lost. His neck was exaggeratedly long, and his Adam's apple bulged. Between his

426

lips, like a cigarette, hung a toothpick which he shifted from time to time. He was looking out into the street as though he were expecting something, as though he were sitting at a table in the coffee shop of some train station and at any moment the person he was anxiously awaiting would come in. His face gave one the sense of that longing uneasiness, but the bitterness of his mouth, turned down at the corners, showed that the wait was almost surely futile. There was no doubt about it: the man was Humberto J. D'Arcangelo, known by people during the old days as Tito. All he needed was the rolled up *Crítica* under his arm. And Chichín was missing, too, who for so many years had stood wiping the glasses and reciting, when he was asked, the lineup of the 1915 Boca Juniors.

From a nearby table someone in a loud voice asked him, "What about you, don Humberto, what's your opinion?"

"About what?" D'Arcangelo replied grudgingly.

"About what Armando said on television."

He half-turned his sharp head.

"About what? Armando?"

Uh-huh, Armando—about what Alberto J. Armando had said on TV.

He considered the men at the next table a moment, and everyone sat in silence, as though before an implacable but utterly fairminded judge. Tito did not reply; he looked out at the street, Pinzón, and sank once more into that solitary universe, while one of the men who had sought his verdict (the cripple Acuña? Loiácono?) commented, in a tone of triumph, "See? See?" What was he thinking about? His father had surely died by now. He could see him (imagine him) in his frayed, greenish homburg, sitting in his little rush-bottom chair at the door of his rooming house, with that gnarled walking stick of his, muttering "eh, yes," shaking his head from side to side as though with the gesture making a comment to some invisible interlocutor on some nostalgic event. "That's the way things were." What things? Little things, always the same things: that ocean he had contemplated from the top of the mountain, with his flute in his hand, those Christmas times when it snowed, those shepherds playing their pipes. Bruno could see Tito, drinking his *mate* there beside the old man, and himself half ironically and half affectionately asking him what it was the shepherds were singing. And the

427

old man, closing his eyes, with a shy, embarrassed little smile, softly
singing:

> La notte de Natale
> è una festa principale
> que nació nostro Signore
> a una povera mangiatura.

That's what they were singing, eh, yes. . . . And was there lots of
snow, old fellow? Eh, yes . . . the snow. . . . And he sat there meditating on that fabulous land, while Tito winked at Martín and smiled
a smile of pity, sorrow veiled by concern for the old fellow's feelings,
and melancholy irony:

"See, child? Always the same story. That's all he ever thinks
about. The little town he lived in . . . If I was a rich man . . ."

And now he must surely be dead. A van from the city had come
and taken his little corpse away and Tito had gone with the body to
a numbered, anonymous deposit in Chacarita where the corpse of
his father would rot among blocks of cement. Not in the land of his
distant village, with the Ionian Sea of his ancestors spread out before
it, but rather there, in the fourth subterranean chamber of a cement
cemetery with numbered niches.

Bruno looked at D'Arcangelo again, scrutinized that longing for
the absolute that was reflected in his face, that mixture of naive
scepticism and kindness, that not-understanding of a world every
day more chaotic and mad—a world in which soccer players no
longer played for love of their jerseys but for money, in which Chichín no longer poured out the vermouth with bitters, in which the
old Boca team was little more than a painful memory. A world in
which that sweet, tender rooming house with its chickens and roos-
ters and occasional horse had been divided into cells of plywood
and cement, with no room anymore for old lame victories. Perhaps
in his little room the old Boca pennant still hung on the wall, and
that signed photograph of the great Tesorieri sat on the table beside
the Victrola. But those treasures doubtlessly survived as sadly as
their owner himself did, in one room, in a place where one no longer
heard the cackling of the hens at sunrise or smelt that odor of wis-
teria mixed with dung.

428

He left the café and walked along the streets which had been transformed as well. That train embankment, those houses with wrought-iron gates and wide porches, where were they? Humble lines of poetry, written by some scribbler, came into his spirit:

> The asphalt wiped out with one swipe of its hand
> the old neighborhood
> that saw me born.

Nothing was left in the ghost city that had been raised upon the desert: it was another desert, of almost nine million people who sensed nothing behind it, who could not even refer to, call on, lean on that simulacrum of eternity that other nations had, the monuments of stone erected in honor of the past. Nothing.

He walked, aimlessly.

IT WAS PAST MIDNIGHT
when he returned to the house that had been the Olmoses'. He approached it silently, as though it were some sleeping creature he did not want to awake, whose sleep, a fragile, precious thing, one wishes to protect. Ah, if only it were possible to return to certain periods of one's life as easily as one could return to the places those periods were lived in, he thought. The same places that twenty years ago had heard his somber voice recite a Machado poem. Rescue that moment from the silent, secret, yet inexorable passing of time, that instant of reality which now barely existed in a memory growing dimmer every day.

His life had been one long running after ghosts and unreal things, or at least after those things that practical people judge to be unreal. One long letting the present go so it might become the past, become nostalgic memory, faded dreams, images to be invoked as he had just then—and always in vain, when it was too late for anyone, anything ever to come back again, when the hand of the person we had once loved could no longer so much as touch our cheek, as Georgina had touched his thirty years ago in that very garden, on a night very much like the night that now found him alone. He felt himself a failure, and he felt the failure as a sense of guilt, brought on perhaps

429

by the memory of that energetic, gruff man that had been his father: one of those men who face with courage their fleeting, cruel lives (yet lives marvelous at every second of the present). He, Bruno, on the other hand, had always been a contemplative man, a man who could acutely and painfully feel the sensation of time passing, and carrying with it all that we would wish eternal. But instead of struggling with time, he had surrendered from the outset, later trying, in melancholy, to remember it all, invoking its specters, imagining that he could somehow fix them in a poem or a novel, trying—and what was worse, kidding himself that he tried—to succeed at that undertaking out of all proportion to his strength, trying to at least achieve some fragment of eternity, even if only the tiniest, most familiar, most modest fragment, a few names, an inscription full of meaning, before which other creatures, other men and women of days to come, sad and meditative men and women like himself, and out of similar motives, might halt the dizzying course of their days and feel, even if only for a few moments, as he had, the illusion of eternity.

Georgina, he murmured, caressing the rusted gate and contemplating the magnolia tree, as though among the ruins of the abandoned garden his spirit might call her up, call up even the appearance of her body, with that trace of a wrinkle on her forehead that seemed to be asking about the meaning of life, about the dreams and frustrations of existence, but in the least puzzled or perplexed sort of way, with the same reserve and modesty she asked all her questions. *Georgina*, he whispered again into the shadows.
Among the ravages of your body,
among the hungry, feverish worms,
even there will my soul be,
like some old inhabitant of a devastated land,
an old man without home or country anymore,
like an orphan searching for his loved ones,
in the midst of anonymous cries
and rubble.

He wandered about until sunrise, and then returned to his home and tried to sleep. His sleep was agitated and suffering. And suddenly he dreamed that he was alone, in some strange, uncertain place. Someone seemed to be calling him. It was arduous, making out the person's features, both because of the lack of light and because of the leprous state of the person's skin, which was falling off in shreds and tatters. He realized that it was a corpse trying to make itself understood: the corpse of his father.

He woke up in anguish, with a terrible pain around his heart.

And once again he was seized with the idea of his failure. And the betrayal of the spirit of the race from which he had come. It made him ashamed of himself.

BRUNO'S UNEXPECTED ACTIVITY WHEN HE WOKE UP

HE WENT STRAIGHT TO THE CHACARITA STATION, which lay in an area of Buenos Aires that he had painfully stayed away from, forever, since that year, 1953, in which his father had died. And now, another twenty years later, he felt impelled to revisit his hometown. What was he going to do? What did he think he would accomplish?

A JOURNEY TO CAPITÁN OLMOS, PERHAPS THE LAST

HE HAD DREAMS THAT HE TRIED much later to get to the bottom of. How is it that no one can ever get to the bottom of their dreams?

"Capitán Olmos," he heard through a haze of sleep. And it seemed to him it was old don Pancho whispering to him from his mummified lips.

He looked around. No, no one. Medina must have finally died. And Commissioner Bengoa, surely, too. Or maybe there weren't any commissioners anymore.

He slowly walked toward the house he had been born in, and again he felt the inward commotion he had felt when his father was dying and he had heard the steady, regular pounding of the machinery. He stopped in mid-block and sensed that he would never enter the house or see his brothers alive again, although at the moment he didn't know why. Instead, he turned toward the plaza and sat down on one of the benches near the little grove of palm trees he used to hide in on summer nights long ago. Colón Movie Theater: from the depths of their eternity he could feel William S. Hart and Eddie Polo, dressed up as cowboys, as Mounties, gazing down on him.

Then he went to the cemetery. The old brick crypts, painted

431

pink or sky blue, with their hedges of spiny Jerusalem thorn or cactus.

In the waning afternoon light he wandered about, deciphering the inscriptions, the names out of his childhood, the names of families that had disappeared, been swallowed up by that Buenos Aires of the thirties, when all these country villages had been decimated by the crisis, their dead left more alone than ever.

The Peñas. There was Escolástica's tomb. The mysterious spinster lady, covered with lace and flounces, accenting her words on the "wrong" syllables, her manners and her speech out of the Argentina of the old days. And the Prados, the Olmoses, families that had fought off the Indian attacks of a century ago. And the Murrays, too:

> In loving memory
> of
> John C. Murray
> Who departed this life
> January 25th. 1882
> at the age of 40 yrs.
> Erected by his fond wife and children.

And then at last he came to the grave of his mother, whose headstone now leaned a little to one side:

> María Zeno de Bassán
> Nacida en Venecia en 1870.
> Muerta en este pueblo en 1913.

And his father's grave, beside it, and the graves of his brothers. He stood there for a long time. Then he realized that it was useless, it was too late, he might as well go.
Stones turned in upon themselves,
stones lost in thought,
their eyes turned toward what countries of silence
witnesses of the void
certificates of the final fate
of a race eager, forward-straining, and discontent
abandoned mines

432

where once
there were explosions
now cobwebs.

He began to walk toward the exit, seeing, or glimpsing, other names out of his childhood: Audiffred, Despuys, Murphy, Martelli. Until suddenly he was shocked to see a tombstone that said:

Ernesto Sabato
Who wished to be buried in this ground
with a single word above his grave—
PEACE

He leaned on a little wall and closed his eyes. Then, when he opened them again, and walked out of the cemetery, he felt an emotion that had nothing of the tragic about it: the gloomy cypresses, the silence of the quickly advancing night, the breeze with its faint fragrance of the pampas, those subtle, muted beckonings from his childhood (like a traveler going away forever who waves shyly, tentatively from the window of the train) produced in him not a sense of tragedy but rather that melancholy restfulness that a child feels when he lays his head in his mother's lap and closes his eyes still filled with tears, after the terrors of a nightmare.

"Peace." Yes, it was surely that, perhaps *only* that which Sabato needed, he mused. But why had he seen him buried in Capitán Olmos instead of in Rojas, his true hometown? And what did that vision mean? A wish, a premonition, a friendly remembrance of Sabato by his friend? But how could anyone think it was friendly to imagine him dead and buried? At any rate, be that as it might, it was peace that S. doubtlessly needed and yearned after—the peace needed by every creator, by every man born under the curse of refusing to resign himself to the life he was given to live, by every man for whom the universe is horrible, or tragically transitory and imperfect. Peace—for there is no such thing as absolute happiness, he thought. It comes to us in fleeting, fragile moments, and art is a way of eternalizing (or trying to eternalize) those instants of love or ecstasy. Peace—for all our hopes sooner or later become awkward, ungainly realities—for we are all frustrated in one way or another, and if we triumph in one thing we fail in another, for frustration is

433

the inevitable fate of every person who is born to die; and peace, because we are all alone, or wind up alone someday: the lover without
the beloved, the parent without children or the children without the
parent, the pure revolutionary confronted with the sad materialization
of those ideals which a few years ago he defended with his suffering
through savage, unimaginable tortures. Peace, because all life is a perpetual losing, a falling away, a farewell, and we meet someone on our
path, but we don't love that person when that person loves us, or we
love the person when the person no longer cares for us, or after the
person is dead, when our love is futile, and wasted. Peace because
nothing of what once was can ever come again, and things, men, women,
children are no longer what they once were, and the house of our
childhood is no longer that place which hid our treasures and our
secrets, and our father dies without speaking to us those perhaps fundamental words, and when we do finally understand, he is no longer
with us and we cannot heal his old wounds, gladden his old sadnesses,
repay or repair all the old losses and misunderstandings. Peace, because
the town is changed, and the school where we learned to read doesn't
have those pictures that made us daydream anymore, and the circuses
have been displaced by television, and there aren't any organ-grinders
anymore, or carousels, and the plaza of our childhood is absurdly small
when we go back to visit it.

Oh, my brother, he thought in high-sounding words, hiding his
sadness from himself by the tone of irony he gave them, you who
at least attempted what I never had the strength to do, what for me
was never more than will-less dream, you who tried to achieve what
that aching Negro with his blues, in that sordid room in a dirty,
apocalyptic city was trying for, too—how I understand you, to have
wanted to see you buried, resting on these pampas you loved, and
yearned for, and to have dreamed that on your tombstone there
should have been carved one small word to protect you at last from
so much pain and loneliness!

His steps took him quietly through the night to his childhood
home, now the home of someone else. There were lights on. Who
were those people?

Is the soul a stranger in the land?
Where do its steps lead it?

434

It is the moonlit voice of the sister through the holy night he hears
the pilgrim
the somber soul
in its night ship
in the moonlit pools
among the rotting thicket of branches, leprous walls.
The raving man is dead
the stranger is buried.
Sister of tempestuous sadness,
look!
A grieving ship is wrecked, it runs aground
under the stars
beneath the silent gaze of night.

Because there is no festive poetry, someone once said, since one may only speak about time and the irreparable. And someone once said, too (but who was it? and when?), that one day everything will be past and gone, forgotten, obliterated, even the formidable walls and the great moat that encircled the impregnable fortress.

ABOUT THE AUTHOR

ERNESTO SABATO was born in Rojas, Argentina, in 1911. In the late 1930s, he moved to Paris to pursue his studies in science and, while there, was influenced by the surrealist movement. He abandoned his scientific career in favor of a literary one, and his first essays were published in *Sur*, the leading Argentine literary magazine.

Sabato is the recipient of Spain's Miguel de Cervantes Prize, France's Prix de Meilleur Livre Etranger, the Jerusalem Prize, and many other literary awards from several countries. His work has been translated into twenty-one languages.

He lives in Buenos Aires, Argentina.

ABOUT THE TRANSLATOR

ANDREW HURLEY is Professor of English at the University of Puerto Rico. He has published several articles on translation and is well known for his translations of works by Reinaldo Arenas, Fernando Arrabal, Jorge Luis Borges, Gustavo Sainz, and Armando Valladares.